THE RACE TO THE BLACKENED NEVERS

BOOK ONE
THE WOEFUL WAGER

DOUGLAS BAIN

The Woeful Wager by Douglas Bain.

Book One of the dark fantasy series *The Race to the Blackened Nevers.*

Toronto, Canada. First edition.

DouglasBain@blackenednevers.com

www.blackenednevers.com

ISBN: 978-1-9991802-0-1

For Lesley.

Wait here.

Cast of Characters

The Gods

Aelic:	The god of fate. His cords tie him to every mortuant in creation.
Aris:	The god of the brae. His temple lies in the Gudfin Mountain.
Bragnal:	The prince of the gods. With his scale he weighs god and mortuant alike.
Civiak:	The god of jest and tricks. Long of tongue and sharp of wit.
Corvii:	The god of time. Husband of *Vestialis*. Father of *Louthe* who he has hidden in the dark tangles of Bedlam's Thicket.
Dhoorval:	The god of law and His High Majesty's court.
Digrir:	The god of wayward children.
Fitzhiff:	The cursed god of music. One of the three gods punished by *Bragnal* for starting a race.
Forrar:	Child goddess of autumn. Daughter of *Corvii.*
Georwrith:	Child goddess of winter. Daughter of *Corvii.*
Gollunt:	Patron god of the 12th Leggat.

Kellcrim: Connachen's god of compassion, a trait unwelcome among the condemned men of the 12th Leggat.

Krynon: The god of the Rowlach people who shuns his own creations.

Louthe: Wandering child god. Son of *Corvii* and *Vestialis.*

Mag: Colmrakken god of gambling.

Methulla: The god of truth surrounded by his six birds.

Morven: - ? -

Rawl: The god of strength. Stoic, indeed, utterly silent.

Salagrim: The god of vision. One-eyed and forever searching.

Sowrug: Child goddess of summer. Daughter of *Corvii.*

Vestialis: The goddess of love. One of three gods punished by *Bragnal* for starting a race.

Woadbrek: The god of drink.

Yaarach: Child goddess of spring. Daughter of *Corvii.*

Zernebruk: The god of harvest. One of three gods punished by *Bragnal* for starting a race.

The Drudges

Amariss and *Juliet*: *Fitzhiff's* singing ghouls.

Chezepock: Husband of *Pennylegion.*

Macionica: Drudge to *Morven* and keeper of her Wall of Yearning.

Mulloch Furdie: Minder of the Lysergic and Amphetamined fires.

Nyqueed: Drudge to *Fitzhiff.* Known as *the Black Song Man.* Three chords and a tale of woe.

Ogham: Many-armed accomplice of the infamous Theft of Krosst's Thimble.

Pennylegion: Drudge to *Vestialis.* Wife of *Chezepock.*

Quindecum: Drudge to *Zernebruk.*

The Carvers

Creche of the Donlands: Virtuoso. His aesthetic is to fill every inch of his work.

Frew the Elder: Official sculptor to His High Majesty.

Frew the Younger: Iconoclastic and snide. His signature is a carved explosion.

Jegs: 'The people's carver.'

The Mortuants

Adalbane: Member of the order of the *Brothers of Digrir.*

Agajin Hiscum: Brae priest of Aris.

Aramis: Captain of His High Majesty's Samidian knights.

Balkan: Former court attendant to the chief justice of His High Majesty's court. Last of the Rowlach.

Bashquake: Dwarf. Tutor of Scramhammer. Hater of humans.

Bockum: Silver-tongued soldier of the 12th Leggat.

Charlotte: Orphan in the care of the *Brothers of Digrir.*

Chim Wiscum: Brae boy. Brother of Phae. As penitent as his sister is sceptical.

Connachen: Captain of His High Majesty's 12th Leggat: *The Thunder that Wanders.*

The Court:	Chief Justice Sova, and Justices Uby, Tock, Orade, Haud, Ramnach, and Lain.
Fiddich:	Fastidious priest of Bragnal.
Fignith:	The last Rowlach girl.
Gogarburn:	Healer in His High Majesty's 12th Leggat. Noted arsonist.
Griscomb:	Kindly prison guard of the Clovenstone Stockade.
Kaif:	One of two vanturian guards in the 12th Leggat.
Lostrus:	Captain of the gendarme in Quardinal's Brawn.
Lumsden:	Old, grizzled denizen of the 13th Step.
Madrigan:	The finest connoisseur of pitch in all of Quardinal's Brawn.
Manion:	Old Methullian knight. Serving below his station.
Mogh:	Torrefact outcast.
Ostaig:	Colmrakken prisoner of the Clovenstone Stockade.
Phae Wiscum:	Brae girl. Sister of Chim. As sceptical as her brother is penitent.
Rothesay:	Groundskeeper of the Quardinal's Brawn cemetery.
Scramhammer:	Dwarven king-to-be.
Scrieve:	Official scribe to the 12th Leggat.
Thaltis:	Criminal overlord of Quardinal's Brawn.
Wergoyle:	Loyal advisor to Bockum, and keeper of doves.
Wulfric:	One of two vanturian guards in the 12th Leggat. A tall, Jarlspeen bundle of woe.
Zollern:	Soldier in His High Majesty's 12th Leggat. Thinks wrapping his halberd in twine will convince his god Rawl to speak. It doesn't.

PROLOGUE

THE OLD CARVER stilled his hammer and drew down his chisel. He brushed away the grit and dust from the obelisk and would have carved more, but he felt a touch on his shoulder. He drew back to let the next carve his verses into the stone.

This second carver worked elegant as a hunting heron. His chisel finally still, his breath heavy in his chest, he too drew back letting the next have access to the obelisk.

The third carver worked angry, with heavy blows that took more of the rock than needed. The fourth was nervous. He worked through six new moons. But finally, he too stepped back. They looked upon the obelisk and this is what they'd written:

There have been not one, not two, but three,
Races of the gods to the world's periphery.

And no less true is he who won:
Bragnal the quick with his iron tongue.

How he mocked, how he laughed,
How the races did craft,
From the bloody fracas of their careen,
Bragnal's justice swift and clean.

To the god who started the first,
He forged the crypt for that accused.

A horrid thing, my brother.

To the god who started the second,
To the crypt nevermore to be reckoned.

A horrid thing, my brother.

To the god who started the third,
Add his wails to the two interred.

A horrid thing, my brother.

Is Bragnal's claim less than a sun,
To swallow all night as it rises at dawn?
Bragnal's scales were weighed and tipped,
And all three pretenders thrown in his crypt!

I heard another?
Shhh, brother. Listen. Do you hear?

A fourth race now? Are the gods to run?
Called by none other than a mortuant's son?

Never!

What say you brothers? Do we let it flow?
And see if Bragnal's pace has slowed?

Never!

But we say yes, let them run for the Nevers,
Let us delight once again in their fool endeavours.

Perhaps your Bragnal this time will trip.
Perhaps mine will dash on keen worship.

And perhaps I will carve another,
To wrench this race from you all, my brothers.

Never!
Never!
Never!

PART I

Fitzhiff's Race

CHAPTER 1

THE SHINE IN THE DISTANCE

ROTHESAY HALTED HIS rake. There was the voice again.

"We've been watching you."

He stopped chewing his piece of licorice root and looked up. The sun was bright overhead, but as its rays passed through the canopy of ash and birch leaves and fell onto the cemetery grounds, they lost their luster. They spilled on the grass like watery milk.

"We've been watching you."

Rothesay whipped around and bent down to look under his wheelbarrow—nothing. He righted himself.

He was standing in the far corner of the graveyard. His favorite corner. It was always quiet, so little to weed, so little to rake. The graves were ancient and obscured by overgrowth. But despite their weathering, the images carved into the gravestones were still visible: Methulla with his six birds, Woadbrek stumbling and raising his tankard, Aelic and his tangle of black cords, Salagrim with his giant eye searching beneath a rock. They were all there on the faded markers.

"We know your name, Rothesay."

The voice came from beyond the tall black ironworks that surrounded the old crypt. The vault was overgrown, lost in brambles and weeds as tall as a man. Deadwood, gray from years under a thirsty sun, wove through its iron fencing up to the ornamental urn carved into the roof of the crypt. The squat vessel was etched with panels. The first showed the image of great Bragnal pressing the vault door closed. The second revealed three gods cowering on the other side.

The first god was Fitzhiff, the god of music, clutching at his ear, his bag of flutes and pipes, lutes and drums opened and its contents scattered broken at his feet. The second was Vestialis, the beautiful goddess of love, tearing at her long black hair. And the third was Zernebruk, the god of harvest, a wicker basket on his back, struggling as his arms and legs drew him down into the earth. The corner of the urn had crumbled away, taking with it most of the fourth image. All that remained was a single hand reaching toward Bragnal.

"Rothesay!" It was a woman's voice now, urgent and insistent, as though she were afraid Rothesay's search for the voice might wander from the overgrown crypt.

Rothesay slowly nodded. His head dipped so low the licorice juice burst its banks and dribbled down his chin.

"You hear. Good. For a moment it seemed as if the gods had stolen that from you as well."

Rothesay shook his head. Why, he couldn't tell. Whose voice was this? His eyes raced over the tangle of vegetation along the crypt's ironwork. Images of the rabbits, foxes, and squirrels of the stories his mother would read to him came to mind. Disbelief tightened on his face as one by one he dismissed the creatures. They were not the source of the voice. They couldn't be. Then what was?

Thin strains of a flute, its notes warped and out of time, suddenly floated on the air. A man spoke now.

"We are not well, Rothesay. We've been shunned. Excluded. Left to rot like forgotten hymns. And your neglect has been the worst."

Rothesay blushed and looked back to the keeper's cottage. *Shhh*, he thought, *Johan might hear you. And that's a lie!*

Rothesay knew he worked hard. He neglected none of the flowers and plants in the cemetery—only this corner and the old, forgotten crypt. The one no one came to. And Johan had told him on the day he'd started: he'd said, "Leave that old crypt alone, boy. Don't you be wastin' your time."

"Enough, Fitzhiff, you treacherous goat!" This new voice was dark and raspy, cold and crackly, like mice feet on tile. "Ignore him, Rothesay. See the cherry blossoms, boy," it whispered. Rothesay craned his neck up to the line of cherry trees in their thunderous display of blossoms.

"They are full, they are strong—magnificent! Pumping with rich blood; pushing skyward! Yet look at me, stunted and gnarled. You mock me with their blooms, Rothesay." Rothesay shook his head in a weak display of defiance. "And what of the Bluebells, Rothesay? Those are yours, are they not?" Rothesay took in the thick patch of blooms and nodded.

"They bulge with vigor, strong enough to peel back their veins and show us what runs inside them. I can smell their scent, Rothesay. Those vital veins reach down to suck the manna from the skulls beneath us. And what of Zernebruk? Hmm?" His voice darkened. "What have you fed me?"

Vestialis took over again. "*Shhh*, Zernebruk. Let the poor mortuant think."

As she spoke a perfume flooded the crypt. Nausea crept over Rothesay like a wet shawl. He stumbled back and steadied himself on his wheelbarrow, again looking for assistance from the keeper's cottage. These voices, they were not right. Something was wrong.

"No, Rothesay," she continued, "don't be afraid. We too have felt fear. Just like you. We have felt their mistrust, their disgust, their rejection."

Rothesay reached up and traced the mangled contours of his face: his misshapen nose, heavy brow, and slack, protruding jaw. He looked as if a sculptor had battered him with a chisel and hammer.

"But we aren't scared of you, Rothesay, not like the others," Vestialis said. Rothesay could have sworn her perfume was reaching out to caress his cheek. "Will you fear us?" Rothesay shook his head, tears streaming down his cheeks. "Will you mock us, tease us? Will you hate us? As they do you?" Rothesay shook his head more insistently. "Can we trust you, Rothesay?"

Just then a soft wind shook the twisted vegetation. The vines, brambles, and thorns all quivered. In a clump of dried and rotted poet's jasmine, a dead flower trembled. As if two invisible hands had wrapped around its lips, the dead flower tore apart. It rolled back on itself like a scroll throwing off dust and pieces of vegetative gore.

From the desiccated bud appeared the tip of a red claw, its nails pinched together like the head of a swan. The claw grew up like an arm pushing through a jacket sleeve, curling and twisting until it freed itself from the dead bloom. There it stopped on a thin appendage, pinched together, its red skin cracked, weathered, and torn, its nails jagged and broken. The claw then bloomed. It parted in slow animation and from it tumbled a dozen tiny red spheres.

Like a child drawn to a shiny object, Rothesay stepped forward. He grabbed his rake, drew the orbs to him, and picked one up. It was moving; contracting and pulsing as though gasping for air.

"Sparrow hearts, Rothesay," Zernebruk hissed. "In that tiny pumping vessel is where that god Bragnal holds his pity. In a bird too fast for the grasp. How vile of him. Well, while they may be too fast for mortuants, they aren't for gods. And so these are for you. A gift, Rothesay. From us. A small token of our sympathy for the beastly neglect that Bragnal and his ilk have shown you. The beastly neglect they have shown us all."

Rothesay threw the hearts down and kicked them away.

"Does he deny our gifts?" Fitzhiff shrieked as the strains of the flute quickened and bent even more discordantly. "What does he say? What does he say?"

Rothesay tumbled backward and fell over his wheelbarrow. He threw his rake into it and grabbed its handles. The voice changed again.

"No, Rothesay. No, don't run. Think, boy," Zernebruk said. "If you sprint now, what will happen to your little Charlotte?"

Rothesay froze. He looked back at the crypt, feeling heavy with dread.

"I've been watching her, Rothesay." A chill ran down Rothesay's back. He slowly let the wheelbarrow down. "The little girl who likes to roam this graveyard, looking in vain for a hint of a family to call her own, who doesn't shy away from you like the others. The one who shares her stolen plums with you. You know the one, don't you?" Rothesay clutched at the locket around his neck.

"I've cursed her, Rothesay, with a vex, black and crumbly like new loam, drawn deep from the rotten core of an old elm tree. A vex ready to pluck her bud before its bloom."

Rothesay checked the keeper's house again. *Where was Johan? He would know what to do.*

"I can see her now, Rothesay. My vision sways in the buds of the willow tree above her head. She's bent over the banks of the high road river just beyond the gates. Where the bridge is. You know it, don't you?" Rothesay gave a terrified nod.

"While her fellow orphans beg for food, she sees a fish, Rothesay. A tiny salmon swimming below the water. Little Charlotte wants to reach for it, bless her. She wants to touch the fish. But I know even more! For, you see, the dirt beneath her tiny feet was placed there in my time. I settled it loosely, laid it in tatters, and shod it with no rock. It stands like dust waiting for the wind."

The gods carved on the stone urn above the crypt all turned to look at Rothesay. "We knew this day would come, Rothesay," they said together. "We knew another race would begin, and Bragnal would leave us out in the cold."

Rothesay slammed his dirty hands over his ears to block their words. But it was no use. Zernebruk resumed his narrative.

"For you see, in this dirt, this mud and filth, I have friends, Rothesay. Black seeds and thick tars, tendrils and shards, columns of vapors, discarded thug thorns. With a word, I can brace the ground beneath her. With a word, my friends can bind the bank, and Charlotte's little hand will reach for the fish and return to her safely. Or they can let it fall. And her with it. Would you like that, Rothesay?"

Rothesay fell to his knees pleading with outstretched hands. Tears ran off his chin. His bottom lip slackened. The piece of licorice root fell from his mouth.

"Then you must be quick. There isn't a moment to lose. I can see little Charlotte. She is reaching, Rothesay. Reaching! What will she find at the end of her trembling little fingers?"

Rothesay rushed forward and shook the iron gates.

"Yes, Rothesay, good. See that thorny vine wrapped around the lock. Tear it away."

Rothesay reached for the vine, but its sharp thorns tore his skin. He took off his coat, wrapped it around his hands, and pulled the vine from the old iron lock. He fell back as the gate slowly opened to the thin distant strumming of a lute.

"Charlotte reaches, Rothesay," Zernebruk continued, "and the salmon swims. My bandits in the bank have stayed firm. She turns now, called by her friend who has found a piece of bread. She's racing to him, drops of water flying off her tiny fingers. A touch of awe at the powers of creation has come to rest on her mortuant soul. How lovely!"

Rothesay lifted up the handles of his wheelbarrow and made to leave.

"Ah, but Rothesay, what of tomorrow?"

Rothesay stopped. He felt his heart beating in his throat.

"What powers might act to snip Charlotte's flower tomorrow, Rothesay? Or the day after? Or the day after that?"

Rothesay dropped his head into his hands. Vestialis took over now, her perfume flooding over him once again.

"Tend our garden, my good, sweet Rothesay. Tend it with love. Clean away the rot and tangle. Free us. For we have called our drudges back to their labors. And so our garden must be ready for them. *We* must be ready for them and so you must tend it well. This is what we ask. And in return, we promise you Charlotte's bloom will see the full light of day."

Another bloom woven into the iron gate burst and disgorged its claw. Then another. And another.

"But if you do not, Rothesay," Zernebruk hissed, "this I also promise you: we are not like the other gods you see carved on the tombstones in this place of death. We are not soft, addled, and idle. We are the gods who dared to score ourselves equal to that bastard Bragnal." The claws extended from their blooms on limbs as long as a ferryman's pole.

"And so I promise you this, Rothesay. If you do not help us, I will see that Charlotte's roots rot beneath her. They will drag her below to the worms and the muck. And I will take her hand and see her descend farther still. Into a loam and rock of such ancient horror that she will be cursed to bloom her guts in the night, as the blossom of a horrid little flower lost in the tangles of Bedlam's Thicket." The red stalks pressed in on him, swirling like leaves in a cyclone. Rothesay watched in horror as they collected the sparrow hearts from the ground.

"But do as we command, Rothesay, and if you survive what is about to unfold, you will be the first mortuant to know, won't you?" A claw grabbed his chin and wrenched his head up. The voices then united.

"You'll know what embarrasses even the sun. What makes these cherry blossoms blush with shame. That something shines brighter and more dazzling than them all. A shine in the distance bright enough… *to cause even the gods to run!*"

The claws wrenched Rothesay's mouth open and rammed the sparrow hearts down his throat.

CHAPTER 2

RUINS IN THE DESERT

THE SETTING SUN now touched the dusty desert horizon. The long train of soldiers that snaked from the orange ball looked like a fuse taking up a flame. Like tiny sparks off of saltpeter, their crimson cloaks and banners snapped in the breeze as the battered men of the 12th Leggat marched past their collapsed captain. Not a single one of them broke rank to help him. They passed with eyes full of scorn and contempt.

Connachen struggled to his knees and stared at the line of his men spilling from the waning sun. His armor—filthy, dented, and scoured—spilled desert sand from its crooks. More sand stuck to his forehead from when he'd fallen, as if his mind had joined the exodus.

"How? How did he know?" he whispered. He jerked his head around to a young pikeman filing past. "How did he know it wouldn't burn, boy? *How?*"

The youth glanced about, nervous that his comrades had heard the captain address him of all people. Suddenly a horse skidded to a halt in front of him. The rider spurred the horse around and pulled in close to Connachen, blocking the young soldier's view with the flank of the beast.

"Move on, damn you!" Gogarburn roared as he dropped from his horse and spread his cloak to shield even more of the 12th Leggat's broken captain. The old healer held firm until the youth and the rest of his confused comrades passed, then turned to his young assistant.

"Quick, boy. Dust of sleep." The boy nodded and ran off to his horse's saddlebag. Gogarburn kneeled beside Connachen. "There, there, captain," he whispered. "This will pass like the others."

He snapped his fingers as his attendant withdrew a tiny fold of parchment paper. All the while the soldiers of the 12th Leggat continued to file past, the rattle of their weapons in their scabbards like the hiss of a dying flame.

"Lean back." Gogarburn guided Connachen's head down to the sand.

As he did, a tall swordsman from the ranks of the infantry sneered at them as he marched past. "Would you look at that, boys? Our captain's broken again. Never seen Bockum broken like that, have you?" His partner shook his head, full of equal contempt.

Gogarburn waited for them to pass. The young boy handed him the parchment, which he unfolded, exposing a pinch of blue dust. He held it over Connachen's lips. "Now, open your mouth, captain. This will quiet your demons."

A sharp pain in his elbow rattled Gogarburn's arm back. The blue dust sprinkled off into the wind and twinkled in the fading sunlight.

Scrieve drew back the stylus he'd jabbed into the old healer's arm. Bent like a probing heron, he clutched an oversized book to his chest. He was younger than Connachen, with dark hair and fine features, and he wore the gray robes, edged with gold, of a court scribe.

"Are you trying to choke the flow of the oracle before it even begins?" Scrieve said as he wiped the tip of his stylus on his robes.

"I'm trying to soothe his tempers, man. As any good healer would."

Scrieve drew his stylus over his tongue. "Yet you prescribe leeches for the blood, do you not? To urge it to flow in times of distemper? So why would we not let our captain's mind flow freely, to purge itself of its distemper?"

Gogarburn got to his feet. "Aye, leech you are, scribe. That much is clear. But he is no blasted oracle. I won't watch him suffer."

"I won't watch him suffer." Scrieve nodded, unconvinced. "Won't you, now?"

He cracked open his giant book. Alternating his energy between the scorn he cast toward Gogarburn and the pages he lazily swiped through, he found his mark. He cleared his throat, checked that no one was listening, and read from the page.

"'Bockum lies.'" He stopped and glared at Gogarburn, letting the words foul the air between them for a minute before resuming. "'Bockum waits like a snake in the grass to strike. He is a traitor and a liar.'"

Scrieve looked up from the book. "I do believe I'd watch our good captain's skull split in twain if he were inclined to elaborate on that point, wouldn't you?" Scrieve drew in close. "And may I remind you of the whispers that float through our camp at night, healer? The seditious, mutinous whispers. It would seem to me that our captain's assessment of Bockum is quite correct indeed."

The cavalry of the 12th Leggat passed now. Their bridles and tack tinkled and jangled as if Scrieve's point were rolling around in a tin can. "Ave Bockum," one rider bellowed. The salutation echoed down the ranks. "May Gollunt grace us with his quick return and this one's quick end." The soldier looked toward Connachen and spat into the sand.

A smile grew on the scribe's lips as the healer drew his young assistant to him.

"Nothing good will come of this," Gogarburn said.

Scrieve flicked his fingers for the healer to retreat further. "I'll be sure to record your hesitations," he snapped as he kneeled beside Connachen's head.

"Now, captain," he said, testing his stylus on a clean page. "Have no fear. It's Scrieve, your trusted scribe."

Connachen's eyes fixed well past him to a scene unfolding before his mind's eye. Scrieve dipped his stylus into its ink and waited until the siege machine, groaning and rumbling over the desert sand like a toppling marble pillar, passed them by. Only then did his interrogation begin.

"Now, my dear captain, I believe I heard you earlier. You said he knew it wouldn't burn. *Who* knew it wouldn't burn? Do you speak of Bockum again? Is that who you mean?" He readied his stylus on the page; his hand trembled with anticipation.

Connachen nodded. Scrieve recorded the gesture in his book in long elegant cursive. "Bockum knew *what* wouldn't burn, captain?"

"Our cage," Connachen whispered, staring off into the setting sun.

"How did he know it wouldn't burn?"

"He said he could read it, in the way the saltpeter spilled from the leather pouch as the executioner walked back to his flame."

Scrieve locked eyes with Gogarburn to register his utter contempt at the latter's earlier efforts to still this broken oracle. "So His High Majesty condemned you to burn, then, is that it? Before he threw you into the Leggat?"

Gogarburn surged forward, angry at the vile question, but Scrieve held him at bay with his stylus. Connachen nodded.

"Bockum said the saltpeter was a language. He said it was Civiak himself writing in the falling dust, laughing at us, mocking our fears, telling him that the flame would never catch."

Scrieve finished the entry. "Be clear, captain. Clear as you can. Was Bockum *in* the cage, or out?"

"He was in. Right there beside me clutching its bars. Ready to burn," Connachen whispered. "With an old murderous sailor and a Torrefact witch."

The dusty wagons of the 12th Leggat were passing now. Their meagre contents rolled and slid across the full breadth of the wood. The sound seemed to penetrate Connachen's fugue. His eyes settled on the young scribe, earnest as a penitent's.

"The witch and the murderer deserved their sentence. As did I. But my sentence was mine. Not Bockum's. It was me. I killed him."

Scrieve looked to Gogarburn to register his shock. But a more worrisome development had taken the healer's attention. Wulfric, the tall Jarlspeen vanturian guard, was the last soldier in the line. He walked alone, the ball of sun behind him giving him an aura of flame. A faint wisp of smoke rose from between his fingers as he walked.

Scrieve looked back at Connachen. "Then why did His High Majesty condemn Bockum to die? Why was Bockum in the cage with you, captain? Quickly, you must tell me."

Connachen grabbed Scrieve's collar. He drew the scribe in close. "Because he lied. As he is lying to us now."

"Why? Why would he lie, captain?" There was urgency in Scrieve's voice. Wulfric was closing on them.

"Only the gods know," Connachen replied, faint and defeated. He let Scrieve go and dropped his head into his hands.

"No! No, captain—*you know*," Scrieve said. He flipped back a few pages, found his mark, and read as fast as he could.

"'I found my wife's killer in the tavern. The Ragged Heel. I tracked him like a wolf. I could hear that fat bastard's voice down the alleyway.'" Scrieve looked at Connachen. It was enough for Connachen to find his thread. He nodded and took up the story.

"I–I sat there. Listening with the others, didn't I? Quiet as a mouse. Not saying a word. Then I asked Kellcrim for forgiveness for what I was about to do. I folded my blacksmith's apron and I stood up. I walked up behind him. He was so loud and drunk. So loud. I..." Connachen formed a circle with his fingers. "I choked the words right back down his fat throat. Right in front of the whole tavern."

"And Bockum?" Scrieve pressed.

"Bockum stood up, didn't he? Just as that fat bastard's body crumbled to the floor. He–he stood with me over the body. And..."

"And what, Connachen? Quick, man."

"Bockum made them swear. All of them. In the tavern. With

that golden tongue of his. To tell them… *that we'd killed that bastard together.*"

Connachen collapsed, unconscious on the sand as Wulfric arrived. He was a bear of a man, tall with wide shoulders and scarred from years of battle. A large wooden carving of Gollunt—the patron god of the Leggat—hung around his neck. The pendant depicted dozens of spears and arrows puncturing the god's flanks and limbs, fanning from him like spokes to the carving's rim.

Wulfric took the rolled tobacco from his mouth and released a cloud of smoke. He pointed with it over Scrieve's shoulder. The scribe turned and stared at the thick arm of black smoke now visible on the far horizon.

"What town is it this time?" Wulfric asked in a low growl. He drew another breath from his tobacco as Scrieve again flipped through his book.

"Torvisk."

"Torvisk? Of the learned Lyceum?" Wulfric said. "And? What of their rhetoric? Did it repel a single blow?"

"Apparently not. Reports are that all are dead."

"When?"

"Two days ago."

"Then they've quickened their pace, haven't they, captain?" Wulfic yelled down at Connachen.

"He's suffering another spell, Wulfric," Gogarburn said, stepping forward.

"Is he now? Looks fine to me, healer. Strong as an ox, in fact." Wulfric dragged Connachen to his feet. "Duty calls, captain," he whispered as he shoved the broken leader of the 12th Leggat forward.

ঌ

As his horse galloped over the sand, the cool twilight wind was enough to sober Connachen. He drew a deep breath and opened his eyes. The spire of the Torvisk Lyceum loomed in the distance, white against the black smoke.

This would be the third town in ten days. How far were they from Quardinal's Brawn? How long they had been marching through the dusty, forgotten corridors of his country? How many dead had they counted? Only a fool could tell. Or Scrieve's infernal book. There you'd find the exact measure of the carnage. There you'd learn the tally under every category of trauma and pain.

He was surging over the desert sand alone now. His men had simply watched as Wulfric had spurred Connachen's horse to a gallop toward the thick black smoke on the horizon. Though he was still their captain, his pains drew no sympathy from them. And why should they? His torment and anguish was his due, as it was everyone's in the 12th Leggat. Each man faced their god's rebukes alone, whether he be cook or captain.

An image flashed before his eyes as his horse closed on the arm of smoke rising on the horizon: the Ragged Heel tavern in Quardinal's Brawn, clear as if he'd just stumbled across its doorway. He could hear the merriment within and saw his hand pressing the door open and, in that sliver of vision, his wife's killer throwing back his head for a heavy gulp from his tankard.

He slammed his eyes shut and clung to his horse as if she were a barrel from a shipwreck. "Kellcrim, please," he whispered to no avail. The vision playing out in his mind's eye widened as if in time to the opening of the tavern door. He could see his wife's killer clearly now, the patrons around him listening keenly as he spoke. And in the corner of the room, quiet and still, sat Bockum, gesturing for Connachen to come inside.

His horse suddenly skidded to a halt, wrenching him from his visions. He tugged on the reins and struggled for control as they contested the tiny patch of sand, the horse refusing to settle or go any further.

"Quiet, girl. What's spooked the finest horse in the 12th Leggat?"

She finally relented, though the boil in her belly was made clear by the blasts from her snout. Connachen leaned forward, caressed her, then looked up to see what had frightened her.

Where the cobble-stoned road leading from the gates of Torvisk ended and the sand of the desert began, he saw three ramshackle columns, spaced and symmetrical like the ruins of an old wall. A few paces behind them, facing back toward Torvisk, was a tower stitched together from leather, broken wood, and wagon wheels.

"Is this what's spooked you?"

He tried to spur her forward, but she wouldn't move. He dropped from his saddle and drew in close. The horse nuzzled him and he reassured her with a few pats to the neck. It was enough. He gave a gentle tug on her reins and she walked forward.

His feet sunk into the loose sand as he led her. The desert seemed to want to hold him back, to pull him away, to turn him from his path and the new visions that had begun to beset him. They flashed in front of him once again: he was standing at his table in the grimy tavern in Quardinal's Brawn, watching the smile of the farmer he knocked aside fade as he closed on his wife's killer. He could smell the ale splashing from the patrons' tankards, could see his wife's killer slam his own down on the bar and gesture for a refill. And he could see Bockum standing up from his table in the corner of the tavern and begin to weave through the crowd. He braced himself against his horse's flank and closed his eyes again.

A flock of vultures took to the air, leaving behind the bones of their latest scavenge. The *clickety-clack* of mandible and rib tumbling back to their sandy grave shattered the dreadful vision.

I thought you forgave me, Kellcrim. Why, then, do you besiege me with these memories?

He wiped his eyes. His horse looked on calmly as he took up her reins and they resumed their approach toward the strange columns.

They came upon the first in the line: a stack of clay pots, each brimming with water. He cupped some and brought it to his nose.

It smelled fresh. He tossed the water back into the pot and wiped his hand on his chest.

The next column was a pile of blankets that reached to his shoulder. He peeled back the corner of one. The smell of bergamot and lavender filled his nose. It was of the finest wool and would have easily warded off the evening cold. Yet here they were piled like firewood in the desert.

Rough wooden crates filled with food formed the third column, stacked straight and tall, and rising above his head. The smell of roasted meats, apples, oranges, cheese, and bread made his mouth water. Everything looked plump despite the effects of the hot desert sun.

Connachen wiped his brow and turned back toward the distant hum of his soldiers. He could see their shimmering image over the sand now. They were bathed in the same amber and ochre glow that hung in the clouds above from the setting sun.

He slipped between the column of food and the stack of blankets. The road to the white walls of Torvisk lay ahead. As did the tall makeshift platform he'd seen earlier.

His horse drew to a halt again.

Kellcrim preserve, girl. Do you think I have a choice? Do you think I relish this?

His patience gone, he wrenched the reins hard, like a sailor tugging his rigging in a storm. The horse could do nothing but submit. And so they resumed their approach, both of them skittish and angry.

The top of the makeshift tower came into view. It held a recessed platform. On it was the crumpled body of an old man still grasping two smoldering torches. Their smoke had blackened the wood of the surrounding platform.

Connachen turned back to find Scrieve's horse taking the scribe through the stacked columns. His book was open on his lap and he wrote as he went.

"What do you make of it, captain?" he said as he approached.

"What I make of things no longer matters," Connachen barked. The anxiety was building in his chest again. He shut his eyes and strained to hold it back.

Scrieve pointed with his stylus to an onyx stone beside the platform, half-buried in the sand. A rough furrow carved across its breadth obliterated the fine etchings it once held. The furrow was full of black soot and bones, straw, leather, and strips of fabric. Tiny tendrils of smoke still rose from it.

"This stone looks like it was pried from the steps of the staircase at the Hallist temple," Scrieve said. His tone went impish. "The first town northward from the Lomhar Pass."

"That stone could be from anywhere, scribe."

Scrieve nodded, unconvinced. "Then what shall I write, captain? That it is *not* from the Hallist temple? His High Majesty will, of course, want a record." His stylus hovered over his book.

"To hell with your book, scribe!" Connachen roared. "What sickness would want to record this madness?"

"The king's truth must be recorded," Scrieve said without emotion.

"And what exactly is that truth, Scrieve? That his world is dead? Well, I wager he'll know that himself soon enough."

CHAPTER 3
THE MANY HANDS OF THE GUDFIN BLADE

"CAN YOU BELIEVE some stupid brae is willing to pay five hundred for that?" Lostrus said as he pointed into the window.

The early morning mist hung in this back alley of Quardinal's Brawn. It was wet and cloying, as though the night had come to a rolling boil and its steam was slowly descending back to the earth. And it had, in a sense. The *Strabismus of Salagrim* had been feted the night before. The square beyond the alley was still littered with its detritus: keys, empty wallets, socks, spectacles, and the thousands of folded pieces of parchment with "I've lost my heart" or "I've lost my senses" or "I've lost my way" written on them and thrown up into the air at the stroke of midnight.

And so it was not surprising that the thieves had picked this morning. Every year Salagrim's adherents, in a ceremony of stupendous irony meant to mimic their god's eternal searching, celebrated the god of vision with such ardour it led to them waking the next morning half blind.

Lostrus steamed the windowpane as he spoke. "I mean, really.

Five hundred for that? Looks like a turnip peeler to me. Aelic's black chords!" He shook his head. "There's always a bigger fool, isn't there?" He ducked his head under the window and slid down the stone wall into a crouch. "Is he still looking? Manion? Is he still looking?"

"I don't care to know," returned a stern voice.

"Helpful as always, novice."

Lostrus peeked over the corner of the window. Satisfied that he wasn't being watched, he retook his position. "According to the trollop I bedded last night, some brae thinks that that rusty blade right there is divine. Can you believe it? He calls it 'the Gudfin blade' or some such nonsense." He startled, winced, and then shook his head as if he'd sucked a lemon.

"Those fools are making a right bungle of it. Look, Manion." He pointed again into the window. "That one's hogtied the owner with the strap of an oxen bell. And he's left the bell on! Hah!" He looked to the heavens. "They'll have the whole gendarme down on them with that racket."

Lostrus's voice died away. His reflection in the window had captured his attention. He licked his thumbs and forefingers and smoothed his moustache out along his cheekbones. "And wouldn't that be embarrassing," he muttered as he admired himself and the gold embroidery of his gendarme badge from the side.

"This is disgraceful," Manion said. The tall white mare beneath him was twitchy and fractious. He patted the horse to still it, half wishing the old beast would rebel and instead carry him from the alley.

Like we did across the Roth Sea, eh, Cawthra? On the backs of sea turtles and whales, leaving that thieving bastard king back on the Jura Isle.

Cawthra warmed to his touch a moment then shook her head. Manion righted himself. "Aye. Aye, girl, you know how far we've fallen, don't you?"

A cool wind whipped through the alley. It billowed Manion's white beard and plunged down his collar. A younger Manion would have ignored the rupture, but his arthritic joints capitulated. A shiver rattled him. He reached back and pulled around his blue gendarme cloak.

"*Shhh*," Lostrus said. "They're going for the door now." He slid from the window and flattened himself against the stone wall. His own blue cloak spun around him, crashing against his thighs, ebbing and flowing as though he stood in a tide.

A door hinge creaked at the end of the alleyway. Two shapes stepped into the street. The second gently closed the door behind them and passed off a bulging sack to his brethren. Both shot suspicious glances left and right.

"There, they've taken the infernal treasure," Manion said between clenched teeth. "You've made your fifteen gold pieces."

"They missed the candelabra!" Lostrus pointed into the window. He turned from it, baffled. "How the muhk did they miss that?"

"Can we be done with this foul work?"

"Afraid not, novice. Why, we haven't even begun. We have another stop to make. You'd know that"—Lostrus turned back to the window and adjusted his badge in the reflection—"but you don't listen very well, do you, old man?" Satisfied with his preening, he spun around and shot Manion a withering look. He steadied himself on the wall and pulled off his black leather boot.

"I suppose that explains why you're still a lowly novice. At your age." He shook out the boot and out fell a pebble. "I'm sure you won't mind me saying this," said Lostrus, pointing his boot at Manion. "But if you ask me, it's a disgrace. If it weren't for the current state of discord in the land, I doubt the gendarme corps would be as charitable as to whom they grant the blue cloak." He put the boot back on.

"I blame the law courts and our feckless magistrates. As any good citizen should." Lostrus pulled out his kerchief. "If this keeps up, we'll be stocking the ranks from the graves." He slapped a shine on his boot with two quick snaps of the cloth.

Something caught Manion's eye: the thieves were bounding from shadow to shadow in the square beyond the alley. He spurred Cawthra forward.

"Novice!" Lostrus said in a commanding voice. He stood tall and tucked away his kerchief. Manion brought his horse to a halt. "Dismount!"

Manion didn't move. How he wanted to rush his old horse forward and gallop from the alley, overtake those bandits, and run them through.

Like the Charge at the Millean Gate, eh, Cawthra? Methulla's wings! How we flew down on them. I cut into that Bracken swordsman like a bear's claw. Do you remember? Hah! It was marvelous. He withered like a...

A roar from Lostrus shook him from his reverie.

"I said dismount, novice, this instant!"

Manion held firm. Lostrus stepped to his side, drew his sword, and held it to Cawthra's neck. "I will run your old mule in with my blade if you disobey me again."

Manion relented. A smile crept over Lostrus's face. "What is she again, Manion?" He stroked Cawthra's cheek. "Pure Al-ghaneen blood? First horse through the... the something gate?"

"*The Millean Gate!*" The words burst from Manion's lips like steam from a kettle. He dropped the reins and spoke more calmly. "She was the first horse through the Millean Gate." He gave her another pat on the neck.

"Was she, now?" Lostrus said, taking the horse's reins. "And she'll be the last horse to eat tonight for your insolence. She can thank you for that. Now dismount, novice."

Lostrus watched the spectacle of Manion's slow, creaky clambering down with amusement. He added to it a well-timed prod to the mare with the pommel of his sword. Cawthra jolted and Manion fell.

"Come on, novice," Lostrus said with feigned impatience.

Manion stood and wiped his knees. Lostrus was a man of

twenty-five; tall, to be sure, but Manion had been taller in his day. And Lostrus was well built, his arms and chest full of power and vitality. But Manion had known more raw strength in his day. And Lostrus's gendarme uniform, perfectly measured to the young man's body, was nothing—nothing—compared to the armor Manion had once worn. *Not worth the rivet of my breastplate*, Manion thought as he stiffened and scowled at the young man.

Lostrus's eyes were cool and bright. There was intelligence in them, to be sure. But Manion at the same time of his life had already scoured the edges of the world and served three kings: mountain, sea, and plains. He'd seen ships forged as large as continents move whole nations in exodus. He'd learned four tongues and crept single-handedly into a lair to save Marian of the famous painting. He'd had more wisdom in the bend of his piss. More than this boy would ever know.

Lostrus's mouth curled in a self-satisfied smirk. "Do you have something to tell me, Manion?" he said as he picked at his teeth. Manion was silent, but his eyes couldn't help but betray his contempt. "Go on, Manion. You can speak freely." Lostrus nodded to the cobblestones.

"I was..."

Lostrus cut him off with a disappointed shake of the head and a crisp "Tut."

"Really, Manion? I know the duties of a novice can be overwhelming to some but, still, we must insist on dignity." Lostrus adjusted the embroidered badge on Manion's chest that had shifted when he'd fallen. "There. Now you look the part of a gendarme at least."

He patted Manion's chest, signaling the work was done. He stepped back a foot, looked at the old knight, and gave him a nod. "Go ahead, Manion, I'm listening." He narrowed his eyes and tented his fingers.

Manion cleared his throat. "When I... that is, when we"—he nodded to Cawthra—"when we first crested the Millean Gate it was overrun by Fieratu, you see. A sea of them. So deep the Bracken were lost in their numbers." His hands set the scene as he spoke.

"The jump across the flames had carried us too far, you see. I only had time for one strike." Manion grasped the hilt of his sword. "Now I saw before me two Bracken warriors locked in combat, sword on sword. A titanic struggle it was."

Lostrus crossed his arms and looked down the alley; a heavy sigh escaped him.

"I raised my weapon. And in that instant, as Cawthra flew through the air, in the blink of an eye I made my decision. And which one do you think I struck down?"

"I couldn't give a pint of Woadbrek's eternal piss."

"In the split second before I loosed *this sword*"—Manion rattled it in its scabbard for effect—"I saw their eyes. They betrayed them like a chest of whispers. I sunk my sword into the heart of the Bracken on the right. And the Bracken on the left was left to live."

"Fascinating, Manion." Lostrus retreated to his horse. "Now mount your damned mule and let's be off."

"Don't you want to know *why* I chose the one on the left?"

"No."

"Don't you want to know what I saw in the Bracken's eyes?" Manion's brow furrowed in disbelief. "What spurred me to strike the one down and not the other?"

"No."

Rage erupted in Manion. "It would illustrate the point that so needs making here, captain. As we sit and watch those thieves make off, trading in our dignity for a bag of gold!"

"And why should I take lessons from a novice?" Lostrus asked, adjusting his horse's halter.

Manion surged forward, full of mighty indignation. "I didn't have my blood spilled at the Millean Gate to—to watch my dignity and honor be frittered away in some dank alley for the price of a stewed cabbage!"

"Did you not?"

"No, I did not! I pledged myself to a higher calling!" Manion was trembling, his eyes blazing.

"Well, that's really something, Manion." Lostrus nodded. "And now, using those powers of deduction that proved so useful to you at places like the Millean Gate, has it occurred to you that while you were sputtering and puffing here, those thieves are now long gone." The point struck Manion cold. He mumbled in protest but could mount no defense.

"That's right. Even if I was somehow impressed by your stories and taken in a swoon at your sentimentality. And let's pretend for the moment that I was inclined to change my mind by the sheer power of your bearing, which, of course, I'm not. You're so bloody self-righteous and pompous that, here again, you trip over your own feet." He looked Manion up and down. "You're simply a foolish, ineffectual old man stuck in the past!"

Manion's eyes bore into Lostrus's.

"So?" the young man pressed. "Anything more to add, old man? Any more stories? Wise teachings? Anecdotes?"

"No," Manion muttered.

"Good. Can I speak now?"

Manion relented with a nod that was quickly followed by Lostrus's blade under his chin. "You will go with me to The Ragged Heel. We will deliver our message for Thaltis and we will play our part. I will get my fifteen gold coins and I will whore like a king tonight. And if you're lucky, I might throw you a shilling or two."

He nodded at Manion's waist. The old man's sword was too big for his scabbard. It stuck out like a quill from an ink well. "For a start, you might consider buying yourselves a sword worthy of your position."

"This sword cut the chains of Piuthar at the battle of Seoras. That act alone changed the course of the whole war. You owe your life to this bla–"

"No one cares, Manion!" Lostrus shrieked. "Do you understand me, old man? No one cares. I don't care. Our brothers in the gendarme don't care. Nobody bloody cares!" Lostrus pressed his sword. A small tint of red spread out at the point and dyed Manion's white beard. It forced the old knight to tilt his head to relieve the pressure.

"Now let me tell you a story of my own," Lostrus whispered, drawing close to Manion's ear. "It's about an old man standing before a man a third his age. In a filthy alley, at the break of dawn, with a sword under his chin. In this story, the old man is, what? Well, he's a novice, isn't he? A gendarme first entrant. He's at the twilight of his life and he finds himself no further ahead than a farmer's son opening the door of His High Majesty's garrison for the first time. If the young man wanted to, he could order the old man to wash his breeches in his mouth. He could order him to kneel on his hands and knees so the young man could have a seated lunch."

Lostrus withdrew the blade and tapped Manion's chest with it. "What a terrible story. A veritable nightmare." He sheathed his sword.

"And so, no. No one believes you, Manion. You, a Methullian knight?" He scoffed. "Yeah, and my father was a Colmrakken war chief." He walked back to his horse and readied to mount.

"If a Colmrakken war chief produced a weakling like you he'd have thrown himself from a cliff," Manion said under his breath.

"What did you say?" Lostrus covered the distance between them in a heartbeat. "What did you say, novice?" He was inches from Manion's face. "I'm warning you, old man. You're not a knight anymore. You wash horse stalls and trail behind your betters."

Manion maintained his defiant stare. Lostrus relented, shaking his head in disbelief.

"I've tried to be nice to you, old man. I have. But you're incorrigible. You're fouling your own bed. And now, now I don't care. You want to speak candidly. Fine, let's do so. Your talk of old days isn't going unnoticed," Lostrus said. "Why do you think they glare at you around the garrison? You interrupt the present with some gloried past full of preening and preaching."

"It was a glorious time. A time of men. *A time of honor!*" Manion's face flushed red as he yelled. "Unlike this wicked feast."

Lostrus punched Manion in the gut. The old knight fell to one knee. When he was young he wouldn't have, but now his body could only break. Lostrus turned back to his horse and climbed into the saddle.

"We've thrown your time away, Manion. Years ago. We cracked every memory of it we could find. And then you show up, squawking about virtue and honor, interrupting the forgetting." He steadied his horse. "Well, let me be the first to inform you, old man: honor's gone. And your virtue? Long, long dead."

He swung his horse around and leaned down to look at Manion. "Let me put it to you clearly, saintly knight. In a way even your moldy, old brain can understand."

The morning mist was burning off, but enough lingered so that it gave each man, in the eyes of the other, the impression they were fading away.

"You had best watch out that your talk of old days doesn't rob you of new ones."

CHAPTER 4

A SPOONFUL OF SHIVERY COFFINFIT

MADRIGAN FELL BACK onto the wall with his heart beating wildly. He felt like he was being turned in a vice, pressed by a team of oxen. They squeezed out every bit of juice from his broken psyche. Out it fell onto the filthy cobblestones.

Do you hear my whispers? Because I–I don't hear you. Not anymore. Where have you gone? Please... d-don't leave me.

He pushed himself off the wall. The vice twisted again. Everything in him fell to the ground with the liquid from his stomach: all he knew, all he remembered, every fact and memory splashed into the alley. He wiped his chin. He stared at the white fluid and searched for his thoughts in its froth and steam.

His bones began their revolt. They shifted position; they rearranged themselves like a bag of sticks. He fell to his knees and vomited again. Then his bowels gave way.

Madrigan sat back on his haunches and picked at the scabs on his arms. His pupils were gone; the whites of his eyes were red. He heard nothing beyond his skin. His heart thumped like an axe into wood. A storm twisted in his lungs. Every stretch of his muscles was a hundred creaky doors.

Fumbling in his robe pocket, his fingers curled around a coin. Or was it a sword, a feather, an apple? He pulled the pocket wide and peered in. It was an old iron fence overgrown with weeds. He reached in. Red claws burst from the desiccated buds and clamped down on his wrist. He screamed. He pulled and pulled until he drew out the coin.

"If it's your hide he's looking for, pity for Salagrim," came the voice suddenly from the shadows. But Madrigan could no longer hear, or, if he could, his ears shirked their work. He pinched the coin between his lips and scratched at his face and arms, trying to carve out the burrowing horde he imagined lay within.

Crummock left his corner of the alleyway. His long black coat made him look like a layer peeling away from the shadows. He bent down and blew gold powder into Madigan's face. Madrigan crashed to the cobblestones like a stack of plates. Then, like curtains thrown open by a busy maid, his eyes opened and he gasped for breath.

He took the coin from his mouth. "Glorious powers like that, Crummock," he whispered as he rolled onto his back and stared up at the night sky. "And yet we still worship the gods!"

"You're an animal, Madrigan. Weren't you here yesterday?" Crummock said, eyeing the alley's shadows.

"Aye. And the day before that. And the day before that." Madrigan wiped his palms on his wet pants. "You have no idea how profound this Shivery Coffinfit is, good Crummock. I've heard things; I've *seen* things. Things I–I could scarcely…"

"Aye, it is something, ain't it, pitchie? I hear its amphetamined rattle is so strong it's shaken Mulloch Furdie himself from his perch.

Bet that little drudge is as jealous as a popinjay." His voice dropped to a murmur. "So? What is it? You want another then?"

"Another? I want another five!"

"Five?" Crummock drew back into the shadows. "You should have made arrangements, pitchie."

"Should I ask someone more successful in the trade?" Madrigan sneered as he righted himself.

Crummock surged from the shadows and slapped Madrigan across the cheek. It sent him tumbling back to the ground. "You go around me, boy, and I'll slit your throat." Crummock looked back down the alley, searching for prying eyes. "Let's see your coins."

"Coins? Well, as it turns out, Crummock, I no longer have the two I started out with. You see, a charismatic young merchant in Velveteen Cromide waylaid me."

Crummock snarled then turned to leave. Madrigan sped up.

"No, wait. I left my biggest coin for you, Crummock. Look, it's as big as a horse!" He held up the coin as if it were a star from the heavens. "His High Majesty's finest gold. Pressed just for this august transaction."

Crummock flashed the point of a small sword from inside his coat. "You do anything and I'll gut you—gut you good. Your reputation is starting to sour, pitchie." He grabbed the coin from Madrigan's hand.

"Is that your view, or the view of Thaltis?" Madrigan spit blood onto the cobblestones.

"Thaltis? That muhk lost his step years ago. He's grown fat and stupid. His day will come." Crummock held the coin up to his eye then snarled.

Madrigan had not produced a coin. He'd produced one of the slim terracotta tiles carved by the mysterious 'people's carver' known as Jegs. Every week his tiles would appear on doorsteps, in boots, in hearths, at the bottom of finished tankards, on windowsills. Each was pressed quick and rough from its mold. A simple sketch, only three flourishes of the artist's knife. Enough to identify the god. The god in the lead. This time it was Methulla.

Crummock threw the tile to the ground. "This is one of Jegs's trinkets, you bastard."

Madrigan scrambled on his hands and knees to the terracotta tile. He looked up like a startled deer and waved for Crummock to stay. With his other hand, he reached into his pocket. "Forgive me, Crummock, please." He produced a dirty gold coin and handed it over. Crummock took even longer examining this one.

"It's good, isn't it?" Madrigan whimpered. Crummock's grunt released Madrigan's tension. "There, you see, I've shown you mine, Crummock. It's only fair you show me yours." Madrigan's tongue slipped over his bottom lip. "To be sure you're an honest tradesman."

Crummock reached into his pocket and drew out his fist, halting it just proud. His eyes narrowed. "Do you really think it's proper, Madrigan? During your Salagrim's *Strabismus?* For you to be engaging in such… immoral conduct?"

"Immoral conduct?" Madrigan clutched at his chest. "On the contrary, Crummock. I have it on good authority that my all-seeing god turns a blind eye at my little extravagances. An indulgence he's granted me ever since I walked in on my father sawing through my mother's chest with his filet knife. It's a lesser-known dispensation of his church known as a *Salagrimistic Blinding*."

Crummock snorted then opened his hand. In his palm was a clear orb the size of an egg. Light sparked inside its confines, metered and crooked like lightning. Fog swirled like water down a drain, and sleet and hail sloshed and spun inside its transparent skin. A layer of frost jacketed the bottom of the membrane like the scaly belly of a beast.

"The s-same as before?" Madrigan whispered, transfixed. "It m-must be the same as before."

"It is, don't you worry." Crummock stared proudly at the orb. "This is pure Shivery Coffinfit."

Madrigan narrowed his eyes. He looked over his shoulder,

clutching the pendant of Salagrim that hung around his neck. "I take it Thaltis is omitted from this little transaction as well?"

Crummock put the orb back in his pocket. "Thaltis is blinded by old allegiances. He can't see how the world is changing. Pitchies are looking for a stronger bit of pitch these days, aren't they?"

Madrigan broke into a broad smile and gave an encouraging nod. "Well said, Crummock. And I say good on you, I do. Thaltis *has* gotten rusty. And the market can always benefit from a shake-up, can't it?" Madrigan surged forward on his knees. "Besides, I've always been of the opinion that the Gailicans are amateurs with their pitch. They crush it in their grain mills. Barley chaff can mix with the fluid in the bones and cause the shoulders to grind." He pursed his lips in disgust. "I know a pitchie who sounds like a rusty door when she walks. Why Thaltis buys from them, I'll never know."

Crummock checked the shadows again. "Look, you want it or not?"

"Of course I want it, my dear Crummock. When have I ever *not* wanted your fine wares? Particularly this wonderful Coffinfit you've introduced me to. And as your first and only customer, I–I feel truly blessed and honored by the faith you've shown me."

Crummock grabbed him by the collar and threw him against the wall. "What are you saying? You think I'm only fit to sell to you?" The blade flashed again, this time close to Madrigan's ear. "I sell anywhere I want in Quardinal's Brawn. Not just to you sick alley-scum. Why even the King's court…"

Crummock suddenly noticed the stain on Madrigan's collar and let him go. He stepped back in disgust. "Muhking pitchie," he muttered, looking around for somewhere to wipe his hand.

"Well, I hope you haven't sold too much of your new pitch, Crummock," Madrigan said with a sly smile. "Word tends to travel fast. Or that is… Thaltis seems to listen quicker than the rest."

Crummock wiped his hand on the sewer grate and locked eyes with Madrigan. "Let him," he growled.

"Yes, let him." Madrigan clapped his hands together, snapping the tension from the air. He shuffled forward. "Well, you'll get no reservations from me, Crummock. I remain as loyal as ever." He bowed. "I would love to purchase your new wares."

"Would you?" Crummock replied with ice in his voice. "And who says it's for sale?" The words sent a quiver across Madrigan's face.

"Letting the t-tension b-build, are we?" Madrigan said. He stumbled and crashed to the cobblestones. The horde was burrowing into his skin again.

Crummock sneered. "You can never gauge exactly when that stuff will wear off." He sniffed at the fingers that had held the powder he'd blown into Madrigan's face.

The poor pitchie shook uncontrollably now. The confusion returned. The vice tightened once again.

"Two gold coins, pitchie," Crummock growled.

"Two? I h-haven't got two! I only have the one."

Crummock palmed the coin, spat on the ground, and made to leave.

"No, wait! A different payment, then!"

"What does a muhk-smeared pitchie have to offer me?"

"I..." Madrigan searched in the growing fog for a gambit. "That Shivery Coffinfit, I tell you, Crummock. It–it grants power, power like I've... I've never seen."

"That's it. I'm leaving." Crummock began walking down the alleyway.

"Wait!" Madrigan screamed, lunging for his leg. "You were gone, weren't you? For a fortnight, were you not? Last month. Arrested by the gendarme?"

Crummock stopped. He looked down at Madrigan.

"Now, w-why? How could those fat, sleepy fools, how could they know a–a clever cautious man like yourself would be in possession of pitch? I could tell you which birdie w-whispered to them, if you let me."

"How?"

"The Shivery Coffinfit, Crummock." Madrigan nodded at the man's pocket. "I tell you, there's some sort of magic in those vapors. Magic, Crummock! I haven't just *seen* things. I've... I've *done* things. You let me s-spin that pitch and I'll find out for you, good and quick."

Crummock considered the words a moment. He grabbed Madrigan's collar and yanked him to his feet. "You thieve from me, you sick little muhk of a pitchie, and I'll gut you. I'll gut you like a deer. Do you hear me?"

"Of course, Crummock. Of course."

Crummock let Madrigan go with a rough shove. He pressed the orb into the pitchie's dirty hand. Madrigan wiped his finger over its length.

"Ooh, this will do. This will do just fine," he whispered, savouring the taste of his finger in his mouth. He fell to his knees and set the orb down as he would a baby. "The secret is to... is to hear your words before you say them."

"Hurry up, pitchie," Crummock grumbled.

Madrigan nodded. His fingers, impossibly poised and calm now, waved over the orb. And his lips, impossibly delicate and precise now, spilled a whispered incantation.

"Magic, eh?" Crummock snorted as he watched on with disdain. "Doesn't look like magic to..."

The egg suddenly began to distend and contract as if Madrigan's hovering fingers were kneading it like dough. The pitchie's whispers quickened. The orb rose above the cobblestones and hovered at the height of his eyes. He threw back his head and let his tongue fall from his open mouth like the lid of a can.

As Crummock leaned forward to get a closer look at this baffling display, the orb burst with a giant *boom* that rang through the alley. Mist poured over Madrigan's face like steam off a kettle. Crummock darted back into the shadows.

A bolt of lightning descended from the frothing, undulating

storm in front of Madrigan's face. It unfurled like a monkey's tail. He positioned himself under it as if he were trying to drink from a leaky pipe. The bolt of lightning seemed to play with him, gently dodging left and right as the pitchie followed, mouth open, neck stretched.

Then it shot down his throat, and the whole storm with it. Madrigan's jaws snapped shut; his body jerked and spasmed. He crumbled, motionless, onto the cobblestones.

Crummock, flat against the wall, listened for any sign of movement, then drew his collar over his ears and stepped forward.

The pitchie's skin was translucent now, and an effervescence was visible under it. The gases reached their limit at the crown of Madrigan's head. There they parted like bubbles trapped under winter ice.

Crummock was so enthralled he almost missed the sound of breathing close to his left shoulder. When he finally registered it, he made up for his lost attention with a mad scramble to the far wall, devoid of all dignity.

He looked back. The shadows moved. A flutter here. A twist there. Then, like a tarp being removed from an old armoire, they bunched at the middle, combining into a single shape, and slid off the wall.

The shadow moved to stand over Madrigan's body. It was silent. It didn't move. But a series of ripples over its length and breadth slowly generated the creature's detail.

Whatever abomination stood before Crummock, it was hidden completely in long, black robes. The only obvious detail was a stack of pendants around its neck. Where the creature's head would have been was a wide flaccid cowl, the edges of which sputtered like oil in a heated pan.

Then, without warning, without measure, without any cause Crummock could discern, the cowl burst into full form like a sail taking wind. The pendants around the creature's neck began to spin like stones in a sling, slowly at first, then faster and faster.

The creature bent at the waist, presenting its cowl as if it were a volcano presenting its crater. Its hands drew up and disappeared into it. The creature struggled a moment as it bound its prey and then drew its hands free. There, hanging in its grasp, was the ethereal image of a man's head whispering into a gendarme's ear.

"Thaltis!" Crummock whispered. He swung his sword at the image, dissipating both it and the creature that produced it. He glowered down at Madrigan as if he might strike the pitchie as well, but he settled on a roar of anger then ran from the alley.

All went silent. Even the wind seemed to pull up at the threshold to the narrow passage. There Madrigan lay comatose and riddled with the strange gases for quite some time. How much time passed was impossible to tell. But it was long enough to draw the inquisitive denizens of that alley from their lairs. Rats sniffed and pigeons pecked the wet cobblestones.

An old black cat appeared at the alley's entrance. The tip of its mangy tail curled around a tiny burlap sack small enough to have been pilfered from the last mouse dispatched for dinner. The cat sniffed at the threshold then meandered toward Madrigan. It pawed at the mortar in the wall, sniffed at a stream of sludge, then toured Madrigan's body in a slow ramble.

It dropped to its haunches, licked its flank, yawned, then went still. Its bright yellow eyes fixed on Madrigan and its tail gently thumped the bag on the cobblestones.

The cat seemed of a piece with the shadows and silence in that dark alley. That is, until its left eye quivered. The quiver turned into a shake. The shake turned into a spin. The eye turned and turned until its movement whizzed red hot then came to a halt. With another ratchet to the right, the eye fell away and tumbled to the ground like a manhole cover. A tiny hand appeared in the hole and batted away the plume of steam escaping from it.

The feline's tail curled toward the eye socket. The hand wrenched the sack free. There it hung like a dislodged eyeball until a second hand appeared from the cat's eye socket and opened the sack.

The gases filling Madrigan's mouth broke their invisible boundary and spilled out into the alley. The hands rattled the sack as if enticing a pet to dinner. The tendrils of gas rose into the air, braided together, and snaked toward the sack—slowly, cautiously. The hands shook it again, signaling their impatience. The gases startled, drew up, found their courage, and then disappeared into the burlap.

CHAPTER 5
BIND UP THE BLADES

THE 12TH LEGGAT caught up with Connachen as the sun finally set and the veil of night was beginning to draw over the desert. They made a quick camp on the outskirts of Torvisk, giving the strange columns and platform a wide berth. The next morning Connachen ordered his army to overturn the jugs of water and smash the food into the sand. Even the blankets were ordered torn to shreds. The soldiers looked at him resentfully as they worked under the scorching sun, contemplating their evening's rations of thin soup and dirty water. So it went for the men condemned to The Thunder that Wanders.

Connachen had also ordered the platform destroyed and the sickly spectacle of the dead man on high wiped from the desert canvas. Presently a young soldier began climbing the black tower to retrieve the body. A group of Leggat soldiers stood by and watched, torches in their hands, ready to touch them to the wood.

The young soldier laid the corpse on the sand. The dead man's white robes were edged in brilliant blue and he wore a thick gold pendant. It was the unmistakable work of Frew the Elder, the senior sculptor to His High Majesty. In perfect proportion and outstanding detail, it showed Methulla, Aelic, Digrir, Civiak, and Salagrim each pouring a pitcher of water. The water streamed down to a young girl holding a cup to receive it. Each pitcher was stamped with the likeness of Bragnal staring, radiant and powerful, back at the viewer. The gods looked down at their pitchers with unmistakable disgust. All save Salagrim. Frew the Elder had rendered the single-eyed god awestruck and staring off to the horizon as if something had taken his attention.

"I can't at this very moment account for his method of death, captain," Gogarburn said finally as he stood up from the body. "At first glance, it looks like he died of apoplexy. The spasms peculiar to Leff's Wandering Gripe come to mind."

"What of the arms?" Connachen asked. The dead man's arms were black, as were his wrists and hands.

"Soot from the torches, I should imagine. Quite curiously, they were bound to his arms there and there." He pointed to ropes still wrapped around the man's hands. He snapped his fingers and his young attendant ran forward to untie them. He presented the ropes to Connachen with a bowed head.

"I want to know how this man died, Gogarburn. And not in a fortnight," Connachen said, ignoring the boy. He turned to Wulfric, who was tapping his rolled tobacco on the sand and examining the body for himself.

"Assemble a vanguard, Wulfric."

The tall Jarlspeen raised his head. The Jarlspeen tribes of the north were known for their bluntness. Their ways were often as cold as the winds that whipped their villages. "Why?" he said loudly enough for all to hear.

Connachen pulled him in close. "Because I aim to follow our orders, Wulfric."

"Follow our orders?" Wulfric pulled the rolled tobacco from his mouth and inspected the ember. "'S'funny, I don't remember signing on for orders like these. To be a gang of whipping boys. I feel fairly confident in saying I don't think any of these boys have such a recollection, either, of the day they were tossed into the 12th."

"Be plain with your meaning, Wulfric."

"It's plain you'd like, is it? Okay." The big man jabbed his finger into Connachen's chest.

"I think this trail of misery and death is *your* fault, captain. That's what I think. And it's not just me who thinks it. I think you've gone and cursed us beyond our station. I think you're going to get us all killed following the whispers of your bastard god Kellcrim. We should be long gone by now." His voice had risen.

"Like Bockum said we should be, right, boys? And the sooner we meet up with him and his men, the better."

"Just follow your orders, Wulfric, and assemble a vanguard." Connachen struggled to keep the growing panic out of his voice.

"Aye, orders. For now, Connachen. For now."

Wulfric set his fingers in his mouth and whistled. It was too loud and too close; it rang painfully in Connachen's ears.

"We will ride to the town," Connachen yelled. His words sent surprise skipping down the line of men. He turned back to Wulfric. "Destroy what's left. When you're finished, ride to the gates and wait for us there."

Wulfric sucked his teeth and spat in the sand. "The compassion of that Kellcrim of yours has you going potted, little toad. And us with it."

Connachen made to reply, but Scrieve grabbed his elbow. "Shall I come with you, captain?"

"And miss detailing each severed limb and cup of human blood?" Connachen said mockingly as he mounted his horse. "Would His High Majesty countenance such shoddy craft from his appointed scribe?"

Connachen tore off for the Lyceum gates. The soldiers mounted their horses and scrambled to follow their captain. Scrieve watched them gallop away toward the looming Lyceum spire like leaves blown back toward their tree, then bent down to the corpse.

The old man smelled of decay and damp earth, like an old firepit doused with rain. Scrieve grabbed one of his blackened hands. The soot felt odd between his fingers. It was heavy, almost wet. He wiped the man's blackened wrist against his robes and fell back in shock. Instead of leaving a stain, the soot moved and shifted on the fabric to form words: *Polymonious XVI.*

Scrieve looked up. None of the remaining soldiers had seen. He blotted the words out and stood. Soldiers were filing past him, torches and axes in hand. The piles were being set to. Kicked over. Scattered.

He drew out his book and turned to a fresh page. Elbows bumped him. He had to sway away from flame and blade but managed to write "Polymonious XVI" in shaky handwriting. He waited a breath until, under his writing, in cursive long and tight, came back the following words: "Astounding. How quick they…"

Too terrified to watch the sentence finish, Scrieve slammed the book shut and stumbled through the Leggatmen to his horse.

The town of Torvisk was walled in limestone, fifteen feet high. The intense desert sun had withered it to a bone-white. At either side of the gate stood more marble statues carved by the great Frew the Elder. On the left, there were five. One each for Methulla, Aelic, Digrir, Civiak, and Salagrim, each pouring a pitcher of water engraved with the proud, mocking face of Bragnal.

The space afforded by the gate had given Frew the Elder more room to work. And the carver had taken advantage of it. Methulla's pitcher was held aloft by the god's six birds. Aelic's was bound by the hundreds of cords flowing off his hands. Digrir's was held by the group of children at the god's feet. Civiak poured his pitcher with his long tongue. The flow of water from the four pitchers arced over the gate to the statue of a young girl holding her cup to receive it. But Frew the Elder had rendered Salagrim's pitcher fallen and shattered, for Salagrim had fixed his giant eye on the horizon, and his finger pointed to something in the distance.

Beyond the gate, the Lyceum tower stood eighty feet high. It was the tallest structure in the empty desert for miles. In a land perpetually reshaped by wind and sand, it stood as a monument to the permanent and the eternal.

Connachen and his men had dismounted by the time Scrieve caught up to them. Each set about his quiet, cautious inspection alone with his own thoughts. And so Bearach crouched on his haunches. The old Trajean soldier sifted a handful of sand between his fingers and looked on with contempt as Connachen drew the gate from the stone wall, dislodging the weak grasses and vines that tangled through it.

"It was never even closed," Bearach said. "There wasn't even a bloody dam in the way of this flood."

"Shall I make the entry?" Scrieve asked.

Connachen let the gate go. It swung back against the limestone. He signaled for the men to follow him, and Scrieve closed his book.

Bearach slapped his hands clean of the sand and stood up. He locked eyes with the young Gailican soldier beside him who was leaning against his halberd. "Maybe your god Rawl has a sense of humor?" Bearach grumbled.

"Maybe. But doubtful," Zollern replied. "I'm sure he has better things to do than laugh." He was a fresh-faced youth of no more than twenty. He sported a patchy red beard and long red hair. The shaft of his halberd had long ago split, and he kept its end wrapped with whatever twine and rope he could find. It bulged like the knot of a tree now.

"Better things to do than laugh? Like what, boy?" Bearach turned to follow the men into the town.

"Well, for one thing, judging by your stench, Bearach, he's obviously preoccupied with brewing something foul in your undergarments."

The old soldier smiled at the insult. "Oh, he's a bountiful god, then, is he?"

Zollern inverted his halberd and whispered into the knot of twine and rope. "How should I know what he is? He doesn't speak to me, does he?" He looked up at Bearach with wild eyes. "But I know one thing he surely isn't."

"And what's that, lad?" Bearach said, looking back at the young soldier.

"I know he isn't happy to watch the 12th Leggat follow this cursed muhk and his Kellcrim as he plays the hero." Zollern nodded toward Connachen. "It's because of him we wandered into the Lomhar Pass. Bockum warned us, didn't he? We should be making for the canyon as fast as possible. The quicker we meet up with Bockum the better."

"Don't be so sure, young Zollern."

"Don't be so sure? That man's cursed, you old fool. He's picked the wrong god. Just as Bockum told us."

"Maybe. Or maybe your silent god Rawl is fixing a bridge of redemption for you, boy. One built on our mad captain's back. One that'll lead you straight out of The Thunder that Wanders and into Rawl's mead hall. Did you ever think of that?"

Zollern snorted. "Is that what your god is telling you, old man?"

"Aye. Unlike your Rawl, who seems to always have his mouth full of pigeon meat and spruce bark or whatever it is you Gailicans fill your bellies with, my god deigns to speak to me. I know exactly what he has waiting for me."

Zollern pounded the butt of his halberd into the sand. "Well, if that's the aim of my Rawl too, then Rawl can burn in the fires of Hadrich for all I care. I'm sick of following that mad muhk. He's going to get us all killed!"

"Fine priest of Rawl you'll make." Bearach eyed the Torvisk spire.

"Finest in all Medurham, old man. You'll see."

"No, son. Gollunt willing, I won't," Bearach murmured as he followed the soldiers through the gates and into Torvisk.

All was still. Nothing save the fluttering of the banners on the Lyceum tower pierced the strange, eerie silence. But in the nothing, there is always something. That lesson had come quickly to the condemned men of The Thunder that Wanders. So they drew their swords. And their gaze darted over every window and door as they progressed deeper into the town.

They soon came to the square. There were more stacks here. Stacks of the dead: men, women, and children all separated, all piled one on top of each other like so many sacks of grain.

Tiny fires still burned; banners lay torn and stomped into the ground; furniture hung out of windows; horses and oxen lay charred and bent in smoldering firepits. And the white walls of the town were no longer white. Tendrils of black soot had washed over their tips as though they had caught a stain on the wind. In the charcoal mottle and smear, curled in a strange cursive, were the words *Polymonious XVI.*

In the middle of the square stood a circular, slightly raised, marble stage. In the middle of it, a burnt-out cage sat on a wagon. Connachen targeted it first, his hand poised on the hilt of his blade.

A metal plate had been attached to the wood at the cage's peak. The shape of Civiak, his hands intertwined, his long tongue curling down to them, was still clear despite the damage caused by the flames. As was Civiak's maxim: *a cage for a beast or a lawyer at least.*

Soot covered the cage bars and ceiling, and a large hole had been burned in the floor. A pile of ash and debris on the ground beneath spoke of the flames that had engulfed the wagon. There, sticking out like branches in sand, were the burnt remains of three bodies. Among the remains, Connachen could see the charred edges of swords and axes.

"Well," Scrieve said humorlessly, "at least they caged and dispatched some of the aggressors." He opened his book and wrote.

Connachen kicked the cage door. It had taken the brunt of the flames. The wood was thin and brittle, and it broke easily under his foot. He reached in, drew a sword from the pile, and inspected it.

"No," he said, "change that. This weapon isn't Ghorak. The Ghorak use rock. This is a human sword, forged in Harodim's Wish, judging by the pommel." He threw the sword on the ground. "These three were men."

"One could… take a different view." Scrieve looked over the top of his glasses. "May I remind you, captain, that no difference lies between a Ghorak and a human skeleton."

"I was at the Lomhar Pass, scribe. Don't lecture me on the material properties of burnt remains. While you were chronicling those flames at length, I was being burned by them."

Connachen bent under the cage. He kicked at the pile of ash and soot, knocking the scorched skulls into the square. His eyes glimpsed metal. He reached into the ash.

"And tell me, scribe, what Ghorak wears a Lyceum band?" Connachen tossed the charred metal necklace onto the ground in front of Scrieve. As with the one they'd found on the dead body outside the town, the contours of the gods pouring their pitchers were still visible despite the ravages of the flames.

Zollern leaned off his halberd and into the door of the cage for a view. "Then the Ghorak burned these men," he muttered before righting himself. "And that'd be the lot of 'em. All dead. Like all the rest. What are we traipsin' through the rubble for, then? Let's be off and join up with Bockum."

"Locked them in a cage of wood with swords and an axe?" Connachen shook his head. "No, these men entered this cage of their own free will. And they submitted to their death. There isn't a single blow to the wood."

He snatched the metal band from Scrieve, who had retrieved it.

"You're so fond of the truth, scribe, put that in His High Majesty's official account: town burns its warriors and plies its attackers with meats, blankets, and water." He turned away from them. He could feel his anxiety growing like a tide climbing up its harbour. He needed air, just a single breath of clean air.

Scrieve shut his book and scurried up to Connachen. "Captain." He kept his voice contained so as to not reach the other soldiers. "You and I both know that some of the more confounding aspects of this epoch we stride are a matter of *interpretation*."

Connachen ignored him. He was struggling for breath and trying to rub his nerves calm through his forehead. Images of the tavern in Quardinal's Brawn—his folded blacksmith's apron, his plate of food, his wife's killer clanging his empty tavern on the bar—flooded back before his mind's eye.

Scrieve stepped in front of Connachen, blocking his path. It was a small mercy. It focused Connachen's tilting world.

The scribe put his palm on his book. "I believe you forget that we are witnessing the writing of a particularly hazardous portion of our history."

"I've known no other type of history, scribe," Connachen said flatly.

Scrieve forced a smile. "Well, then, on that we agree. And, so, consider this, commander. Were you to lose your life, or be swallowed in this expanse of desert, your words and deeds would become, how shall we say, open to interpretation. I should think you would welcome the power to work with, well, the chisel as it carves the tablet."

"Let us not mince words, scribe." Connachen wiped the sweat from his brow. "While history is being written before my eyes, I will not let you edit it. Not anymore."

"You seemed much more open to the proposition after the unfortunate events of the Lomhar Pass."

"And I seem to recall you didn't take the invitation." Connachen seethed. "I seem to recall your pen feverishly stabbing your pages while the Ghorak feverishly stabbed my men."

Scrieve cleared his throat. "Well, the battle was one of exceeding interest to the realm." His gaze fell nervously to his book, which he closed and drew behind his back. "And as you know, it was an exceedingly one-sided affair. It would take dramatic flourishes even I don't possess to cleanse that account."

Connachen grabbed the scribe by the collar. "So you would foul the honor of these men?"

"No! No, great captain. I would reclaim it!" But the scribe's words only made Connachen tighten his grip.

"Let me write a new narrative, captain. Let me show His High Majesty all the forces you were up against. The destructive force. The insurmountable odds. The certainty of death. For the good of the kingdom… for the 12th Leggat's honor!"

Connachen released his hold. "And who decides what's good for the kingdom? You?" Connachen looked away. "You pluck the strings of truth when it fits you. You have no concept of honor."

"Do I have you correct?" Scrieve asked, pointing back to the burnt cage. "You think the good of the kingdom is served by recording the capitulation of its own people?"

"I know this, scribe: this world would be far better off without your truths and accounts." Connachen turned and walked away.

"We both need my truths and my lies!" Scrieve yelled after him. "You would be wise not to forget that, *captain at the Lomhar Pass!*"

CHAPTER 6

SCRAMHAMMER AND BASHQUAKE WALK INTO A TAVERN

THE BARKEEP STARED at the two dwarves and tilted his head contemptuously.

"Look at this one. Probably pulled the cork on the race himself," Bashquake whispered to Scramhammer as he stared at the barman. "And then he has the cheek to sell the rest of us drinks to wash it down with." Scramhammer could smell the campfire and mole meat on the old dwarf's breath.

"Are you going to order or just stare?" The barkeep swatted a mosquito with his cloth.

"Beer," Scramhammer said, flipping a gold coin onto the bar. The bartender slid it into his hand and dropped it in a mug behind the counter. The handle of the mug was carved into the form of Woadbrek. The god was steadying himself on the mug to gather his balance as three gnomes poured more beer down his throat.

The bartender filled a wooden mug from the keg. He gave it to Scramhammer and resumed drying his mugs. Scramhammer turned and faced the room of the Ragged Heel pub. He inhaled the malty smell of the beer and smiled.

His beard stretched down to his clavicle; it had been parted in two and dipped in crimson dye. He wore leather armor and a bronze manica that ran the length of his right shoulder to his right hand. A spiked mace dangled from his belt. Like Bashquake, he carried his outsized shield on his back. It made the dwarf appear like a high-relief sculpture freed from its rock but with a chunk of its substrate it couldn't shake off.

He walked a few steps, gulping prodigiously from the mug, then collapsed onto a bench as froth from his beer leapt into the air. Bashquake followed, his gaze spinning the length and breadth of the bar, wearing his contempt with pride. The old dwarf's hair was gray and matted from neglect. His beard went to his navel, split into three, and was died aquamarine. He wore old leather armor and a wolf's pelt over his shoulders. A war hammer hung at his waist.

Scramhammer took another sip of his beer. A young human couple huddled over a single tankard caught his attention. Bashquake noticed and leaned in.

"Now that human wouldn't hurt a fly. Bet he asks her permission to blow on his own soup. Looks like a blind mole, doesn't he? When the race starts, he'll cry and beg, mark my words."

He took a gulp from Scramhammer's mug and wiped his mouth with the back of his hand. Scramhammer's attention hadn't moved, so he continued.

"Now human women," he said, "mad as swans. They'd talk down a man's sword at the neck of the devil." He tried for another sip but Scramhammer pulled his beer closer. He'd noticed the bundle on the woman's lap. Bashquake trailed this observation as well.

"Good. *Good,*" the old dwarf said. "You see well, pup-king. But make you no mistake. That wean is a human wean. Soft now, but he'll harden. Quick as your blink. Mark you this: that sweet little wean will soon be the curse in some dwarf's throat. You watch." He grabbed Scramhammer's collar and pulled the young dwarf in closer, knocking the tankard into a wobble.

"And that brings us to another point, wretched pup-king." He caught the tankard. "You'd do well to be wary of just where you drop your own seed." He released Scramhammer and took up the tankard again. "A kingdom's strength will depend on it."

The door of the tavern opened. Two men eyed the room as they walked to the bar. Bashquake leaned in again.

"Now those two humans, look at 'em. Beady eyes and heavy foreheads. I imagine even a worthless king-to-be can tell criminals when he sees them."

Scramhammer watched them keenly as the old dwarf spoke.

"That first one's a dimwit. Sure as granite. Look how the nostrils hang lower than the ear lobe. Molly-brained from birth or I'm a muhk. And the second…" Bashquake narrowed his eyes as he considered the point. "That's a Calamagarian chin, I'd bet my hammer on it. He can sniff the scent of your coins before his breath reaches his nose."

The strangers sat down on two stools. "Beer," barked the first man as he placed a leather bag on the bar and wrapped his arms around it like it was a pillow. The bartender put two mugs in front of the men.

"May Woadbrek leave the drinks to the mortals," the Calamagarian said as he raised his mug.

"You put the marble back, right?" the other asked as he reluctantly raised his own mug.

"Crystop, my good friend, you worry too much." The Calamagarian turned to survey the room.

"And you don't worry enough, Supa." As Crystop swivelled his chair to face the room, his elbow caught on the leather drawstring of the bag. It fell to the floor with a huge clatter. The impact caused the string to slacken, and a gold plate slid out. He sprang from his chair after it.

"Why are we here?" he grumbled, stuffing the plate back in the bag. "We should be at the goddamn smith's."

"Hard work merits a drink," Supa replied. "And what's the use of work if no one knows you're working?"

"The smith knows."

"Yeah, but his purse is as dull as his swords." Supa took another sip.

"Well, hurry up and get this stupid spectacle over with." His partner dropped the sack back onto the bar.

"A few more eyes yet, Crystop, my friend," he whispered as he scanned the room.

Meanwhile, Scramhammer was seething, curling his hand into a fist. "Grimy human thieves."

"Good. Good pup-king!" Bashquake said. "And what of them?"

"Guilty of human thievery. Plain as kraken breath."

"*Human* thievery?" Bashquake slapped the young dwarf. "What makes you think they stole human goods?"

Scramhammer worked his jaw out. "You implying they stole from dwarves?"

Bashquake cocked his head. "Aye, I am, pup-king. Did you not see that plate? Dwarven it was, or I'm a muhk."

Scramhammer sputtered and spun in his seat to look back at the bar. "Which kingdom?" His eyes flashed with anger.

"Hard to say, pup-king. Winchpry Hall, perhaps. Or the Jig-stricken Fissures. Or perhaps the Festerbilge Muds." Bashquake lingered on this last option to see if there was any spark in the young dwarf's eyes. There was none.

"Not the Mightenthew Fortress, surely." Scramhammer replied, ignoring him and stroking his beard. "They'd never climb those walls."

"Aye, likely not Mightenthew. Likely from a less formidable kingdom. But even the lowliest of dwarven kingdoms has value."

The words seemed to sour the air before Scramhammer. He looked back at the old dwarf as if he'd sucked a lemon. "Bah! Then let them have it."

"*Let them have it*, the muhk-sire says. And if the pup-king's coronation chair *doesn't* lie in the kingdom of Mightenthew? If it lies in a less auspicious locale—the Festerbilge Muds, for example. What then?"

Scramhammer bashed his fist on the table. "Anything less than Mightenthew and I'll refuse. You tell them that." He made to drink, but more words came to mind. More invective. He paused the tankard at his chin. "I'm no two-piece thane, Bashquake, fit to walk a land of mud and crumbly flint," he snarled. "I won't accept. You just watch. They can't force me."

"Can they not?" Bashquake replied as he settled back in his seat.

Meanwhile, Supa was whispering behind his raised mug of beer. "Pull out the tankard."

Crystop glared back at him.

"Do it!"

Crystop undid the drawstring of the leather bag, reached in, and set the silver tankard on the bar. Supa leaned over and slid it down the wood to show it off.

"He's making a mockery of us," Crystop said. "Here we are on display like a bunch of popinjays. We should be off the streets and at the smith's."

Supa sucked his teeth. "Well, true: no one likes to feel the fool." He finished the last of his beer. "Put out the dagger."

Crystop hesitated again.

"Do it, you muhk!"

Muttering like a glugging drain, Crystop drew out the dagger and slid it down the bar. It glimmered in the faint candlelight.

Scramhammer's blood went cold when he saw it. He pulled the old dwarf toward him, but Bashquake got the first word in. "Yes. Yes, *a scoush*, pup-king. Now that is surely dwarven."

"Filthy human filches." Scramhammer spat. "We should close our doors. Now! Let them all burn!"

"Ah, but the doors of the Mightenthew Fortress are not yours, pup-king. Not yet. Perhaps not ever."

"And so these filthy humans filch our wealth and we do nothing?"

"Is this nothing, pup-king?" Bashquake leaned in close again, sliding the mug away from them both. "You're watching and you're learning. Every inch of their foul nature. You're seeing that the human look is the human take. And the human take is always a take from someone else. Always. Never forget."

Scramhammer turned at the sound of two chairs sliding against the stone floor. The man and woman had stood up and were approaching the bar. The man's voice trembled as he spoke.

"He'll take the blade."

"He will, will he?" Supa leaned off the bar. "How much?"

"Three hundred coins."

"Show me."

"What? Here?" The man looked nervously over his shoulder but relented under Supa's intense stare. He nodded to his wife.

She put the bundle on a table and unfolded the blankets. The naked baby kicked at the air. A tiny silver pendant of Digrir—on his knee before a mother and child—rattled around his neck as he fretted and squirmed. She hushed him and slid her arm along his back, finding a coin purse and handing it to her husband. Supa snatched the purse, looked inside, and threw it back.

"Three hundred coins," he said quietly, nodding his head before his voice galloped to a roar. "You insult us, Thaltis!"

Every head in the tavern turned; every conversation withered. "Five hundred coins! Not a single coin less!"

"But w-we can't," the man replied. "He only gave us… He doesn't let us negotiate. And we don't know who…" His voice trailed off as his wife touched his wrist. She stepped forward.

"Please, take the purse. Just give us—"

Supa grabbed the baby by his chubby leg, shaking him free from his swaddling. As the infant hung upside down, he searched the bundle of blankets for more coins.

"He sent you here with three hundred coins? He presumed to

tell Supa what he'll pay? Does Thaltis take me for a naked beggar?" Supa laid the baby out onto the bar and drew out his sword. "Well, Supa is no beggar. You'll get me my five hundred coins. Now! Or this babe's brains polish the bar."

He swung his sword toward the child's head. The woman screamed; at the last second Supa diverted his sword so it glanced off the bar.

The man rushed at him, but Crystop drew his own sword. He slashed the man's side and kicked him back. The man crumpled to the ground. Crystop glared at the other patrons, daring them to come forward.

"When the babe's dead, take the dagger," Bashquake said as he drank the last of Scramhammer's beer.

"When the babe's dead?"

"Yes, you muhk-clotted pup-king! To hell with the human child. Have you not been listening? Let its brains run. One less criminal, I say. Besides, who plants a seed in the midst of the race, anyway?"

Scramhammer nodded. He undid the knot of his mace and stood up from the table, but Bashquake jerked him down. "Make a mess of this, you dreg-brained scion, and I will carve your family's name into the lily-white skin of your backside."

Just then the tavern door opened. Manion lingered by the door, blushing and fidgeting at his oversized sword, as Lostrus strutted toward the bar.

"I hear whispers of a threat to the peace here in Quardinal's Brawn!"

"No, no threat to the king's peace. Just a lively conversation heated through good ale," Supa replied with a crooked smile.

"Please," the woman said. "He took our baby; threatened to kill him."

Lostrus turned to Supa. "Is this true?"

"Sir, please. Much drink has been spilled down our throats tonight. Some of us have let our imaginations get the better of us." He glared at the woman.

"Quite true, Calamagarian." Lostrus frowned and crossed his arms. "How else to explain five hundred coins? Four hundred is the reasonable sum. Not a penny more."

Supa startled. The child's father protested. But Lostrus held him quiet with a hand in the air as he took a gulp from Crystop's tankard.

"You will take the four hundred coins," he said, smacking his lips, "and as for the child…" He leaned over to stare at the bawling baby. "Do with him what you like. I can't imagine he's of any concern to Thaltis." He raised his sword to Supa's throat. "Between us, if you don't take his offer you have the brains of a drak."

Lostrus finished Supa's beer, smiled, bowed, and retreated. Manion followed him out the door under a cloud of gloom.

Supa grinned after him. He turned to the room and bellowed. "You bargain like a god, Thaltis! I accept!"

The mother rushed forward and grabbed her son. She hugged him close to her chest and drew back.

"Run," the father whispered.

But Crystop grabbed the man by the collar and yanked him back. Putting his blade to the man's neck, he sneered, "Not so fast. You owe us four hundred coins."

"But I–I," the man sputtered. "He only sent us with three hundred."

"Then who's paying the sum? Hmm?" Supa looked around the room. "Which one of you bastards has it?" His gaze settled on Scramhammer, who now stood beside them watching quietly.

"You!" He pointed with his sword. "It's you, isn't it?"

"Yeah. Sure. It's me."

"Well, pay up, dwarf. And don't touch the money. We want a profit, not the plague."

Supa turned to signal the barkeep to fill his tankard just as Scramhammer swung his mace. In a flash, it had caved in Crystop's jaw. Teeth and blood poured out of his mouth as the man dropped his sword and grabbed at the wound.

Supa turned back and attacked. But his swing carried such force he couldn't stop his sword's downward thrust, and Scramhammer dodged it easily. The sword clanged off the stone floor. With a mighty backswing Scramhammer mashed the Calamagarian's nose to pieces. It exploded in blood, and Supa fell to the floor unconscious.

Scramhammer glared at the trembling man now freed from Crystop's grasp. "Filthy human filches."

The man nodded and gathered up his wife, and they disappeared out the tavern door.

Scramhammer returned his mace to his belt. He finished Crystop's beer in one gulp and picked up the scoush. Bashquake snatched it from him as patrons were crashing over each other to escape out the door.

"Thieved from the Carbor Quicks." Bashquake held the hilt of the dagger close to his eye. "Deep within the Festerbilge Muds, if I don't miss my mark." He again lingered on the name, hoping for a dazzle in the young dwarf's eyes.

But the glee on Scramhammer's face withered at the mention of the Muds. He snatched the scoush back and ran his finger over the blade. "Festerbilge Muds?" His nods grew bigger as he surveyed the length of the old, rusted blade. "Course it is. Tip's broken. It's as rusty as an old nail. What the muhk do we want with this piece of flinty tin?"

A young girl, her apron full of apples and her cheeks rosy from the day's exertion, called from the doorway. "He'll give you three hundred for the dagger. Just walk down the road and enter the butcher's shop. Your gold will be waiting for you there." With that, she slipped away into the muddy street.

Scramhammer glared at his old companion. "You made me leave my drink to reclaim a rusty little needle forged by the halfwits of the Festerbilge Muds?"

Bashquake wrapped his arm around the young dwarf's shoulder and steered him to the door of the tavern. "But a dwarven scoush is a dwarven scoush, pup-king. Whether it comes from the raging forges of the Mightenthew Fortress or the baked muds of the Festerbilge. Don't be so quick to disregard the baubles of even the lowliest of dwarven kingdoms."

The sun was setting as they stepped outside. The roads of Quardinal's Brawn were now busy with men and women rushing home after their day's labors.

"That blade is useless to you. Not worth your time. And the longer you keep it, the less he'll pay. Two-fifty now." The words came from a man kneeling in the mud. In his hands was a basket of bread baked into the form of the god Digrir. A group of filthy children hovered around him, snatching at the knotted loaves.

"What is going on, Bashquake?" Scramhammer whispered, breaking his tutor's embrace and retreating from the children.

"The imbecile heir is as baffled as a donkey," said a man as he passed by carrying a pile of wood. Scramhammer ran after him and pushed him over, scattering his load into the muddy street.

"Give the dagger to the boy in red," shouted a man leading an ox.

Scramhammer turned to him and put his hand to his hilt. "Treacherous, filthy, contemptuous humans!"

"It's a hundred now," said a boy rushing after a dog.

"Give it to the jeweler, dwarf. He'll have your money," said a man on horseback. Scramhammer roared at him like a caged bear.

"Well, pup-king, what will you do?" Bashquake whispered. "Shall we keep this thieved dwarven treasure form the Festerbilge Muds, or cast it back to these thieving, grubby humans?"

"Keep it? Why should we keep it? This piece of flinty muhk's-work has been trouble enough. If it were a battle axe forged in the fires of Mightenthew, it would be a different story entirely. I'd slit the throats of any one of these humans who so much as reached for it. But *this*." He rattled the scoush in his hand. "What king-to-be cares for a blade carved in that muhk-smeared, rotten little kingdom?

"There is no rotten corner if dwarves reside in it, pup-king. Each has its place. As king, you'd do well to remember that."

"You're potted," Scramhammer muttered as he scanned the crowd. He spotted an old man on the far side of the road and gave a resigned nod. "He's lucky I don't bury this rotten scoush in his chest for all the trouble it's caused us."

Scramhammer walked over, grabbed the man by the shoulders, and swung him around. "Here!" He thrust the dwarven dagger at the frightened man. "Take your bloody thievery. May the race consume you all. And may you humans all rot in hell!"

CHAPTER 7
The Ballad of the Black Song Man

NYQUEED LOOKED AT the two unearthed graves and the fresh piles of disturbed earth that walled the deep pits. The caskets at the bottom lay broken, as if bolts of lightning had welled up from the cob-webbed depths of the wooden boxes and shattered their lids. A thin slide of dirt in each pit testified to the escape of what had lain within.

The light of the moon came into fullness in the wake of two parting clouds. It illuminated the first line of the epitaph on the tombstone to the left: "Black Song Man," it read.

"Black Song Man." Nyqueed traced his hand over the headstone, scattering the tattered remains of a bouquet of roses. "Reminds me of a song I once knew." The faintest echo of a melody rattled through his mind. It vanished as quickly as it had arrived.

He looked over his shoulder as if the memory of the melody had been delivered by a tapping finger. Discerning nothing in the shadows of the silent cemetery, he knelt down to the tombstone. He followed the epitaph with his fingers as he read:

Black Song Man,
Tell Amariss,
Buried in rot and ruin,
How the roses wane,
Robbed of her kiss,
By your black heart's doing.

He stood up. "Black heart's doing?" He repeated the phrase as he wiped his hand over his mouth. It awoke a faint memory like a rhyme of childhood. "I've heard that before, haven't I? But where?"

In his other hand was a note, which he unfolded: "Quardinal's Brawn. Cemetery. At midnight."

His eyes narrowed. He strained them past the blooming cherry trees, black hollyhock, and blazing red forsythias that lined the dirt path. "So? Where is he, then?" He stepped away from the grave, knocking the fresh soil from his boots as he went.

The second tombstone was half-buried in the excavated earth. He cleared away the dirt from its epitaph. It was older than the first; weather-whipped and rich with moss:

Black Song Man,
Tell Juliet,
Buried in mud and mire,
That your thievin' plans,
Were twice as sweet,
As her love you set afire.

"Thievin' plans?" He rubbed his chin. "Man after my own heart." He chuckled and glanced at the black velvet pouch in his hand. Checking over his shoulder again, he loosened the drawstring a fraction.

Just a glimpse. Enough to be sure it didn't fall in the mud. Where's the harm in that?

He opened the pouch wider then thought better of it. He shut it with a taut jerk of the drawstring. "And risk Salagrim finding it with that bloody eye of his?"

He twisted about, staring into each of the cemetery's shadowy corners. "Risk that one-eyed god finding me with his prize? Here? Standing over a grave. Saving him the bother of digging one." Nyqueed shook his head. "No, you best get this done, Nyqueed, quick and easy. Get your money. And get out."

The wind picked up. It drew the wayward dirt and rocks into the hole. His cloak billowed after them. It seemed to take his patience as well.

"Enough of this, Thaltis!" he said as loudly as he dared. "Show yourself!"

Nothing.

"There's a deal to be struck!"

Still nothing.

"You were right," he pressed. "It was exactly where you said it would be. That Salagrim might as well be blind as well as mute. There it was, under his eye the whole time." He rattled the pouch above his head. "So, show your damned face."

Only the wind through the cherry blossoms high overhead and the creaking of the willow and sycamore trees answered him. That is, until a woman's voice in sing-song broke upon the night air,

"Juliet and Amariss,
Sweet as midnight bloom,
Crept up on that Black Song Man
Like ivy on a tomb."

"Like ivy on a tomb?" The words hit Nyqueed hard. He knew them. He'd heard them countless times. But when? Where? The shock sent him scrambling back from the grave and the black pouch tumbling from his hand. He grabbed it up and wiped off the dirt.

"Enough games, Thaltis. Show yourself!"

But the woman's voice replied,

> *"Juliet whispers to Amariss:*
> *What do you think he stole?*
> *The Gudfin blade, a widow's kiss,*
> *Or the ring from the devil's toll?"*

A chill ran down his back and his swallow stuck in his throat. He knew those words as well. All of them. Every damned word. But how? He retreated farther. As he caught his balance in the skidding dirt, a second woman's voice sounded from the other side of the path.

> *"Amariss whispers to Juliet:*
> *Sister, you mustn't forget,*
> *Nyqueed's fingers may have the sleight*
> *But it's Fitzhiff's on the fret."*

The last of her words struck him like a whip. "Fitzhiff," he whispered. As he said the name, a melody flooded in again, loud as a rung bell. A melody he hadn't heard in ages. A melody more familiar, it seemed, than the beating of his own heart. He grabbed at his head as memories clattered back to life.

"Poor, poor Nyqueed," sang the first voice. "He never had a chance."

"While all around him began to run, the thiever could only dance," sang the second.

Nyqueed stumbled from the grave mound and onto the dirt path. "Who are you? What do you want?"

Something rustled in the hedge behind him. He turned to find Rothesay blocking his way, a dagger in his filthy hands.

The women sang together now. "Poor, poor Nyqueed. He never

had a chance. While all around him began to run, the thiever could only dance." Their voices were louder, clearer, unobstructed.

Nyqueed twisted away from Rothesay and his threatening dagger to see a beautiful female ghoul in a frayed yellow dress emerge from a grove of lilacs. She sashayed to the tilted trunk of a windswept birch tree. There she lay back, drawing up one of her legs to reveal a length of her pearl-white flesh.

"Who are you?" Nyqueed yelled. "Where is Thaltis?"

"Who am I? I'm Juliet, of course." The ghoul rose from the trunk in a fit of indignation. "Have you forgotten your own song, dear Nyqueed?" Her eyes fell bashful. "And how brutishly you treated me?"

On the opposite side of the dirt path, another ghoul emerged from a patch of nightshade and joined the first at the birch tree. Her rotten and torn dress matched Juliet's.

"He forgets his song, sister." Juliet pointed at him.

"Forgets it?" Amariss said when she reached the tree. "Could it be? Fitzhiff never taught him his own tune?"

There was that word again, *Fitzhiff.* "What are you talking about?" Nyqueed shouted.

"He's returned, Black Song Man." Juliet swung around the birch trunk and embraced it. "He is free!"

Amariss held out her hand to him. "They all are. And they are calling their drudges home. It's time, little melody, to return to your instrument and serve your god again."

Rothesay growled and raised his dagger. Nyqueed stumbled back from it, falling into Amariss and Juliet, who took him by his arms.

Juliet said in his ear, "He lives, little tune. The strings call you back. Let us show you."

"W-who lives?" Nyqueed whispered.

"Fitzhiff, of course," she replied.

Again the melody thundered in Nyqueed's mind, and with it came a flash of memory so strong, so vital, it drew him to a halt. "B-but that's not possible. He's gone. Bragnal imprisoned him f-for starting the race."

Amariss put her finger to his lips. She pointed down the path toward the iron gate of the crypt. As the two ghouls let go, Rothesay gave Nyqueed a rough shove. He tumbled into the gate, where the thin strains of a discordant tune, as if the flute had been filled with rubble, came to his ears. This was not the echo of a memory anymore. This melody lived on the night air now.

He leaned toward it over the gate. With each inch he pressed forward, the sound intensified, until the song found the marrow of his old memory, sparking it to life again. Wide-eyed and trembling, his face ashen, he looked back at the ghouls. They nodded.

"Yes, Nyqueed," they seemed to say. "Fitzhiff is free."

Amariss passed by, close to his cheek. She reached forward to lift the gate latch. The old iron mechanism released and the doorway swung open. "Poor, poor Nyqueed," she sang. "He never had a chance. While all around him began to run…"

"The thiever could only dance," Nyqueed finished under his breath.

The inner garden of the crypt was now open to him. Rothesay's wheelbarrow lay upturned in the corner. Scythes, pruning shears, rakes, and shovels were scattered on the ground. A flagstone path led to a bronze basin, its still water reflecting in the moonlight. The large stone door of the crypt was open, and the strains of the ugly melody echoed from within.

Rothesay shoved him again and he tumbled into the mud and dirt. Nyqueed stared up at Rothesay with pity, his fist quivering before his chin and emitting tiny sparks of light. He opened his hand. A silver locket flashed in the moonlight, revealing a tiny, amateurish portrait of a little girl in its frame. Rothesay looked down at his coat as the power that had plumbed it extinguished. His pocket fell limp like a rabbit's ear against his hip. He bolted forward and snatched back the locket.

"I–I remember my song now." Nyqueed stared up at the old crypt.

"All of it?" Amariss shared a quick look of concern with Juliet when a voice suddenly emerged from the crypt.

"My Black Song Man. My little whistle and strum," Fitzhiff sang, accompanied by the contorted strains of a fiddle. Amariss danced past Nyqueed and embraced the crypt door.

"Yes, he's come back to you, master." She twirled her arms above her head like two entwined serpents.

"Does he have it?" Fitzhiff was blunt as a boulder. The fiddle extended its horrid note as he waited for a reply. It was Juliet's turn to race past Nyqueed. She fell to her knees by the door.

"He does, master. He has it. I heard him calling out, and I saw him hold the pouch up to the moonlight."

"Good. Good. My little three chords and tale of woe has done well," Fitzhiff said. "I had thought the tempo of his little ditty too much for him, at first."

The words stung Nyqueed. He winced and got to his feet. That jab of pain cleared his head, and a measure of strength returned. "I'm not your song, Fitzhiff. Not anymore." His eyes darted around the crypt for an escape.

Rothesay read his intentions. He sent him back down into the dirt with a rough push as Amariss and Juliet shrieked.

"How dare you!" Amariss hissed.

"What? What does he say?" Fitzhiff screamed from within the crypt.

"Nothing. Nothing, master," Amariss bellowed into the darkness beyond the door. "Your little tune. He—he simply weeps before his songsmith, thankful to be the melody from your divine lips." She shot Nyqueed a withering glance.

"He says no such thing, you deaf old fool." It was now Vestialis's voice from deep inside the crypt. As she spoke, perfume flooded the tiny garden and sent Amariss curling away from the door. "Your songs are not as sweet as they used to be, Fitzhiff, before Bragnal scarred you," she chided. "They clatter and scrape. They rattle and grind. No wonder your drudge looks upon you with dread."

The fiddle's discordant notes grew darker. "And perhaps your charms are not what they once were either, fair Vestialis," Fitzhiff replied in an angry growl. "For while my song has returned to me, I don't see your drudge falling at your feet. Has she forgotten you? Like the rest of humanity?"

Amariss and Juliet picked up the taunt, rising and twirling in the dirt. "Poor Vestialis, once again forgotten. Or has Pennylegion's love finally grown rotten?" they sang.

The smell of perfume intensified. Oil spread upon the still water in the basin. The moon's reflection in it shattered as a wavy, ethereal image of Vestialis appeared in the water.

"Fools," Vestialis shrieked. "While you mock me, my drudge Pennylegion is busy finding my child. He will be mine again. And so will the location of the Blackened Nevers. And you, poor Fitzhiff, will find nothing more with the stolen goods your Black Song Man has thieved for you than the dust of my footprints!"

The water rippled as if a giant stone had fallen into it; the image of Vestialis shattered and disappeared, as did the perfume that had pervaded the tiny garden.

Just then a solitary red shoot freed itself from the mud. It grew up on a long stem and bloomed a gray tongue that unfurled like a fern. It licked at Amariss and Juliet's legs; they replied with hisses.

"And where is my drudge, Quindecum, you pathetic mortuant?" Zernebruk's voice boomed at Rothesay.

The brute fell to his knees as his dagger tumbled into the mud. He pleaded his case silently with trembling hands.

"Perhaps her attention has been taken by another, Zernebruk?" Fitzhiff said. "She was ever free in her affections, monstrously free, if I remember correctly. Your garden having sat dead for so long, no doubt she moved on to greener pastures."

Another shoot exploded from the dirt. It rose into the night and disgorged a claw that curled back and pointed to the crypt door. "This is your doing, Fitzhiff, isn't it? You and that perfumed wench, Vestialis. Do you think I didn't hear you two plotting against me in the dark corners of our prison? Your laughter. Your mockery. I heard you two scheme and conspire. You've turned my drudge against me, haven't you? Like Bragnal turned the very earth against me. Haven't you? *Haven't you?*"

"You have spent too long harvesting suspicion and hatred from your garden, Zernebruk," Fitzhiff said. "It has left you rotten and blighted."

A dozen more shoots burst from the earth around Amariss and Juliet. The tendrils peeled back on themselves and bloomed red claws that grasped toward the moonlight.

"You will pay for this," Zernebruk screeched. "Mark my words. I will win this race. With my drudge or without her. And when I reach the Blackened Nevers first, I will see you and that goddess of love buried deeper than death."

Zernebruk's limbs dove toward the ground. They buried deep and then, as if the vital fluids were sucked away, fell limp and brittle like old stalks of corn. And the crypt fell silent.

The ghouls closed around Nyqueed. They gently drew him to his feet and dragged him to the open crypt door.

CHAPTER 8
A COLD MORNING'S COMING DOWN

"DISGUSTING." LOSTRUS KICKED Madrigan's body over like a rotten piece of timber. His breath formed clouds in the cold morning air that whipped as he spat out the husk of a sunflower seed.

Manion had held back at the alleyway entrance. He wanted no part of being here. He was sorry he even had to tread over the threshold to this dank artery. Its battered cobblestones seemed to sink deeper than the streets beyond. A gray efflorescence snaked up the stone walls, as if ground-up bones were seeping from the masonry. And the stench in the alley was horrid. *Like the intestines of a Bracken war dog*, he thought, putting his hand over his nose and mouth.

"Is he dead?" he yelled.

"Close enough." Lostrus reached forward and pried open Madrigan's eyes, careful to avoid the yellow foamy substance that had dribbled out his nostrils. "That new pitch, Shivery Coffinfit, be my guess."

Lostrus stood up and spat out a husk. He leaned over and picked up the cracked Jegs tile beside Madrigan's body.

"Would you look at that, Manion? That carvin' little bastard Jegs says it's Aelic in the lead now! Fat chance."

As he tossed the tile aside he added under his breath, "He's probably tripped and is sitting tangled in his own cords."

A trickle of sewage dripped into an askew sewer grate forged into the shape of Civiak. The god gestured vulgarly at his audience. His long tongue curled down toward his interlocked fingers to form the grating of the metal cover. One of his bawdy maxims was etched into the top: *The arse spits cleaner than the mouth that feeds her.* A warm fetid stench rose from it, as though an abomination native to the alley were boiling the sewage below in a clay pot.

Manion shook his head as he took in Madrigan's crumpled body. *Imagine, choosing to be so cursed. Like some shambling ghoul. It's an utter scandal.*

His voice caught up to his musings. "It's filth like that that's breaking apart this realm. His father must be mortified."

"I do believe the old knight is speaking from experience. Did someone's vices leave you wanting, old man?" Lostrus said.

"My son is dead," Manion said gruffly, turning his head. "Thank Methulla."

"Failed to live up to your lofty expectations, eh, old knight?" he muttered. "I wonder what that must be like." He poked the blood trickling from Madrigan's mouth and rubbed it between his fingers. "Still red."

His voice rose to reach Manion. "Cracked his shell about… two hours ago, I'd wager!" He righted himself. "I don't fault them, myself. Not anymore. For some, a shot of pitch is the only thing that keeps them going in these black days. Bragnal's scales, some days I could join them. Just listening to you for a day makes me want to crack my shell."

Madrigan suddenly gasped for breath. Lostrus did not react. He stood quietly working another sunflower seed between his teeth. "Apparently this one didn't crack his shell, after all."

Madrigan rolled onto his side and evacuated his stomach. The pool joined the rivulet of sewage trickling toward Civiak's sewer grate. Lostrus examined his boots for defilement. He shook his head, shared a glance of contempt with Manion, and leaned down to the young man.

"Welcome back, pitchie!" he yelled.

Madrigan brushed Lostrus away, his hand limp with surrender.

"We thought we'd found another dead pitchie! But you're not dead, are you, my good man?"

Madrigan pushed himself up from the ground. The lantern's light made him wince. He slid away from it into the shadows. There he shivered, his head twisting and turning in fits and starts.

Manion looked on in horror. *He's alive. Methulla, please. Please don't let this get tricky.*

"Bad pitch, was it?" Lostrus said, spitting another seed. "Well, no matter. Not your fault, pitchie. No shortage of that going around. Can't fault yourself."

Madrigan slithered further into the shadows.

"But we wouldn't be doing our sworn duty if we didn't make sure you came back intact." Lostrus glanced at Manion. "Wouldn't want you to come back only to find that that pitch has stolen your mind, now would we?"

The words jolted a memory in Madrigan. His head whipped left and right, up and down, turning and craning for all angles.

"You okay? You broken, boy?"

Lostrus looked at Manion, the full devilish proposition clear in his eyes.

He's considering it. Methulla's heron! Please, not again. Manion looked out of the alley to the civilized streets of Quardinal's Brawn. They were empty. As they always were at this hour.

Madigan scurried out of the shadows and clung to the lamppost. With manic jolts of action, he drew every inch of his body into its soft glow. He trembled; his eyes quivered like an animal in a trap.

"No, no, no," Lostrus said, reaching out and grabbing Madrigan's collar. "You're not going anywhere, lad. You've got some explaining to do. Pitch is pitch, after all." He pinned Madrigan in place with the point of his sword.

"Where are you from, boy? Any family about? Hmm? Answer me." Lostrus cracked another sunflower seed. He shot Manion a glance, priming him, telegraphing for him to prepare. Madrigan lifted his head but couldn't manage a sound.

"Mute as well. Lovely!" Lostrus stuffed another sunflower seed between his lips, then Madigan let out a terrified moan.

Lostrus raised his blade to the young man's throat. "Shut your mouth, pitchie," he grumbled, looking over his shoulder. "You'll wake the whole muhking neighbourhood."

"But I–I saw it all… the–the gods… the race," Madrigan began in a weak, quivering voice.

"Sure you did, pitchie." Lostrus lifted Madrigan's cloak with the end of his sword to see if the man was armed. "I'm sure you saw all sorts of interesting things. *Unarmed!*" he yelled back to Manion.

Manion glanced back at the street beyond the alley. *Confound it. Where are they all? Methulla, please, throw someone up out of this darkness. Just one witness. That's all it'll take to cool him off.*

"Can you walk?" Lostrus sheathed his sword and grabbed Madrigan under the arm. "Course you can walk. Young man like you. You're just shaken up from the pitch, that's all. What we wouldn't *pay* to be young again, eh, Manion?"

Madrigan's knees buckled. Lostrus caught him and leaned him up against the post. "There, there, pitchie. We'll heal you up good, don't you worry about that." He slipped his hand into Madigan's pocket, pulled out two tiny silver cubes, and held them to the light. "Well, well, well, what have we here? Two cubes of Velveteen Cromide? And what were you going to do with that, eh, pitchie?"

But Madrigan heard none of it. His eyes were searching the shadows. Lostrus grabbed his chin and looked into his eyes.

"Tell you what we're gonna do. We aren't going to arrest you, pitchie. Not that you don't deserve it, mind. I've seen His High Majesty's courts of justice toss pitchies half your age into the Clovenstone Stockade for having just one of these cubes." He spat another husk of seed onto the ground.

"No. No, with you, I think me and this good gentleman here are going to help you instead. Help you rid yourself of this terrible affliction, aren't we, Manion?"

From the corner of his eye Manion spotted two men walking toward them. Lostrus muttered at his disinterest and turned back to Madrigan.

"In the Milkwood Market. We know a man. A good, honorable man. He specializes in helping young men like yourself locked in this miserable struggle. We'll take you there. Cost you nothing. And we'll see that Velveteen Cromide off His High Majesty's streets as well. How does that sound?"

"N-no," Madrigan clutched the lamppost. "No, I can't… I can't leave the light."

"Leave the light, son? No, my boy, we're going to return you to the light. Return you to Aelic's bosom, or Methulla's, or Bragnal's, or…" It was then he glimpsed the Salagrim pendant around Madrigan's neck and lifted it free of the pitchie's robes.

"Or Salagrim's." Lostrus leaned in. "Though let's hope your ever-searching little god doesn't see this little predicament you find yourself in, eh, boy?"

"The boy said something about the race," Manion yelled. "Ask him what he means." The strangers were too far away. He needed to buy more time.

Lostrus glared back at him. "Who gives a rutt about the ravings of a muhking pitchie? He's addled. Look at him." Lostrus wrenched Madrigan's chin up.

"I think we should let him talk," Manion said, his gaze trained on the approaching men.

Lostrus let Madrigan go. "What did you say, novice? Are you forgetting your rank again, old man? We will do *what* I say *when* I say it." Lostrus closed the distance between them and lowered his voice.

"And that means we're taking this young man to the Milkwood Market. And you'll stand quiet and docile as a whipped mule while they peel back the edges of that fat leather purse of theirs and pour out a filthy pile of gold. And like a muhking mute, you're not going to say a word. Not a word, novice, do you hear me? For if you say anything, old man, I'll order that wrinkly throat of yours slit. And, trust me: there are a dozen men in the gendarme who'd line up for the work. Do you hear me?"

Madigan howled again. He pointed into the shadows of the alley. "There!" he screamed. "F-Fitzhiff. H-he's found me! There he is. Look!"

Lostrus turned around. He followed Madrigan's finger, peering into the dark corner. His eyes narrowed. He played with a sunflower between his teeth for a moment. "You playing with me now, pitchie? Hmm? Don't play with me. Don't play with me, boy. You don't want to know me when I'm angry."

"But he's there!" Madrigan screamed.

Lostrus rushed back and slapped him. Madrigan slid down the lamppost, his lips quivering. "He's there, I swear. He's looking at us. *He's looking for me!*"

Lostrus called to Manion. "Novice. Get your old carcass over here. Now!"

Manion could now hear the blessed footfalls of the two men. They were close. It was only a matter of seconds.

"Novice! Don't make me ask again, you old…"

Manion began to walk down the alley.

"And draw your muhking sword, you old idiot!"

Manion did as he was told.

Madrigan let out another moan; he pointed again. A tiny stream of blood emerged from the corner of the alley. Lostrus drew back in shock, the sunflower seed dropping from his lip.

"Investigate the corner, novice. Now! Do it before I carve both your bellies."

Manion was alongside them now. He could hear gurgling from the corner. Just then the mysterious men reached the head of the alleyway. They stopped. Manion looked back at them. They were only shadows themselves, featureless and silent.

"Go on, now, citizens," Lostrus yelled. "Official gendarme business."

But the men did not move. Madrigan screamed and pointed again. "He's moving. He's coming for me!"

"I said go on, citizens," Lostrus roared. "This is official gendarme business."

He turned back to Manion. "Investigate what's bothering this muhking pitchie, old man, or so help me you'll be wishing you'd died in those glory days you love so much."

"Yes, search the corner, Manion," said one of the men at the top of the alley. He was standing legs wide. They could hear a cascade of coins falling from one of his hands to the other. "Go on, old knight. Have a look!"

Lostrus was boiling now. "Leave, citizen! I warn you: stay another second, and you'll see the bars of the Clovenstone Stockade!"

He kicked Manion forward. The old knight collected himself, raised his sword, and slowly approached the corner.

"It's a foul world we live in. Full of darkness and treachery," yelled the stranger, the coins still cascading into his hand. "Isn't it… Madrigan?"

The name jolted the broken pitchie's attention to the entrance. "Thaltis!" he whispered.

"Th-Thaltis?" Lostrus stammered in shock. He turned to the stranger. "Please accept my apologies. I didn't recognize…"

A hand suddenly tore from the shadows in the corner of the alleyway and grabbed at Manion. The old knight swung his sword. He severed the arm in a clean stroke, but the momentum that carried it forward continued. As the shadows peeled off it, Crummock's body crumbled at Manion's feet. Blood seeped from a dozen wounds and a rattle escaped his mouth.

"I see you've found Crummock," shouted Thaltis from the top of alley. "Impetuous and reaching in death as he was in life." He pointed to Madrigan. "I'd like this young, filthy pitchie slapped in irons and thrown into the Clovenstone for this. What do you say, Lostrus? Do you think you can get those instructions right?"

Manion stumbled back and fell against the wall. His sword dropped from his hand. His heart raced. He closed his eyes and took a deep breath. His mind returned to the gardens of the Methullian Keep: the rose bushes, the wood sorrel, and the violets that grew by the low stone wall. He'd rested his helmet on that stone. The strong, firm, eternal wall of the Keep. He could smell the lavender that grew at its base and he could see Morven at the moment she had leaned in to kiss him. The wind through the hemlocks and jack pines had pressed her hair against his cheek. A caress of pure beauty. One he carried with him forever.

What have I become?

He opened his eyes at the sound of Madrigan pleading with Lostrus. The gendarme struck him then clapped his wrists into manacles. Thaltis tossed his coins in the air like confetti, turned, and disappeared into the shadows of Quardinal's Brawn as the gold drummed onto the cobblestones.

CHAPTER 9

WHEN THE VERSES BLEED

"BEARACH, ZOLLERN, WITH me." Connachen barked the order as he and Scrieve slipped through the broken doorway of the Lyceum tower.

The soldiers chuckled at their captain's choice. Zollern struck the door of the tower, laying limp on its hinges, in frustration. It crashed to the ground. The Shemetesh soldier next to him grabbed the young man and spun him around.

"What the hell are you doing, lad? Why don't you just ring the Ghoraks's bloody dinner bell?"

Bearach pulled the man's hand off Zollern's shoulder. "Leave him be."

"Leave him be?" the soldier snapped. "And who the hell do you think you are, old man?"

"Who do I think I am? I was in the Thunder when your mother was a school girl. Now leave the boy alone."

"Ah, yes, the infamous crimes of Bearach. So ghastly they've had you wander in the Thunder for fifty years to pay your debt. Isn't that right, old man?"

"I thought it was sixty years," the soldier behind him chirped.

"I heard seventy," said another.

The first soldier bent down to Bearach and rattled his fists at him. "I killed two Torrefacts with my own hands, old man. Broad daylight. Not a drop of drink in me. I'll do as I bloody well like while I'm in the Thunder."

"Will you, now? So you choose to tremble like a baby, then, afraid the Ghorak might tumble out of these windows or climb out a potted plant, is that it?" Bearach looked at them all, mystified.

"Careful, old man. No one's afraid. We're just smart." The soldier tapped his temple. "I plan on surviving the Thunder and paying my debt. And then I plan on going back and finding the judge who put me here. And I plan on giving him a taste of my Torrefact skills."

Bearach stepped back and stared at the soldiers. "Is that the same for the lot of you? You're all hoping to survive the Thunder?"

The soldiers nodded sheepishly.

"Even you, boy?" Bearach asked Zollern. The young man shrugged.

Bearach roared with amusement. "Then you're all bigger fools than I thought. You're not being punished, you muhks. You're the meat frying in the pan. Can't you see that? You're doomed." He turned back to the soldier and tapped his own temple.

"And there's no getting out of the pan, boy. And there's no calling off the meal."

Bearach howled with laughter as he pushed Zollern through the broken doorway.

ↂ

"Why?" Zollern ran from the top of the stairs and grabbed Connachen's hand. "Why are we opening this goddamn door? We should rejoin Bockum. *Bearach!*" he called over his shoulder.

Bearach had crested the last step and was catching his breath from the climb. The going had been slow. The hallways showed the ravages of the flames that had run through them; they were strewn with debris, damaged furniture, overturned bookcases, and torn tapestries. The door before them was the oddity; it was free of any damage.

"Leave your captain be, Zollern," Bearach said as he came to stand before them. He put his hands on his knees, gathered his breath, and nodded at Connachen to open the door. "He's building a bridge of redemption on his back, aren't you, captain?" he said with a wink. "And if that leads through this door, then so be it."

"No," Zollern roared. "Enough! I might not know what my god Rawl puts behind doors in the middle of the desert, but I know what he *doesn't* put there: my supper and warm bedroll. This is a muhk's errand. We should leave and be done with this foul place. We should join up with Bockum. And you know it."

"Is that what your god believes, boy, or is that what you believe?" Connachen said. "Enlighten me. Which one's the coward?"

Zollern wedged his thumbs into his belt, pining his halberd into his elbow. "Rawl? A coward? Never. He hates cowards."

"And how would you know? Your Rawl holds his tongue, doesn't he?"

Zollern blushed and looked askance. "He hasn't told me that directly, I'll concede that." He shook the knot of twine and rope on his halberd. "But I'm no fool, Connachen. I see the way he treats you. And so I can deduce the contempt he holds for cowards."

Zollern's wit pleased Bearach. The old man clapped his hands in amusement and winked at his younger comrade. Scrieve was also amused; his stylus glided over a clean page.

"You know, you aren't the only one deducing a god's intentions, Zollern," Connachen replied. "I'm cursed to lead condemned men through a burning world. I'm left, therefore, with only one conclusion as to my god's intentions. Do you want to know what it is?"

Zollern shook his head. "I couldn't give a pint of Woadbrek's piss what that Kellcrim of yours thinks. Following him has gotten us into this mess."

Bearach looked at him coldly. "Forgive the boy, captain," he said. "He's new to the Leggat. Doesn't understand its ways, do you, boy?

Look at you. Muttering and sputtering. No respect for the whispers of a man's god. You should be ashamed."

Zollern blushed again. He lashed out with the end of his halberd. "Whispers of a god?" he said incredulously. He leaned down to Bearach. "You know as well as I do his ramblings are madness, not some god's whispers."

"And who are you to tell that, boy? Hmm?" Bearach turned to Connachen. "The gods work in strange and mysterious ways, don't they, captain? Especially for the men condemned to The Thunder that Wanders." He nodded for Connachen to continue.

Connachen pointed to the door. "Kellcrim knows what's behind that door. So does your Rawl, Zollern. And so does your Gollunt, Bearach. But you know what none of them know?"

"What?" Zollern muttered.

"What's in here." Connachen pointed to his heart. "What we're going to do in this sea of despair. And you want to know another thing?" He stared up at the burnt and torn tapestries hanging limply above them. "I think Kellcrim and Rawl—and all the other gods besides—are growing bored with the fires that burn outside men. No, I think they're more interested in seeing the fires that burn *inside* them. What fire burns inside you, young Zollern?"

Bearach smiled and looked back at the young soldier with a twinkle in his eyes. Zollern scowled and crossed his arms when a sound emerged from behind the door. Bearach turned to it and rubbed his hands.

"Speaking of a god's intentions, I believe I hear mine setting my place at his mead hall. Now if you three sewer rats will excuse me." He reached for the handle and opened the door. As it swung open they were hit by the musty air of old books and scrolls.

They stepped into a great library with bookcases lining its walls from floor to ceiling. At a desk in the far corner was an old man. He wore white robes with brilliant blue edging, identical to the robes the man on the platform had worn.

"You!" Connachen bellowed. "Present yourself."

The man looked up from his reading and stared over his spectacles. A smile came to his lips. "I am Cious, professor with the Lyceum." He got to his feet and gave a tiny bow.

"And what do you study, professor?" Connachen asked as he scanned a shelf of old books.

"The humanities, ancient civilizations, the histories," Cious said calmly as he set his spectacles on the desk.

"Well, your study of warfare is abysmal." Connachen dug out his leather pouch and opened it. "Your people lie murdered."

"Ah, war. Yes, I prefer to study war's aftermath. I'm particularly well studied in the generations of pain it leaves in its wake and the battered psyches of its perpetrators."

Connachen grunted. "Hard to quantify the pain that would result if wars never happened, though, isn't it, professor?" He unwrapped the object he'd produced from his pouch. It was a crest of the king's army: a beautiful silver eagle encircled in a ring of woven chains sculpted by none other than Frew the Elder himself.

"His High Majesty's 12th Leggat!" Cious exclaimed. "The Thunder that Wanders." He came out from behind the desk. "We had thought you all died at the Lomhar Pass."

"Did you? And by what account?" Connachen replied.

"Oh, the word traveled fast, captain, I assure you. But it was limited to result, not cause. Please, enlighten me."

Scrieve grabbed Connachen's arm before he could answer. "The battle was heavy," the scribe said. "The king's men were pressed upon by hordes of Ghorak. But thanks to the courage of the Thunder they drove them off to heavy losses." He cast a sympathetic look toward Connachen.

Cious's eyes narrowed. He pulled his robes tight and looked the men up and down. "Really, scribe? We heard half your men were slaughtered. That they were driven like cattle from the pass by the strength of the Ghorak *hordes*, as you call them."

"And speaking of courage," Connachen said. "What happened here?"

"The men and women fell," Cious replied. "They whimpered and cried like babes. Beyond the east wall, you will see their courage." He walked to the window and pointed down.

"Walk ten paces and you'll find the bodies of the children first, discarded by their parents. Walk twenty more and you'll find their mothers felled where they ran, having abandoned their offspring. Walk thirty more paces and you'll find the bodies of the men having, well, having abandoned them both." He turned back wearing a smile. "All struck down by the Ghorak hordes, as you put it."

"Did no one come to the defence of the city?" Zollern asked in disbelief.

"Our blood was about to run like a river in spring. Our world was about to crumble and our city was about to burn." A unsettling serenity came over Cious. "So we met the scourge as you might expect. With sweetmeats, water, and oaths of friendship."

"I would have expected a little more"—Connachen's voice galloped to a roar—"before you watched your women and children be slaughtered!"

"You put more faith in man than you should," Cious said.

"And where does your faith lie, professor?"

"Where all good humans should put their faith. In truth, science, and knowledge. Not the dull instruments of warfare."

Scrieve stepped forward. "What does 'Polymonious XVI' mean?"

Cious bowed gracefully. "Ah, the scribe sees more than the warrior. Polymonious was a famous philosopher. A founder of the Lyceum. It is a citation to a page in his *Principia Naturalis*." Cious walked to a shelf and took down a book. He thumbed through its pages until he found his mark.

"Polymonious long ago deduced the inviolate nature of peace. And I will admit, when the Ghorak first appeared on the horizon, we all—to a one—forgot this truth. Those in the cage in the square were the most forgetful. They almost held the day, men being the simple and fickle things that they are. But then we received a… *divine recollection*." Cious looked up from the book.

"It was as though our scourge was edifying us. In our darkest hour, our conquerors were recalling us to our noblest intentions. Their whispers were as angels."

He quoted now, his chin quivering with emotion, one finger to the sky. "'Violence destroys only the perpetrator.'" He slammed the book closed, lingering on its spine as he slid it back into place. He turned to them.

"It came to us on smoke—thick, alive, glorious smoke. It landed on our walls, scrawling our greatest vision, rousing us to our better impulses. We decided to burn the violent heretics among us and send forth welcome and supplies."

"And you alone were spared?" Connachen asked.

"Not without barter," Cious said, wounded at the implication. "Else I would have gladly died."

The words stiffened the soldiers. "What barter?" Connachen unsheathed his sword and pointed it at his neck. Cious's smile broadened.

"Would you like to know what I've learned, commander of The Thunder that Wanders? About the Ghorak, that is?" Cious's eyes emitted a green glow as he struggled to keep his neck above the blade. "We know everything that you know. All of it. And yet you know nothing of us."

Connachen gestured to his men, and in a sharp display of unison they drew their weapons.

"You can't even identify the agents of your own destruction," Cious screeched.

"We know you butcher women and children," Connachen said defiantly. "And that you have no honor."

"Honor? You speak of honor. What honor is there in self-destruction, human?" Cious's voice raised like a banshee. "It wasn't the Ghorak who kept these gates open, who burned their warriors and sent women and children to give water and bread to an enemy. No, captain of the Thunder, you were falling long before the Ghorak set their sights on your land. Honor escaped you long ago. It scurried away as timidly and fearfully as you escaped the Lomhar Pass."

The old professor choked and trembled now. Spittle frothed on his lips. All around them the books began to quiver and rattle on their shelves. Thin black threads seeped from their spines.

"The race has begun, warrior. What will you do?" Cious sputtered. "How will you stop it all from slipping from your grasp?"

The black liquid streaming down the bookcases pooled on the floor, swirling and eddying before pulsing to the window. There the stream climbed the rock wall and began leaching through the mortar and the gaps between the panes.

"Kill him!" Scrieve screamed. He was clutching his book to his chest, fighting to choke off the effect of the thin black threads bleeding from it no differently than the books around them. His work was collecting at his feet and surging toward the window. "Kill him, you fool!"

Cious smiled and raised his arms to his sides. "It leaches away, captain of The Thunder that Wanders. All of it. All of what you know… gone!"

Connachen's breath grew short. Images of the Lomhar Pass flooded his mind: his fallen men, the Ghorak blades flashing in the sun, the dusty tumble of their retreat, buffeted and whipped by the fiends like a sheet on a clothesline. He saw the blood and the carnage. All that horrid blood.

His mind turned to Scrieve's book, the chronicle of the Lomhar Pass. The scribe's pen had recorded each man's dying breath, each horn of retreat, each slashing blow of the Ghorak horde, each fretful stab of indecision he'd faced as he watched his men die. He closed his eyes; he could hear Cious laughing and Scrieve screaming for him to act.

A while longer. Kellcrim, please… just a little while longer.

And in that instant, a calm descended. He drew a deep breath, a glorious, fresh, clear breath. He opened his eyes and thrust his sword forward.

It sank into Cious's neck. The old man reached for his throat and fell back against the bookcase, blood streaming down his chest. He fell to his knees staring placidly, almost smiling, at Connachen, then crumpled to the floor.

A yell rose from the courtyard. Zollern ran to the window. "Ghorak!"

Connachen joined him. The leaching black liquid had made it to the base of the tower and was pooling in the courtyard. A few paces beyond, at the stack of corpses, a Ghorak lifted the body of an old man from the stack and threw him to the ground. It latched onto the lower jaw and dragged the body over the dusty ground. It stopped at the pooled black ooze, then snapped back the corpse's head and yanked his jaw open.

The Ghorak cupped the black liquid with one hand and with the other jerked the dead man's tongue forward. It punched the liquid down into his throat.

It drew another cup, and then another and another until the man's stomach distended. Then, from nowhere it seemed, the Ghorak produced a rough cord attached to a needle. It stitched the dead man's mouth three times and snapped the needle free.

"Kellcrim's armor," Connachen whispered. He turned from the window to see Scrieve holding up his ruined book.

"You did that, didn't you? Look at it!" he screamed, pulling the tattered pages apart. "It's all gone. Including the account of your abject failure at the Lomhar Pass. How convenient!"

As soon as the words were out of his mouth he realized his mistake. Zollern reached out to grab him, but Bearach caught his hand.

"He'll have his time, son," the old soldier muttered. "Men of vile imaginations like his are sure to meet gods equally creative."

Zollern glowered at the scribe while Bearach moved to the

window and watched the Ghorak drag another corpse across the dusty courtyard toward the pooling liquid. He threw open the window and screamed down to the soldiers huddling at the base of the tower.

"Step back. All of you! Gollunt sets my place at his mead hall, and I aim to join him!"

⁂

They burst out the door of the tower into the midday sun.

"Zollern! The cavalry horn!" Connachen roared.

But the young soldier ignored him. He patted Bearach on the back and whispered into his ear. "If you see Rawl, tell him to raise his voice." He rattled the shaft of his halberd and held the knot to his ear.

"I will, lad." Bearach turned to the soldiers gathered at the door. "To never again be downwind from Kaelan on a march." He punched the warrior warmly. "That'll be glorious indeed."

Kaelan gave a weak smile as punches rained down on him from his comrades. Bearach then stiffened himself. "Right. See you in Gollunt's mead hall, boys."

He broke from the ranks and made to step into the courtyard, only to find Connachen blocking his way. "I can't let you do this, Bearach. Let me call for the cavalry."

Bearach shook his head. "No, no cavalry. This is my god's will, captain. And a divine grace it is to be rid of the Thunder, finally."

"His will?" Connachen replied. "His will is for you to die for no reason?"

Bearach looked at him questioningly. "To be free of the Thunder strikes me as reason enough. I've paid my debt, captain. But if I'm wrong, don't you fret." He patted Connachen on the cheek. "When I learn his reasons, I'll whisper them back to you in your dreams." He pressed past Connachen and walked out into the courtyard.

The Ghorak turned at his approach and dropped the corpse in its hand.

"Gollunt, forgive me. Let this pay for my lost honor. Let this make right my debts. To my wife, to my child." Bearach turned back to the soldiers and smiled a weak smile. "To my Leggat."

He closed his eyes and took a deep breath. His old, shaky fingers curled around the hilt of his sword. "Forgive me," he whispered.

He raised his sword and lunged. In a flash of dust and wind, he was thrown into the air. He sailed across the courtyard and crashed against the stone wall, dead as a broken branch.

Connachen stepped forward and roared his command. Zollern, paralyzed by shock, fumbled with the horn a moment and then blew. Its piercing blast filled the courtyard.

In the distance, another horn responded. The courtyard shook. The cavalry of the 12th Leggat suddenly burst through the gates and skidded to a halt, enveloped by a giant plume of dust and sand that settled like fog on the Ghorak. It turned its thick neck, its claws clenched, and roared in defiance.

Connachen screamed at Zollern. The soldier gave a second blow on the horn. A dozen heavy lances lowered. With the third blow of the horn they charged.

The horses careened toward the beast, their riders' lances out like tusks, and drove it into the limestone wall. Pinned against it, the Ghorak screeched and wailed and soon poured out the last drops of its blood against the bone-white barricade.

CHAPTER 10
A SUNSET FOR OUR KNIGHT

"HERE," SAID THE young man, pointing to the stream. Verica gave her signal, and the party drew to a halt. The young man was at the river's edge before the others had dismounted. "It's here," he said.

"I shall have your head on a silver platter." The merchant struggled to disengage himself from his horse. He wore a fine silk tunic that bulged with the rolls of his fat.

"No, you won't. This is the king's business now," Verica said. She had joined the boy at the river's edge. "Touch him and I'll have *your* head on a platter." She gave the young man a heavy swat on the back of his head. "Where is it, you little fool?"

"There!" He pointed to a group of reeds beside a submerged stone.

"Manion!" Verica called out without looking back. "Wade into the river and retrieve it."

Manion finished tying his horse to a yew tree, brushed its mane with his hand, then turned. "Could you repeat that, captain? My left ear's been a bit lame, you see, ever since I threw myself upon the Bew Stone and saved that Plantonian king's life."

"I said wade into the river and retrieve it, you old fool!"

"Captain," he said, relenting with a bow. He reached down to untie his boots.

"No, now," Verica snapped.

"These boots have tread the steps of the Millean Gate, madam," he sputtered.

"Spare me, novice. We don't have all day. Get in that river or I'll see your hide strung up."

Manion relented once again. He approached the river's edge and followed the young man's hand to the tiny plot of the riverbed. Little flotillas of ice still sailed along the current from the spring thaw.

Broth and woollens this evening.

He braced himself and stepped into the river. The cold shot up his legs and rang between his eyes. He gasped and fought to gain his balance on the wet rocks.

"Aelic's straps! Do hurry up, good knight," Verica yelled.

By the time he reached his destination, Manion was shivering. "I can't see anything!"

"You can't see a hay wagon from three paces, old knight!" Verica replied.

"It's there. That's where I put it," the young man insisted.

The merchant glared at him.

"You rotten little scoundrel!"

Verica gestured for them to be quiet. "Reach down and feel with your hands," she said, winking at the boy.

Manion sighed. *Like Lord Midvale hacking the frost at the Battle of Delbon Hill.*

He reached into the frigid water and his joints clamped shut instantly with the shock. He shook like a flag in a gale. "There's nothing here," he bellowed.

"Have you taken a vow against work as well, old knight? Keep looking."

Methulla asked the fattened calf to take two breaths and give three back.

He steeled himself with a long breath then plunged his hands back into the water.

"Well, novice?" Verica yelled.

"There's nothing here." He stood up, freezing water pouring from his sleeves.

"That bastard of yours is covering for the boy," the merchant said. "He's had his side from the beginning."

I won't freeze while these three bargain and bicker.

Manion stumbled to the river's edge. Water glugged out of his leather boots as he stepped onto the grass, clutching his chest and shivering.

"Order him back in!" the merchant yelled. "Order him this instant."

"Captain," Manion said quietly, "if something had been there I would have seen it."

"I'll get it," the young man said.

"No!" Verica grabbed the boy by the arm. "This fool knight is going to wade back into the water. And he will keep searching until we find what we came for."

"Captain…"

"Now, novice!"

Manion bowed as low as his shivering body would let him and returned to the water just as the wind picked up. His cloak, tethered to his calves where it had soaked up the freezing water, filled like a sail.

Methulla asked the fattened calf to take two breaths and give three back. The refrain revolved in his mind as he searched blindly in the water.

"Farther to your left!" the boy yelled.

Manion adjusted himself, lost his balance and crashed into the river.

"I see our goodly knight swims as well as he mucks stalls." Verica laughed and clapped her hands together. Manion got to his feet. The cold water drained from every tuck and button of his uniform. "Go on, knight," she pressed.

He nodded, bent over, and thrust his hands back into the stream. Finally, his cold, cramped hands bumped against something foreign. He pinned it between them, pulled it out, and held it aloft, cold water dripping onto his head and beard.

"Hah!" the fat merchant shrieked. He turned to the young man and shook his fist. "I'll see you thrown into a Leggat for this, boy. Mark my words."

"It was a trick, that's all," the boy said imploringly. "I did it to impress Yashdle."

Manion climbed out of the river, handed the statue to Verica, and wrapped himself tightly in his cloak. Though his vision rattled from his shivers, he could see that the side of the statue's left arm had been eroded by the water as was the back of the head.

"You leave my daughter out of this, you little fiend," the merchant growled as he leaned in to inspect the statue. "Ah!" he exclaimed. "Look! The left arm is withered." He glared at the youth and held up his left hand. "Mine's been taking lame since the winter, you weasel. And look. The aches in my head." He covered his anguished mouth as he pointed to the figure's head.

"You did this to me! You planted this *thing*. You'd have me wither away to nothing, like this… this clay abomination. Murderer!" He turned to Verica. "I want this boy arrested and hung in a fortnight."

The young man bumped into Manion as he recoiled. Tears streamed down his face.

"Captain, please," Manion said. "There is no magic here." He nodded disparagingly at the merchant. "If that man has been withering, then he must have started out as a solstice hog."

The merchant raged. "I want that boy arrested. Arrested, damn you!"

"Manion, you will speak when I tell you to speak!" Verica's voice was as icy as the stream.

"But, captain," Manion said. "Surely you don't aim to…" He nodded down to the terrified boy.

"I see. You presume to understand my aims now, do you? Well, then, please enlighten me, goodly knight. What would you have me do?" Verica crossed her arms, pinning the effigy in the crook of her elbow.

Manion was startled by the deference. He looked down at the boy. He couldn't have been more than fifteen years old. His clothes were filthy, his fingernails packed with dirt, his shoes cracked and torn.

If anyone's been withering, it's this poor child.

Manion cleared his voice and bent to the boy. "My son, what was the point of this mischief?"

"I just… I wanted to impress Yashdle. I formed it from clay in the riverbed. As a joke. I made it look like her father." He caught the merchant's gaze. "She thought it was funny."

The merchant glared at him and made to speak his rebuke, but Manion held him off with a raised hand. "And? Other than Yashdle's smiles and giggles, what magic did you think this trinket would produce?"

"Nothing!" the youth exclaimed. "What do I know about magic?"

"You see?" Manion said, nodding at Verica. "This was just the lad's naive attempt at expressing affection, wasn't it, boy?"

The boy nodded.

"Never!" the merchant roared. "I am ailing just as it does. Look, damn you." He held up his arm.

Manion ignored him. He leaned down to the boy again. "Let me tell you a secret, boy. A secret whispered to me by my god Methulla. Do you know the god Methulla? The god of truth and his six birds?" This drew a sigh of exasperation from Verica. The boy shook his head.

"Well, Methulla is a wise god, a caring god. A god who refuses to sit idle and watch corruption occur. He has birds that do his work. Work of all kinds. Flying high and diving low to see the path of mankind set true. And he tells us that a man who sets his sights on miracles will always find them. But not necessarily where he thought they were."

"This is outrageous!" the merchant sputtered.

"While you busied yourself with this chicanery, you missed presenting Yashdle with the wonders of the world, did you know that?"

The boy looked up at him, confused. Manion nodded and turned him toward the river.

"Did you notice the school of trout in the stream? They have jets of silver on their flanks like lightning strikes. They swam circles around my ankles just now. They're hungry for a spring meal. Didn't you notice?"

The young boy wiped his nose with the back of his hand. "No."

"And when you entered the river, did you see the Gilden moss on the bank? It's beginning to wake. It glows fire red when you look at it upside down. Did you see that?"

"No."

"Now," Manion whispered gently. "Imagine you'd shown Yashdle these wonders. Imagine how impressed she would have been. Instead, you traded on this mischief."

The young boy looked askance and nodded.

Manion followed and looked deeply into his eyes. "A boy who misses beauty and chases after mischief becomes a man who misses redemption and chases after evil." He nodded toward the merchant. "Now, son. Do you think it was wise to play with this man's feelings like this?"

"No." The boy stifled a sniffle.

"Well, then. There's only one thing left to do, now, isn't there?"

The boy readied himself for the blow.

"Seek this man's forgiveness, boy," Manion said.

He opened his eyes. "What do you mean, 'forgiveness'?"

"Repent for what you have done, son, and you will be forgiven."

The boy stared at him in shock. "You mean you won't arrest me?"

"Of course I won't arrest you."

"Repent and I'm free to go?"

"That's right."

The words hung in the air as the young man processed their full meaning.

"Then I repent!" he blurted. He started defiantly at the merchant.

"Methulla bless," Manion said as he ruffled the boy's hair.

"This is outrageous!" the merchant roared.

Verica gave a weak clap. "Well done, goodly knight. A model of His High Majesty's justice." She handed Manion the figurine. "I suppose there is only one thing left to do to put this mischief behind us. Destroy the effigy, knight and let's ride home for a warm dinner. Get you out of those wet clothes."

Manion lingered a moment, examining the effigy and the meaning in Verica's eyes. Tiny flakes of snow were falling now; they were thin, like dust off of sandpaper.

"Well, go on. Be done with it, goodly knight." Verica stemmed the merchant's protest with her hand.

Manion held up the statue and crushed it. As he did, the merchant tore apart. The head cracked from the clay body and so too did the head of the merchant. As Manion's grip severed the statue's legs and torso, the merchant's torso split in half, spilling entrails and blood onto the soft dirt trail. Manion threw down the effigy in disgust and fell to his knees.

Verica flashed a coy smile. She leaned forward and whispered into his ear. "Thaltis thanks you. This merchant had many debts, long ignored. And I assure you," she continued with a crooked smile, "being in his good books far exceeds being in the good books of that bastard Methulla. Now, observe the real *truth*, old knight."

Verica grabbed the boy by the scruff of his neck and pulled him down to the ground. She put one foot on his chest and drew her sword. The boy cowered beneath its gleaming tip. As she drove it toward the young man's head, Manion lurched forward to grab her arm but the cold in his blood bound his old joints. He fell limp. The sword struck.

A sudden burst of light overcame the young man.

"There's your justice, old knight. A game of lies and fantasies,"

Verica spat as her sword sunk into the soil where the boy's head would have been.

The boy was an old man now. He pressed himself up from the dirt, withered and wrinkled. He wore the filthy tunic of a prisoner of the Clovenstone Stockade, and his legs, like his feet, were bare and caked with dirt and mud.

He scurried to the remaining fragments of the effigy and stuffed them greedily into a pouch he made from the end of his tunic. As he did, Verica drove her sword into Manion's shoulder. She reached over and unsheathed his own as he fell over, gasping from pain.

"How an old fool like you was able to walk through the Quardinal garrison without being relieved of this exquisite prize is itself a mystery of creation." She walked to her horse and slid the sword under her saddle. "Be quick, Chezepock," she muttered as she passed the old man.

Chezepock brought his finger and thumb up to his eye and squinted through them, measuring Manion in the gap. He then brought his hand down and began stirring the broken pieces of clay with his finger. A green glow overcame them. They bubbled and stretched and churned in his hand until they took on the pure likeness of Manion.

"Now, break him."

"He *has* been a bad boy, hasn't he?" Chezepock sneered as he brought out a piece of deer antler. He rapped the effigy's head with it, causing a thin crack. Manion, in turn, tumbled over, grasping his head in pain. The old man then scampered into the stream. Mumbling an incantation, he laid the effigy on the bottom of the river bed.

"Why have you done this?" Manion whispered.

The tiny wisps and threads of snow had grown. The clearing was filling with their effervescence. What little heat there was left in Manion was leaving him. His lips were blue; his hands felt brittle.

"Did you really think a garrison of sons and daughters of

muhk-poor peasants would let a doddering old fool embarrass them?" Verica spat.

"But I never…"

Verica stepped forward and pointed her sword down at him. "Hmm? What did you think, old fool? After walking through the piss and garbage of the slums of Quardinal's Brawn? After plucking arrows from their limbs, protecting the scum of that filthy city from the horrors sprouting from this race? After all this death and horror? What? They'd want to hear your tales of heroes? Of far-off crusades? They'd want their supper spoiled with your braggart's talk of ancient war banners, enchanted weapons, and loving gods?" Verica sneered. "They loathe you, Manion. They loathe everything you stand for. But apparently to some god, you're worth a coin or two."

She sheathed her sword and mounted her horse just as Chezepock stepped from the icy water. "Kill his horse," she barked.

"No!" Manion tried to get up, but his frozen joints failed him.

Chezepock smiled and nodded. He drew the antler behind his back and approached Cawthra, half stalking her, half whispering his pale assurances. He grabbed her reins and stroked her beautiful golden mane. As the old horse slowly grew calm, he struck.

The tip of the antler plunged into her neck. He heaved downward with all his might, tearing through the horse's flesh. Cawthra screamed, made to buck, but her hind legs gave way. She collapsed on her side and bled out into the grass beneath the yew tree.

Chezepock drew back, his chest wracked with heavy breaths. And in the movement, he transformed once again into the young man. In a flash, he was on his horse, waiting for Verica's signal.

"Now, old knight. Please go ahead and bleed what remains of your addled mind. And then die."

Verica turned her horse and galloped off into the twisting filaments of snow.

CHAPTER 11
A MOUTH FOR AN EYE

GRISCOMB SLID OFF the door. The light from the hallway behind him dimmed as it swung back into place. He steadied the wobbling tray he carried. It held a mug of water and a fold of parchment paper.

He eyed the cell at the end of the room. At the foot of the bars was a fat beeswax candle moulded into the shape of Salagrim. The tiny flame had melted the top of the god's head, and the burning halo was descending to threaten his giant eye. Huddled beside the candle, his head bent forward and his knees drawn tight to his chest, sat Madrigan.

"I tucked a kerchief under the door," Griscomb said, nodding over his shoulder. "To stop the drafts. They were coming in fast. I could see old Salagrim here was beginning to sputter." Griscomb sat on the bench beside the cell. His ring of keys splayed out on the rough wood as he set the tray next to him.

"Good to see it's still strong, though. That's good. I'm sure the presence of your god Salagrim is bringing you much comfort in these trying times, Madrigan." He rubbed his thighs and sucked in a breath.

"You know, it's not right," he went on. "Young man like you. In here. With *them*." He gestured with his thumb to the door then leaned in for a whisper. "And I hope you won't mind me saying this, but you aren't exactly built for stale bread and thin sheets, now, are you?"

Madrigan withdrew from him, languid as a ghoul.

"You never did tell me which one it was that threw you in here." Griscomb turned the handle of the mug on the tray, angling its position aimlessly. "My guess would be Justice Tock. He is a bastard, that one. You know I heard that if a Kaopsin man steps foot in his court he immediately forfeits his shoe. Always the left one. Right there in front of everyone. Then he says to the poor man, 'You Kaopsin are all crooked. Only fair we make it clear for all to see.'"

He leaned his head against the wall and crossed his arms. "No, wouldn't surprise me at all if he was the bastard that sent you to the Clovenstone Stockade."

"It was no judge," Madrigan muttered.

"No judge? Who then?"

He brushed his hand across the flame. "Thaltis did this to me."

"Oh!" Griscomb's eyes bulged. "Oh." He leaned back again. "Thaltis, eh? More powerful than the court combined, he is."

Madrigan turned and stared at the prison guard wide-eyed. "But he's fouled up far more than he knows, Griscomb. I've seen things. Amazing things! I saw them, Griscomb: Fitzhiff, Vestialis, and Zernebruk. They're free, and the race is on."

He took in the shadows of the cell as if they had ears to overhear. "And I–I can't help but think that it's… it's running right at me."

Griscomb rolled his eyes. "There, there, Madrigan. Don't work yourself up. You take some warmth from ol' Salagrim there, burning warm and true. Whatever horrible turn that pitch gave you, you're safe now."

Madrigan retreated into the cage, shaking his head, and Griscomb returned to adjusting the angle of the mug.

"Do you want to know what I heard? I heard the Aelic and Methulla gangs in the east wing have been screaming back and forth to each other about a bargain. A bargain struck between the gods and a mortuant. They say it's what started the race. They're rattling their cages and making a right racket about it."

Griscomb chuckled and stared up at the ceiling. "I don't imagine old Salagrim here has lifted his lid and whispered any of that to you?" The color drained from his face, and he descended into a tangle of sputtering and recrimination.

"Oh, forgive me, Madrigan. I'm sorry. I–I didn't mean to." He shook his head and dropped his gaze to the stone floor. "How could ol' Salagrim whisper? He can't exactly *say* anything, now can he? Not given, you know…" Griscomb trailed off awkwardly, pointing at his mouth.

"Please, Griscomb, can't we talk about something more uplifting?" Madrigan ran his fingers through the candle's flame.

Griscomb picked up the tray and made to leave. "Oh, what's the use? All I do is prattle on about nonsense, making things worse. I–I should just go. You don't need my stupid mouth bubbling over."

Madrigan grasped the bars of his cell. "No, please, Griscomb, don't go." He dissolved back into his cell, eyeing the shadows nervously. "Your stories please me today, as ever."

This brought a smile to Griscomb's lips. He sat down and deposited the tray on the bench. "I *can* tease a laugh out of you, can't I, Madrigan?" He resumed adjusting the mug.

"Let's see. What other rumors have I heard? Two hundred men were condemned to a new Leggat. That's news."

He turned to Madrigan, proud at his next point. "And that Bockum with his silver tongue was among them. The one who laughed in the cage when the executioner's saltpeter failed to light. Do you remember?"

Madrigan returned a languid nod.

"He asked for a Leggat to be commissioned instead. A hundred prisoners followed his silver tongue, happy as weasels going into a hen house. Can you believe that? His High Majesty must have spit out his tea when he heard."

Madrigan waved the story forward with an impatient rotation of his thin, sallow hand.

"What else?" Griscomb searched his mind as he traced the edge of the tray. "Of course! I can't believe I haven't mentioned this already. You know the Civiak boys, in the north wing? Well, they've been howling for two weeks straight. They say they've found a special brick in one of their cells. If you knock it three times and say 'Who's there?' Civiak will whisper a punch line through the mortar. Can you believe it?" Griscomb beamed, well satisfied with his story. He slapped his thigh and leaned in, bright as the sun.

"Just imagine your Salagrim there was to lift his lid and whisper to you a little chuckle about a horse every time you fanned his flame…"

The flush returned to his cheeks and he dropped his forehead into his hands. "By the gods, Madrigan, I am sorry. What is wrong with me? How could Salagrim whisper anything? He has no"—his voice fell under his breath—"mouth." He looked away. "I'm just a fool. I should just go." He grabbed the tray and stood.

Madrigan surged to the bars again; he was paler than chalk and drawn even more gaunt by the shadows thrown by the emaciated flame. He stared off into the far corner of the room as he spoke. "P-perhaps you're right, Griscomb, old friend. Perhaps tonight is not a good night for idle chat. Maybe what's best is for you to leave." His gaze drew down to the parchment on the tray. "But if any pity remains in your heart for a poor, broken, old pitchie, you'll leave that tray of yours."

Griscomb read Madrigan's intentions in the instant. He grinned and wagged his finger. "Now, now. I'm no fool, Madrigan. You can't get rid of me that easy. I know what you want. But you can't scare me off."

He held up the parchment paper. "You'll have it soon enough, friend. All I ask is a little chat in return. A little chat will probably warm you even more than ol' Salagrim's flame. I don't ask much, and it seems a fair price for the food, and the blankets, and the candle I brought you, no?"

Madrigan drew himself up onto the bars. His eyes were wild and his chin quivered. "You're right, Griscomb. Right again, as always. But you see, the thing is..."

"Are you okay, Madrigan? You look pale."

"I'm fine, Griscomb. That is, what I mean to say is..." He startled as if a snake had crawled into his robes. "I–I'd feel better at the present, if–if I were... less inhibited."

"Inhibited?" Griscomb's gaze fell to the lock on the cell. "You don't mean...?"

Madrigan shook his head. He glanced at the powder on the tray. "Just a drop, Griscomb, to–to help focus the mind for what's about to happen."

Griscomb breathed a sigh of relief. He pushed the tray away from the cell. "Soon enough, Madrigan. And, now, tell me. What is it you think is about to happen, friend?"

"Enough, Griscomb. You should run. Please. For I think... I think..."

"You think *what*, Madrigan?"

"I–I think he's here with us, Griscomb. Right now."

"Who's here, Madrigan?"

A sound emerged from the corner of the room, a shifting of bulk and a tapping of hands on the cold stone floor. It sent Madrigan back from the bars. Griscomb turned to see Rothesay slowly get to his feet with his pitchfork rattling over the stone floor.

"Well, hello, friend. Now, how did you get out of your cell?" Griscomb looked at Madrigan to share a wink, but the pitchie could only return a helpless shake of his head.

Rothesay reached back into the shadows from which he'd emerged and drew Nyqueed to his feet. The drudge made to run, but Rothesay collared him and threw him to the ground, pinning his left hand to the stone floor between two tines of his pitchfork.

Nyqueed dug into his pocket and removed the black pouch. He undid the drawstring with his teeth and upturned it. A metal tile fell through the air and hit the floor, reverberating like a drum until it came to a halt.

Griscomb took a few uncertain steps forward, angling his head to look at the tile. "Madrigan!" he whispered. "Would you look at that? That right there is *a mouth!* A bloody tin mouth! And here's us—just now—talking about your ol' Salagrim's lack of..." His voice trailed off; his fingers fretted again at his lips.

The floor of the room suddenly quivered; the dust in its mortar pulsed into the air on the force of the rhythmic impacts. The distant sound of footfalls flooded in on them, distant at first but quickly growing louder as if horns were alternating call and answer. Nyqueed tried to scramble back from the tile, but Rothesay's pitchfork bound him in place.

The sound of heavy breathing leaked through the brick walls. It was as if the room were lodged in the throat of a sprinter. It quickened, too. Soon all of it—the steps, the breath, the shaking of the floor—grew to a fevered pitch.

The sounds stopped; the rumbling withered away; the dust returned to its nooks in the mortar. A thin breeze poured across the room in its wake, sending the flame on Madrigan's candle sideways.

"Madrigan?" Griscomb whispered over his shoulder. "You seeing this? There's a bloody tin mouth on the floor of this room, and I'm beginning to think..."

Two floating blue hands suddenly flashed above the tin tile. One of them reached down, halted, and drew back. The other advanced. It too stopped. The hands then joined and wrung with indecision for a moment before finding their resolve. They slowly reached down together.

Meanwhile, Griscomb reached into Madrigan's cell. He lifted the candle from the floor, drew it carefully through the bars, and pressed it toward the ethereal hands. Its broadened light revealed the figure in full. The god's giant eye constricted at the candlelight. One hand rose and shaded it while the other held the tin mouth up to its face like a pair of armless spectacles for his chin. There it moved as though the god were working it out after long years of neglect.

Griscomb furrowed his brow. "Wait a second. Aren't you–?"

Griscomb turned back to Madrigan. "Madrigan, is that– is this– is this... *your Salagrim?* Why, surely it is!"

He turned back to the strange blue figure and wiped his hand over his mouth. "As I live and breathe, *that*, my friend, is your Salagrim!"

Salagrim stepped back and licked his new lips.

"I bet he's going to speak, Madrigan." Griscomb stepped closer to Salagrim. "At long last, son, you'll hear the words of your god above..."

Rothesay struck like a wolf waiting in the grass. He grabbed Salagrim's arm and wrenched it back, forcing the god to his knees. The impact dislodged the tin mouth. It sat vertically now, like a horrid caricature on the terrified god's face.

The door to the room suddenly opened on a long *creak*, like the protracted draw of a violin bow. Amariss and Juliet sashayed over the threshold and into the dim candlelight. Behind them trailed a female prison guard humming a light, airy tune.

Juliet swanned up to Salagrim. "Hello, Salagrim. How long has it been? No, please, *don't speak*," she added with a caustic sneer. "Best you simply listen." She turned back to her sister and nodded.

Amariss led the prison guard forward and drew away from her in a low bow. The woman began to sing. Her thin, reedy melody filled the room until she arrived at a soaring note. There, the woman's song warbled.

She grabbed at her throat, struggling for breath, when a bird's head wiggled out from between her lips. A charred, bloodied, half-skeletal, half-rotten bird opened its beak and continued the woman's song.

"He's here, Salagrim," Juliet whispered. "He's come all this way for you. You should be honored."

The bird struggled free. It beat its threshed wings twice then fell, thrashing on the stone floor until it went still. In its wake came two red eyes peering out from the woman's throat.

"Hello again, Salagrim." It was Fitzhiff's voice.

The woman fell to her knees as her neck engorged. A gray hand burst from her mouth, followed by a second. Her jaw widened beyond its worldly limit as Fitzhiff's head birthed into the room. He looked up, leaking gore from the holes where his ears had once been, and focused on Amariss and Juliet.

"How did my song sound, my sweets?" he said.

"Beautiful, master," they replied in chorus. "Sweet as a symphony. You have outdone yourself."

"Good. For a symphony is exactly what we require on this auspicious occasion, don't we, Salagrim? To give your sacrifice the due it deserves. Now, where is my Black Song Man?"

Fitzhiff pulled the rest of his body free of the prison guard's mouth.

"He is here, master." Juliet ran to Nyqueed.

"Hello, little tune."

"I–I am not your tune," Nyqueed replied, shaking his head.

"What does he say?" Fitzhiff shrieked, slipping in the protoplasmic slimes that had delivered him from the prison guard's mouth.

"He refuses you, master," Juliet snapped.

"He refuses, does he?" He scowled at Nyqueed. "It seems that while I rotted in my cell you have grown off-key, little tune."

With the verve of a toreador snapping his cape, Fitzhiff tore off his left arm. He tested it on his thigh—*tap, tap, tap*.

"Sing my wayward little tune his part, my dears," he said scornfully. "Let his ears fill with his beautiful refrain." With that he whipped his arm over his chest and began to drum on his sternum.

Amariss danced forward on the beat of her master and sang.

"The Black Song Man,
Had more work yet,
Fouler than the devil can,
Wrangle with his net."

Rothesay threw his dagger, which landed at Nyqueed's feet. He wrenched Salagrim up from the ground and bound his head like a vice between his big hands. He tilted it back, exposing the giant eye, and nodded at Nyqueed.

Fitzhiff's beat grew faster and louder. Juliet's dancing grew manic and wild.

"No," Nyqueed pleaded.

"But your song is written, drudge," Juliet replied. "You have no choice."

"This is *not* my song. It–it can't be." Nyqueed backed away.

Fitzhiff's rhythm increased. He stepped closer and cocked his head, leaking more blood from the hole where his ear had been. He smiled as he watched Nyqueed's right hand reach for the dagger; the drudge was powerless to stop it.

Nyqueed grabbed his traitor hand with the other and pulled with all his might, but it was useless. He drew the dagger up from the floor.

Fitzhiff's rhythm increased to a furious pace. It took on a timbre and crash like the hammer falls of blacksmiths on glowing iron.

"No. No, please," Nyqueed whispered as his foot slid forward. The other followed. He closed on Salagrim.

"Please," he whimpered. "I can't. I won't." But his body was no longer his own. He was above Salagrim now. The dagger in his hand rose. Nyqueed closed his eyes and turned his head.

The dagger fell. Salagrim gurgled and his body buckled. The god's mouth, a hard metal tile again, clattered onto the stone floor.

Fitzhiff's rhythm eased. The two ghouls came forward, hand in hand, breathless. Nyqueed opened his eyes and lurched in horror, for in his right hand was the detached mess of Salagrim's eye spilling blinding blood, bright as the sun.

Juliet snatched it from him. "I have it, master," she squealed. "Look!"

"Good. *Good!*" Fitzhiff threw off his battered arm. "Now. Where is the follower of this blinded little god? Where is the sick mortuant we smelled on the air?"

Griscomb suddenly felt something throttling his neck. He turned just as Madrigan scurried to the far wall of his cage. The pitchie raised his trembling finger as if pointing to a murderer.

"He's here!" Madrigan screamed. "Salagrim's fool is here."

"B-but I…?" Griscomb sputtered. He looked at the Salagrim candle in his hand. The light illuminated the Salagrim pendant coming to stasis around his neck. His jaw dropped.

"What did he say? What did the mortuant say?" Fitzhiff shrieked.

"We've found him, master." Amariss took in the length and breadth of Griscomb like a wolf sizing up its prey.

"No. No, you don't understand," Griscomb protested. He pointed back to Madrigan. "These are *his*. He's the follower of Salagrim. Not me."

"What are you waiting for? Brand him! Quick, while the eye sluices with his god's hot juice!" Fitzhiff screamed.

Griscomb crashed up against the iron bars. "What are you doing," he cried as the ghouls grabbed him. "I'm not Madrigan. That's Madrigan, in there! Tell them, Madrigan. Why won't you tell them?"

But Madrigan had withdrawn into the far shadows, holding his breath, still as a board. Two lines of silver powder led to his nostrils. Beside him lay Griscomb's tray, overturned, and an empty piece of parchment paper.

Amariss grabbed the prison guard's arm and unfurled his hand. She put her finger to Griscomb's lips.

"*Shhh*, mortuant. *Shhh*. With this gift, you will carry Fitzhiff's vision back to what has already been seen. You will read what can no longer be read."

"B-but I'm not Madrigan," Griscomb whimpered.

"There, there, mortuant. You will return to the Lomhar Pass," Juliet whispered in his ear. "The eye shall see what must be seen. And when the eye and the mouth are reunited, Salagrim will tell Fitzhiff the location of the Blackened Nevers. And the race will be his for the taking!"

Amariss bent over Griscomb's hand and hummed. As the prison guard looked on in horror, one of the pebble bones in his palm quivered. It separated from the rest and floated out of its cavity, raising his skin like a tent. Amariss kissed it then clapped her hands. The bone burst through his flesh, arced like a jet of water, and rattled onto the stone floor. It was too much for Griscomb. His light faded and he collapsed into unconsciousness.

Juliet joined her sister. She held up Salagrim's dripping eye. Amariss nodded and she let it go. As it fell, the eye grew smaller and smaller, until it was no bigger than Griscomb's extracted bone when it landed on his palm.

It swirled around his wound like water around a drain until it disappeared into his hand and the skin covered over. The ghouls let him go and Griscomb crumpled to the floor.

Amariss and Juliet joined hands over his body and began to spin. So too did the eye buried inside Griscomb's palm. Faster and faster they went until, heads thrown back and shrieking, they released each other. The ghouls split apart and disappeared with Fitzhiff into the shadows.

And in like manner, Salagrim's eye shot off like a bolt of lightning deeper into Griscomb's body, where it was lost in the deep recesses of his flesh. The room fell silent.

The thin sound of metal scraping against stone punctured the stillness. Rothesay turned to see Nyqueed slip the tin mouth of Salagrim into his pocket. The big man snarled and drew up his pitchfork; Nyqueed retreated and stumbled over Griscomb's body.

"I told you. This is not my song," Nyqueed whispered.

He ran. And their race was on.

CHAPTER 12
AS THE THREADS UNRAVEL

BY THE TIME Connachen and his men had returned from Torvisk, the sun was setting. News of what the men had seen in the town had traveled fast among the soldiers of the 12th Leggat. It was met with a mixture of bland curiosity and resignation. It was simply another town, another tragedy, another sick reminder of the spread of death.

Connachen had ordered them back to the march the moment he'd returned. They'd mustered into rank and file, listless and sullen. He watched them now from his horse while his mind replayed the events in the Lyceum over and over. Had Scrieve not tugged at his arm to rouse him, he would have blindly watched his army slip away.

Scrieve's book was open on his lap. It was warped and bowed as if it had spent an age gumming up a sewer pipe, and its pages cracked apart like a rotted log of wood. The scribe held his stylus at the ready and turned to Connachen. "I shall write that you refused to leave men to protect the Lyceum."

"To protect what?" Connachen replied. "You saw for yourself, scribe. It's gone. It's all gone."

"You'd like to think that, wouldn't you?" Scrieve said. "That it's all wiped from the ledger. All gone. All forgotten. A bit of mercy from that bastard Kellcrim of yours, is that it? A bit of bountiful intervention for the benefit of the humiliated, mad captain of the 12th Leggat?"

They were slowly making their way to the front of the army. The sun bathed everything in its rich golden hue. The path before them, now illuminated like a thread of yellow flame, snaked toward a canyon rising in the distance.

"Or maybe, scribe, it's the gods' way of telling you that they read your chronicles. And they found them wanting."

Scrieve spurred his horse and closed alongside Connachen. "I will begin again, captain. You just rest assured of that. This time it will be the true reflection of *everything* I see and hear. A true account of the world. And I promise you this: your accursed position in it will live forever!"

Scrieve waited for his reply, but Connachen had abandoned the fight. His sight was fixed on the canyon walls ahead as a tiny cloud of dust emerged from between the soaring rocks. He raised his hand and signalled for the 12th Leggat to halt. The soldiers obeyed. All except Wulfric.

The tall Jarlspeen walked proud of the line and planted his halberd in the sand. It might as well have been Connachen's thigh, for the weapon now held strips of fabric written with thick, stolid Jarlspeen runes. It was a vulgar standard. And it was at the head of Connachen's army.

"Vanturian guard, present!" Connachen bellowed.

Kaif, the thick-muscled Dinafatari vanturian, walked past him without the slightest recognition of his order. He joined Wulfric, and they shared a whisper as they kept their eyes on the cloud of dust in the distance. Scrieve's eyes danced with delight as he registered the defiance. Having finished their exchange, Wulfric passed his halberd to Kaif and stepped back toward Connachen, tucking his tunic into his belt. He brushed too close to his captain's horse; the beast jerked back, and Connachen struggled to settle her.

"*Ave praesidium*," Wulfric murmured. The plume of dust emerging from the canyon now revealed a galloping horse at its core.

"Bring a line of archers forward," Connachen commanded.

"And miss all the fun?" Wulfric turned to see the contours of the fresh-faced soldier riding the horse come into focus. He struck a flame to his rolled tobacco. "Anything else, *captain?*" he said with disdain. He waited a breath then lumbered back to join Kaif.

Seconds later the young soldier skidded to a halt in front of the two vanturian guards. Connachen made to speak, but Wulfric beat him to the mark.

"State your business, soldier."

His eyes darted between Wulfric and Connachen. The boy's voice faltered as he tried to speak and he blushed.

"Speak, boy," Connachen said finally.

"Bah, do we need the boy to tell us what we already know?" Wulfric's voice rose to address the Leggat in full. "The canyon is abandoned, isn't it, whelp? Bockum and his men are long gone, aren't they?"

The young soldier's mouth framed his words but he couldn't speak.

"Well, soldier?" said Connachen.

"The canyon is empty, captain. He speaks the truth."

"Empty?" Scrieve exclaimed. "Are you saying half a Leggat simply disappeared into the dust?"

Connachen straightened himself in his saddle as the men mumbled behind him. "Were there any signs of where they went?"

"Far from the 12th, I'd wager!" Wulfric released a giant curl of smoke. Chuckles rang out among the men.

"There are signs, captain. To the east," the boy said.

"Captain?" Wulfric interjected. He tapped his smoke sending ash tumbling to the sand. "He's going by *captain* still? This mad toad says he's our captain, boys. What do we think of that?"

The men roared with laughter. Connachen had to turn now. There was no choice.

He tugged the reins of his horse and the assembled men came into view. They had lost their marching form. They were pressed in close, formed into a rough semi-circle. The ragged aspect was not lost on Connachen. The army was a place of angles and lines. The loss of them was a portent of destruction on the battlefield or anywhere else. What was also clear was that Wulfric was speaking their singular voice. Not a man attempted to avoid his gaze. They were united. He could feel it. Something was coming apart in his hands.

"We've lost Bockum and his men. We're doomed. Doomed!" came a voice from the crowd. The words stung Connachen like a whip.

"We are not doomed!" he roared. "We carry on. Make for the canyon. Set up our camp. Send riders to Bockum's men. They may have moved on for any number of reasons."

Kaif's whisper into Wulfric's ear failed him; it carried to Connachen. Connachen turned back to see another horse suddenly emerge from the desert path that ran eastward from the mouth of the canyon.

"Who is this rider, boy?" Wulfric growled as he pointed to the distant cloud of dust.

"I–I don't know." The young soldier shifted in his saddle to stare back at the approaching rider. "The canyon was empty when I…"

"Who sent this rider?" Wulfric bellowed to the assembled men. The cloud kicked up by the horse grew bigger and bigger. They could hear the hooves now like the distant echo of thunder.

"Bloody Torrefact," said one of the soldiers. "Torrefact scum!" said another.

Scrieve pulled tight alongside Connachen. "This was you, wasn't it? No wonder you offered shelter to those wretches."

Connachen jerked his horse away and fixed his gaze on the approaching rider. Mogh's form was becoming clear against the desert sand as he rode his horse hard.

Many months ago, a dozen Torrefact had emerged from the forest by the Eperon River. The women and children they carried in their arms or dragged behind them were little more than corpses, maimed in some violence the men would not speak of. They had thrown down their weapons at the first sight of the 12th Leggat, and their curious surrender had left Connachen cautious. Nothing the Torrefact did was by happenstance. How had these outcasts known where the 12th would march? What had they fled? What was their purpose? Whatever it was, the Torrefact men wouldn't answer.

But the men of the 12th had not been shy in their answer. They had sneered at them like rats, like walking disease. So Connachen had ordered the 12th to throw down a day's rations and their sanctuary in the 12th rejected. And he would have stuck to the rule, too, but Mogh had stepped forward. He remembered the fear and desperation in the man's eyes, and how he'd held up a broken child in his arms as if it proved the contours of some profound horror.

Scrieve had challenged Connachen: the kingdom of His High Majesty had rejected the nomads of the Torrefact and so must the Leggat, he'd said. It was written, he'd said, pounding his leather book. It was then Connachen had heard the whisper of Kellcrim in his ear. And no man in the Thunder can deny his god's whispers.

Connachen had relished the look on Scrieve's face when he'd ordered the Torrefacts searched. But he also knew well enough they couldn't take the line. No man would have suffered to walk with a Torrefact. So he ordered them to walk beside the 12th.

But what the murderers and rapists of the 12th would accept by day, they would not accept by night. On the first morning, he'd found a body beside the firepit burned from the torso up. There was another body the following morning. From then on Connachen ordered the Torrefact to sleep in the tent beside his own. But as the ranks of his men continued to thin with each engagement, it wasn't long before the Torrefact were sworn into the Thunder with the grudging acceptance of his bloodied, scarred, and bruised men.

Mogh's horse now skidded to a halt twenty paces from the Leggat. He was shirtless, and the vibrant red cloak of the 12th Leggat draped over his shoulders was a study in contrast to the skin beneath it. Runes and symbols covered every inch of it. So busy was the work that each embellishment was lost in the weave of the other.

"Careful," came a voice from the assembled ranks. "He'd slice yer neck as soon as shake yer hand."

"Now, now, lads," Wulfric replied, flicking his rolled tobacco onto the sand and raising his hand in a gesture of silence. "I'm sure the Torrefact fulfilled a very important mission for our toad of a captain, didn't you, boy? It must have been. Given you're all that stands between us and our captain's head." He glared back at Connachen. "So, go on, tell us, Torrefact. Tell us what you saw."

"Bockum and his men have abandoned His High Majesty's 12th Leggat," Mogh said. A gasp rang out from the assembled men. Connachen watched Scrieve take up his stylus and record the news.

"Bockum has left us?" came a voice from the crowd. "We're doomed!"

"He left because he knows the Thunder is a nest of curses!" came another. Echoes of agreement followed.

"Now, now, lads." Wulfric lifted his hand to calm the crowd. "Let him finish. Go on. Tell us, Torrefact. Where have they gone?"

"They are two leagues away. Moving toward the Clovenstone Stockade."

"Sounds to me," Wulfric bellowed, clapping his hands, "like Bockum and his men had the good sense to abandon our captain as quick as they could. Why, then, should we delay any further?"

Connachen drew his sword and pointed it at Wulfric. "That is enough! If I hear you challenge my authority again, soldier, I will have you whipped."

"You lift a finger against me and twelve pikes will run you through. There's not a pikeman, archer, lance, or bloody standard bearer in this army that could give a pint of Woadbrek's piss for you or your command now, you cursed prick!"

Connachen didn't need to turn. He could hear the jostle of weapons from the assembled men lending credence to Wulfric's words.

Scrieve brought his horse alongside Connachen's. "You are losing this battle, Connachen, like all the others," he whispered. "While your men know themselves to be condemned to the Thunder, apparently even thieves and murderers draw the line at following a mad and addled captain cursed by a failing god."

"That's how the chronicle will read, is it?"

"Oh, you can count on it, captain. I imagine His High Majesty will relish this particular passage the most."

"Listen to the scribe, Connachen," Wulfric yelled. "The 12th has suffered under you long enough. Your black star has ruined us for too long." He stepped toward his comrades and threw up his hands.

"How many more of us need to die because of him and the whispers of his cursed god? How much honor and blood must we spill following this mad toad? And to think Bockum warned us all along that Connachen is vexed. That we would be cursed with the shame of the Lomhar Pass and cursed to wander under his dark cloud. Well, I say: no longer."

Connachen opened his mouth but Wulfric cut off his response. "No! No more lies. We end it here." He drew out his sword. A thunderous roar rang out from the men, followed by the slow unsheathing of their swords.

Mogh spurred his horse forward. "There is something else I have learned."

"And what is that, Torrefact?" Wulfric sneered, his eyes narrow.

"Your defeat at the Lomhar Pass."

"What of it?"

"Was because Bockum and his men betrayed you."

Gasps erupted from the men of the 12th Leggat. Wulfric doused them by stepping forward and holding up his hands.

"Bockum betrayed us? *Never.*" He pointed at Connachen. "It was this mad toad that cost us the Pass. Bockum warned us, didn't he?

He warned us this *captain* of ours would lead us to our deaths. And so it was. Besides, you would trust the word of a Torrefact, sent by our pathetic captain to conjure up doubt among us? They'd kill their own mothers for a taste of blood." He looked Mogh up and down.

"I don't ask you to trust the word of a Torrefact," Mogh replied, settling his twitchy horse. "I say what I say because I found *this*." He undid the strap around his horse's flank and produced a Leggat shield. He threw it at Wulfric's feet, where it landed half-buried in the sand.

"A shield?" Wulfric mocked. "The Torrefact produces a shield?"

"Let him finish," Connachen said.

Wulfric whipped around. "You'd like that, wouldn't you, captain? To put us all in the thrall of this wretch. Well, I say, no. We've had our fill of you and your cursed god. And no Torrefact games will change that, will it, boys?"

But no bellow of agreement arrived. Instead, a lone voice emerged from the assembled men.

"That's Bockum shield, Wulfric."

"What of it? Who knows what this Torrefact has done to it? Who knows what traps and lures he's baked into—?"

"The top left corner," Mogh said.

"Listen, Torrefact..." Wulfric was taken from his curse by the object that hit him in the gut. He picked up the silver Leggat crest from the sand.

"This is not a plaything to give away, toad," he hissed, glaring at Connachen.

"The top left corner, Wulfric," Connachen said.

Wulfric wiped his hand over his mouth then spat into the sand. He rattled the Leggat crest for all to see, then stepped to the half-sunken shield. It was as he imagined it would be, battered and scratched and mauled by countless sword and arrow strikes.

"A warrior's shield. What of it?" he rumbled.

But just then, his eyes settled on the corner of the shield and his breath stilled in his chest. He placed the Leggat crest alongside and looked up at Mogh, powerless to speak.

The scratches and dents in the corner of that shield were no longer haphazard marks of war. They were the clear pattern and relief of the crest of His High Majesty's 12th Leggat.

The assembled men exclaimed in shock. Soldiers jockeyed at the edges of the group for a view.

"Impossible," Wulfric whispered. "Pure chance!" he bellowed. He looked up at Mogh. "How have you done this, Torrefact?"

Mogh made no effort to answer him. He addressed his next words to the men of the 12th. "There is more, more script describing your ruin."

Whispers and murmurs raced through the assembly. "What? What is there?" someone yelled from the ranks.

Wulfric turned to the voice. "Don't you see what he's doing? The Torrefact is beguiling you. He plays games with your head. Our captain sent him to sow doubt among us when we have our truth. Our captain is cursed. It is his fault we entered the Lomhar Pass. We should have done as Bockum suggested and aimed south."

"Liar!" Connachen roared. "It was Bockum who suggested the path north to the Pass. Not me."

A silence fell. The conviction the men had placed in their betrayal was shaken. The faith that had united them around campfires, the unity that had expressed itself in furtive whispers as they dug their camps at night, the resolve the men shared in oaths and mutters as they sharpened their swords and undid the bridles of their horses—it was rocked to its foundation. The Torrefact's revelation was as scouring as the desert sand that whipped them. A confusion settled over the men as obvious as the canyon in the distance.

None of them dared to meet Wulfric's glare as he paced among them, searching their eyes for someone courageous enough to speak. But no one ventured to disrespect him, not alone, not by themselves.

That is, until the solitary voice of someone who knew his gambit could not be denied rose from their ranks.

"Let the Torrefact speak!"

The men parted to reveal Zollern holding his halberd high.

"Why?" Wulfric menaced.

"Because my god Rawl… h-he spoke to me." This sent new whispers through the Leggat.

"Your Rawl is a mute, boy. And you should follow his form," Wulfric barked.

"No, I swear, I heard him." Zollern shook the bulge of twine on his halberd next to his ear. "Rawl spoke to me. Just now. And he says to let the Torrefact speak."

"Your Rawl? Whispering? A likely story, boy."

"He does," Zollern protested, staring at the troops. "I swear it."

"The boy is lying!" Wulfric said. "He's muddling our minds for his own ends. Like the Torrefact. Like our toad of a captain. His god is a deaf-mute. We all know it."

But Wulfric's passion had pushed him too far. The men looked at him contemptuously now. Their silence was colder than any wind that had whipped them in their northern marches, more oppressive than any heat that had assaulted them in the southern swamps.

Connachen locked eyes with Mogh. *What if Wulfric is right? What if I am cursed? Have I not felt something in me? Something growing? Something invading my mind? Maybe a curse is exactly what it is. Maybe Kellcrim wants all this. Maybe he's caused it all. They have a right to know, don't they?*

"Fine!" Wulfric lit his rolled tobacco and drew in heavily. "Go ahead with this farce, if you want. But I'll take no part. Let the Torrefact fill your head with lies." His growls were soon lost in a cloud of smoke.

The men of the 12th Leggat pulled in tight around Mogh as he undid the clasp of his Leggat cloak to reveal the square symbol on his collarbone. He turned slowly in his saddle so all the soldiers could see it. He nodded to the old warrior standing, arms crossed, directly in front of Bockum's shield. "Look in the middle, by the axe strike," he said.

"The Torrefact is beguiling us," Wulfric protested. "We are fools to listen."

But as the old soldier peered at the shield, his face drained of color. "Gollunt's spear," he whispered.

The men boxed him out as they leaned in. Sure as the sun above them, the symbol on Mogh's chest was there on Bockum's shield, formed from a cluster of scratches, dents, and cuts.

It was Scrieve's turn to examine the shield. He'd dropped from his horse and wiggled through the crowd of soldiers and was now bending low for his own view, clutching his damaged book to his chest. He too went white as a ghost. It was the first time Connachen had seen him so affected.

Mogh lifted his elbow and pointed to another strange rune covering the skin. "The bottom," he said, "where the sword strike pierced the leather." The men drew in toward the shield again, and more gasps flew among them.

"What are they?" a soldier asked.

"I do not know," Mogh said. "I did not seek these scars. They arrived from the heavens, and my family and I were banished from our village as heretics."

"But what do they mean?" said another soldier.

Mogh stared off at the setting sun. "I do not know. But I believe they speak of ruin and pain. See this one." He held up the palm of his left hand. "It was burned into my skin the night my tribesmen came after us and killed my family. My heart tells me this means *despair* in this strange language that cloaks me."

"And this one." He pointed to a symbol on his cheek. Mogh's lips trembled. "This one appeared the night before the attack. I embraced my wife's brother that night, and he kissed me here after we'd pledged our lives to one another. When I turned from him I felt it burn into my flesh."

He scowled as he looked at the fingers that drew off his cheek. "I found out later that it was he who led my tribesmen to our camp. I believe this to be true: it means *betrayal*."

He pointed to the like symbol on Bockum's shield. The men leaned in again, and a dark rumble, made of curses and oaths of revenge, came from them. Mogh lifted his next words over their growing anger.

"Bockum and his men visited both upon you: despair and betrayal. He divided you. He split you. He aims to turn Leggat brother against Leggat brother. Why? I do not know." He looked at Connachen now as if they were the only two standing in that dusty arena.

"But of that I am certain, captain of The Thunder that Wanders."

CHAPTER 13
THE BRIG IS BUST!

"PRESS!" THE LIEUTENANT ran his cudgel along the planks of the wooden shelter that enclosed the battering ram. Behind him, the Leggatmen pushed with all their might.

"We're coming to the petticoat, sods," he yelled, peering out. The men returned a raucous laugh as they struggled with the beams. "Soon be at the girdle."

Cannonballs landing around them sent up blasts of soil and mud. Burning arrows flew in deadly arcs through the night sky. A clatter of crashes and cracks shook the wooden structure. Smoke choked the air inside. Drops of burning oil pierced the hide casing and dripped onto their shoulders. It took men off their beams to swat away the pain. A tin plate, now wet with the hot oil, had been nailed into the ceiling beam; the plate was engraved with the god Civiak's face. His long tongue curled down to the letters of his maxim: *The gods are there, but I wouldn't stare!*

Three large boulders hit the ram in quick succession. It skidded to a halt on the muddy terrain. The prison guards on the parapet of the Clovenstone Stockade cheered at their successful attack and the wounded machine beneath them.

"Looks like she forgot to tell her husband about our little tryst," the lieutenant yelled. His exhausted men managed a few tired laughs as they regained their posts. "But he's an impotent bastard, isn't he, boys?" He pointed his cudgel down the muddy road. "Put her feet to heaven!"

The men pushed again. The battering ram righted course. It lurched forward and gradually turned the corner of the washed-out road. It now faced the wooden gate of the Clovenstone Stockade twenty yards away.

"Hold! Let's inspect the beauty." The lieutenant cupped his ear and listened. The lull held. He poked his head from the enclosure.

"Warden of Clovenstone!" He banged his cudgel on an iron bell hanging at the entrance of the machine. "Call off your men!"

He waited. Silence.

"If the ram touches, there will be no quarter!"

Silence again. The lieutenant turned back to his men. "Mustn't lose our manners in the heat of passion, right, boys?" he said with a black-toothed grin.

An arrow sailed past his head. He gritted his teeth, spat in the mud, and barked his order.

The Leggatmen strained to their labors again. They slipped and slid, struggling for footing in the mud. It churned deep like a sticky stew, but the great ram moved, a foot at a time, until it finally came to rest before the thick wooden doors.

"Hold!" The lieutenant's head emerged again from the machine. "Once more, in the name of His High Majesty's 12th Leggat, I beseech you: for the lives of your men, surrender!"

Suddenly the latch on the gate jingled. The creak and moan of heavy wood brought into motion came to their ears as the smaller wooden door within the gate opened. From it strode two prison guards dressed in leather armor. Their contrast to the muck and dirt was stark, as it was with the shackled man they led through the door.

The guards wasted no time. They positioned the man between them and the battering ram, and then, in unison, struck at his shackles. They were back through the door before the rusty irons fell to the mud. The bolt of the door tumbled into place, and the scene fell silent.

The man stood immobile, frozen as if his hands were still shackled. His hair was dark and long, and his beard was cinched by a knot of rope. He was naked save for rough iron bracers on his wrists, a dirty cloth around his mid-section, and heavy sandals on his feet. Scars from fierce lashings covered his back, chest, and arms, which were three times the size of an average man. He straightened; his giant bulk obscured completely the portal he'd emerged from.

"Do you surrender?" the lieutenant barked.

The giant man rubbed his wrists. He squinted at the light thrown off by the blazing torches on either side of the gate.

"Do you surrender?"

The giant located the source of the words. His eyes narrowed; his lips curled.

"Bah! We didn't come for a cuddle and a pinch, did we, boys? Paint the gate with his brains!"

The giant man put his hand to his forehead to block the light. He caught only faint glimpses of the machine. But he heard it. The sound of men rushing to beams, pulling, pressing; oak groaning; chords snapping taut. He looked back to the gate then to the machine. His snarl tightened.

At the head of the battering ram jutted a massive timber, two feet in diameter. The tip of the ram was covered in iron molded into the shape of a man's face. It wore a ghastly grimace and around it was a halo of six birds all woven together.

"Methulla, savage!" the lieutenant yelled. "Giver of truth," he added with a rotten grin.

"And taker of innocence," came a raspy voice from behind him. The men chuckled.

"No sign o' that here, boys." The lieutenant pointed his cudgel at the prisoner. "Now stand aside, savage. What do you care for the

Clovenstone Stockade? Why would the animal defend the cage that holds it?"

The big man said nothing.

"The men who lashed you, they are behind those walls. The men who shut you in darkness. They are in there. Do you understand?"

The giant dug his feet into the soft ground. He reached down and grabbed a handful of dirt and mud. He wiped the earth on his chest and shoulders and in a deep ominous snarl, with an accent rough like iron ore, he spoke.

"This is no cage. And I am no animal."

Charlotte stopped. There it was again. She gazed toward the horizon as the *boom* echoed away. But it wasn't long before the slack on her rope was consumed. With a jarring tug, she was pulled forward again.

An arc of burning arrows took to the air in the distance like a rainbow on fire. This time she leaned back, dug in her heels, and pulled. The knot around her waist dug into her skin, but finally the boys ahead of her stopped. Shuppan and Mastiel glared at her. She pointed. They followed her finger as another volley crossed the sky.

Mastiel was quiet for a moment then shrugged. Shuppan, in the middle of the rope, echoed the shrug. They both made to resume their pace, but Charlotte planted her legs and pulled again.

"What are you doing?" Mastiel said in a tight whisper.

Shuppan echoed it: "He said, what are you doing?"

"That's the Clovenstone Stockade," Charlotte replied. "I think it's under attack."

Shuppan began to repeat her words, but Mastiel waved him off. "I can hear her, you ninny." He looked past Shuppan to Charlotte. "So what if it is?"

"What do you mean *so what if it is?*" Charlotte said. "We should raise the alarm."

"Alarm? Brother Adalbane didn't tell us to raise any alarms. He told us to find a boy, wandering alone. The one he'd seen in his vision, under the Quardinal Bridge, right there." He pointed to the arc of the golden bridge a hundred feet up the road.

"He's right, Charlotte," Shuppan ventured, twisting around to her. "Besides, wouldn't that mean speaking with the gendarme?" he added nervously.

Mastiel closed on Shuppan and put his hand on the young boy's shoulder. "That's right, Shuppan. We'd have to speak to the gendarme. Do you want to do that?" Shuppan shook his head. "No? Well, neither do I." Mastiel glared at Charlotte.

"But the stockade is under attack. What if there are children in there?" she said. "They might be hungry and scared. And what if they're getting hurt? Doesn't that outweigh one wandering boy?"

Mastiel left Shuppan and stood before her, bending to look into her eyes. "Are you forgetting what life was like before the good graces of the Brothers of Digrir, Charlotte? Are you forgetting what it was like to sleep in Quardinal's sewers, surrounded by discarded shoes and apple cores? Remember that, Charlotte? Remember the growl in your belly so loud it would keep you from falling asleep?"

Charlotte had no response; she could only look away. Mastiel bloomed with confidence at her apparent retreat. "Well, I do. I remember it. And if it weren't for the Brothers of Digrir, that's where I'd still be. You too, Shuppan. And you too, Charlotte."

A crack and rumble sounded in the distance as a wall of the Clovenstone Stockade toppled. It took Charlotte's attention, but Mastiel stepped into it.

"The brothers gave us warmth, shelter, food in our bellies. When no one else would. Certainly not those evil gendarmes. Everyone else would have let us starve, or worse. And they've only asked *one* thing in return: to help find other poor, wayward children who are probably just as scared and hungry and alone as we were."

Charlotte blushed as Mastiel's points piled up.

"So if you two want to take their charity and throw it back in their faces, fine! But I won't. And I'm certainly not going to do the gendarme any favors. So? What's it going to be?" He gestured as if he were about to undo the knot around his waist.

"Charlotte, I–I think he's right," Shuppan whispered. "We can't talk to the gendarme. Who knows what they'd do to us? And I sure don't want to go back on the street. Not ever."

Mastiel saw victory and let the rope go. He retreated with swagger until the rope between them was taut. Shuppan shrugged at Charlotte, turned and followed. Their combined strength dragged her forward. They were right. She'd be a fool to speak to the gendarme. Who knew what they'd do to her?

Darting from shadow to shadow, they soon passed by the Clovenstone Stockade. It was as Charlotte feared. The jail was under siege by a phalanx of red-cloaked Leggatmen. But there was no lingering. Mastiel tugged on the rope, and she tumbled forward past the fires and crumbling stones.

They soon reached the Quardinal Bridge. Ducking to keep below its low railing, they scrambled across it following the series of carved panels that arched with the bridge as it traversed the river. Each of the kingdom's artists had been given a panel.

The first panel, leading onto the bridge, had been carved by Frew the Elder. He'd rendered His High Majesty resplendent on one knee, palms open like they were a book. Before him was Bragnal, pointing the way as the gods stepped into the king's hands.

As the arch curved to its apex, the work gave way to the panel of Frew the Younger. The gods were taller here. And as was his signature, he had carved the corner jagged and punctured, as if some unknown subject had emerged from the carving.

On the far side of the bridge was the panel carved by Jegs. The procession of gods was half the height of the panel now. It was rumored that their faces were those of the downtrodden and disadvantaged members of Quardinal's underbelly, a style Jegs was famous for.

The bridge ended with the panel of Creche of the Donlands. The gods now filled the entire work, their heads bent and stooped to fit within the border. Every inch was crammed with exotic symbols, arabesques, filigrees, and old runes woven together.

Mastiel scrambled off the golden bridge and raced for the rocky embankment that sloped down to the high road river gurgling below. The other two children weren't half as courageous. They looked at each other and silently reflected on the significance of where they now stood: on the *other side* of the Quardinal Bridge, something neither of them had done before.

The bridge's torchlight didn't penetrate the darkness beneath the bridge at all; it was thick with shadow and echoed with babbling water. It reminded Charlotte of when the gendarmes would cover the sewer grates with horse dung and cloth in their efforts to ferret the city's unwanted children from their burrows.

"Hello?" Mastiel whispered. "Hello?" He waited for a moment. "We're wards of the god Digrir. We're here to help." He elbowed Shuppan forward.

"I–I know what it's like, friend," Shuppan said quietly into the darkness. "My father, he wasn't kind to me. So I ran too. And I hid. And I grew hungry and scared, like you. But not anymore. The Brothers of Digrir have been so kind. They found me. I don't know how they did it, but they did. And I have shoes now. I have food. I have a warm place to sleep. You should come out."

Mastiel turned to Charlotte. His eyes told her it was her turn. She dropped to her knees and leaned down the embankment as far as she dared.

"My mother…" Her voice trailed off as she caught sight of a Stockade tower igniting.

Mastiel followed her gaze and gave an exasperated shake of his head. He slapped the back of her head, and Charlotte reluctantly shifted her attention.

"My mother died. Not too long ago. And when it happened, I

was so scared. I had no one. But the Brothers of Digrir found me. I'm warm. And I'm safe. You should join us."

She stood up and glared at Mastiel. They waited. But they heard nothing.

"Maybe he's walked into the woods." Shuppan pointed to the forest that swallowed the high road as it led away from the city. "Or maybe he's taken the high road to the next town?"

"No," Mastiel said. "The Brothers specifically said this bridge."

There was a sudden splash from the river below. From its far side, a figure draped in shadows had entered the stream.

"It's him. We found him!" Shuppan exclaimed.

"No, it can't be. He's too tall," Mastiel whispered.

The figure stopped in the middle. The jingle of his armor was audible, and the line of his scabbard hanging around his waist was clear as it parted the water.

"That's not a child," Charlotte said. Her words had carried to the stranger in the river, for he looked up from washing his hands in the stream.

"You must sound the alarm, children." He righted himself and shook the water from his hands. "My army is laying siege to the Clovenstone Stockade. My men fight ferociously, and they may appear strong now, but I assure you"—he flicked the last water drops free—"we're at the crucial point of the engagement. An attack now by the gendarme of Quardinal's Brawn would surely break them, would it not?"

The children stood in stunned silence until Mastiel drew them into a tight congress.

"Did he say *my army?*" Shuppan whispered. He looked like a rung bell.

"That's what I heard." Charlotte nodded.

"Brother Adalbane didn't mention an army." Shuppan sounded stupefied. He and Charlotte looked at Mastiel. The boy grimaced and broke from their huddle.

"What do you mean *my army?*" he shouted at the stranger.

But now, at the far side of the river, an old man in simple white robes stepped from the underbrush. He strode to the riverbank, tested the water with his sandaled foot, and thought the better of wading in.

"A Colmrakken barbarian," the old man yelled, holding a glass vial over his head. "He's delaying our men at the entrance. If you want my advice, we shake the remaining grains of powdered shipwreck in this here vial along a piece of birch bark held up…"

The soldier in the river turned to face the robed man and put his finger to his lips. "Hush, Wergoyle. That is, unless you think you have something better to say than the gods themselves?"

He pointed to the children on the far bank. Wergoyle followed his gesture, sighed deeply, and shook his head.

"No, Bockum, I do not. But I might ask how it could be anything but folly to tempt your own defeat by instructing these scamps to warn the gendarme of our attack on the stockade? Surely victory is best achieved by not *promoting its defeat?*"

Bockum gestured toward the three children. "I'm simply offering a bit of honesty, steward. To cleanse the air. Is it really your counsel that I should commerce with the gods laden with deception and half-truths?"

Wergoyle shook his head. "No, captain." He muttered the rest of his opinions into his chest.

The children formed their tight congress again. "Did he say *commerce with the gods?*" Shuppan asked. "Brother Adalbane definitely didn't mention anything like that."

"Whoever he is, I think he's right," Charlotte said. "We should sound the alarm. We can't just let the Stockade be overrun. It's full of criminals a-and worse."

Mastiel scowled as he mulled her words over. "But why would someone want to bring about his own defeat? That makes no sense."

"Maybe it's a trap," Shuppan said. "To make us go away. So he can…" The immensity of the point drew his breath from him.

"Find the boy himself!" Mastiel finished, slamming his fist into his palm.

"Exactly!" Shuppan said.

Mastiel broke from the huddle. "Go ahead! Burn it down for all we care. We have other things to attend to. More important things."

"Like finding Corvii's delightful little boy?"

Bockum emerged from the river and held up his lantern. They could see his fine features: his bright blue eyes and long blond hair. And the Leggat eagle that dangled from his neck.

"How do you know that?" Shuppan said. Mastiel gave him a sharp elbow in the ribs for his misstep.

"It turns out that I'm a master of all sorts of strange languages. And some of them are in the least expected places. Consider the rope around your belly. There's a whole tirade written in its weave. In long, flowing cursive." He lifted his lamp and pointed to the rope around their waists. "You only have to pause in the midst of all this chaos and read it."

Shuppan brought the rope up before his eyes in wonder, but Charlotte swatted it away. "We need to sound the alarm!"

"Why? So we can go home to Brother Adalbane empty-handed?" Mastiel said. "And let the gendarme throw us in their dungeon, besides? No way."

"Well, I don't care what you two think. I'm going!" Charlotte backed away from them, fumbling to release herself from the knot around her waist.

"Oh no you're not." Mastiel grabbed the rope and tugged it before her fingers could finish their work. The force knocked Charlotte to her knees, and the flinty edge of the embankment gave way. She slid down as far as the rope would allow and dangled at its end like a fish on a hook before Bockum.

Bockum locked eyes with Charlotte then dropped his gaze to the knot around her waist, now tightening under her weight. His eyes widened with delight.

"My dear, that knot was written by none other than the god Aelic himself, master of the threads of fate. Can you not see? Look at the clean lines of his script. When your fingers tangle in a million directions one must be nothing but exact."

He stepped toward her. Charlotte scrambled backward in the loose rock and dirt, fighting for footing.

"*Shhh.* There, there, girl. There's no need to worry. Aelic clearly finds you amusing. And if you've won *his* heart, then you've won mine." He crouched down and caressed the rope above her head.

"Look here. He writes that when you stopped on the high road just now and saw my siege in the distance, he too thought it wrong. That it went against all laws of providence and fate." He startled and covered his mouth.

"Why, look at that!" He pointed to the rope. "He writes that he even reached out from the heavens and loosened your knot. Had you run then for the gendarme it would have fallen about your feet. Why did you not?"

Charlotte struggled to find purchase in the rocks and dirt. Her efforts sent her twisting where she dangled.

"But now look. That same rope holds you tight like a vice. One can only conclude from such a strange turn of events"—Bockum looked up into the sky—"that the great god Aelic has changed his mind. He has reconsidered the offer I wrote upon my shield at the Lomhar Pass. And he now agrees."

A tiny rock fall grew to a tumble, and soon Mastiel and Shuppan were at Bockum's feet.

"Ah, now the joker replies!" Bockum pointed to the knot around Mastiel's waist. "Not to be outdone, it would appear that Civiak too has considered my bargain. And he pulls you both toward it with his usual comedy."

Shuppan managed to untie his knot. He wiggled free and let the rope fall away. Bockum reached for it and drew it like strands of silver across his palm.

"Well, look at that. Even righteous Dhoorval has joined his cursive to the work. He writes to say that he accepts my offer." He drew more of the rope and pointed at it. "So does Woadbrek and diminutive Mag."

By now all the children had undone the knots around their waists. They threw the cord down and Bockum pulled its length toward him.

"So too does Gollunt." He spoke in breathless wonder as the rope sifted through his fingers. "Even Rawl relents with his usual cold, stiff tone." He looked up, eyes wild as a banshee's. "But no Methulla. The god of truth balks. Well, no matter. He will enter my bargain in time." He drew his gaze back to Shuppan.

"My offer at the Lomhar Pass is accepted, then. The siege of the Clovenstone will succeed; the Blackened Nevers will be reached. And brother shall once again kill brother. Glory be to the gods!"

Charlotte and Mastiel shrank back farther. Charlotte tried to draw Shuppan with them but the little boy knocked her arm off his shoulder.

"Y-you didn't mention Bragnal. He didn't mention Bragnal," he repeated to Charlotte. "He was… he was my mother's god. Before she died. She said not to worry because Bragnal would hold her in the palm of his hand. You can see them, can't you? You can *talk* to them. Well, go on. Ask them. Is she with Bragnal? Tell me, does he speak of my mother?"

Meanwhile, a row of six Leggatmen had appeared from the forest on the far side of the river. Wergoyle could not avoid it any longer. With a sick look on his face, he joined them as they waded through the water.

Bockum stared into the little boy's eyes. "No, son," he said sympathetically. "No, if a length of this rope was twisted and burned, rotted and frayed, then I would think of Bragnal. If it burned me with hot treachery, then I would think of Bragnal."

The jangle of the soldiers' weapons and armor, and the splash of their progress through the water, echoed under the bridge. Mastiel pulled Charlotte back and shoved her up the embankment, fighting her every effort to turn back to Shuppan.

The soldiers reached their side of the river. Bockum motioned to a tall Shemetesh warrior to come forward. "Hold him," he said. The soldier nodded, came behind Shuppan, and held the little boy fast.

"I want to tell you a little story, boy. Is that ok? Will you let me tell you a story?"

Bockum dropped to his knees before Shuppan. He held the rope up to the lamplight and teased out the four strands that formed it, laying them out in his palm like the roots of a tree. He singled out the first with his finger. As Bockum prepared to speak, Wergoyle gathered up the rest of the rope that lay slack behind Bockum and threw it into the air as if releasing a dove. It floated aimless for a moment then twisted like a dying snake, curling, spinning, and warping until it formed the profiles of a dozen faces that all bent to look down at Bockum's hand.

"This is the *when*, my son. This is when the story ends. It was a long, long time ago. Before dreams, before men, before cities and kings, before races."

He winked at Shuppan, whose eyes were full of tears. "Long before apple custards and sweet breads. During a winter that spanned an eon. I want to return to it. Isn't that exciting?" He pushed the strand aside with his finger and teased out the next.

"This one is *where*. Where it will happen. For now, we draw the finish line at the mountains we call the Blackened Nevers. I aim to find them again, boy, with the help of an old woman and her husband presently bound in that jail I'm laying siege to. And as it once was, so it will be again." He pushed the strand aside and drew out the third.

"Haven't we said enough, Bockum?" Wergoyle said in an angry whisper.

"This one is the *what*. The *what* is the good stuff, isn't it, boy? The meat of it all." The faces in the rope closed in to peer into Bockum's palm.

"Now imagine a giant battle. Brother versus brother. You had a brother once, didn't you, Shuppan? Before Bragnal took him as he did your mother."

"Why are you telling me this?" Shuppan cried, tears staining his cheeks.

"I would echo the boy's sentiment, captain," Wergoyle said.

"Why am I telling you this? Because the gods are fickle, aren't they, Shuppan?" He turned to the faces in the rope. "Exchange with them demands scrupulous honesty, doesn't it?"

Wergoyle stepped in. "Bockum, I must insist…" Bockum turned on him and Wergoyle limped into retreat.

"The gods move the very celestial bodies and bind the firmament beneath us, don't they, Shuppan? Are they not entitled to know exactly what my bargain entails, in case they decide to abandon it?" Bockum turned back to the frightened boy. He inched forward on his knees and wiped away Shuppan's tears.

"And so, if any one of them, with this knowledge, wishes to see my gambit foiled, well then, they now see my honesty extends to such lengths that I have whispered my plans in full into your ears. And, in turn, created the very vessel that can foil them, haven't I, little Shuppan?"

Shuppan looked at him wide-eyed and trembling. Bockum snapped the length of rope taut. The faces in it fell away and it tumbled to the dirt. The soldier behind the boy wrapped the cord around the little boy's neck and wrenched a knot.

"But, alas, honesty is not foolishness, Shuppan," Bockum said as he got to his feet. "Even the gods don't expect that. Bring him."

~

"Bah. Protect your foul crate," the lieutenant yelled.

He let his cudgel fall. The trigger tripped. The men set to. The limbs and rope of the machine began to cycle. On the beats of their chant, the massive timber slowly drew backward, gaining height with each pull. The lieutenant roared again. The timber burst from the structure with a harrowing groan. The iron face of Methulla, agape and pained as if he'd just been informed of a great sin, rushed toward the barbarian.

The giant man caught the ram in his chest. The impact forced the air out of him, and he felt his ribs crack. He tried to lean forward but leverage was gone. The force dug him two trenches through the mud. Still, he kept his position, straining to absorb the shock and bring the movement of the ram to a halt.

The head of Methulla pushed the giant backward, closer and closer to the great wooden doors of the Clovenstone Stockade. He pressed with all his might; his biceps bulged; his shoulders trembled. The doors loomed behind him. He gave one last great effort, drawing up every inch of strength. Gradually the momentum of the ram began to lessen. He fell to one knee in the mud as it came to a halt.

All was silence; the men were stunned. No one moved. Then a voice rose out of the giant man like the roar of a bear.

"I am Ostaig Colmrakken!" he screamed as he stood up. He drew a breath and stepped forward. "I am the son of Thon Colmrakken!"

He pushed forward. The strength trapped in the man's massive thighs released and he advanced a step.

"My blood burst from the fire hills!" He moved his other foot forward. "My mother drank granite to build my bones!"

The giant siege machine shuddered and groaned. It ratcheted backward. The men in the shelter set to their beams with all their strength but were powerless to stop the action.

"The ram and bear pledged my limbs!" Ostaig took another step forward. "Buckthorn and oak grew my heart!"

The battering ram gave out an unholy screech. Its cords frayed; its gears ground. The oaths came fast now. Ostaig began to run.

"Eagles hatched my eyes! My fists were carved from bison hoof!"

With this last declaration, Ostaig summoned all his strength and gave one last mighty push. The ram careened away from him, its great structure torquing and trampling the men inside. It surged backward, caught on a rock, and upended. The great iron face arced upward, its mouth agape and wild, until the momentum was spent. The ram came crashing back down again and split in half. Methulla's head with its laurel of birds drove deep into the mud and was lost to the light.

⁂

High atop a hill, Bockum watched his siege of the Clovenstone Stockade slowly turn from stalemate to victory. A surge of his men against the western wall had succeeded in breaching it. They poured into the prison now. Even more miraculous was what transpired at the gate; once barred by the giant Colmrakken, it now lay breached, its timbers succumbing to a porcupine's hide worth of flaming arrows. It seemed to him an embarrassment of divine interventions.

He gestured to Wergoyle. The steward nodded. He retreated to the cage in the corner of the tent. There he drew out a dove, whispered to it, and threw it into the air.

It flew ragged at first, shaky and awkward. But it righted its path as it crested the Quardinal Bridge. From there its course was straight, over the broken siege machine, over the top of the Clovenstone Stockade, and down into the courtyard, where it landed on a gooseberry bush.

From a window at his station, Lucian, officer of the watch, noted the dove landing. He plucked a set of keys from the wall and whistled as he walked down the corridor.

CHAPTER 14
A CELL TO SELL

PRISONERS STREAMED THROUGH the halls and courtyards of the Clovenstone Stockade. Murderers and rapists, thieves and con artists, molesters and seditionists, all clamoring for weapons: a bar, a brick, a shard of ceramic.

The air was thick with pails, stools, rocks, and wood set to flight; the stockade guards being set upon from all sides. None of them stood a chance.

But the tide of prisoners parted when it crashed against Ostaig. He walked slowly against the flow, one arm over his aching ribs. The rods, bars, and bricks in the prisoners' hands were lowered as they passed him only to be raised again for the plunder and murder continuing in his wake.

He cleared the courtyard and came to the doorway leading to his hall. The door lay on the ground, splintered and cracked after having been blown from its hinges. As Ostaig grabbed it to throw it free from his path, a bearded Kaopsin man slipped out from the shadows. The man sneered. He held a third of a chair.

"Out of my way, Colmrakken pig."

The Kaopsin lunged. Ostaig swung the heavy door. It took the man on the head, pinning him against the stone wall with a sickening thud. He pulled it away. The man's head was caved in like a pumpkin. Ostaig kicked the body aside, entered the hallway, and wedged the broken door back into place.

He ran his fingers along the stone walls as he walked. The muffled din of the violence outside was the only sound. He turned the corner; now every six feet of stone wall made way for eight feet of rusted iron bars. The cells were empty, their contents overturned.

He walked the thirty paces to his cell and slipped in. He closed the door behind him and sat down on the rough hay bunk. With a deep, satisfied breath, he lifted his hand from his ribs. He felt the area with his fingers: four cracked. A glorious gift from Mag above.

Suddenly Griscomb skidded to a halt on his knees in front of the iron bars.

"Ostaig!" He looked over his shoulder. "Let me in. Let me in the cell. You've no idea what's happened to me. No one will. But we'll talk about that later. Please, they're coming. Let me in!"

The guard reached for the door handle, but Ostaig slammed it shut with a kick.

"It's me, damn you. Griscomb! Don't you remember?" He gestured to the dirty plates on the cell floor. "The beets? I'm the guard who brought you beets on Tuesday evenings. Remember?"

Ostaig looked at the ceiling and closed his eyes.

"Damn you, Colmrakken," Griscomb screamed, shaking the bars. "I should have given those beets to another prisoner. I was a fool to help you, to spare your lumbering hide."

Ostaig grunted. "You spared me? And who asked you for that?"

"The bloody impulse of humanity, of sympathy, you brute."

"Bah! Is that all humans ever care about? Alleviating suffering? No wonder your gods are weak and thin, and they choke under their debts."

Approaching footsteps brought fresh urgency to Griscomb's voice. But it was too late. He turned to parry the thrust of a sharpened ladder's leg. "Ostaig!"

He parried another blow and lost his grip on his sword. It crashed to the stone floor.

Ostaig lumbered to the iron bars and rattled them. "Take your bloody wounds, you filthy weakling!" Spittle and froth flew from his mouth, and tiny flakes of dust took to the air where the metal bars he shook met the stone ceiling.

The noise startled the three attackers and they paused their assault. A tall Jarlspeen man with long blond hair and thick sideburns leaned toward the Colmrakken's cage. He tapped the bars with his makeshift sword.

"Well, what do we have here, gentlemen? The famous Colmrakken. And the bull's been left locked in his cage." He kicked the bars. The two men behind him laughed.

"That Colmrakken pig stopped the Civiak riot. Caved in my friend's head," snarled a fat Dinafatari man holding a sharpened piece of pottery.

"That's him, isn't it? The Wednesday Whip," the third man added. He was a thin Gailican youth not more than twenty-five. He held a club made of a ball of shattered glass affixed with strips of torn bedding to a piece of wood.

"The bloody Wednesday Whip," the tall Jarlspeen repeated with a nod.

"You couldn't yield just once, brute? Eh? Just once?" the Dinafatari yelled. "For your brothers?"

"Of course not," said the Jarlspeen. "We had to bask in his vaunted Colmrakken stubbornness. And so we all got to climb into our bunks hungry." He turned to the Gailican youth. "How were your Wednesdays, Mast?"

"I ate mice."

"You, Rol?"

"Straw. From my mattress."

"That's *your* fault, Colmrakken," the Jarlspeen sneered, tapping the bars again.

"Bah! You're all cowards and invalids." Ostaig let go of the bars. "Suckled on petty comforts." He returned to his mattress. "You would beggar the millstone to pity the chaff."

"I went hungry, savage. Hungry! Cuz of you!" the Jarlspeen roared.

Ostaig gave a snort and cocked his chin contemptuously. It brought a snarl to the Jarlspeen's lips. He grabbed Griscomb, pressed him against the bars, and put his sword between the man's legs. "I'll cut his balls off!"

Ostaig looked at him blankly.

"I will. I'll cut his balls off and bleed him right here!"

"You'll not find any balls on that one," Ostaig muttered.

"I–I brought you clean water!" Beads of sweat streamed down Griscomb's forehead. "Every Thursday. Drawn from the stream. So you could clean your wounds."

"I never asked for water."

"You never asked for water? To clean wounds? You can't be serious. You'd be dead by now without…" Griscomb suddenly howled in pain. He raised his tunic to see the skin lifting above his navel. It domed as if an egg were poking against it from inside his belly. He doubled over and held his stomach.

The Jarlspeen took this with surprise that quickly turned to disgust. He smashed him back onto the bars but Griscomb was a hollow shell of himself now.

"I would have died, and I would have been happy doing so." Ostaig lay back on his mattress and closed his eyes. "Resigned to my fate. Fortunate to be blessed with clearing a trunk's worth of Mag's debts. So his dice may roll on. Not grasping and whimpering, begging to everyone around me like a newborn babe." Ostaig rolled over and faced the wall.

"If you had any balls, prison guard, you would grab the door to my cell with your left hand. You would swing it open with all your might and smash it into that Jarlspeen's head. Then you'd grab his sword and plunge it into that fat Dinafatari next to him. From his stench, you could do it blindfolded. Then you'd push his corpulent body into that Gailican child, pinning the little prick with a sound kick." He calmly turned his head back to them.

"If any vitality remains in your broken manhood, that is."

The Gailican youth put his hand on the Jarlspeen's shoulder. "D-did he say the door was… was unlocked?"

The Jarlspeen pushed the youth away. He licked his lips as he considered the situation. The fires from the courtyard had entered the corridor now. They were illuminating the ceiling beams in hues of red and orange.

"Where's the key?" he roared. He gave Griscomb a shake.

"I–I don't have the key," he whispered, overcome with pain. "There are no keys. Not anymore."

Ostaig roused from his mattress and glared at him. "What do you mean?"

"I mean the keys are gone, you ignorant brute," Griscomb muttered. He inched up the bars to get away from the Jarlspeen's blade.

The hallway suddenly shook as a ceiling beam collapsed. The sparks crashing off it spilled onto the floor.

"Who holds me, then?" Ostaig stood up.

"You just shut up in there," the Jarlspeen said. He crashed his fist on the bars for emphasis.

"Let's leave it, Mok." The Dinafatari man backed away from the cell.

"I said *who holds me?*" Ostaig's bellow sent the Gailican youth running down the hall. He disappeared into the smoke and flames.

"No one, you oaf. The brig is bust. You're as free in here as a bloody cockroach," Griscomb yelled, pushing himself higher on the bars.

In a flash, Ostaig threw open the door to his cell. It knocked the Jarlspeen man back and cut a trench into Griscomb's thigh as he fell. The Dinafatari raised his weapon, but Ostaig's punch snapped his head back. It dangled from the man's neck like the broken stalk of a banana. He crumpled to the floor.

The Jarlspeen quickly recovered and drove his sword forward. Ostaig darted out of the way and clamped his massive hands on either side of his head, pressing them together as if squeezing a tomato. The man's struggles ebbed away with his life.

"Grab the sword, fool," Ostaig said as he let the limp body go.

"A-are there more?" Griscomb looked around.

"Grab the sword!"

Griscomb nodded and picked it up. Ostaig grabbed the hilt, binding Griscomb's grip tight under his, then drove the sword deep into his own stomach.

"Nice strike," the giant growled, looking down. "The wound is deep." He closed his eyes. "It clefts my stomach and perhaps my spleen. The rot and pain will be immense. Mag will roll his dice hot tonight!" He flashed Griscomb a grin.

Griscomb stumbled back, bewildered.

"Stop your mollycoddling, guard. You did well. It's a fine wound. Just deep enough to prevent my escape."

"Th-that wound is not my doing," Griscomb stammered, "and you're not escaping. The brig is busted clean, you big oaf. It's burning to the ground!"

He made to run, but Ostaig caught him. The flames stretched along the wooden ceiling now. Smoke filled the corridor and sparks dropped all around them.

"Remove it." Ostaig stared down at the sword. "Remove it and clamp me in irons."

"I'm not touching that thing. A-and I'm not clamping you in bloody irons!" he screamed before doubling over from the pain in his stomach.

The beams on either side of them collapsed. The impact threw stones and cinders into the air of the narrow hall.

"You will hold me captive. You will drive me under lock and key until my sentence is served." Ostaig looked up. The fire rolling toward them across the ceiling was freeing great piles of debris into the hallway. "Or you will be buried alive."

He returned to his cell and his mattress. He leaned back, hands behind his head, and closed his eyes. The sword dangling from his side was slowly carving and spreading the wound in his gut.

Griscomb stared at the giant, dumbfounded. “Fine. Fine! I’ll imprison you. I’ll–I’ll drive you under lock and key. Just get us out of here!”

Ostaig rose and presented his belly. Griscomb grabbed the hilt of the sword and, wincing in disgust, pulled it free of the giant’s midriff. He tossed it to the ground, which drew a vicious glare from Ostaig. Griscomb returned a look of profound confusion.

“In case I try to escape.” Ostaig nodded toward the sword.

Griscomb swallowed hard. There was no use in protesting. He relented and picked up the sword as Ostaig raced from the cell and, blood spilling from his gaping wound, began to dig their path to freedom.

CHAPTER 15
THE DAEMONIUS CONCENTRIC

LUCIAN STOOD BEFORE the door, paralyzed with indecision. The key ring in his hand held one that was intricately carved and oversized. And the door before him was intricately carved and oversized. This obvious corollary would have struck the passerby as cause for no indecision at all. The path was clear. But the indecision for Lucian involved something far more profound.

It was not *which* key would open the door to the Daemonius Concentric. That was obvious. It was one particularly nauseating possibility that was giving him pause: what if they choose to torture everyone by inserting giant needles up the back of their legs?

The door was far grander than any other in the Clovenstone Stockade, carved by the great Frew the Elder himself in one of his last public commissions. At its top were the sun, moon, and the stars; below them, a chain of giant mountains; below them, the assembly of the gods.

Bragnal was etched in the middle, his left fist on his scales. The opposite weighing pan was high above, and on it stood Zernebruk, Vestialis, and Fitzhiff.

Beside him was Aelic, the thousands of cords trailing from his hands twisted down to the bottom of the door. There, hundreds of tiny human bodies busied themselves with the tasks of living: washing linen, sowing seeds, trading goods, and laughing and dancing. At the edge of the door, a group drew back a woman who had thrown a brooch into a dark forest. Frew the Elder had rendered the brooch in mid-flight with a weaving filigree from the forest twisting around it. Two eyes peered from inside the deep cuts and cross-hatchings the Elder had used to represent the tangle of trees.

Civiak was depicted between two of the mountain peaks high on the door. His hands grasped them and his tongue, like a ribbon, wove through the peaks and curled around his axiom: *Grim is the prayer to a god who won't care.*

Methulla was next. The god had been rendered prostrate in a circle of six birds, each with a different object in its mouth. The tiny swallow, a sprig of laurel; the raven, a key; the pheasant, an acorn; the hawk, a snake; the dove, a ball of light; and the long graceful heron, an iron ring.

Next to Methulla stood Digrir, his hands spread to embrace a group of street children. Their collected tears formed a stream that washed down the middle of the door to Woadbrek. The short, squat old man drew his tankard from the stream while four attendants steadied the teetering god and stood ready to refill it. Behind him, young Mag sat cross-legged, rearing back to throw his dice, a pile of bones and hearts and heads between him and a minotaur.

No one Lucian knew had ever touched the door, let alone opened it. The closest he had come to seeing inside the Daemonius Concentric was once, ages ago, when a retinue of Samidian knights had stood by while the warden unlocked it. Even then, all he'd seen was the flicker of torchlight on the condensation as the knights pressed their prisoner down its steps and into darkness.

What if they choose to burn all the old ladies in their beds? His fingers shook as they pinched the giant key.

What if they choose to knot all the puppy legs together? You'll be responsible for that too. He slid the key into the lock and paused. *Then you had best think of a way to not be responsible, Lucian Agroft.*

So there Lucian stood, hunched before the door, key in the lock, while he waited for fate to intervene.

Suddenly, a terrific impact of something hitting the wall showered him in dust. It was just enough, perfectly enough, for Lucian to foment a startle. He shook and twisted, and in doing so made certain the hand that held the key twisted as well. It turned over. Lucian jumped back.

That wasn't me! I didn't do that! He held up his hands in surrender. *You should've looked after that door a little better, Bragnal. Imagine, letting little ol' Lucian Agroft's hand twist like that.* He moved cautiously back toward the door.

But I want something made absolutely crystal clear, Bragnal. He took another tentative step. *Any dragons they might whistle for. Or demons. Those can't be laid at my feet either.* He leaned forward.

All of that, from here on in, is your damn fault, not mine. Imagine, letting little ol' Lucian Agroft's hand just land...

He closed his eyes and reached out his hand.

... wherever...

He grabbed the handle and turned it.

... it felt like.

The handle rotated in his hand like a warm corn cob on a stick of butter. Lucian opened his eyes. He was almost there. All he needed was one more tiny bolt of inspiration. He scrunched his brow deep in thought, and then it hit him.

You know as well as me, don't you, Bragnal, just how hard your poor Lucian slaves. Each and every day. Up at dawn, sweeping the stalls, with nothing more than one slice of bread with no jam.

Lucian Agroft put the side of his head, then his shoulder, on the door.

So you can't be surprised when your poor, exhausted servant Lucian succumbs to his mortal failings. And he takes his wee pause. His tiny, wee rest. To keep himself from an early grave.

With that, he pressed his entire weight against the door. Nothing. He added ever so slight a touch of muscle flex. But it didn't move.

"Glory be to Bragnal," he grumbled under his breath as he retreated.

While his futile efforts had been playing out, he had held in his left hand an envelope bent by his fingers and dampened with his sweat. It hung limp as Lucian contemplated the situation.

He tried the door again, thumping his shoulder against it, but still it refused to budge. He examined the other keys on the chain and tried a few. They did nothing.

Well, it seems we're at an impasse here, aren't we, Bragnal? He hugged his stomach and picked his teeth. *A proper god would do more, I think. A proper god would send his good servant a message, wouldn't he?*

It was then that he thought of the envelope pinched between his fingers. He stepped back with delight and slapped it with his other hand.

Blessed be your works, Bragnal. Blessed! Straight from your worktable to your faithful servant Lucian Agroft.

He drew the paper out from the envelope and unfolded it. He held it up to the flickering light of the torch sconce and knitted his eyebrows.

How you curse me, Bragnal.

Lucian Agroft let it drop to his side. He brought it back before his eyes and muttered again. It was no use. He'd expected a loving god would have used pictures. Bragnal, it seemed, was anything but loving.

It had been years since Lucian Agroft had tried to read anything. And even then, it had been a sign on the high road pointing to his daughter's village. He'd spent a full ten minutes trying to mouth the words before a farmhand blurted it out for him with a laugh as he trotted by on a mule. But this was something entirely different. There were at least a dozen words written in large cursive on this paper.

He stared at them as though he believed the secret lay in his eye muscles. But the words remained indecipherable. He crumpled the paper in a fit of pique and threw it at the door.

Your will is truly inscrutable, Bragnal!

Four pale, wrinkled fingers suddenly wiggled at the base of the door. They curled around the note and drew it under. Lucian registered the movement in awe. He looked up at the ceiling.

Now you saw that, didn't you? I had nothing to do with that. Nothing!

"There is a switch, my boy," came an old woman's voice from under the door. It was creaky and shrill like the gears of a windmill. Lucian put his ear close.

"The switch is made from the tip of Civiak's tongue. You need to turn it." Lucian heard paper crinkle. "Clockwise, my dear."

He nodded and stepped back to examine the carvings on the door. He spied Civiak's tongue twisting up off the mountains when a chill hit him. He darted away from the door.

"Now just a minute," he whispered. "I know what *I'm* doing—well, not doing. And I know what Bragnal is doing." He crossed his arms over his chest. "But I don't know what you're doing."

"I see," the old woman whispered. "Perhaps you have a touch more integrity than we first imagined, Lucian Agroft?"

"It's nothing of the sort." He pressed his finger into a deep furrow of the black forest etching on the door. "It's just, well, I just think I need… another thought. The ones I have aren't doing the job. What I think I need is something more…"

"A rationale, good Lucian?"

Lucian nodded. "Yes. Yes, that sounds right. A rationale."

"Well, as you can hear, I am an old woman, aren't I? And this is clearly a locked door, isn't it? And… I'm stuck! Yes, that's it. I'm stuck down here. And I'm hurt as well." She paused. "Will that be enough?"

Lucian frowned and rubbed his chin. "An old woman? Stuck, you say?" He shrugged his shoulders. "Bit of a fanciful story, don't you think? Might need a little more meat on the bones. Just how does an old woman find herself stuck in the Daemonius Concentric?"

"You'll never believe me."

"Give it a try."

The woman's whisper was stronger now. She'd moved to the keyhole. "Behind the olive grove on the high road, near the Quardinal Bridge, there's a cave. My husband Chezepock and I were walking in the woods when we heard a cat meowing. Yes. It seemed so hungry. So we followed it into the cave. And one thing led to another, and we found ourselves in this terrible place. It's full of awful drudges, Lucian. Sick, mean servants. So, please, Lucian. Please, my darling. For a hurt, old grandmother with bad knees, you simply must open this door."

Lucian traced his finger along the wall bashfully. "What you're really saying is you're looking for a hero."

"Absolutely, Lucian."

"To help you out of this horrible situation."

"Oh, the most horrible."

Lucian winked to the heavens. "Yes, I think that should do the trick just fine." He dropped to his knees before Civiak's tongue.

"In truth, you really had no choice, my boy," the woman said, breathless with excitement.

"None," he whispered as he grasped Civiak's tongue and turned it. A giant bolt fell in its mechanism and sent off a tiny stream of dust from the lock. Lucian stepped back, but a final wave of hesitation hit him.

What the muhk's bucket am I doing? What if those drudges pull down the sun and it's a thousand days of night? What if they send ghouls through the pipes? I can't do this.

"My boy, I can't open it myself." The old woman spoke under obvious strain. "It's too heavy for me."

Lucian was debating a quick flight from the door. The sword blows and explosions seemed closer. He could smell the smoke and it was drawing off his resolve.

"You aren't hesitating again, are you, Lucian?" Her words led his focus back to the door. "Your great-great-grandfather was ever the hesitator." Her voice was as sharp as a wasp's sting. "So you come by it naturally. Did he ever tell you I offered myself to him? Oh, that's many, many moons ago. But, like you, he hesitated. And, well, look where it got him. He was forced to plant his seed in that rotted womb of your ancient mother. And lo and behold, the cycle of hesitation spins anon."

Lucian stepped back from the door.

Who the muhk is this? What has Bragnal done?

"Bragnal wants this, Lucian." She seemed to have read his thoughts. "Think for a moment. He put you here, now, before this door. And he gave you all the tools you need to open it. Tools he refused other men."

Someone called out in the corridor behind him. Lucian turned to see Wergoyle emerge into the flickering light. The old steward bent his torch to the sconce. It took up the flame and illuminated the white dove in his other hand. The bird startled at the sudden brightness. Wergoyle soothed it calm.

"Were the instructions too difficult for you, Lucian?" he said.

"Far too difficult," the old woman said.

"Then I might ask you, Pennylegion, if I might, why you saw any utility in using such a dunce in the first place?"

"He's at the door, isn't he?" she hissed. "Better men would not be."

Wergoyle brought the dove up before his eyes. "True, better men are prone to all manner of failings, aren't they, bishop?"

"B-bishop?" Lucian said.

"Why, yes, Lucian." Wergoyle held the dove out. "This little feathered courier is none other than the cardinal bishop of Bragnal, Bishop Lansdowne. Differently attired, I granted you. But it was him who flew to you with my note. Speaking of which, where is Lord Bishop's missive?"

Lucian snapped out of his confusion. He pointed to the door. Wergoyle sighed and came alongside it.

"Why have you stolen this man's note, Pennylegion?" Then he aimed his venom at the dove. "No man should be stolen from, should they, Bishop?"

"H-he stole from you." Lucian stammered in bewilderment.

"Oh, indeed he did, Lucian. Bishop Lansdowne here stole my wife from me and threw me into the 12th Leggat, didn't you, Bishop? But now look at the distinguished man of the robe. He finds himself in an awful twist of fate, don't you, Bishop? For now, it is *him* who is condemned to die." He fingered the tiny hangman's noose around the dove's neck.

"He buys a reprieve from the anointed moment of his hanging in bundles of hours paid for in service to me, don't you, Lansdowne? But that trade will quickly vanish if he keeps coming up feeble and ineffectual! Now, where is the note?" he screamed at the little bird.

"If that feathered specimen is the cardinal bishop of Bragnal, then I am Woadbrek's lead privy," Pennylegion said as she pushed the note back under the door.

"Lo, Bishop!" Wergoyle exclaimed. "Fortune shines upon you." He picked up the note. When he finished reading it, he glared at Lucian. "The instructions are as clear as day, Lucian. Why then is this door not open? Was the task too difficult for you?"

"That…the…" Lucian pointed to the door. Wergoyle followed.

"Who? Her? Yes, I can imagine she might cast a ghoulish cloud. But, my good man, you really must recall that the divine race is once again afoot. Doors are opening all around us with all manner of abominations bursting from them. If we were to hold all our keys to our chest, then when the time came to use them…" Wergoyle's voice went soft as he reached out and righted Bragnal's scale. A series of clicks and shudders ran through the door. He grabbed the handle.

"We might find ourselves with no more locks to open."

He pulled. The heavy ornate door groaned open on its rusted hinges. Wergoyle's torch pecked at the darkness beyond, illuminating a dark passage that led to steep stairs descending in a spiral. The outline of Pennylegion's dress was also caught in the glow. The old woman pushed herself off the wall into the light, clutching a doll to her chest.

She was haggard. Deep wrinkles criss-crossed her face. Patches of baldness thinned her long white hair. She had sunken eyes and was missing half her teeth. Her left cheek was permanently pitted. Every one of her movements came with trembles and shakes. She fretted with the black lace shawl over her shoulders as she looked expectantly at Lucian. But it was Wergoyle's icy voice that broke the silence.

"Has your husband Chezepock returned from his frolic by the river? Has the effigy of the knight been placed?"

"It has," Pennylegion replied. "And he has returned. I must warn you, though, he has warmed to the freedom terribly, Wergoyle."

"Then I suppose you'll want that old bag of a husband of yours broken free as well."

"I would be forever in Bockum's debt."

Wergoyle brought the dove up close to his eye. "Mess this up, Bishop, and it'll be the rack before the swing. Mark my words."

With that Wergoyle threw the dove into the staircase, gave a weak bow, and strode off the way he'd come.

CHAPTER 16

PENNYLEGION'S BASTARD TREE

PENNYLEGION OFFERED HER elbow to Lucian. "Help an old woman, would you, dear?" He instinctively drew back and a reflexive "No" escaped his lips.

"You would deny me?" Her voice trembled with indignation. "Seventy-seven generations have sprouted from my womb. The very milk that you sipped from your mother—that milk first fell from my breast." Pennylegion tapped her chest before stabbing toward his.

"Your heart beats blood first mixed in my belly." Her expression read equal parts galled and pleading. "And you would deny me? A simple steady hand, Lucian? To see me safely down these treacherous steps. That's all I ask."

Pennylegion gestured toward the stairs. The small effort brought forth a stumble. Lucian stepped forward and grabbed her.

"Fine. Take my arm."

Pennylegion looked up at him. "Bless you, my son."

They started slowly down the stairs, Pennylegion leaning on Lucian's arm. "Now, as you heard, I am Pennylegion. And you must be Lucian."

"Of course I'm Lucian," he snapped as he steadied himself on the wall.

"Now, now, my boy. What are we in this life if we can't be cordial to one another? Now my dear." She tapped his arm with her finger. "You must tell me about this promise of divinity Bockum gave you. I read it in your note. How exciting for you! I know the opinion of an old woman doesn't carry much sway in the world any longer, but I can tell you the life of a drudge is a wonderful life, full of adventure and intrigue. Unless of course, one finds oneself a drudge rotting in the Daemonius Concentric for six centuries. Then I would be remiss not to remark that the immortality does tend to weigh."

"You're one of them?"

"A drudge? Yes, my boy. The drudge to Vestialis herself. We are all drudges down here. As you will be soon if I heard correctly. Now, my darling." She crested the step. "You simply must tell me, which type did you pick?"

The question shocked Lucian dumb. She tapped his arm to bring him back to the conversation. "Go on. No secrets from an old granny."

"I said I wanted to be a drudge to a–a god of thunder. I like thunder." He blushed.

"Oooh." Pennylegion's voice bubbled with warmth. "That is exciting. You'll make such noise and light." They negotiated the next step.

"I've always liked thunder," Lucian replied. "It was thunder, or it was a god of earthquakes. It was between those two."

"Oh, well, you did make the right choice, my boy. As I understand it, earthquakes are a perennial affair. That god would keep you up at all hours of the night, and they work a terrible effect on the ears."

"Yes, I like to think so." Lucian sounded chuffed at his choice. They negotiated another step. "Bragnal, it's hot in here." He drew his tunic from his sweaty neck.

"Yes, but what will that be to you soon enough?" Pennylegion gave him a wry smile. "Soak it in while you can, my darling. You'll soon have nothing but your memories of such mortal concerns."

"I suppose you're right," Lucian said, licking his lips.

"Because what you do today is so profound, Lucian, so heroic. It rivals when Vestialis first drank from the chalice of love."

"It *was* me that opened that door, wasn't it?"

"Absolutely it was." Pennylegion tapped his forearm again. "Thus your handsome reward, my boy."

They stepped off the final step and stood at the threshold of the Daemonius Concentric.

"We all saw your work today, Lucian, my dear. And you did wonderfully." Pennylegion gave him a warm smile, and he blushed. "Shall we?"

Lucian nodded, and they stepped forward into the octagonal chamber.

It was a large room, forty feet by forty feet. The walls were broken by the rusted bars of eight prison cells, each one set in shadows. A number of torches struggled to produce light in their sconces. The smell of filth and decay was overwhelming.

"Well, here we are," Pennylegion said. "Smaller than you imagined, isn't it? And that smell! That smell is exactly why I always say that a drudge, like a god, should insist on showing their faces so seldom. What would mortals think if they knew the stench the divine give off?"

She turned to Lucian and pointed a pedagogical finger at him.

"The myth is always affected when the mortal encounters it. Remember that, Lucian. It invariably takes some of the sheen off." She whispered, "And a sheen is all some of these have."

Lucian's stared into the room, mouth agape. He started toward a cell, but Pennylegion fixed him firm. "Please, my darling. My legs aren't what they used to be. I'll need your arm still."

"Your mind isn't what it used to be either, Pennylegion," came a raspy voice from the shadows of a cell.

"You'll hold that tongue, Ratcha, or I'll see you thrown deeper than this pit," Pennylegion growled. "My Vestialis is free," she preened. "And she has half a Leggat behind her. Soon I will join her. And she will win this race, of that, there can be no doubt."

A man slid on to the bars of his cell. Pressing against the iron made the shadowy figure look as though the metal had sawn him into quarters.

"Will she now?" Ratcha reached up into the shadows around his face. His hand jerked, and in a flash a bleeding tongue fell at their feet. Lucian scrambled back.

"Now what, you doddering old biddy?" Ratcha spoke as though the tongue were still in place.

"This one will stay in his cage," Pennylegion said before her voice galloped to a roar. "And anyone else among you who'd like to rattle a few more curses my way."

She held up the keys in Lucian's hand. "That's right." She nodded. "Lucian Agroft decides who stays and who leaves! And he's with me!"

Pennylegion ushered him forward before he could deny her words. As they moved, a woman came to stand before the bars of her cell. The shard of glass in her hand rattled against the metal. She was naked from the waist up and her belly was full and distended. A jagged wound ran across it, thick with hardened blood. A rat's tail dangled from the cut, and the skin of her stomach undulated with quick, skitterish movements.

"Pennylegion, I beg of you. Is Zernebruk with you? Is he coming to free me? Can't he see I'm with child? This is no place for a drudge to raise her young! I need a warm and safe environment. Not this pit surrounded by these… these wretches and beasts."

She turned to Lucian and pursed her lips. "You will be freeing me, won't you, Mr. Lucian? Can't I help my god Zernebruk run as well?"

As the woman spoke the soft earth beyond her cage trembled, and three red shoots burst from the ground. They curled through the bars and bloomed within its shadows, leaving a faint cloud of dust in their wake.

Lucian began to stammer a response but Pennylegion stamped it out. "Of course he will, won't you, Lucian? Though a few more centuries of reflection on your indiscretions would do you a world of good, Quindecum."

In the cell next to Quindecum's, a man's voice announced itself.

"You'd *better* free her, Lucian. For if I have to listen to any more wailing and stitching, I'll hang myself."

"You shut up, Macionica," Quindecum shrieked. "It's your fault I'm in this condition. Using a woman so. And then abandoning her. I should have known. Letting myself be wooed so by a drudge of seduction."

A rustle of hay; the sound of naked feet on stone. Macionica's hands suddenly grasped the bars of his cell. Each hand held no more than two fingers, the others having been burned or torn away, and they glistened with a sheen of oil that dripped onto the stone floor.

"A drudge of seduction?" Macionica chuckled. He receded into the shadows of his cell. "You tell yourself whatever you need to, you lusty sprite. You reached out to me. Like all of them do!"

Pennylegion prodded Lucian. "Go on, unlock the cells." He stared at her in disbelief. "It won't do for the drudge of a god of thunder to tremble, boy."

Lucian stepped forward. Quindecum looked longingly at him as more red shoots curled around her. She twisted one over her finger as he fumbled with the keys. "The drudges make love too, Lucian Agroft." She cradled her belly. "And much besides."

He found the key, unlocked the cell, and then darted back.

"Now the other," Pennylegion shouted. Lucian shook his head.

"Lucian! Enough of this! Unlock the cell!"

Lucian gathered his wits and nodded. He approached Macionica's cell, tore through the keys, and unlocked the cage in as swift a maneuver as he could manage. He was at Pennylegion's side before the cell door clanged open.

Pennylegion patted his arm reassuringly and ushered him to the next cell. As they walked, she stared into his eyes. "You know, Lucian, my darling, you have your father's eyes."

"No. No, I don't… I don't think so."

"No, I'm afraid you do. I remember his father too. A suckled pig.

I beat him black and blue but still, he grew so soft. He wouldn't rise to meet the morning without a drink of fermented goat's milk. Same with his son, and his son after him. It seems you simply can't carve that smut from the seed. And I tried, Lucian. Believe me, I tried."

They reached the next cell and Lucian paused once again drawing more of Pennylegion's ire. "Go on. Lucian, my darling, please, you're embarrassing me."

Still nothing.

"Lucian!" Her voice was full of rebuke. "Enough of this. Turn the damned key, boy."

"I–I'm not so sure anymore." Lucian looked back at the path of cells they'd already traced. "This feels like madness." He locked eyes with Pennylegion, but the old woman's patience had reached its ebb.

"Madness, is it?" she scoffed. "Allow me to tell you what madness really is, boy. Madness is the thought of a blighted mortuant like you joining our ranks."

Behind her, the freed drudges slowly emerged from their cells. They turned and looked at him. Those still in their cells moved in similar unity, their hands on their cell bars, their heads cocked to listen.

"You are the son of Poetic and of Silber and of Coate." Pennylegion spit out each name and counted them on her bony fingers. "And you are the son of Tlas and of At, and"—her lips curled into a vicious sneer—"you are the son of that rat, Malc!" She pointed at Lucian.

"No wonder your eyes droop like a turtle's shell. That scar is borne by all the bastard children of that rat's feculent manhood."

Macionica, standing with the freed drudges, raised an accusing finger at her. "Listen to Pennylegion waxing on, chastising him! Enlightening him! Why, she thinks of herself as a god of creation, doesn't she? Such arrogance could only come from the drudge of that witch Vestialis."

Pennylegion turned to Macionica in a black fury. "I will take all the time I need, Macionica. Who are you to judge? You, whose god lies dead in that foul, dirty crypt."

The shock of her words was plain on Macionica's face. "Morven is not dead," he retorted, slapping away Quindecum's sympathetic hand.

"So she abandons you, then. For here you stand, unclaimed and useless. Though the bars of your cell lie wide open for her to claim you. And yet… she does not. I wonder why?"

Macionica smiled slyly. "You are a fool, aren't you, Pennylegion? Still following Vestialis blind as a puppy."

"She is the goddess of love, drudge. A true emotion the likes of which you will never know."

"Love? She is pure corruption of love," Macionica hissed. "We all see it. Better to be unclaimed than the drudge of a false god."

Pennylegion didn't deign to look over her shoulder at him. "Careful with your words, Macionica, I warn you."

"Says the drudge of love," Macionica said as he returned to his cell.

Meanwhile, Lucian had retreated from Pennylegion, stumbling backward into the bars of the next cell. He instinctively grabbed at them and the keys in his hands clanged against the metal and fell to the floor.

"Pick up your keys, Lucian Agroft," Pennylegion hissed.

"No. T-this is madness."

"Aye, madness it is, Lucian," she replied as she closed on him.

"I–I don't want it anymore," he whimpered. "I take it all back. Tell Bockum. Tell him I don't want to be a drudge any longer."

"Do you presume divinity so cheap?" Pennylegion grabbed his neck with a grip as firm as iron. His head crashed into the bars and the impact knocked the breath from him.

"You? A drudge? Hah! You have been a disappointment from the start, Lucian Agroft. A degeneration, a corruption! As have all your kind!" Spittle pooled on her lips as she barked her insults. "Just you wait until your father hears about this. In fact, I think I hear him home from his ramblings now."

Just then, from inside the cell, a bony wrinkled hand reached out and grabbed Lucian's hair. It pulled hard and stretched his neck upward. A voice came to his ear.

"Yes, my dear, I can smell it. This one is indeed a fruit from our bastard tree." The man's voice was a creaky, rotten whisper. "Best we hurry and prune it. Before the weed grows any wilder."

A deer antler, stained with horse blood, flashed in the shadows in the cell. It slipped through the bars bound in the old man's grip. Lucian struggled against Pennylegion's hold as he watched it rise toward his neck. But Lucian Agroft was no god. He was no drudge. He was mortuant through and through. And so, as mortuants have since time immemorial, he was witness to the stark reality that his struggles, though assembled from every mortal fibre of his being, were as nothing before the exercise of true divine force. The antler pierced his mortuant shell and released the flow of his blood. And Lucian Agroft's life fell away onto the stone floor of the Daemonius Concentric.

CHAPTER 17
FOLLOW THE BURROWING EYE

TRESTLES FROM THE collapsed ceiling blocked their path. The air was thick with smoke and zipping embers. Ostaig blew on his singed fingers. "It's too much, guard!" he called back to Griscomb before throwing aside another beam. "We need to find another way."

He turned to find Griscomb hunched over, cradling his stomach.

"Didn't you hear me? There must be another way out of this bonfire."

"Ostaig, I can b-barely stand. Something's not right."

"Of course something isn't right, man. We're trapped like rats." He drew Griscomb up by the collar.

"This is not an auspicious start," he sneered. "You promised to guard me. To see your prisoner's sentence served. Not to curl into a ball and wait to die. Think, damn you. There must be another way through the Clovenstone."

Griscomb's face contracted in agony. "I–I don't know. I only know the way from the kitchen to the cells. That's it. I'm not allowed..."

"Follow the eye!" came a voice from behind them.

Ostaig let Griscomb go. He thrust his hand out blindly into the smoke. When he drew it back, Madrigan dangled at the end of his grip. He glowered at the pitchie. "Who the muhk are you?"

Griscomb managed to rise to one knee. "H-he did this to me. That pitchie!" His voice was hot with anger.

Ostaig sneered at Griscomb. "You take your bloody pain as it comes, man. And pray to Mag that when he collapses this hallway he blesses you with a rusted bolt through the shoulder." He let the image gather steam a moment in his mind's eye. "Creating a wound that will fester. So you might free him from the shackles of another poorly made wager.

"And speaking of poorly made wagers." He turned to Madrigan and tightened his grip on his collar. "Speak quick, stranger. Explain why you're babbling to me in the midst of an inferno."

Three timbers crashed down. Their embers flew into Ostaig like driving rain. He paid them no mind.

"F-follow the eye," Madrigan said.

Ostaig's eyes narrowed. He looked Madrigan up and down. "He's right, isn't he? You're a blasted pitchie, aren't you?" His grip tightened. "I hate muhk-sodden pitchies."

"Please. His shirt. Lift it up!" Madrigan sputtered. Clouds of smoke were chugging along the belly of the stone ceiling. The giant hesitated.

"Do it, you fool!" Madrigan pressed.

Ostaig threw Madrigan down and yanked the shirt up from the guard's stomach. Madrigan held out his sputtering candle to illuminate the quivering bulge tenting the skin of Griscomb's sternum.

"What is that?" Ostaig said.

"My god's eye. Now turn him around. In a circle."

"Now you'd have us dancing?"

"Just do it, you lummox!"

Another ceiling timber crashed into the corridor. Ostaig relented. He spun the prison guard and, as he did, Griscomb screamed out in agony.

"Stop!" Madrigan yelled. He brought the candle forward again. They watched as the sphere slithered up the guard's chest. "This way!" He pointed back down the hallway. He made to move, but Ostaig fixed him in position with a sharp tug.

"That way leads back into the prison, pitchie."

Another timber fell to the floor beside them, showering him in flame and ember. Madrigan broke his grasp and, shaky as a newborn calf, fumbled down the hall as best his broken body would let him.

Ostaig watched Madrigan disappear. He looked back at the approaching flames, snorted, and pulled Griscomb to his feet. The prison guard cradled his chest as if his lungs would spill. "Under which rock did you find that one?" Ostaig growled as he pushed him down the hall.

They made slow progress, dodging debris and ducking under smoke. Before long they came to a junction. Four separate corridors branched from it. They found Madrigan propped against the wall, gathering his breath.

"Spin him," he whispered between gasps.

Ostaig set the prison guard into motion. Madigan peeled himself off the wall and joined him. His candle showed the eye moving up and boring into Griscomb's shoulder. "This way!"

"How far will this egg move?" Ostaig dragged the prison guard behind him.

"It wants to return to his hand!"

"Then you'd best stop, pitchie!"

Madrigan skidded to a halt. Ostaig held up Griscomb's right arm. The eye had slipped over his shoulder and was now in the plump flesh of his bicep, its quivering iris clearly visible under the guard's thin skin, straining to take in the massive wooden door beside it. Ostaig leaned in and sneered at it. The eyeball drew back.

"No, it must be wrong," Madrigan shouted. "We need to keep going!"

"Wrong? It isn't wrong, pitchie. This eyeball is threatening to burst out of his bloody skin." The flames behind them were licking across the ceiling; trestles and rocks tumbled into the corridor.

"No, no. It's wrong; it must be." Madrigan shrank back to the wall.

Ostaig pulled the door to the Daemonius Concentric wide. He took in the spiral staircase beyond it. "What's the matter, pitchie? You afraid of shadows?"

The words forced Madrigan forward. "There are things down there, Colmrakken, that your simple barbarian mind cannot fathom. Monstrous things. Things that should be left locked up for the ages as their treacherous gods were locked up."

"Then why is the door open? If these monstrous things are indeed so monstrous?"

"I–I don't know."

"Mag above, you humans are a cowardly lot. Pain is leading the prison guard, as it rightly should. But if you're too gutless to follow its path, then fine! We'll go on alone."

He pulled Griscomb up from the floor. "Come on. Let's see where this curse of yours leads." He pushed the ailing prison guard through the open door and down the spiral staircase.

Madrigan fell back onto the wall. Down the hallway, a door burst from its hinges with a blast of flames. He cringed until they subsided. He could feel the ache and twitch in his fingers; they wanted to burrow, like worms. He tried to shake the urge from them as if wringing water from his hands, but it was no use. They were intent to burrow, and burrow they would.

He reached into his pocket. Another crash broke out in the passage. More embers took to the air. His fingers settled over the cube he'd stitched into the fabric, and he pulled out the tiny piece of Velveteen Cromide.

Another explosion; the Velveteen Cromide fell to the stone floor. Madrigan searched frantically in the dust and debris until he recovered it. He leaned back against the wall, shut his eyes, and swallowed it—slivers, dust, and all.

The Cromide broke into his bloodstream, granting him a flush of calm. His cheeks were radiant. His eyelids grew heavy. The clatter and din around him withered away.

That is, until a sound beneath his nose reclaimed his attention. He opened his languid eyes to see a tower of three rats in front of him. The shaky rodent stack tilted forward, bringing the top rat's eye within an inch of Madrigan's.

The rat's mouth opened. He heard a clatter down its gullet: metal crashing, heavy creaks like wood bending, and frustrated mutters. Suddenly the stomach of the rat at the bottom of the column bulged. The bulge moved up its neck and head. Then the stomach of the second rat swelled, as if what was inside the stack of rats were climbing up.

The stomach of the third rat distended. So too did its neck until, in a storm of muttering, a tiny hand reached up from its throat, grasped the rat's tongue, and dumped an old burlap sack onto it. A tiny man clambered up after it.

He paused a moment, gathering his breath, one hand up to hold Madrigan's questions. He was as thin as a wire, with long white hair pulled into a tight ponytail. It was bent up like a chimney, and smoke chugged out of it.

"What do think you're doing, pitchie?" the man said. He leaned out the rat's mouth and stared down the corridor. "Look at you, curled up in a ball. Brain wrung clean from Cromide. Limp as a rag!"

"M-Mulloch Furdie?" Madrigan said in awe.

The tiny man ignored him. He upturned his sack and picked a long, corkscrewed thigh bone from the pile. He walked to the edge of the mouth and, grabbing one of the rat's whiskers, launched himself like a sailor dangling from the forestay of a ship.

Mulloch Furdie tapped Madrigan's forehead with the bone; the lush in his bloodstream evaporated. The sudden sobriety was like a slap on the cheek. Mulloch swung back into the rat's snout and threw the bone onto the pile.

Madrigan leaned forward, pleading like a convicted felon. "Mulloch, please."

"Mulloch, nothing!" the little man roared. "You fool. You have no idea what you've done. Sucking on that new pitch, that... that Shivery Coffinfit. That's what it's called, isn't it? Did you think a drudge of lysergic medicaments wouldn't notice you going behind his back? Don't think I haven't watched you. I watch all my pitchies. And don't for a moment think I haven't tasted the vapors as they spilled out of your limp, pathetic nostrils." He drew in close to the frightened pitchie.

"I should be inclined to punish you viciously for wandering from me. But it occurred to me that without your intrepid treachery, I wouldn't have shared in your little visions, now, would I?" His words and his sinister smile drained the color from Madrigan's face.

"You've seen—?" But Mulloch cut him off.

"I have seen it all, pitchie." He reached up and unscrewed one of the rat's teeth as if it were a light bulb.

"But perhaps, most importantly, without you I wouldn't have known the divine race was on. Me, a lowly drudge—how would I ever have known?"

He upturned the tooth like an old jar, and a small ribcage fell out. Madrigan went white.

"M-Mulloch, I–I..."

"Save it, pitchie. Now is not the time for your groveling. I have a task for you. It's time for you to see this little intrepid adventure of yours through to the end."

The words sent Madrigan crashing back into the wall. "Th-the Lomhar Pass?"

"Oh, yes. I saw that, too, through your vapors. Now"—Mulloch knotted two of the ribs with a tight yank—"you will follow those two mortuants down those stairs. And you will look to see what caused the race, do you hear me? Who announced it? And when? And why?

Who put the first step forward? In what direction? All this you will relate to me. Do you understand?"

Madrigan looked away as if he were a child refusing a spoonful of food.

"Straighten yourself up, pitchie." Mulloch spoke with reproach, looking around as if prying ears were near. "You're embarrassing me." He knotted another rib. "Now, open wide, boy."

"W-what is it?" Madrigan flattened against the wall and bit his lips shut.

"Did I hear you right? Did you say 'What is it'?" Mulloch knotted the last of the ribs. "Oh, my dear little pitchie," he sneered. "Your days of choice in the matters between us are long, long gone."

CHAPTER 18
MACIONICA'S WALL OF YEARNING

MADRIGAN STUMBLED DOWN the spiral staircase leading to the Daemonius Concentric. The going had been rough. The knotted bone Mulloch Furdie had forced him to swallow had taken effect instantly, and he'd negotiated the stairs feeling as though he were upside down. He felt the cold stone floor on the crown of his head, and the flickering torchlight seemed to make his big toes expand like dilated pupils.

When he stepped from the last step and into the chamber, he found Griscomb on his knees. The prison guard held his hand in front of him as if it had been dunked in a vat of plague. Where his arm connected to his wrist the bulging eye lifted his skin into an angry welt. Beside him, Ostaig had thieved a torch from a sconce and was casting its light into an empty cell.

Griscomb turned to Madrigan. "What have you done to me?" he cried.

A sound came from the cell on the opposite side of the room. The three of them turned to see the brambles and weeds that had burst from the stone floor and overgrown the cell. Shards of the broken slate hung in the twisted vines. Poet's jasmine and honeysuckle wove their way through the bars. Ivy stretched into the room like the arms of a dying man crawling toward water.

Quindecum drew aside the vegetation. She cradled her distended stomach and leaned back against the bars as if she were proud of her development: a black tarry sludge bubbling up from a fresh scar along her belly. Above her head, a single red claw dropped from the weave of brambles like a spider on a strand of web. It curled down to her cheek and caressed it. She closed her eyes, warming to its touch.

"Zernebruk is free, Macionica," she yelled. The red claw moved to her other cheek.

"He is awake once again," she said quietly. Then her voice rose to fill the chamber again. "Do you hear that, Macionica? Zernebruk is free, and I serve him again!" She rolled on the bars to face the three adventurers. She seemed eager to share her next words with them.

"And he won't take lightly to the way you've been treating me."

Macionica's disfigured hands clamped onto his cell bars. They glistened with oil and their drips echoed through the chamber like moisture dripping in a cave. "Zernebruk is awake? And how do you know that?" His voice was frail and distant.

"Because he's come to me, hasn't he?" The claw caressed her cheek again then retreated into the moss and vines.

"He's whispered to me news you can scarce imagine, Macionica. If I'd had this news, why, I would never have given in to you." She traced the cold steel of her cell door. "News that would make any mother think twice about bringing new life into this world."

"Enough remonstrations, woman." Macionica tightened his grip on the metal bars. "Tell me what he told you."

"If I do, will you promise to never leave me? Will you promise to do good by me? Given the wretched sin we both fell into."

She ran her finger over a bar and her voice dropped to a whisper. "I would… I would leave him, Macionica. I would. For you."

"Enough, Quindecum. Tell me what Zernebruk has told you."

"They are all free," she said.

"All of them? Free?" Macionica replied breathlessly. "Morven as well?"

Her name sobered Quindecum. "Forgive me, Macionica. I–I spoke too soon. Not all of them are free." She bowed her head and sobbed.

"Morven died in that crypt, didn't she?" Macionica seethed. "Like Pennylegion said."

"She did," Quindecum said quietly. "But say the word, Macionica, and I will never leave you. I will tell Zernebruk that I am different now." She cradled her belly. "I will tell him I have to stay. To see to my lover. To care for him. To nurture him in this time of despair. I will tell him that… *that I am in love.* That is what we have, isn't it, Macionica?"

He left her words unanswered. "Then the world is even more despair than I thought it was." He drew back into the shadows.

"Who the muhk was that?" Ostaig growled. "And who the muhk are you?" he asked Quindecum.

Griscomb suddenly roared in pain. He held his arm up high and watched as the eye of Salagrim surged to the meaty flesh of his palm. It appeared clearer under his skin than it ever had. He rocketed to his feet.

"The eye. It's calling him forward." Madrigan said as he backed against the wall.

"What did I do to you, pitchie, that you curse me so?" Griscomb whispered as he staggered toward Macionica's cell. The door slowly opened. The eye pulsed again. Griscomb stumbled into the cell and, in a flash, was swallowed by the darkness.

Ostaig roared. He raced to the cell and pulled the door wide. A match struck within and a candle sputtered to life. The darkness peeled away to reveal Griscomb bound to the wall by dozens of hands reaching through bored-out stones. They held the prison guard at every corner and span of his body: wrists, neck, thighs, shoulders, calves.

Beside him, holding a thick wax candle in his broken and mangled fingers, stood Macionica, hunched over with his long, matted hair greased down his head and neck. It formed a precise black stripe over his white skin. At his feet was a wooden bucket. A heavy, greenish crust floated on the liquid, congealed with dead flies and spiders, stones and hair, twigs and tiny bones.

"Who the muhk are you?" Ostaig demanded.

"I am Macionica, Morven's drudge. I listen to those who still yearn for her." His voice shook with emotion as he waved his hand over the wall.

"Are you now?" Ostaig's grumble was as menacing as a distant storm. "Well, be thankful I don't yearn for your broken jaw, you little muhk. Now, let my prison guard down."

Macionica didn't move. Ostaig started to charge but stopped when Madrigan put his hand on his elbow.

"Don't, you stupid lummox. He'll send them back into the wall. Griscomb will be cleaved into a dozen pieces."

Ostaig yanked his arm back. As he did, Macionica shuffled to the hand that held Griscomb's chin.

"Look! Look, how they still grasp. They yearn for her as strongly as they did before Bragnal threw her in that crypt. Before her light was extinguished." Macionica stared at the hand, a broken, trembling drudge shattered by the death of his god.

"What can they possibly remember of her now?" he whimpered. "Whispers? Memories? Faint recollections passed down from grandmother to child?" He nodded down to the bucket at his feet.

"And look at what thin substance sustains them. I had no choice. I had to dilute her essence year after year, and now—now it's thin as gruel. A shade of her former divinity, more foul, brackish water than her loving presence. And it's all my fault, isn't it, Quindecum?"

"No, my love. This was Bragnal's black doing. Not yours. You are hurt and confused. But I'm here now." They all turned at her voice.

Quindecum leaned up against the cell, cradling her belly. The black tarry froth from the stitches across her stomach bubbled between her fingers now like scum in a pot.

Macionica shuffled across the wall to a woman's hand binding Griscomb's left shin. Her fingers were lithe and adorned with gold rings.

"Take this one, for example." Macionica held his candle close to the fingers. "She has groped to reach my beloved Morven for fifty years. So earnest. So trusting. Never giving up on her god. Reaching into the darkness with unimaginable faith. Waiting all the while for her to return. Now what? Now what do I tell her?" He stared at them, shaking his head, baffled and confused.

He bent and punctured the green crust in the bucket. The ooze that ran off his hand bedazzled him for a moment. "That there is no meaning left. None." He clenched his fist. "That their yearnings have been for naught." He looked up at them with a face twisted into a deep, angry scowl.

"Perhaps it is time, then. Time they should know the truth."

He smeared the woman's hand with the oily substance. Then, shaking like a leaf, he lifted his candle up to it. Her fingers ignited in a brilliant blaze of flame and the hand disappeared into the wall.

Macionica stared at its vanishing point. "Thus is communion with the gods now in Bragnal's black, black world."

He shuffled next to a child's fingers. He held the candle up and caressed them, cautious and stingy with his touch as though playing with the head of a cobra. He dunked his hand into the bucket again and raised it to the little hand.

"Enough, Macionica," Quindecum said. "Not the child. Anyone but the child. Besides." She caressed her belly again. "I feel weak, Macionica. Weak and tired."

"The world is weak and tired, woman." Macionica seethed, tears in his eyes.

"But I thought," Quindecum said, "that in such dank and

miserable circumstances, I might… we might… seek some comfort at each other's side."

Macionica looked away as he blinked back his tears. "Never. I'll never leave this cell. The fires of hell could rage all around me, but I will never leave." He shook his head to confirm his conviction. "I will see to it that the world knows of Bragnal's treachery. I will see to it that any mortuant who reaches for my beloved Morven will feel the burn of that bastard Bragnal instead."

"Then I will stay here with you." Quindecum stepped deeper into the cell. "And I–I could love you."

Meanwhile, behind her, the floor of the Daemonius Concentric had begun to fill with red shoots like a gathering of snakes. A ripple, as if in shock at Quindecum's words, tore through the mass. The ripple heaved and roiled the shoots, knotting them together into thick limbs that thrashed against the stone floor like a child in a tantrum.

Macionica looked up at her, his chin quivering. "You are, in truth, all the light that remains in my dark world now, Quindecum."

"And you are my light, Macionica."

As she spoke, a long thin appendage curled through the cell bars and slithered over the stone like a snake. It twisted around Quindecum's ankle and climbed her leg. In three twists it was up and over her belly. There it scurried over its breadth and burrowed into her fresh, bubbling scar.

Quindecum came alongside Macionica and draped over his shoulder. "Will you love me as you loved Morven?" she whispered.

As Quindecum and Macionica stared into each other's eyes, the claw re-emerged from Quindecum's belly. It slithered away from her up the wall, aiming for a single hand with filthy fingers stained red with ochre and clutching tiny bones.

"Look! Her church lies in ruins," Macionica whispered as he took in the hand. "All Morven has left to worship her are woodland shamans, heretics and madmen. They try to divine her essence from the bones of gophers and pigeons because that is all they have, Quindecum. In the face of her raging silence, *that is all they have!*"

The claw opened, revealing a black tarry matrix in its grasp. It twisted around the hand, and the black soot pulsed as if alive. It spread over the fingers and thumb and continued up the wrist before disappearing into the wall, the hand with it.

Quindecum pointed to where it had been. What remained of the black tarry mix evaporated on the bricks like a spill of water under an intense sun. "I choose to think of it differently, Macionica. I like to think that hand has been touched by the warmth of our love. And word of what we have is spreading. Morven's legacy will be rekindled by the strength of our union, you'll see."

Just then the flame on Macionica's candle soared. The rest of the hands retreated into the wall like startled spiders, leaving Griscomb to tumble to the floor. Ostaig was on him as the wall gave way in a shower of dust and rubble.

Griscomb was soon shrieking in pain. He held up his hand again. The eye quivered. It drew Griscomb to his feet, and he stumbled forward.

The dust from the collapsed wall thinned to reveal a solitary hand. It wore a battered and scarred Leggat gauntlet and was balled into a fist. The eye saw it in the parting cloud and surged toward it.

It scanned its length and breadth, dragging Griscomb in tow until, suddenly, the trap was sprung. The hand clamped around Griscomb's arm and the remaining bricks fell away.

The wall was a void of white light now. The hand retreated into it, drawing Griscomb with it. In a flash, he was gone.

Ostaig roared. He grabbed Madrigan and shoved the startled pitchie into the light then jumped after him.

All fell to black with the sound of rushing air. Ostaig tumbled, twisted and spun until, in an instant, everything returned: sight, sound, gravity, and force all announced with supreme alacrity. His senses coalesced on the most pressing revelation now, a blinding glint of light right before him: the cutting edge of a weapon barreling down on him.

He surged up onto his toes to fight the force of momentum as the Ghorak's eyes fixed on him. Its rocky, jagged mouth was curled into a sneer, and the sharp edge of its flint was aimed at his neck.

CHAPTER 19

THE VERGE OF ONE WORLD MEETS THE CUSP OF ANOTHER

MADRIGAN TUMBLED OVER the ground like a teetered tornado until he crashed into a Ghorak's leg. It didn't move. He could have hit a barrel of Woadbrek's cider. The impact took his breath. He slid off the creature and onto his back, struggling to breathe.

In the air above his head, like flotsam floating on an ocean, two squirrels were frozen in mid-jump, their bodies twisted to avoid the Ghorak Madrigan had just collided with. He got to his hands and knees and touched one. It was as firm as a stone.

Where am I?

Like the two squirrels above him, the Ghorak was also frozen but in a full sprint. The creature's skin was rough like rock and its body proportions were uneven. One leg was thicker than the other, the left hand smaller than the right. And the creature seemed to end above its eyes. There the skin and shape changed. Its form became angular and roughly hewn. And in this blocky substrate of a skull, a number had been ground: 389.

Behind the Ghorak was another, frozen in mid-charge, and

another behind it. And behind them both were hundreds of Ghorak, frozen as they charged down the side of a mountain. But something was wrong. Something about the mountain. Something that drew Madrigan forward on his knees in a mystified haze.

The mountain looked like a rough wooden bowl turned on its side, the hollowed out slope more like the pit of a man's palm. More of the rock, tiny hills in themselves, rose from the valley floor fifty yards from its base. They resembled the tips of fingers emerging from a pool of water.

As Madrigan looked on, breathless and awestruck, the texture of the mountain gave way. Its rough, rocky veneer changed to the color and consistency of skin. All of a sudden, Madrigan found himself on all fours beneath a giant hand frozen as it reached out into the valley.

He scrambled to his feet, his heart pounding in his chest.

Mulloch, w-what did you give me?

He felt his face: still there. Still warm. Still alive. But any reassurance this brought quickly faded. His wonder surged once more as he took in the escarpment, a sheer cliff, short and squat, made of deep black granite, on the other side of the narrow valley. At its base, frozen in disarray, were the ranks of a Leggat army. They'd been startled and had struggled to respond.

Like the Ghorak, the Leggatmen had drawn their weapons. But they had moved in haste, reactive and frightened. And just like the mysterious mountain behind him, the escarpment flickered before his eyes; the verge of one world met the cusp of another.

The crags and fissures of the escarpment vanished. It took on the polished veneer of metal. Gems materialized on its flank. Short tines topped with pearls appeared where its cliff had been. Madrigan was no longer staring at an escarpment at all; he was staring out the side of Bragnal's crown. But that was nothing compared to what he saw in the sky behind it.

Looming like a colossus was a man collapsed onto a table. He held a set of scales in one hand. One set of the weighing platforms was pinned under his head with a small stream his drool pouring off it. On the other platform, high above his head, was a small man. His head was back, his mouth was open, and three goblins were frozen in the act of pouring the remnants of a tankard in it. A fourth goblin was in the midst of gesturing his refusal at a young boy who sat cross-legged with a pile of bones in the space between them. The dice he'd thrown down were paused in mid-air.

Behind them, a man stood aloof from the scene. Six birds were in mid-swirl around his head. The man was frozen in the act of swatting his raven away and, brow furrowed, bringing his chalice to his lips.

Beside him, similarly frozen, another man in simple white robes was trying to cover the eyes of three filthy children in his embrace. A girl had forced his hand away from her eyes and stared wide-eyed at the feast table.

Behind them, receding toward the horizon, were dozens more of the looming figures; some sat at the table, some stood, some were bent in conversation. Some wore armor, some wore simple robes. Some were frozen with grapes tumbling into their mouths, some slapping a shoulder in good humor. Others stood scowling, arms crossed as they refused an offer of meat.

Madrigan turned back to the grasping hand superimposed on the mountain behind him. The sky above had also taken on form now. A channel of black cloth led up from the hand to a shoulder and above it to a cowl. The cowl was leaned away, cocked, furtive, and a long, thin tongue dangled out of it.

"That's Civiak," Madrigan whispered. "Mulloch, you've baked me mad."

Suddenly the mouth of the squirrel highest in the air beside him pried open. Its cheek ruffled and Mulloch Furdie got to his feet on its tongue. He wore a leather apron, filthy from caked blood, and held a wooden timepiece.

"I'm still spinning, aren't I?" Madrigan said.

Mulloch Furdie nodded. "Oh, yes. You're spinning alright,

pitchie. You're spinning immaculately!" He looked up at the gods then down at his timepiece. "Pray you are spinning quick enough to get a good, solid look."

"A look? A look at what? What's happening to me?"

"To you—why, nothing. To the world—well, everything." Mulloch checked his timepiece again and pointed back to the Leggat lines.

"This is when it starts, pitchie. Right here, right now."

"Starts?" Madrigan swallowed hard. "What's starting?"

"The race, you fool. Now *shhh*."

Mulloch Furdie held further questions at bay as he walked to the back of the squirrel's mouth and tilted his ear toward its throat.

"The backside of the rib cage has been drilled." Mulloch's voice carried a slight echo. "It took me hours. The fat around the lungs should be slowly liquefying. It's sifting through a tube of braided whiskers as we speak. Once it renders it should dissolve on the tongue like butter. You'll find the bucket wedged between the spleen and stomach. Remember—the spleen and the stomach."

"W-what do you mean?" Madrigan stuttered.

But a hiss escaping the squirrel's throat stole Mulloch Furdie's attention. He stepped out of the way of a cloud of green steam that chugged up onto the squirrel's tongue. The squirrel spasmed, and he braced himself on its cheek.

"Now, listen carefully, pitchie," he said, dodging another cloud. "Three ichors should soon spill into that bucket. The heart will leach at least three more. I have turned the squirrel up for you; he'll be hot as an oven soon. But you must let the ichors cool. Their color should be thick red like a beet."

"But I–I…"

Mulloch Furdie glared at him. "Look, pitchie, do you want to return from this or not? It makes no difference to me, for I am presently being serenaded by crickets on the side of the high road river, having consumed a modest bucket's worth of Speckled Frommorrow."

He presented proof of his aspect by passing his hand through the squirrel's cheek as if he were a ghost.

Madrigan nodded gravely.

"Right, so we understand each other," Mulloch said. "Now, you will need to carve the bucket from its guts. Hold it in the palm of your hand like so. Then press your right eyeball into the liquid."

Suddenly Ostaig's fist, quick on the heels of a mighty roar, hit the Ghorak beside them on the chin. The only result of this massive impact was a fine mist of yellow light, as though the big man had struck morning dew from a rose bush.

"These devils won't budge. I've felled timber with the blows I've landed on this lot," he said, doubled over and panting.

"Ostaig," Madrigan whispered.

Ostaig righted himself and drew his long dark hair back over his head. "What is it, pitchie?"

"D-do you not see them?" Madrigan pointed to the sky. "The gods."

"Are you having another of your visions, pitchie? If so, keep them to yourself." The big man spun around to survey the Ghorak. "I'm sure I've seen fogs out my backside more profound than your visions."

The air was thick with suspended dust and sand kicked up by the charging Ghorak. Arrows loosed from the Leggat bows hung in it, as did the vultures circling overhead waiting to descend to the dead.

It was now Griscomb's turn to tumble to the ground beside them, dirty, flailing, and out of breath. "What have you done to me, Madrigan?" he shrieked, holding up his arm. The eye was tenting the skin of his hand like a grotesque scepter. "What did I ever do to you to deserve this?"

Just then a peal of thunder broke over the pass. It sent Madrigan and Griscomb tumbling to the floor, but Ostaig lifted his nose like an old wolf. The big man's eyes narrowed as a cold silence fell.

"Do you feel that?" Griscomb whispered.

"Feel what?" Ostaig was bent over, rubbing dirt onto his hands and thighs.

"The wind."

"Aye, there's wind."

"Yes, but why is there wind if nothing else is moving?"

"A fine observation, prison guard. You may be more than the miserable, little worm that you present," the big man grumbled.

But Griscomb would have none of his humor. He retreated in a half stumble, half crawl.

"Where in Mag's dice do you think you're going?" Ostaig barked.

Just then, a hiss, like gas escaping a pressurised cylinder, emerged from within the ranks of the charging Ghorak. It sapped the last of Griscomb's courage. He made to run, but Ostaig grabbed him and threw him down.

"You'll not hide like some mangy field mouse. And you'll not abandon your prisoner!"

The look of fear on Griscomb's face bemused the big man. He checked Madrigan; the pitchie was cowering in an equally pitiful display. Ostaig chuckled and let the guard go.

"I see." He inspected the grit on his fingers. "I find myself in the path of one of your civilized nightmares, do I? Passed down, no doubt, from generation to generation of you quivering varlets. Do your pathetic gods rattle their sabers in the sky above, is that it? Well, damn your cowardly myths." His voice reached full gallop. "And damn your gods!"

"Ostaig, no!" Madrigan reached for the giant Colmrakken as a colossal *boom* filled the canyon.

As though a crate had overturned over the Lomhar Pass, the air was suddenly criss-crossed with thick black strappings leading from the hands of the Leggat soldiers up into the air. There they collected in the grasp of the god Aelic, seated at the feast table.

Madrigan and Ostaig stumbled back in shock as the scene of the gods dining above them came into view.

"I–I told you," Madrigan stammered. "I was trying–"

But Griscomb's roar of agony drowned him out. The prison guard held his hand out like a boom on a mast. It trembled, and the skin distended until the eye burst free from his palm. It took to the air, twisting left and right, shedding remnants of blood and gore. The eye settled on its mark and flew off quick as a bumblebee toward the Leggat ranks.

Ostaig rounded on Madrigan. "What is happening, pitchie?"

"I–I don't know," Madrigan whimpered.

The eye wove through the line of Leggat pikemen and rose along the flank of Bockum's horse until it hovered before his shield. In a series of fits and starts, it traced the length and breadth of the shield as if it were reading a passage of script written in its battle scars.

"It looks like it's… it's reading," Griscomb stammered.

Salagrim's eye started back from the shield as if the last words it had read had cast a spell of fear. It trembled and spun around, looking about for something behind them. Griscomb swallowed hard and turned.

A young boy stepped from the Ghorak ranks. His skin was bluish white, and his little neck was scarred from what seemed to be a dozen deep knife cuts. He looked about in wonder, as if he were a soul newly born. He felt the texture of the Ghorak beside him, bent to run his fingers through the grass, and then looked up at the gods above, smelling the scent of it all on his fingers.

"Who the devil are you?" Ostaig bellowed.

The boy looked over his shoulder nervously, then with one finger on his lips whispered, "Don't tell father."

"Father?" Ostaig barked. "I'll tell the whores of Medura if I–"

That was all Ostaig was allowed. The boy pressed his finger deeper into his lips and the Colmrakken fell to his knees, powerless to move.

The boy walked forward with the air of a mischievous imp and grabbed one of the straps criss-crossing the air. He pinched it, and the tremble he caused on the line shot up to Aelic's fingers and along to Bockum's right hand.

"Look up, mortuants." The boy pointed to the gods.

Methulla and Aelic, Digrir and Dhoorval, Rawl and Civiak, Mag and Gollunt, and the countless other gods besides, now stared down at the child. All but Bragnal. His head remained on the feast table.

"They're stuck, like sticks in mud? They've all read Bockum's offer. All save that bloated Bragnal. But it was never destined for his eyes, now, was it? It's the most profound offer any mortuant has presented in all the ages of creation. And they all must agree. Look how their tongues slacken over their lips as they imagine the look of defeat on Bragnal's face. How their eyes widen with visions of victory."

He struck the cord again, sending another tremble along the line.

"And yet none of them are willing to make the first move. All the promise and excitement of the race at their feet, and they are stuck. I wouldn't be stuck. Not me. Not for all the honey in Bedlam's Thicket would I stay bound in place. Father tries to keep me hidden. But I don't listen to him, do what he will to me. Look at them. It's almost as if Bragnal has beaten the fires from them. Like they wait for their own divine spark, no longer able to provide it themselves. Shall we give it to them?"

The boy spoke true. There was hesitation in the eyes of those gods. They were indeed frozen, waiting like mortuants for another force to intervene. And in that little boy, they found it.

He obliged in the instant. With a short, crisp tug he snapped Aelic's strap leading to Bockum's right hand. A tiny cloud, like a tin of powdered silver spilling onto a glass table, burst into the air as the strap fell to the ground, heavy as a concrete pillar.

"Now," the boy said, hiding his little nose and mouth behind his hands. "Let the race begin!"

❧

The scene burst into life. The charge of the Ghorak resumed. The panic among the Leggatmen resumed. The gods above them again cajoled, whispered, ate, and drank. The dice hit the table. And Civiak's hand, superimposed on the mountain opposite, extended again over the Lomhar Pass to steal Bragnal's crown.

Ghorak howls pierced the air. The whinnies of horses, screams, barked commands, the slide of swords from scabbards—it all swirled in the maelstrom.

Horses reared, pikes jammed into the ground, shields were steadied, swords were drawn. Above it all, the giant ethereal hand of Civiak got closer to Bragnal's crown while the prince of gods slept off his drink.

As Civiak's fingers curled around the crown, the Ghorak and Leggat lines collided. Ostaig and Griscomb were consumed in the fury of dust and metal as Civiak lifted the crown into the air and the Lomhar Pass shook with thunder.

Bragnal lifted his head. The balance of his scales reasserted itself. Mag tumbled; his dice spilled off the table and fell down to the valley below. Woadbrek washed onto the table on a thin stream of ale. Even his languid, sunken eyes fixed on the receding crown.

Bragnal stood up. Methulla was upon him, whispering in his ear, pointing to the retreating crown, and barking at his hawk and heron. The birds broke from the formation, twisting in the air and setting their sights on the crown.

Digrir pressed the children back. He disentangled himself from a boy's hand and joined Bragnal and Methulla.

The table of the gods shook as the rest stood up as one. The meats and fruits, the tankards and wineskins, the plates and knives and candles clattered from the table and fell into the pass.

Eyes narrowed. Muscles coiled. And, as one, the gods ran.

The eye of Salagrim drew back from the colliding armies, dodging blade and hoof and arrow. Corkscrewing through the air, it flew toward Griscomb and burrowed back into his palm. He roared in agony, knees buckling, and fell to the ground.

Above them, the table of the gods upturned; everything upon it rained down into the Lomhar Pass. Madrigan stumbled back as a giant silver knife crashed a few yards from him. He retreated on his hands and knees, trying to get a grip among the grasses and sedges as the ground shook. Above him the gods rushed forward, pushing and elbowing each other.

What do I do? What do I do?

He scrambled to his feet. More Ghorak were charging across the pass. The air was thick with mud and soil and zipping arrows.

He ran, tumbling and dodging the Ghorak rushing by. They paid him no heed. The retreating crown above was like a giant schooner in the sky, and the majesty of it froze him a moment. That is, until inspiration hit.

Mulloch!

There it was: the dead squirrel lay broken and still a few yards away. He ran to it, fell to his knees, and picked it up. He opened its mouth, plumbing its cheeks for Mulloch Furdie. He upturned it and shook. Nothing. Then something collided with him so forcefully it took his breath and knocked the squirrel from his hands.

A Ghorak loomed over him. It gave him another kick. He lurched to the side, but the Ghorak was quicker. It pinned him in place with its heavy foot. As he struggled for breath, he tracked the crown blotting out the sun as it rose to Civiak's furtive eyes. The Ghorak's mistake was to follow his gaze.

Madrigan made his move. He squeezed out from under it and scrambled to his feet. It raised its hand ax, the stone blade like a quartered watermelon. Behind it, the gods were charging pell-mell into the Lomhar Pass.

Madrigan grabbed the squirrel. The Ghorak paused. Its gaze fell to the animal and back to Madrigan's face. Its eyes narrowed and its head cocked. It rechecked its grip on its blade and circled him.

Madrigan grasped a handful of the squirrel's fur and pulled. Fur and blood flew up in a tiny explosion. The Ghorak stood still, uncertain of what it was looking at.

The bare chest of the squirrel was exposed now. Madrigan winced as he tore into it with his teeth. The flesh gave way. He spat out the skin.

The Ghorak stepped forward and Madrigan held out the traumatized rodent as a threat. The Ghorak snorted. It had made its calculation: Madrigan was all bluff. It began to close the distance between them.

Madrigan buried his fingers into the squirrel's chest, choking and gagging as he worked. He brought out a handful of gore and, falling to his knees, sifted the contents in his palm.

Where is it? Where is it, Mulloch, you bastard?

Suddenly Madrigan's vision wrinkled as if a child had pressed flat a crumpled piece of paper. It was followed by the sound of the bones in his finger grinding as they shifted the blood and pulp in his palm. Over that grind was the roar of his breath in his lungs, blaring like flames under a blacksmith's bellows. It was his pitch roil. It was blooming again.

No, no! No, no, no!

At last he found what he thought was the squirrel's heart. He held it up triumphant and threw the body away. The Ghorak picked up the discarded animal and sniffed. It prodded the trauma with its tongue, then scowled, dropped it, and charged.

Madrigan bit down on the heart. It burst in his mouth and dissolved on his tongue tasting of chalk and seaweed. He closed his eyes and braced himself.

Silence.

Madrigan opened his eyes. The Ghorak's blade was an inch from his neck, frozen mid-swing. The creature's mouth was wide in a roar. And there, dangling from its canine tooth, as if he'd been thrown from a listing frigate, was Mulloch Furdie.

"Do you loathe me, pitchie?" Mulloch hissed. He flickered in and out of focus as he spoke. "Why? Why do you hate me so?"

Mulloch threw his sack down onto the Ghorak's tongue, let go, and landed beside it.

"Please, Mulloch…" Madrigan began.

"Why do you not listen to me? Hmm? You had such a simple task."

He turned his focus to the strange sound now coming from down the Ghorak's throat. "I said nothing about the heart, now, did I?" Mulloch whimpered.

The noise in the throat grew louder. He turned back to Madrigan wide-eyed and trembling. "My pitch was collecting in the bucket. *The bucket, you fool!* The one I wedged between the stomach and spleen. I said nothing about the heart. What have you done, you stupid little pitchie!"

Three severed arms crawled onto the Ghorak's tongue. One was thick with muscles; one was thin as a rake; the other, black and brittle.

The muscular arm grabbed the others and flung them forward. They landed by the Ghorak's front teeth. Mulloch Furdie retreated a step and teetered on the edge of the Ghorak's lip.

The thin arm rose like a striking cobra and pointed at Madrigan. The muscular arm threw the burnt, brittle arm to the end of the tongue. It splayed its fingers and ignited, throwing off a thick black smoke. The thin arm raced forward and shaped the smoke with its fingers. The muscular arm waved the smoke forward now in the shape of a distended black skull.

"You fool. You absolute fool!" Mulloch cried.

The cloud floated up to Madrigan. He could not hold his breath any longer. He gasped like a deep-sea diver and drew the smoke into his shuddering lungs.

PART II

VESTIALIS'S RACE

INTERLUDE

Bockum's words filled the pass,
The race was truly on at last.

Is Fitzhiff free? Vestialis too?
Does Zernebruk burrow with his wormy crew?

All are free of Bragnal's crypt,
His judgment broken; his scales tipped.

But this is wrong, my brother.
Fitzhiff is no songsmith, and Vestialis is no mother.

But the race must run, the sprints must spark,
How can the runners stream off in the dark?
Let them each to their way.

Even if her child must pay?

Brother Jegs, your chisel shakes.
Is it now your heart and not the rock that breaks?

But the finish line, have we decided?
We have bickered and fought. Are we still divided?

Brothers, please! There is yet more rock,
Plenty of Jegs's heart to be struck.

Forgive him. The Younger speaks out of turn.

While the Elder is about to learn.
As will you, Jegs, my brother.

Never!
Never!
Never!

CHAPTER 20

WHEREIN FIDDICH BEGINS TO SULLY

THE TINY BEARDED shaman crouched in the ruins of a gopher. Naked from the waist up, he wore frayed animal pelts tied one on top of the other, otter over wolf, wolf over elk, elk over mink.

His skin was dirty and well-tanned from a lifetime of being out in the sun and wind. It was criss-crossed in lines of red ochre. The rich red hue culminated in his hands so intensely they seemed as if they'd been quarried straight from the rock. His heavy white beard was knotted and clumped, torn by a thousand stalks and chases through a universe of thorns, brambles, and bogs.

He gathered the bones as the cabbages rained down on him. He hissed in defiance as he swept up the skull and metatarsus. A tomato took him on the shoulder. The red mass sprayed upon his bare torso. It wet his hair and splashed in his eye. He howled like a wolf and snapped at the air.

The shaman snatched up the last femur and packed it in his leather pouch. He got to his feet, raised his jaw in defiance, then crossed his arms over his chest. He rocked back and forth. The crowd hushed.

Suddenly a burst of vomit—white as ash—shot from his mouth. The crowd roared.

He licked his teeth and screamed an oath. The men and women roared back, enjoying the scene, oblivious to its meaning.

The shaman snorted in disgust then walked to the vomit, flicking what remained off his chin to test the wind.

He bent over, cupped a handful, and sifted it through his fingers, testing its consistency, measuring it against some mysterious spectrum. Satisfied, he stamped the stage with handprints of vomit.

"If your Morven is all-powerful," yelled a tall red-bearded man at the back of the crowd, "then why did she abandon me in the privy last night?" Laughter rippled through the throng.

The shaman looked up from his pattern like a wild dog spooked from a carcass. His nostrils flared. He drew quick agitated breaths as he scanned the crowd for the man who'd spoken.

"I got one," came another voice. "If your Morven is all-knowing, ask her where my wife was last night."

"Couldn't find her in the barn, Seamus?" someone answered.

Another peal of laughter shook the crowd. Someone threw a rat onto the stage. Another tossed a cabbage, then three eggs. The shaman growled and rose from his work.

He studied the men and women who had gathered in the square of Quardinal's Brawn: farmers and potters, merchants and mercenaries, wives and husbands. All of them shouting, laughing; none of them listening.

He clapped the vomit off his hands and held them up in surrender. The crowd roared, and a rock flew by his head. The shaman gathered his leather pouch and retreated from the stage. As he did, he slipped on his handprints. The men and women roared with laughter.

Behind the throng, in the middle of the square, loomed Frew the Younger's sculpture, tall and thick like an oak tree. Made of strong northern ice, the work was a technical masterpiece. Dozens of layers, all of them rendered in great detail, existed within the ice. They had been crafted so the nested images would be unveiled one after the other with the spring thaw.

Frew the Younger had sculpted Bragnal strong and powerful, bicep on his weighing pan jerking his scale out of balance, crown upon his head. But that layer had melted away, seemingly as soon as the cords and timbers were removed that had set the giant sculpture into place.

By dawn of the next day, the melt revealed an image of Bragnal with Morven by the hair. This melted to reveal Bragnal pushing a thick, stone crypt door into place with one hand. The other held out his scale. In each of its weighing pans was a mortal figure in perfect balance. The sculptor had carved Morven petrified and reaching out from behind the crypt door as the slender opening faded away with Bragnal's efforts.

Frew the Younger had timed the layer to appear perfectly with the winds of March. The ice melt was slow enough that the gusts blowing from the north drew the water to the side and froze it there. For a week Bragnal's head, shoulders and arms seemed to burn with flames, like a demon fresh from hell's forge.

The scandalous layer produced whispers from the passing citizens. This soon grew too much for the priests of Bragnal. But there again, it seemed Frew the Younger had anticipated this. The layer of the image melted away just as the foot of Bishop Lansdowne, the cardinal bishop of Bragnal, reached the first step of the castle entrance intent on bending the king's ear to the crisis. It was nothing but a pool of water by the time the bishop, notified by an acolyte's whisper, returned to the square. The image of Morven was gone. The proud, powerful aspect of Bragnal was clear again, but this time the scales were empty and the other gods of the pantheon had been dutifully rendered supplicating at his feet.

Bishop Lansdowne had ordered a watch. And so it was that two young initiates slept rough in the square, keeping an eye on the statue for any more blasphemies. But none came. Each successive image paid homage only to Bragnal's might and strength.

Dripping with tomato and wearing a shroud of cabbage and carrot greens, the tiny bearded shaman slipped past Fiddich standing at the base of the stairs leading up to the stage. The young Bragnal priest, his attention startled away from his leather-bound book, flattened himself against the scaffolding. The stench of vomit filled his nose as he struggled to smile politely at the shirtless man.

Bragnal, give me strength.

Fiddich pointed to a bucket of water with a gracious wave of his hand.

As though divine truth could be discerned in the remains of a gopher.

The tiny shaman dunked his hands in the water. Fiddich watched as he brought a handful over his head.

And, what? Are we to believe you didn't eat the rest of that gopher?

He offered the shaman a handkerchief, which the tiny man snatched up.

Probably took half of it in his jaws as it dangled over the warren he pulled it from.

The shaman handed back the handkerchief. It had turned a sickly yellowy-red from the yolk and tomato he'd washed away. Fiddich awkwardly pinched at its corner.

And? If we take the analogy to its length?

Fiddich examined the handkerchief as he brought it through the air and deposited it on the stairs leading to the stage.

Now half of your god's essence is sitting in your worm-infested stomach? To be added to your feces pit? Abominable!

The shaman's long, tattered hair was now clumped and pressed to his head. He looked like a bison fresh from a muddied pond.

"I thought you were quite inspiring, priest of Morven," Fiddich said, bowing to the small man. "Clearly the reflection of Bragnal in our world is limitless."

"Bragnal?" The shaman's eyes darted up at Fiddich through his matted hair. "You… Bragnal?"

"Well, I am a priest of Bragnal, yes. Not yet divine myself, I'm afraid. But my braised lamb is close to perfection." Fiddich gave a low bow. As he did, a woman in red silk robes passed between them. Her long slender arms held a large copper incense burner that left clouds of perfumed air in her wake. She walked confidently up the steps and onto the stage. The shaman stepped close to Fiddich.

"They do not listen," he said, pointing to the crowd. He drew a shriveled owl's head from his leather pouch. Fiddich covered his mouth with the ends of his robe. "The feathers. They don't move in the wind. Not since the crocus bloomed."

The shaman held the owl's head up to the wind to present the theory. He looked intently at Fiddich. Fiddich's response was nothing but revulsion.

"It's Bragnal!" the shaman exclaimed, souring the air between them. "It's Bragnal's treachery that has brought the race upon us." He stuffed the owl's head back in the pouch and lowered his voice. "It's Bragnal. What do they want with Morven, who has suffered so under his thumb?"

The men and women in the crowd were quiet now. They watched politely as the red-robed priestess kneeled over her pot of incense and blew on the coals.

"How dare you?" Fiddich whispered. He raised his silver scepter. The jewel-encrusted rod was crowned with an orb carved in the image of Bragnal's fist. But Fiddich's gesture was clumsy. The scepter slipped and fell in the mud, which suddenly quivered as if the sceptre had awakened it.

Fiddich grabbed it up, and knocked away a measure of the wet dirt that clung to its intricate carvings. In doing so, he missed the three red shoots that had burst from the mud and stretched after the retreating scepter. The shaman drew back in shock at the sight of the red shoots that quickly slipped back under the mud like a fleet of diving submarines.

In fear. As it should be.

"So that is why the race is on." The shaman gave a resigned nod and pointed to the mud where the scepter had fallen. "The gods have learned to hate your Bragnal. What else has he done to earn their enmity, priest?" The shaman lifted his head to sniff the wind.

"Learned to hate him? Of course they don't hate him." Fiddich fought to calm the indignation creeping into his voice. "Bragnal isn't one of your… your savage totems! To douse with pig urine to ensure fertility." He began to brush out his long, white robes with his delicate fingers.

"Bragnal is a god of strength," he concluded. "The source of all moral authority. The prime mover. All the gods rightly bow before him."

But the shaman had stopped listening. He fell to his knees in the mud, searching for the red shoots. As he parted a handful of clotted earth, a collection of young shoots startled back from his hands like mice uncovered in their warren.

"I see clearly now," he muttered. "Bragnal sits on his throne a fool and a tyrant. Despised and resented." He looked up at Fiddich. "And his priests do nothing."

"Well, we don't soil ourselves for his salvation, if that's what you mean," Fiddich said with disgust. "Look at you."

"Corrupt gods grow old and confused, priest of Bragnal," the shaman said looking up from the mud. "And their priests soon follow."

Fiddich raised his scepter and would have struck the shaman had it not been for the sudden crash from the front of the stage. Two men from the crowd had rushed it and in their zeal disturbed the heavy incense burner. It rocked and reverberated until the energy was spent and the great burner came to rest. By now the men stood on either side of the priestess. She smiled at them, raised her arms and nodded. They pulled off her robes.

"I'll have this god!" a fat man in a worn leather apron yelled from the crowd. The woman next to him slapped him hard on the shoulder. Pockets of laughter broke out.

The priestess grasped each man's hand and bowed. They turned and led her to the incense burner. She tested the burning embers with her naked foot, stepped in, and was engulfed in a perfumed cloud of smoke. It wafted over her, obscuring her body.

She closed her eyes. Her stillness seemed to calm the mists of incense; they rose straight and tall like oak trees. The two men, now ignored, soon lost interest. The awkwardness having grown too much for them, they retreated into the crowd, shoulders hunched. The moment had unfolded nothing like they'd imagined.

Meanwhile, Fiddich raised his scepter high. "There'll be no woodland brutishness here, witchdoctor," he seethed. "Thankfully, it's Bragnal who inspires the men who rule these realms and not the thuggish myths of your poisonous, long-forgotten little goddess Morven. Now you'll stand back and keep your distance!"

To his surprise, the tiny shaman retreated. His gaze had fallen to his hand. He held it palm up and away. Thin columns of smoke rose off it as if it were a smouldering fire. He snarled and glared at Fiddich just as three more shoots burst from the mud and rose toward the shaman's hand.

What on earth is this brute doing?

"I'm not *the* priest of Bragnal!" Fiddich yelled. "I'm just one of them, you woolly imbecile. There are hundreds of us. Hundreds!"

"Then the corruption is worse," the shaman growled as the shoots slithered off his thigh and wrapped around his hand. "The race has begun, priest. And it is your Bragnal's fault they run. His treacheries have caught up to him."

"Oh, please, spare me your boggy revelations," Fiddich said, distracted again by the priestess of Vestialis, who had broken her meditation. And so it was that he missed what transpired behind him.

The buds puckered like lips, twisted around the shaman's hand,

and drew in the smoke off his fingers. It brought new life to them; it smoothed their withered vegetative skins and engorged them. The shoots pulled back and then dove for the mud, disappearing within it.

"Vestialis has long been forgotten by the denizens of Quardinal's Brawn," said the priestess to the crowd. "This neglect has broken her heart. But I have come to tell you, brothers and sisters, that the goddess of love still loves you." She mixed the smoke with her outstretched hands as she spoke.

"Thought I met the goddess of love last night. Or at least she seemed to think so!" More laughter followed the man's heckle.

Fiddich suddenly felt a sharp pain in his shoulder. The force that had produced it quickly increased well beyond the simple sting. It took him in its wake as if he'd been taken by a tumble of logs. He dropped to his knees in the mud.

"What are you d–?" But before the words could escape his mouth, three red shoots wrenched open Fiddich's mouth, another burst its bud, and a cloud of thick, tarry dust enveloped Fiddich's face.

The taste of blood, wet earth, rotten vegetation, and rust broke upon his tongue. He gasped for breath. That very impulse slipped the rotted mass farther down his throat. He gagged, but the shoots forced his mouth closed. More of the mass tumbled down in his panicked swallows.

Fiddich caught one of the elongated limbs and pulled with all his might. It fell to the ground, writhing like a segmented worm, and the rest followed after it. In a flash they retreated down into the mud and disappeared.

"Corrupt gods grow old and confused, priest of Bragnal," the shaman hissed, looking on calmly. "And their priests soon follow."

Fiddich swung his scepter at the shaman's head, but he dodged it, got to his feet, and tore off down the street. He was soon lost in the crowds milling at the fringe of the square.

Fiddich dropped his scepter and doubled over. He coughed and spat out chunks of the tarry matrix. He fell sideways onto the scaffolding, spitting the substance from his mouth, trying not to swallow anymore of it.

Meanwhile, on the stage, enveloped in perfumed mists, the naked priestess of Vestialis continued her sermon. The smoke spilled from her mouth like a waterfall.

"Take heart! Vestialis forgives your neglect. And I come to you with a message from her. Bragnal has called the divine race once again. The gods run again. But he has cheated Vestialis. He has shunned her, imprisoned her, and he has banished her child from her sight."

"Why don't you put your clothes on and tell us why? Why has the race started again?" came a voice from the crowd. It was an older woman's voice, shaky but strong. A chorus of agreement followed.

The priestess smiled. "It is forbidden to know the reasons of the gods."

"Bah! We have no time for your *forbiddens*, priestess," came another shout.

"That acolyte of Methulla gave us no forbiddens, did he?" came another voice. "Or the Brothers of Digrir."

"Children," the priestess began. But the word did nothing to soothe the crowd; instead it seemed to harden it.

"Take solace," she said. "I come with a message of hope. *Vestialis is free!* Free as the wind now. And the goddess of love does not rest; she has not surrendered. She is determined to run the race despite Bragnal's injustices. She will find her child. And the child will point the way. And when the laurels of victory are around her head, a new age of love and peace will dawn."

But the crowd's mood had darkened. Mutters and slurs rolled through it like distant thunder. The priestess felt the change. She split the surrounding smoke into two columns so she would be seen. "I tell you the fires of Vestialis are still burning."

"To hell with your fires," someone in the crowd said. "We want to know why the race is on?" The question echoed through the throng.

"Because..." The priestess smiled sweetly as she waved the smoke back over herself. "Because gods and men have turned their backs on… on love!"

Groans rumbling among the men and women were quickly followed by a rain of "Boo!"s.

Behind the stage Fiddich snorted. *Oh, she's finished.*

A rat flew from the crowd and bounced off the incense burner at the priestess' feet. She jumped and retreated from the burner, spilling red embers onto the stage. She dodged a tomato, then an onion. She bent to collect her robes and took a moment to scan the angry faces in the crowd. But the people's mood had broken irretrievably.

The priestess of Vestialis straightened, turned, and ran from the stage with tears streaming down her face.

CHAPTER 21

A LITTLE STORY ABOUT THE BRAE

EACH BLOW RESONATED over the cobblestones like a heavy burlap sack landing on a midnight dock. The awful sounds seemed to hang in the air like fumes. And when they reached Chim Wiscum's ear, his little brae mind flooded with images of the source of those brutal sounds: a poor, hurt, broken brae was being thumped. And brae were never thumped. They were never thumped or smacked or hit. For the brae of Sefton Skene kept their peace as neat and tidy as they kept their broom closets.

How has it fallen away so fast?

He grimaced at the next volley and leaned back against the cold stone wall. He brought his hands up to cover his ears as his sister leaned out from behind the garbage.

Phae Wiscum was sixteen years of age, younger than Chim, with dark eyes and thin, sharp features. Her hair was knotted and her clothes were dirty and torn, as though she'd slept in ditches and suppered in brambles. She turned to Chim with a wide smile.

How is she smiling? What is wrong with her?

Chim and Phae Wiscum were crouched in a pile of garbage. The jagged peaks of the broken chairs, old stumps of wood, and shattered barrels around them, draped in equally compromised old tarps and soiled linens, seemed the spitting image of the mountain that cradled the little brae city of Sefton Skene. The craggy sides of that mountain rose around the city and narrowed above it, leaving an opening like a carved pumpkin that was covered with a translucent dome set in place by the high priests of Aris. The light of the moon, just now rising to its station in the night, flooded through the dome and seemed intent on illuminating the hidden little brae.

"You'll have to cut one of them," Phae whispered. Another bone-cracking thud rang out. She looked back to follow it as though she'd seen a glow bug out of the corner of her eye. "Oh, you'll definitely have to cut one of them."

Chim dropped his hands from his ears. "Cut one of them? Are you mad? If you think for one second that I'm going to follow you down this horrible path you've set us on, you're crazy." He struggled to keep his voice down.

"Why not?" Phae said. Energy pumped through her words now that a fight was brewing. Chim almost spilled off the wall in his anger.

"Take a long—long—look at what's happening at the end of this alleyway, Phae. Sounds like this haven't rung out in Sefton Skene for five hundred years. And this is all your fault!"

Delight flashed in Phae's eyes. She seemed to smell the trauma in the alley and draw it in as though it were perfume. She would have been a frightening creature, almost foreign, if she weren't cut from the same cloth as Chim.

"This is my fault?" She shook her head. "No. No, don't be a fool, Chim. Our ways were failing well before anything I ever did."

Chim broke. He grabbed his sister's arm. "That brae is being beaten, Phae Wiscum. Robbed of his life!"

Phae yanked her arm back. "And? Why should we care? He's probably a crook. Probably cuts little brae for sport; saves their fingers, puts them in a honey jar. Maybe he steals lockboxes from old widows.

Maybe, Chim, just maybe, he's a murderer himself. And he would have gotten away with it. Just like everyone got away with it before the blessed race. Now people get what they deserve."

"Blessed? The race is blessed now?" His face went hard as a plank of wood. "So you want to stop, then?" He was quivering; his blood roiling. "You want to throw it all away? All this work and effort? Just throw it away?"

"Maybe we should," she said petulantly. "Maybe we'd be better for it."

"Okay. Then let's throw it away." Chim reached for the burlap tucked away in his leather satchel. "It's all hokum and bunk to you, right? Okay, so let's do it." He lifted the wrap out and held it up. They locked eyes.

"I'll do it," Chim pressed. "I don't care. I've done enough for you already. And you don't seem to care one bit. You never seem to care."

"Nah, you won't do it. You're too pious. You care too much."

Their stares intensified. As usual his sister didn't give an inch. And as usual, he let his bluff fall. "You're a selfish, selfish brae, you know that?"

"I just know who I'm dealing with," Phae replied. She turned and engaged once again with the scene at the end of the alley. Chim closed his eyes and took a deep breath.

How did it come to this? How did it all slip away so fast?

He returned the burlap to his satchel and then joined his sister peering out from behind the garbage.

Five brae men with plumes of tobacco smoke rising off them were leaning against the wall. Their faces were obscured but their silhouettes were clear: the brims of tall brae hats, tiny walking sticks jutting out like the legs of an easel, chains looping at their belts, and bottles hanging from their hands. Another brae, the largest of them, lean and muscular, was bent over his victim, punching him into the cobblestones. The other brae egged him on, their voices wet with alcohol, until one pushed himself away from the wall.

"Try the back of your hand, Guindon!" he said. "Aris won't know."

Guindon stopped punching for a moment. He nodded, turned his hand, and slapped his victim with all the force he could muster.

The brae off the wall watched keen as a professor. He pointed his walking stick like a piston as each blow landed. "Any different? Any different, Guindon?" he asked.

"Bah!" Guindon said, panting. "Strikes too clean. I like the fist; it's like thumping mud." He swung again, landing his fist square on the brae's chin, and let him go. The brae crumbled to the cobblestones.

Guindon straightened and gave a mighty whoop of satisfaction. As he caught his breath, another brae man pushed off the wall.

"He must have money," he said excitedly. He checked his trajectory of his idea in the eyes of his compatriots. "We could take it. Aris will never know."

Guindon reached down and pulled a leather pouch from the vest of the beaten brae. "Four coins!" he yelled as the spherical orbs fell into his palm. He kicked the brae in the stomach. "If that's a week's wage, my little brae brother, you should thank the race. No need to slave anymore what with Aris off running, now is there?"

Guindon took the coins from the pouch and tossed the empty sack at the victim. He grabbed a bottle from one of his mates and took a large swig in the full light of the lantern. His face was red from his efforts. His tiny brae nose dripped with beads of sweat, and his fist was bloodied and torn. He wore a broad-rimmed leather hat like the others and a brown leather vest. He stared off down the alley aimlessly as he guzzled from the bottle.

Chim ducked back behind the garbage. "Don't make a sound," he whispered.

"Why not? Won't they believe us? They look like good brae to me," Phae replied with a mischievous grin. "'Our traditions are strong, Chim. We brae trust one another,'" she said, mimicking her brother's voice. "Isn't that what you said? Or do you not believe that anymore now that the race is on? I say we find out."

Chim lunged at her, but it was too late. She darted away and stood up. Her movement knocked an empty wooden box into the drain. Guindon kept his bottle to his lips as he took her in, then slowly lowered it and wiped his mouth with his forearm.

"Well, well, well. What do we havc here?" He pointed the bottle at Phae.

"A wandering brae," said one of the braemen leaning against the wall.

Chim shook his head in frustration. He cursed the day his younger sister had ever been born then rose to stand next to her.

"Two wandering brae!" said another braeman, rolling off the wall.

Guindon pressed his bottle into the gut of his friend and walked toward the pair, shielding his eyes from the lantern's light. "Don't see many braes out after dark. Not with Aris off running his race. You must be lost little piglets."

"Tell them, Chim," Phae whispered. He shook his head.

Phae stepped away from him and pointed back at her brother. "He's on his way to the Gudfin," she said, happy as a blue jay.

The braemen exchanged confused glances.

"Planning on having a prayer, is that it, piglet?"

"Tell them, Chim," Phae said. "Tell them everything. Trust in the strength of our traditions," she finished acerbically.

"Yes, Chim," Guindon yelled. "Tell us, boy."

"Fine," Chim whispered. "W-we want to pay our respects to Aris," he yelled down the alley.

"Hear that, boys? They've got respect for Aris!" Guindon roared. "Well, we wouldn't want old Aris to be deprived of respect, now, would we?" He kicked his victim once more and glared down at him.

"Why shouldn't every brae be afforded the opportunity for a bit of communion with a loving and a generous god"—he took a final swig of alcohol and threw the bottle against the wall—"running away from his creations?" He grabbed another bottle from the braeman beside him and pushed him away. The bottle teetered as he spoke.

"Maybe while you're there—you know, on bended knee, with a few copper candles in your little hands—you could ask him something for an old brae."

"What?" Chim yelled back cautiously.

"Ask him..." Guindon swayed as he went deep into thought, poking at the ground with his walking stick to keep balance. "Ask him... does he plan on ever stopping? Does he plan on taking a moment to catch his breath and have a look back at the brae he's abandoned?"

"Of course." Chim nodded.

"No!" Guindon roared. "I don't think you quite understand my meaning, boy." He held out the bottle level with the cobblestones, the contents threatening to escape.

"What I mean is. What I want you to ask him is. Ask him... is the prick actually going to run away and just leave us to our own devices? Is he actually okay with whatever pours out of us while he's gone?" Guindon poured a measure of alcohol onto the ground.

"I'll ask him that for you, sure."

"You'll do this for me?"

"Yes. Yes, of course."

"Oh, that's grand of you. Eh, boys? This one's a kind piglet," Guindon said over his shoulder. "There's hope in this new generation yet, I'll say that."

But his compatriots weren't listening. They were huddled, holding up their vests to dampen their whispers.

"C'mon," Chim said quietly, grabbing Phae's arm. "They're letting us go."

"You've been gone a long time, brother." Phae gave a nervous chuckle. "Brae words aren't as clear as they used to be now that Aris is gone." Chim ignored her and tugged her forward.

"Where the hell do you think you're going?" Guindon roared. "I said ask the prick. And I meant it. Go on. Ask him. Ask him now!"

"I told you. They won't listen. Not with the race on. You'll have to cut them," Phae whispered.

"Never."

"Say it, boy," Guindon yelled.

"Say it or he'll cuff you!" yelled a brae from the huddle.

"No, no—he'll bite you!"

"Shut up!" Guindon snarled. "Now say the words, boy. Say them. Speak to that prick. I want to hear how he responds to the only two loyal little piglets left in his flock he's abandoned."

Chim glared at his sister, bowed his head, and cleared his throat. "*Quintariuc nu Aris…*"

"Louder!"

"*Quintariuc nu Aris*," Chim repeated, raising his voice to fill the alleyway. "*In tominadec holluc domic stantic sanquic. Mediates unic divine holluc?*"

Guindon swayed, his eyes closed, letting himself absorb the words. Chim grabbed Phae by the arm. "C'mon," he whispered. But as he made to move, Guindon's eyes opened, and he shook his head as though he were trying to throw off an idea.

"Help me a moment, would you, little piglet? What was that last bit you said?" Guindon gave Chim a pained look. Alcohol washed out of the bottle as he swung it. "See, it's been—well, a long, long while since I was last at the Gudfin. What did you ask that prick?"

"I asked him what you wanted me to. If he was planning on catching his breath and looking back at his brae," Chim replied.

"Looking back at what, again, piglet?"

"A-at us. At the brae. That's what you wanted, right?" Chim looked at his sister.

She shook her head and pointed to his satchel as Guindon burst into laughter. The brae behind him chuckled and snorted and came to stand alongside their leader.

Guindon's words were slurring heavily now. "No, piglet. I was wondering if that good and loving Aris was planning on looking back *at me?* Because if he was, he might see that I'm about to bash your brains into these cobblestones."

The braemen roared with laughter. "Elbows! Don't forget elbows!" one said.

It was Phae's turn to grab Chim's arm. "I told you. The brae are lost, Chim Wiscum. Lost! You're going to have to gut them. Gut them from navel to neck! It's the only way."

Meanwhile, Guindon had returned to the body of the brae he'd beaten. "Go ahead, light all the candles you bloody well like. Aris has abandoned us. He's off running his little glory sprint. If he was ever here in the first place. Just ask this little piglet."

He pulled the bloodied head of his victim up from the cobblestones. His eyes were swollen shut and his lip was split. Dried blood spattered his cheeks and forehead.

"This is the brae's world now, piglet." He dropped the head. It fell back with a sickening thump. "Blood, cuts, splits, and breaks." He shifted the brae's head with his foot and stared after it in dark contemplation.

"We're on our own now, piglet, and now anything goes. So, no. No, we won't let you go. We can't. How would that be right? You'd be praying alright. But praying to nothing but that prick's dust!" He took another stiff pull from the bottle and began to walk toward them.

"Can we kick them, Guindon?" one of the brae asked.

"Aye, boys. Kick as you like." Guindon drained the last drop from the bottle and threw it aside.

"Can we pinch them hard, with our nails?" said another.

"Aye, you can pinch. You can thump and whip and whump, too. As you like. It's all fair now."

Chim and Phae inched backward as the braemen came upon them.

"Use it, Chim," Phae whispered.

"Never."

"Use it! They'll scatter like pigeons."

But it was too late. Guindon grabbed Chim's vest and drew him close. "You hearing anything, piglet?" He cupped his free hand to his ear. "Nothing. Seems Aris isn't inclined to look back, now is he?"

"Cut him!" Phae yelled. "Cut him, Chim!"

Her words rifled through the braemen like wind through wheat, throwing up whispers. Guindon wheeled around to her. "Cut me?" he said, bewildered. "Well, well, well. The race really has cracked us to the core, hasn't it?" He grabbed Phae by the hair and drew her near.

"And how would you even do it, girl?" he jeered. "There isn't so much as a sharpened blade of barley for fifty miles. The brae haven't seen a knife in fifteen generations!" He gave out a hearty laugh as he forced her to her knees and drew back his fist.

"No, there'll be no gutting here, piglets. Only a fine display of thumping, slapping, and kicking!"

"Do something, Chim!" she screamed.

Chim swallowed hard. The sight of his little sister bent under the drunken brae's will was too much. He fumbled for the burlap in his pouch. His fingers curled around it and drew it out as Guindon's fist hovered like a comet above his sister's head. He pulled the knot of the string and there, in that dark alley, Chim might as well have stopped time. As the burlap fell away, he held up a rusty dwarven scoush.

The braemen jumped back in shock then ran off down the alley. Guindon's fist crumbled but he recovered quickly. He wiped his mouth with his hand as he stared at the blade.

"Well, would you look at that. You little piglets found a blade. An actual blade. Here in Sefton Skene. Well, I'm game, children. Aris is gone, isn't he? World's in a muhk's state. I say let it fall!" He drew his fist back again.

"Cut him, Chim!" Phae yelled.

Chim ignored her. He had to do this. He had to.

"She's the Gudfin thief," he blurted.

"She's the..." Guindon's words failed him. His expression fell blank. He lowered his fist again and let go of Phae.

"And this is the Gudfin blade. Or so we think." Chim checked his last words in Phae's eyes.

Guindon turned to Phae, his eyes wide in shock. "You filthy muhk!" he roared. He lunged at her, but Chim brushed his sister behind him. "I'd pound you to pieces here and now if I thought you'd get all the blame you were due, you filthy little thief! What do you think? Just because Aris is off running, we brae are free to do whatever we like? Do you know what you've done?"

"B-but that's all a myth," Phae said. "Agajin says you'd have more luck pulling a ruby from the mouth of a trout! Besides, there were thousands and thousands of blades. How could the one I stole be the one keeping the Gudfin asleep?"

Chim turned to her in shock and disbelief. How could she mention that muhk's name? Was he responsible for all this?

"Oh, I see. So now all of Sefton Skene gets to wait to see if you've brought the Gudfin down on us, is that it?" Guindon sneered. "It's one thing to steal, or give out a thump or a slap in the shadows while Aris is off running, but to steal one of the Gudfin blades? Maybe *the* Gudfin blade? What were you thinking, girl?"

"What are you waiting for?" Phae screamed. "Cut him, Chim!"

But the moment had shifted. Guindon's expression now matched Chim's. He snorted, lifted his hat, and wiped back his greasy hair.

"Is she always like this?" he said over a belch.

"Unfortunately, yes," Chim replied.

Guindon heaved forward, caught his balance, and then stiffened as though addressing a royal procession. "The brae don't cut. Or do you forget your traditions, girl?" He turned to Chim. "How did you get it?"

"Outwide. From a Kaopsin trader. I paid him good money in Quardinal's Brawn."

"Quardinal's Brawn? You went to Quardinal's Brawn? Aren't you a precocious little piglet?" Guindon leaned over to inspect the blade. "Looks dwarfish to me."

"Dwarves were at the Gudfin Clash," Chim replied helpfully.

"Aye, they were, boy." Guindon nodded with a hint of admiration. "Aye, they were. But you don't know for sure this is the blade."

Chim shook his head.

"Gonna need a run of luck, piglet." Guindon looked up at the stars shining through the dome over their heads. "Because you don't have much time, now, do you? I wouldn't want to be returning a blade to the Gudfin Mountain with the kiltering feeling so close."

Chim's blood went cold at the word. He even saw a flash of fear in Phae's eyes. They both knew the kiltering might come at any moment. They both knew that in a flash the Gudfin Mountain would disappear from Sefton Skene and the protective cradle of the brae mountain, and into the embrace of another miles away and perhaps miles deep. It was for that reason that wise brae, smart brae, brae keen on preserving themselves, stood close to their hearths when the kiltering was near. Certainly none were foolish enough to wander out to the Gudfin Mountain to pay their respects to Aris, only to run the risk of finding themselves whisked away with it to the back of beyond.

"Might need some intervention," Chim countered with a glint in his eye. It was enough to tease a smile onto Guindon's hard face.

"From that prick?"

"From that prick."

Guindon reached into his vest pocket and thrust the four spherical coins he'd taken from the fallen brae into Chim's hand, almost knocking him over in the effort. He steadied himself, holding Chim's hand in an intense embrace.

"Off you go then, piglet. And you tell Aris. You tell him, Chim. You tell him… these are from Guindon. You tell him to keep running. Tell him there's no need for him to look back at me. I'll be good from here on in. I swear."

CHAPTER 22

JUSTICE ON THE KHALLIN CLIFF

THE MORNING SUN drew a golden hue up the flank of the Khallin Cliff. Its rays changed the gray granite to a rich earthy orange as they climbed the rock. The north wind whistled across the pointy outcrop, throwing rocks and dirt into the air to fall to the valley below.

The granite shelf protruded from a forest dense with tall pines, oaks, and birch trees. Five ornate chairs were placed where the cliff separated from the forest, arranged in a row facing the edge of the rock.

Attendants in long black robes fretted around the chairs, adjusting them, wiping them clean of wayward leaves. Two attendants held a new chair still glistening with lacquer. Their efforts to wedge it into the row drew snarls and rebukes from the other attendants. Each attempt failed miserably, and the pair wound up dragging the new chair to the end of the row.

At the forest edge, huddled in ragtag groups, were the men, women, and children of the Rowlach tribe. They were ruddy-faced and filthy, dressed in furs and leathers. At their feet were bulging sacks, coiled bedrolls, and simple yokes with baskets, buckets, or cauldrons tied at their ends. The women carried babies; the men, rusty swords and chipped battle-axes, discards from battles generations removed.

To the side of the ornate chairs was a magnificent desk carved by Creche of the Donlands, the virtuoso of everything he touched. As was his style, every single inch of the table was filled with a catalogue of each family, clan, city state, or guild that had been successful before the court.

At the desk sat the clerk, his fingers splayed over scrolls, his arms splayed over the table. His skin was white as ivory, his fingers long, thin, and delicate. He was like a fine candelabra lit at its tip by two luminescent blue eyes.

Behind him, on a column of marble, was an oversized ornate stamp thick as an elephant's foot. It gave off a strange mist, blue like the attendant's eyes. The marble stamp had also been sculpted by Creche. It depicted the god of the court, Dhoorval, with a giant book spread open on his knees. The pages of the book were chiseled to look like gleaming swords arcing across one cover to the next.

To the left of the clerk's ornate desk stood Aramis the Samidian. He was dressed in blue armor like his men, who were lazily dispersing over the cliff.

The clerk rolled up his scroll. He scanned the crowd before pointing to two Rowlach men. They stepped from the forest edge and onto the cliff, clutching their battle-axes to their chests. After a few paces, they stopped, turned, and faced the chairs. Behind them the sky loomed stark and broad; it looked as if they'd been called to attend on a cloud.

The gaze of the Rowlach men was fixed on one man. He stood behind the middle chair, the largest and most ornate of the six in the line.

Balkan wore the same black robes as the other attendants. As he adjusted the chair in front of him, brushing a leaf from the cushion, he caught their gaze for a second and looked away.

Stop staring, you brutes, or you'll give it away before it's even begun.

A horn sounded, and the Rowlach at the forest's edge slowly parted. Five men and a woman, wearing blue robes fringed with plush white fur at the necks and cuffs, walked solemnly from the forest in single file.

Balkan stepped forward and grabbed the chair in front of him, steadying it for the woman. She waited for the other five judges of the court to take their seats in the line of chairs before she took her place.

The clerk rose from his desk. "His High Majesty's Court is now in session," he said, solemn as a church bell. "May the gods unshackle us from our illusions," he added in a mutter as he sat down.

The woman gestured Balkan to her ear. "When did *they* arrive?" She nodded toward Aramis's men.

"There are four more at the baggage train, Chief Justice," he replied.

"Well, then." She took a scroll from the small table beside her. "If the king wishes to watch his justice through the eyes of dogs, who are we to prevent him? A study in the law's equanimity might do him well. Though in the future I might choose a less hazardous locale."

"It is sacred to the Rowlach, Chief Justice. A site of much significance." She shot him an iron stare. "Or so I am told," Balkan added quickly, bowing low.

"So you are told." Chief Justice Sova was younger than Balkan, but her eyes asserted complete dominance. "And of what significance is it to you, Balkan?"

"None, ma'am."

"None? Good." She directed the scroll toward him but lingered over its release. "Still, I think it merits saying. I hope you will never forget the effort expended to civilize you, Balkan. It would hurt me greatly to think it was wasted."

"Yes, ma'am." He righted himself from his bow with an icy fever running up his spine.

Does she know?

"The petition of Thalmuir!" The clerk rang a heavy copper bell, drawing the court's attention to the two Rowlach men standing on the cliff. "Exalt to the king." He retook his chair and stirred a pot of wax hovering over a tiny flame.

"Which of you is the Rowlach man named Thalmuir?" Justice Sova took off her glasses.

"That one is Thalmuir." Aramis pointed with his drawn sword. "And the other is Kraalmac."

The chief justice forced a polite smile Aramis's way.

"We must confess that the court…" Her voice gave out. She touched at her throat and gestured to Balkan to pour her some water. She drank it with fervour.

"What I was hoping to say was that the court finds your petition a touch indecipherable," she continued. "Please understand the court has traveled a long distance for your petition at much inconvenience. In these trying times, brevity and concision would be most appreciated. Now, what is it exactly that you seek from His High Majesty's courts?"

"*Ans hoch nac ma teen*," Kraalmac grumbled. He strengthened his grip on his battle-ax.

Balkan's blood chilled as the words tumbled from the man's lips. He raised his hands in protest. "*Doch nur nach ni an stach!*" He repeated it, addressing the Rowlach at the forest's edge. They slowly lowered their weapons.

"Taste of things to come, clerk?" Aramis asked with a coy smile. He crossed his arms over his chest and nodded instruction to two of his knights.

"Enough of this, Aramis. And Balkan, you will translate for the court, not speak for it." Justice Sova waved him forward.

Balkan moved as instructed. But as he stepped onto the rocky outcrop, a young girl tumbled from the Rowlach line. She skidded on the rock and scrambled back, terrified. She was no older than ten and had been roughly handled by the looks of her. Her clothes were filthy and torn, her hair matted, her face bruised and cut.

"*Roch nes an heem,*" Thalmuir yelled, pointing at her. "*Fignith hoc oifis air tha mor an sgiansk theirig tha.*"

The girl stared at him in horror. She ran for the forest but the crowd caught her and threw her back.

"Balkan, please." Justice Sova wearily touched her temple. "Make sense of this, will you."

"The Rowlach ask the girl to speak, Chief Justice. On their behalf," he replied.

"Oh, but that wasn't it, was it?" Aramis pushed himself off the clerk's desk. "It was a bit more than that, wasn't it?" He came to stand beside Balkan. "He said she was cursed, didn't he? And something a tiny bit, well… *threatening* best sums it up, wouldn't you say?"

Balkan ran the back of his hand over his mouth. *H-he speaks Rowlach? By the fates, we're doomed.*

"Yes. Yes, she was described as cursed, justices," he said. "Or to be more precise, 'followed by chaos' in the native imagery. Merely a figure of speech though, justices, to connote her birth rank and season."

"Hah!" Aramis roared. "A joker to the end." He raised his sword to Balkan's throat. "You're lucky I find this amusing, attendant. But you will translate fully next time, or I'll have your tongue on a platter."

"Aramis! Cease this at once!"

Aramis relented. "As you wish, Madam Justice." He bowed deeply. "Reality will break on your soft shores soon enough."

Chief Justice Sova took a moment to compose herself then addressed the Rowlach girl. "Come here, my love." The girl checked with Balkan and took heart from his nod. She stepped forward.

"Do you speak common?"

The child nodded.

"That is very impressive for such a young girl. Particularly considering your circumstances. Now, I'm told you have something to say."

Her eyes were drawn to the bruises on the girl's cheek. "Oh, you poor dear. You look hurt." She reached out to soothe her, but the girl pulled away. The chief justice's eyes darkened and her manner followed.

"Well? What is it you wish to tell the court, Rowlach? Speak!"

The girl looked at Balkan again. This time Justice Uby, seated next to the chief justice, noticed as he shooed away his attendant.

"The girl takes a peculiar fascination with your attendant, Chief Justice. As do our plaintiffs. Is there a dynamic to this petition we don't yet realize? Do you know this girl, clerk?"

"I do not," Balkan replied.

"Hah!" Aramis clapped his hands.

"May I remind the court that we are in a hearing?" Justice Tock bellowed, leaning forward in his chair. The old man quivered as he spoke. "Is the girl going to speak on behalf of the plaintiffs or not? For if not, I move that we dismiss this claim *moto murandis* and be done with this filthy backwater. The spring storms are brewing and, lest I mistake the chill on the wind, we will be forced to cut through Bedlam's Thicket to make our way back to Quardinal's Brawn. The quicker we leave this cursed place, the better!"

Balkan's eyes bore into the girl. "Speak, child." His voice was constrained to a whisper but it was as hard as the granite cliff. She stayed quiet.

"Can the savage not speak?" Justice Uby pounded his fist on the arm of his chair.

The young girl startled at the noise.

"Am I being petitioned by a blasted mute?"

She covered her mouth and cowered back.

Speak, damn you.

"Go on, girl. Speak!" the chief justice commanded.

"The… the race has started," the girl whispered, staring fearfully at the assembled Rowlach.

"The what?" Justice Orade blazed with indignation. A clamor

descended over the judges. As they bickered and their attendants rushed in to soothe the raging disputes, Balkan locked eyes with Thalmuir and Kraalmac.

All this bickering and fighting. It's making them lose hope. They're weighing it up. They're actually weighing it up. Kynon, please. Reach out your divine hand and hold your people firm.

"What is the girl blithering about?" the chief justice shouted.

"I confess, justices I–I do not quite know," Balkan replied. "Perhaps if I were to…"

"Oh, why don't you just tell them the truth, Balkan?" Aramis yelled. He had made his way to the very edge of the cliff, which caused his voice to echo into the gorge. He turned back from the ledge.

"Hmm? For starters, why don't you tell the court why they've convened at this knife's edge of a rock?"

The blood drained from Balkan's face.

"And why don't you do the court the courtesy of telling them why there are so many bones down there in the gorge? Hmm?"

Chief Justice Sova turned to her attendant. "Balkan?"

"It's true, your honors: this site is significant in the religion of the Rowlach. Or so I am informed."

"Significant? Hah! Is that how we're describing it now? Well, I suppose human sacrifice certainly is significant to the one whose neck is sliced and is thrown off this rock!"

Balkan looked askance; his fingers quivered as he searched for a gambit. "That… that aspect of the religion, I must confess, justices, I was ignorant of—"

"Ignorant of?" Aramis strutted like a ram. "Then, please, tell me why we are here, old man? Hmm?"

"*Not for that!*" The words, addressed to the assembled Rowlach as much as to Aramis, erupted from Balkan.

Justice Uby leaned forward. "Are you mocking the court, man?" he snarled. "Because I'll brook no mockery. None."

"*Rein nach no lan ti askhoc,*" Thalmuir suddenly shouted. The Rowlach men at the edge of the forest murmured the words in reply.

What are they doing? Please, just a few more minutes. Let the court decide, damn it.

"Balkan!" The chief justice was fuming now. "Inform these brutes they would be wise to hold their tongues. If they do not, the court shall order those same tongues delivered to the king."

"You know what would be truly wise, Chief Justice?" Aramis said, snapping his fingers. Three of his knights moved to the edge of the forest. The Rowlach drew back at their approach.

"What would be wise would be to seek a translation of what that Rowlach brute just said. Wouldn't it, Balkan?"

He knows. By the gods, he knows.

"The Rowlach men… th-they use terms I no longer recognize," Balkan stammered.

"Terms you no longer recognize? You're a liar and a traitor." Aramis snapped his fingers again. Three more Samidian knights came forward.

"Aramis!" Justice Sova roared. "May I remind you this is a lawful hearing of his High Majesty's Court of Assizes? Your vulgar displays are contemptuous and felonious. You will cease your interference at once."

"But of course, learned justice." Aramis gestured for his men to hold off. "I'll simply retake my seat here and return to enjoying your obvious infallibility."

The chief justice took a moment to let the slight fall away. "Balkan, please. What is going on here?"

Balkan locked eyes with the girl. *Why does she stand there dumb as a mute? Why is she not asking them? I was promised one that could speak.*

"I–I think… if we just let her gather herself," Balkan stammered. "That is, I imagine the girl must have more to say."

The eyes of the court turned to the girl, but she was paralyzed with fear. All she could muster was a terrified retreat.

"*Rein nach no lan ti askhoc*," Thalmuir shouted. He righted his battle-ax. Whatever remnants of patience the man had held on to had left him. That much was clear to all who watched the proceedings on the Khallin Cliff, and particularly to Aramis.

The knight snapped his fingers. His men at the forest's edge raised their swords in turn. The Rowlach shrank back.

"No!" Balkan shouted, "Chief Justice, please. The Rowlach are trying, in their way, to *petition* you, as good, loyal citizens. Aren't they?" He glared at the frightened girl.

Why is she not speaking?

"For an order. Permitting them to flee their lands," he continued. All artifice in him was gone now. "They want the right to leave their lands and head south. Don't you, girl? Don't you?"

But she shrank farther away from him, eyes darting like a cornered rabbit.

Damn it all. She's useless!

Balkan was left with no choice. He dropped what remained of his subterfuge. "The Rowlach petition this court for an order allowing them to abandon their lands and flee south to the mountains they call the Blackened Nevers. Isn't that right, girl?" Balkan pressed, sweat dripping down his forehead. "Tell them. *Tell them, damn it!*"

"Did I just hear what I think I just heard? The lowly Rowlach want an order of this court allowing them to-to just walk? To the Blackened Nevers?" Justice Uby exclaimed.

"*Roch na an sgiansk hoch*," Kraalmac screamed. But the response from the Rowlach was pitiful. Barely a handful remained.

"Enough!" Aramis yelled. He snapped his fingers one last time. Two of his knights stepped forward and knocked the battle-axes from Thalmuir's and Kraalmac's hands. With a punch to their spines they dropped them to their knees.

"Let me translate, learned judges: *Throw them from the cliff*, I believe, is the rough equivalent in our tongue." Aramis savored the looks of horror in the judges' eyes.

"Yes, throw them from the cliff! It was a trap, you blind idiots. You were lured to the Khallin Cliff. The blood of His High Majesty's court was to run off into the wind like the thousands of gutted deer that have come before you. As a sacrifice. The supreme sacrifice. To Krynon. To pay *him* for the release of his people from their lands."

He stepped to Balkan and grabbed the old man by the collar. "That's how the story goes, isn't it, old man?"

"No, their claim was honest. They were supposed to ask. To plead. To–to petition the court. And if the king's justice could have simply issued..."

"And if it didn't, traitor?"

"Chief Justice, I–I..." Balkan stammered but Aramis threw him to the rock beside the girl.

"You see. This, *this* is what happens when the king's court is left to its own devices," the knight muttered. "Trusting in Rowlach."

Aramis nodded. His men raised their swords and let them fly. The heads of Kraalmac and Thalmuir rolled off their torsos. The Rowlach, in turn, broke and ran. Aramis's men disappeared after them.

"Justices, please. This was not the plan," Balkan protested. "She was supposed to speak. The court could have listened. You could have granted it. *Why didn't you grant it?*"

"The court could have granted it?" Justice Sova's face flushed red. "How dare you presume?"

"But... but the race has started, ma'am," Balkan whispered. "And it will consume all in its wake."

"The race? Listen to yourself. You've been attending that god parade in Quardinal's Brawn, haven't you? You've let the woolly myths of your people seep into that brain of yours and dislodge the scaffolding of your civilized form. You've let them corrupt you. And now? Look at the depths you've sunk to. Leading the court to this... this sacrificial altar. The race has started!" The chief justice repeated with contempt.

"I suppose in the end you had no choice. Treachery such as this is baked deep in your blood, isn't it? Borne of irremediable base impulses. Were it not for Aramis and his knights, why, I shudder to imagine how this would have unfolded."

The knight bowed. "How lovely to be recognized. And by such a luminescent mind."

"Without me, without her"—Balkan pointed to the girl—"they would have gutted you the moment you convened the court. But they didn't. They petitioned you. As good subjects. Why did you refuse to listen?"

"Are we to give thanks for this?" Justice Uby exclaimed. "A clerk of this court? Manipulating its process for the ends of his filthy stock? This is high contempt!"

Justice Haud raised his hand and leaned forward in his chair. "This clan. It is the Rowlach, is it not?"

"It is, brother justice."

"Did I not, in Mallus 389, I believe, chronicle the long, unfortunate history of the Rowlach's disadvantage before His High Majesty's courts?"

Justice Uby pounced. "But was it not I, in Septis 34, who chronicled at pains this court's shameful history of neglecting Rowlach claims while the claims of the Tish pass with nary a delay?"

"And surely it is manifest beyond proof," Justice Ramnach added, not to be outdone, "as I said in Sallish 13, that the men of the Rowlach fill the Clovenstone Stockade beyond their proportion. Clamped in irons for no more than the theft of a leek?"

"Beyond proof, brother," Justice Haud offered. He crossed his arms and sank into his chair. "I sometimes feel the truth we distill is only for ourselves."

"It is the shame of the realm."

"But," Justice Tock said, leaning forward, "must we not see the full dimension of the issue? Its true breadth and scheme?"

"We must," Justice Uby agreed.

"Has it not been the saving grace of the Rowlach people that, so mired in their ignorance and misfortune are they, they have never been capable of fathoming the prejudice against them?"

"It is unimpeachably true. That *has* been the state of things." Justice Uby nodded vigorously.

"But now—*look*—we find the seed of knowledge has taken root." Justice Orade scowled at the chief justice as if the reproach were aimed at her. "They speak freely of the race. And what's more, the Blackened Nevers!"

"They do, brother justice. Surely such rot must be weeded?" Justice Ramnach said.

"For if it isn't, will they not measure the true depths of their deprivation?" Justice Orade held his glass up for water.

"Will they not catalog their true misfortune?" Justice Ramnach said.

"Indeed, is it not the court's duty?" Justice Tock and Haud said together.

"To prevent this ignorance from spreading?" the chief justice finished. She looked up and down the row of judges. "Then we are all in agreement?"

The judges nodded as one then turned to Justice Lain at the end of the row. He was younger than the rest, and their eyes on him made him blush and scramble the papers on his lap.

"But s-surely," Justice Lain stammered, "given their misfortune and pain, the court is obliged to—"

"Then we are all in agreement?" the chief justice snapped. The expression of the other judges supported her insistence. Justice Lain relented and nodded.

The old clerk gave a shriek of delight. He looked up from his scroll, his luminescent eyes flaring. He bowed his head, inked his quill, and wrote on the page. Then, licking his lips like the sail of a windmill, he poured a pool of hot wax from the pot onto the scroll.

"Is it so ordered?" The clerk was like a dog waiting to pounce on a bone.

The chief justice glared at Balkan and nodded. "It is."

The clerk stood up from his desk. He turned to grasp the ornate stamp from the marble column and held it like a newborn, beholding it reverently, his fingers lost in its misty blue glow.

"Chief Justice, please!" Balkan pleaded as he retreated. The young girl scrambled to her feet and followed after him.

"Silence, Rowlach!" she replied.

The chief justice grabbed at her throat and raised her empty glass. The attendants exchanged confused looks until a young Dinafatari scribe wrenched the pitcher from an attendant, fending off his protests with an elbow. He darted forward and filled her cup.

Justice Sova looked at the interloper as the water tumbled into her glass. "Let justice be served," she said as she dipped her finger in the water and wet her lips.

Balkan grabbed the young girl and drew her tight to his chest as the old clerk closed his eyes and held the stamp over his head.

"Exalt to the king!" he shrieked as he drove it down toward the pool of wax. A thunderous boom rocked the cliff when it hit.

The rock beneath Balkan criss-crossed with fissures. They grew into deep cracks, and then the cliff shuddered. It fell away, and Balkan and the girl tumbled toward the valley below.

CHAPTER 23

CALTROPS IN A HELMET

MADRIGAN'S HEAD BUMPED over the cobblestones like a child dragging a toy on a string. On the positive side, it did have the effect of drumming him back to consciousness.

The bright nucleus of a lantern passed over him. It was like a dagger to the middle of his head. It forced his eyes closed, and the impression of the lantern followed him into the darkness. He waited what seemed like an eternity for that wound of light to dissipate then opened his eyes again.

The tops of shadowy buildings passed on either side of him. He could make out their gutters, their windows, their eaves and overhangs. He saw a sign hanging over a misted window pane: The Ragged Heel. He could hear the merriment within.

The Ragged Heel? I must be in Quardinal's Brawn. By the gods, how?

The hanging wooden sign was replaced by the bright moon overhead. It sat nested in a moving picture of heavy clouds.

Unbeknownst to Madrigan, a cobblestone ahead sat proud of its brethren. It had been dislodged by the wagon that had brought the ice sculpture of Bragnal, freshly carved by Frew the Younger. The horse pulling it had grown skittish the farther into the city it had gone until it finally broke wild. Madrigan's head now collided with this cobblestone.

His scream of agony was instantly smothered by a black hand, and he was tugged to the side. The hand pressed down harder, stifling his breath. He heard footsteps and managed to turn his head to see the blue cloaks of two gendarmes passing by.

The hand lifted away. It snapped its fingers and a voice, like crickets crushed under a wagon wheel, was in his ear. "They're looking for him. Just like I am. Who do you think will find him first?"

Madrigan's eyes had adjusted to the darkness now. He could see the slow trickle of smoke rising off the hand in the space between its fingers. "Who are you?"

He felt his collar go limp. Two more arms joined the black hand. One was thick and muscular, the other thin and lithe. They leaned in close, crowding around his head.

"Where is he?"

"Where is w-who?" Madrigan sputtered.

"Nyqueed of course, you little muhk. That thieving, treacherous Black Song Man."

Madrigan heard another set of footfalls. The arms turned like hyenas startled from their carrion. Two gendarmes approached on a trajectory more concerning than the first.

The muscular arm balled its hand into a fist and struck, causing Madrigan's world to once again fade to black.

Madrigan's eyes opened just as the stair ground into the back of his neck. He was dragged past a young guard who sat in a heap, clinging to his pike as if it were the mast of a sinking ship. An empty triangular vial lay on its side beside him, and he drew great sonorous breaths in his deep slumber. Impaled on the tip of his pike, sitting like the headache he was sure to have when he woke in the morning, was a rose bud.

The arms pulled Madrigan up the remaining three steps. He and the arms crossed the threshold and entered the home. His head fell sideways. The thin arm bent at the wrist like a grotesque scorpion, raising its forearm behind it erect like the arachnid's stinger. It reached back to the door and closed it. Madrigan's progress became gentler. The arms dragged him forward over a smooth wooden floor now and past two muddy footprints.

His progress slowed again when the arms reached the threshold of the next room. He saw them huddle, their fingers quivering with indecision. As they fretted, Madrigan shifted to peer into the room. There, lifting a tray of jewelery from the dining room table, was Rothesay. The brute sniffed at the tray and his eyes narrowed. He looked under the table, as if he'd caught a mouse in the act, then righted himself and drew his thick finger through the dust that had settled on the shelf behind him. He rubbed it between his fingers and paused in deep thought, sniffing at the air like a wolf.

The arms saw their gambit. The black arm covered Madrigan's mouth, and the pulling resumed. They drew him under the dining room table. Rothesay's feet slid past as he and the arms slithered across the room undetected by the brute.

They slipped through an open door and into the hallway beyond. It was cold. He could hear water drops and smell the rotting earth. In the light cast from the flickering sconces, he saw a door at the far end of the hallway. It was cracked open just enough for a lithe and slender body to slip through. The arms made for it.

It was solid iron and at its belly was a complex lock the size of a man's shield. As they neared it, Madrigan's head and shoulders parted the springs and gears, bolts and tumblers of what had once composed that lock like a frigate through jetsam. Their scratching on the stone floor must have resounded down the corridor, for Rothesay's cold eyes peeked out from the doorway behind them.

The room they'd entered was a makeshift armory. Dozens of swords, pikes, halberds, axes, bows, and shields lined the racks and walls. Suits of armor stood in each corner. One of them was missing its helmet. Two guards were asleep, snoring loudly, and on the tips of their pikes: two more rose buds.

They were quickly through its far doorway. Here hundreds of caltrops had been swept to the side of the earthen passage. A broom leaned against the wall with an upturned helmet brimming with more of the little spikes. A note had been wedged into the helmet: *Empty before wearing.*

They came to a corner. As they rounded it, Rothesay's shadow lumbered out of the armory only to disappear when the arms dragged Madrigan sideways. He and the arms now passed under a sprung trap. A blade, wider than a dinner plate, had been ejected from the ceiling. Frozen mid-swing, it still gave off the whir of its mechanism but its blade no longer spun. A bolt of black metal had been lodged in its axle.

The hallway changed now. It started a slow descent. Dirt ground at Madrigan's head and elbows. He shifted his weight to ease the scouring until it mercifully ended at another door. A guard lay crumpled beside it here as well, asleep and christened with another rose on his blade. This door too was open. In its lock was a wax key that had already begun to melt. Madrigan could hear voices beyond the door, and he could see the faint flicker of candlelight. He was tugged across its threshold just as a loud bang erupted in the room. It seemed to shock even the arms that dragged him, and the journey shuddered to a halt.

"Show him, Joseph. Throw some on the table." The man's voice sounded nervous. Madrigan heard the tinkle of multiple metal objects against wood. "Go on." The voice seemed to address a new target now. "Take it! Take it all, damn you."

Madrigan struggled to turn, to look toward the voice, but the light was too dim. He could make out only bookcases lining the walls, full of glass display boxes teeming with jewelery, and a large oak desk in the middle of the room. Looking under the oak desk, Madrigan could see two sets of human legs against the far bookcase. It leaked books onto the floor as if one of owners of those legs were struggling against it.

A young boy stepped away from the desk, wiping the remnants of the metal from his hand as if it were pepper into a stew. At the bookshelf, a new voice announced itself.

"Do you think I want your filthy gold, jeweler?" Nyqueed hissed. He must have turned, because his voice was directed away from Madrigan now. "I am here for the Gudfin blade and nothing short of it. And you'll give me what I want, man, or I'll see you and your little boy here bled like feast pigs. Do you hear me?"

"I–I don't know what you're talking about," the merchant sputtered.

"Oh, I believe you do. And my patience is wearing thin. The Gudfin blade, mortuant. *Now!*"

The arms dragged Madrigan farther into the room. It was wood floor first, then carpet. Before long the corner of the desk loomed over him. They tugged him its length until he saw the face of the young boy staring down at him, shocked and mystified, like a sun at the horizon.

The desk suddenly banged and jostled. Madrigan could hear the soft drumming of fingers. The desk jostled again; more drumming of fingers. The muscular arm buried itself under Madrigan's back. It found his centre of mass and pressed upward with a burst of strength. Madrigan launched into the air and landed on the desk in an explosion of gold coins. The boy whimpered and ran. He had disappeared down the passage before the reverberations of the coins subsided.

Nyqueed turned at the commotion. He held a dagger to a fat man's neck. The man's silk cravat was stained with a thin line of blood, his velvet vest had been cut open, and his tunic hung untucked from it. A tumble of books lay around his feet as his hands struggled against the bookcase. He trembled like a newborn fawn.

"Do you mind?" Nyqueed hissed. "I'm in the middle of something."

The thin arm produced a dagger. It flipped it playfully in the air as the muscular arm grabbed Madrigan's forehead and held it tight. The thin arm brought the dagger down across his neck.

"Pay up, brigand, or I slit your champion's throat," spoke the black, brittle arm in a voice that sounded like kindling snapping.

"Whatever this relates to, my charred little friend, surely it can wait until I'm done," Nyqueed answered.

"No. No, little tune, it cannot wait. I want my payment. Now! Or I will kill this little mortuant of yours." The muscular arm wrenched Madrigan's head back, exposing even more of his throat, and the thin arm pressed the dagger down.

"Payment?" Nyqueed barked. "What payment? Who the hell are you?"

"You know exactly what payment, you feral little sprite," the hand hissed.

"I'm afraid I don't. And as you can see, I'm a little busy with work at the moment." The jeweler stared at him, bewildered. Nyqueed shrugged. The man managed a sympathetic smile in reply.

"Krosst's Thimble, you muhk!" the arm roared. "Does it ring a bell? We were contracted to steal it."

Surprise blossomed across Nyqueed's face. "Ogham?"

The arm bowed.

"Of course, I *do* recall that caper. Went a touch sideways if I recall correctly. Ball of flame, wasn't it? Triggered when you reached for the..." The word "safe" fell away as a whisper.

The burnt, black hand began to quiver with rage.

"I thought you'd died in that fireball, Ogham."

"Well, I survived, didn't I? Or parts of me, at any rate." The hand curled into a fist and banged the table. "You could have searched for me in the rubble, you muhk. Instead you leave me for dead and make off with the Krosst's Thimble yourself. I should have known, trusting a drudge of your... predilections."

"Searched for you? I had seven angry guards barreling down on me after your little firework display. Besides"—Nyqueed turned back to the merchant to press his point— "setting off that trap was not my doing. It was that stupid little Mulloch Furdie who bungled the whole affair. He was supposed to hide lock picks in that monkey's cage. But not only did that idiot hide the lock picks, he hid the monkey, and his cage as well. It was only when we reached the edge of the roof, with those seven angry guards in tow, did he disclose that he'd hidden the rope as well! I found three empty folds of parchment paper in his pocket when he said that. That fool attended our caper high as the sun on a triple batch of Finder's Weepers!"

The thin arm balled its fist again. The muscular arm rose from Madrigan and laid itself out as a palm. The fist slammed into it. "Enough of this. Pay me or I slit your mortuant's throat."

Nyqueed leaned off the bookcase and examined Madrigan. "My mortuant?" He chuckled. "I'm sorry, Ogham. That blast truly did take your eyes. If that filthy little pitchie is anyone's mortuant, it's that stupid drudge of lysergic torpor, Mulloch Furdie, the idiot who hides things so well that he hides even the things that hide the things that he wants hidden!"

The arms faced one another; their fingers quivered with doubt. Nyqueed turned back to the jeweler and re-established his dagger at his neck. "No, that one is definitely not mine. Do what you like with him. I couldn't care less."

"Liar!" the arm replied, but its voice could not stem its creeping uncertainty. "Pay up, you filthy drudge, or I'll slit his throat."

"I sold that bloody thimble ages ago, Ogham," Nyqueed said over his shoulder. "That money has been well spent. You're out of luck, my friend."

He turned his attentions back to the jeweler. "Now, my good citizen of Quardinal's Brawn, back to our business. The Gudfin Blade. Where is it?"

"I w-warn you." The jeweler directed his words as much to Ogham as to Nyqueed. "I am in Thaltis's camp. He will hear about this."

"Thaltis?" Nyqueed blurted. "He's the muhk who invited me to commerce in that cemetery. Why in the fates am I always hearing that mortuant's name?" He leaned in close to the quivering merchant. "Are you trying to intimidate a drudge? With the reputation of a mortuant?"

"Tell him nothing," Ogham called out to the jeweler. "He will only cheat you."

"Ignore him," Nyqueed said. "An old associate. Angry at the whims of fate. Now." He pressed the dagger harder on the jeweler's neck. "Where is the Gudfin Blade?"

"I–I don't know."

"Don't you?" Nyqueed cupped his hand before the jeweler's face and blew into it. The pockets of the man's vest and pants billowed, burst free of their station, then deflated. Nyqueed opened his hand. In his palm, illuminated in the soft candlelight, were the contents of the jeweler's pockets: three spheres of gold.

"Coins shaped as spheres? Now, I wonder, where do they press their gold into spheres?" Nyqueed asked, enjoying the taunting.

"I don't know," the jeweler sputtered.

"Only the brae press gold like that. To avoid sharp edges that might *cut*." Nyqueed pressed the dagger into the merchant's neck, producing another line of blood. "Now, how did three brae coins come into your possession, I wonder?"

"Don't answer him," Ogham shrieked.

"It was my boy! H-he's a pickpocket. He must have stolen these—that's it!"

"Is that it?" Nyqueed smelled the coins and shook his head. "No, I don't think so. No, that's not it. You see these coins are rank with your scent, mortuant. And the smell of ale." He inhaled deeply over the handful of coins. "And the fumes of congress. The bent and huddled whispers of conspirators. I know that stench well."

The jeweler reached into an open case on the bookshelf and grabbed a necklace. "Here. Here, take it!" He thrust the necklace into Nyqueed's hand. "This is the work of Frew the Elder himself. Only twelve were made. To commemorate this auspicious occasion."

Nyqueed sneered. "What auspicious occasion?"

"The race, of course. It has started again. Do you not know?" The jeweler stared at them, baffled and confused.

Nyqueed took a moment to consider the man's words, then he snatched up the necklace. Seven silver oval tiles were connected by black chains, all overlapping, connecting each tile to the other. The tiles were all different. The first showed the gods and a crown receding from them. From this tile, the viewer's eye could proceed to any of the others depending on which chain the viewer chose to follow. Each tile bore another intricately etched scene.

Nyqueed followed one of the chains to a broken tile. A thin fissure ran across the middle peak of the mountain chain depicted on the tiny sculpture.

"It's cracked. You've given me a worthless piece of junk," he snarled.

"No, I swear—that is how the Elder made it."

Nyqueed grumbled and pocketed the necklace. He glared at the jeweler. "I still want the blade."

"But you don't understand. Thaltis will kill me."

"As will I. But my blade will send you farther than the grave, mortuant," Nyqueed hissed.

"He sold it!" the jeweler screamed as his courage left him. "To a young brae. A fortnight ago."

"Are you sure?"

"Yes."

Nyqueed stepped back and let him go. He picked at his teeth a moment as he fell into deep thought. The poor jeweler, not knowing if this meant he was free or if this was simply an interlude in his agonies, froze where he stood.

His decision reached, Nyqueed turned around and faced Ogham.

He blew into his fist again. His own pockets billowed and a leather pouch appeared within his grasp. He buried his fingers inside and held up a coin. "You know, Ogham, I think you're right. I think it is high time for me to make good on my debts."

The arms turned to one another in shock. "Why now, flotsam of the heavens?" the black arm replied suspiciously.

"Well, for one thing," Nyqueed said, nodding toward Madrigan, "why should this poor mortuant be caught up in our little misunderstanding?"

The muscular arm let go of Madrigan and joined the others. The three hands tented together as they pondered Nyqueed's gambit. "What is your ploy here, Black Song Man?"

"My ploy?" He fished out a handful of coins from his pouch. "No ploy, Ogham. Just a flash of honor. They don't come often enough to the Black Song Man. Mine is a tune of sadness and woe. So grab it while you can. Now, how much? To clear our debt and take this dirty, confused little pitchie off your hands?"

"One hundred gold coins."

Nyqueed glared at the arms.

"Seventy-five gold coins," Ogham countered.

"Seventy-five?" Nyqueed fumed. He stopped counting. He put the coins back into the pouch and threw it. The thin arm caught it in the air. Its heft slid him to the edge of the table.

The arms grabbed up the pouch, scurried down table, and were out of the room before Nyqueed reached Madrigan. He bent low to the shocked pitchie. In doing so he missed Rothesay's hand at the door. The brute silently pushed it wide and stepped into the room unnoticed.

"What say you and I pay your little pitch master Mulloch Furdie a little visit?" Nyqueed hissed. "I think he and I should resume our working relationship."

Rothesay stepped into the candlelight; Nyqueed stumbled back from Madrigan and into the bookshelf. Rothesay lunged. He grabbed Nyqueed around the neck and forced him to his knees.

"Looking f-for Salagrim's Mouth, brute?" Nyqueed sputtered. "How fitting, as yours is so broken."

Rothesay punched him and then jammed his hands into Nyqueed's jacket pocket. But his thick fingers were held up at the threshold. The pocket engorged with bilious energy and pressed free of its hold. It fell inside-out and limp like a dog's ear.

Rothesay snarled. He tried another pocket, then another, but all of them were proud of their binds, limp and empty. Nyqueed shot him an impish grin.

"Too late, brute. Salagrim's Mouth is gone. Looks like your little race isn't over just yet."

CHAPTER 24

PAINTING WITH THE INEVITABLE

"AND HOW IS your drain in the morning? Is it thick or thin? Light or dark?" Gogarburn helped Connachen climb onto the long wooden table in the tent. The captain of the 12th Leggat kept his eyes trained on the scene outside.

The flap of the tent came loose from the knot holding it in place. It fell back over the doorway. Mogh tied it back up and resumed his quiet sentry.

Gogarburn took the black poultice from the bowl and worked it between his fingers. He nodded impatiently at his young assistant. The boy opened and closed the drawers of an old cabinet, working his way down the grid, and stopped three rows down and eight in. He drew out a roll of bandage and handed it to Gogarburn.

Beyond the tent, Connachen could see his men moving through the burned-out village. Mogh noticed his preoccupation and adjusted the knot, drawing up more of the fabric to bring more of the scene to light.

The stacks of bodies were once again divided into men, women, and children. Once again they were bloated and stitched at the mouth.

But it had been what they had found in the courtyard that had caused Connachen to stumble and allow the flint ax of the Ghorak to catch him in his midriff.

A dozen bodies, arranged in a grid formation, filled the tiny courtyard. Each body, hunched on all fours like a boulder, was naked, the steps of their vertebrae clear to the sky. Their arms fought to support their frames from collapsing into the sand.

In the middle of the strange arrangement was a man sitting on a cobbler's bench. His clothes were filthy and his arms were akimbo, his muddy hands splayed on his knees. He didn't move; he didn't speak. He wore a ghoulish grin, eyebrows arched high, and broken stitches around his mouth dangled limp in the wind.

"And your stool, captain?" Gogarburn asked. "How is it? Is it stitched on the flanks, or is it folded as a napkin? Let us pray it is folded. For it would lead me to eliminate Vecktum's Decreptic Hood from the list of what might have caused your peculiar affliction. And more's the thanks. That ill humour can cast a pall over the heart of a weakened man."

"My stool?" Connachen glared at the healer. "Bind my wound, man."

Still working the black poultice in his hands, Gogarburn leaned over to look outside the tent.

"We crossed the Kilarion border this morning, did we not?" He packed the poultice into the wound on Connachen's stomach. "In doing so, we entered the land of the Kaarel, I imagine. This village is one of theirs, is it not?" Gogarburn pressed hard on the poultice. Connachen winced and gritted his teeth.

"If memory serves, it was a Kaarel tradesman who told the gendarmes in Quardinal's Brawn about my little set of fires. Four days later, I'm sentenced to the Thunder. I scarcely had a moment to draw a breath."

He smoothed the poultice along Connachen's flank and smiled.

"How ironic. Now their little village finds itself standing in the path of the most supreme inferno."

Six of Connachen's men had been assigned to the courtyard. They walked silently through the grid of bodies, stumbling in shock. Connachen got to his feet and rushed to the tent entrance.

"The boy, you fools!" he screamed, pointing to the last member of the human grid. For his efforts he fell back coughing and struggling for breath.

"Captain, please, you mustn't strain like that." Gogarburn held a napkin to his mouth to catch the blood and spittle, but Connachen slapped him away.

At the far corner of the courtyard, a naked boy crouched on the ground, back bent like a turtle. His tiny legs were folded beneath him and his arms strained to hold up his torso. His little chest shuddered with broken breaths. The boy's waning life did not go unnoticed. Five feet away, on the perimeter of the courtyard, three vultures waited patiently.

The soldiers turned at Connachen's outburst. He couldn't read their eyes. Were they paralyzed by shock? Revulsion? Or were they content to watch this horror? His men had suffered much; they had seen more cruelty and death than any man should see in a lifetime.

"The boy…" Connachen tried again, but a storm of coughs overtook him.

"Captain, please," Gogarburn said. "How many such villages have we seen in the past fortnight? If you work yourself so at every one, you'll be no use to anyone. Your men will catalog and bury this village. As they have all the rest."

One of the vultures ventured closer. The little child faltered; he slipped an inch closer to his sandy end. The vulture took another greedy step. The devil sitting on the cobbler's bench turned his gaze to the boy, and his grin widened.

Scrieve stood off to the side. The scribe was writing in his leather-bound tomb, looking up at intervals, gauging and calculating the scene to its full measure.

Zollern stood next to him. He had the knot on his halberd's staff close to his ear; he rattled it like it was a broken toy. He whispered something to Scrieve, who gestured for him to stop.

The healer's gaze turned from the scene to his captain. "I'm told that you are also bothered by nightmares. Am I correct?"

He snapped his fingers. His attendant approached with a bandage. Gogarburn wrapped it around the poultice he'd worked into Connachen's belly.

"Who told you that?" Connachen grumbled.

"The scribe, of course, captain. He is very concerned for your health." Gogarburn dismissed his attendant's look of shock with a quick flick of his hand.

"Is he?" Connachen got to his feet again, waving off Gogarburn's protests, and struggled to the doorway. Once there, he locked eyes with Mogh.

"The boy," he whispered. Then he screamed the words into the courtyard.

Scrieve stopped his writing. Connachen pointed. The vulture had inched close enough to nip at the child's leg. Scrieve gestured for Zollern to attend the boy and resumed his entry.

Gogarburn came alongside. "It almost seems as though the Ghorak are now testing their conclusions about us somehow, does it not?"

As if the words had arrived like a gale, Connachen stumbled. Mogh caught his fall. Gogarburn angrily brushed the Torrefact aside and guided Connachen back to the table.

"Captain, please. Your men will see to the cleanup of this forsaken village. You must see to your own health."

Meanwhile, Zollern was walking to the dying boy. He moved slowly, eyes cast down, as if he were stepping through a field of glass, when a shadow crossed his path. He looked up to see Wulfric barring his way.

"And where do you think you're going?"

Zollern nodded his head toward the vulture now probing the flesh of the boy's thigh with its beak.

Wulfric snorted as he took in the boy's fate. "I take it your god is speaking again, then, is he? He's a right babbler of late, ain't he, boy? Has he not seen a dying child before?"

"I imagine he's seen them," Zollern said defiantly. "Just seems he doesn't *like* seeing them."

"Doesn't like it? A sensitive little flower then, is that it? If he doesn't like it, why is he painting so many of them on this bleak canvas?" Wulfric lit his rolled tobacco.

"How should I know?"

"'S'funny how your Rawl has a tendency to fall silent when it suits you." Wulfric throttled Zollern by the collar and drew him close. He grabbed the soldier's halberd and brought it up to Zollern's ear.

"I know you lied back there, boy. Don't think you can fool me. All to save that little toad. I let it go, because while you might not hear your bastard god, *I can*."

Zollern looked like a rung bell.

"That's right, boy. I hear them all, and your Rawl sounds like a wind chime in a gale. He's terrified." Wulfric looked off into the distance as he let Zollern go.

"I can hear them all. Every one of them. They're screaming and wailing and gnashing in this little courtyard. Such a racket a man can barely make sense of it. But I'll tell you one more thing."

He leaned toward Zollern and let out a long plume of smoke. "There's no Kellcrim in the bunch, I'll tell you that."

"Y-you can hear them, Wulfric?"

"Aye, I can hear them, boy. I've heard them my whole life. Who do you think told me to strangle that girl? It's cuz of Gollunt himself that I'm in the Thunder."

"What are they saying now, Wulfric?" Zollern asked, wide-eyed.

"What are they saying?" Wulfric eyes narrowed. He took in the dying boy. The vulture was probing the child's side; the boy hadn't the energy to move in his own defence.

"That's a hard one. See, they're huffing and they're puffing, boy. Maybe they're just catching their breath in this little courtyard."

He startled and raised his finger as though to hold the conversation at bay. "Oh, no. Now, hold on… no, no. Now they're angry."

"About what, Wulfric? Is it me? Is Rawl mad at me?"

Wulfric closed his eyes and concentrated. "You mean because of your little betrayal of your brothers back there in the canyon?"

The color drained from Zollern's face.

"No." Wulfric put his hand on his shoulder. "No, it isn't that. Though it should be, boy. It should be." He leaned in close.

"It's because of *all of this*—everything you see around you, boy. They think they created all of it. But that one." Wulfric pointed to the man sitting on the cobbler's chair. "That one is showing them they aren't the only game in town. And there's nothing they can do about it."

"Nothing?" Zollern asked in wonder. "Even Rawl?"

Wulfric shook his head. "Even Rawl." He looked back at Connachen's tent and drew more smoke into his lungs.

Meanwhile, the effort of yelling had run its course over Connachen. The bandage Gogarburn had wrapped him in was stained with his blood. The healer tutted and unwound it, exposing the poultice again.

"The Ghorak stone cut so very deep," he said as he surveyed the wound. "Like a chisel through clay. You're lucky. Had you not dodged, I believe this would have taken your life."

Kellcrim, why didn't you let it?

Gogarburn's young attendant poured a cup of water then stopped when he saw the scowl it elicited; he blushed at his foolishness. He raced through the drawers of the cabinet again before withdrawing a tiny vial of powder. He poured a small amount into the cup of water and handed it to Gogarburn.

"Here, Connachen. Take this." Gogarburn lifted the cup to Connachen's mouth. "You cannot see to everything, captain. This is too much for one man's shoulders. Let others help you. Let others collect the broken pieces of this world. If they must be collected."

Connachen took a sip.

"Good. Now these strange dreams, captain. These nightmares. What do you remember of them?" Gogarburn bound the wound again.

The man sitting on the cobbler's chair stood up.

Kellcrim, please. Please, by all that's holy, strike him down.

A warm fog settled over Connachen's mind. "I–I remember so little," he whispered.

"How long have you had them?"

"A fortnight. Maybe longer."

"They seem to perplex you. Why is that?"

A numbness arrived. Connachen's eyelids fell heavy. "Because I feel as though… they aren't mine somehow."

As he said this, the man who had stood from the cobbler's bench raised his hands in front of himself.

Do something, Kellcrim! By the gods, do something!

The man closed his thumb and forefinger as though he were pinching a filament of pure divine light stretching from the ground to the heavens. He pinched another with his other hand.

What are they doing? Why don't they stop him?

But Zollern and Wulfric and Scrieve and the other men of the 12th Leggat did nothing. And so the man from the cobbler's chair was free to pluck this invisible strand between his fingers.

The arms of the woman three rows down suddenly gave out. She crashed to the sandy floor of the courtyard, dead. The vultures at its periphery squawked and bobbed their heads. A pair flew into the air. Scrieve did nothing but write. The soldiers did nothing but stare.

The man pivoted to his right. He pulled the other invisible string. The arms of an old man gave out. He too crashed to the sand, dead. The man pulled two more strings at once: two more fell dead. And so he continued, playing the arrival of death like the strings on a celestial harp.

Mogh turned in the doorway of the tent and locked eyes with Connachen. The captain of the 12th Leggat fumbled to respond, but his energy was leaving him. He felt Gogarburn's hands take his head and gently lower it to the pillow.

"Well, if these dreams are not yours, Connachen, then I feel compelled to ask. Whose are they?"

Connachen's world was collapsing, ebbing away. It ended at the bridge of his nose. The healer was but a blur beyond it.

"Do you remember none of them?" Gogarburn pressed.

"Only glimmers and pieces of words," Connachen whispered.

"What words, captain?"

"The charge at the… at the Millean gate."

"Well, you should remedy that at once. Perhaps if you knew their fulsome content, you could see these strange memories banished. I order you to find yourself a scullery maid in one of the villages. Ask her to accompany you to bed one night and listen to your visions. How's that for a healer's prescription?"

The flow of Connachen's senses returned. His world burst back to its full measure. Mogh was still at the door of the tent. His face was impassive, his eyes fixed on the courtyard. More of Connachen's men had piled into the killing floor. And like their brothers they did nothing.

More vultures appeared in the air. But the vulture who had pressed toward the body of the child had them beat. It was on the boy now, testing and probing.

"If this scullery maid can't write what she hears on a piece of parchment paper—and in this god-forsaken Kaarel wasteland that's likely a guarantee—then surely she can relate it to the scribe in the morning. If you're lucky, he'll write the dreams down, and you can consider the forces working within you with a clear mind."

The mysterious man plucked his final string. The boy fell. The vulture struck.

Mogh turned and stared at the captain of the Thunder. Connachen struggled to respond with something—anything: the lift of a brow, the set of a lip, something to express to the Torrefact man that he did not condone this. That this was a sin, a transgression, its own compounding horror. Connachen wanted to scream that Kellcrim's order had no room for such depravity. That what was playing out in the courtyard should have called on the best in his men, not their worst. But the sedative coursing through his blood robbed him of even that. His head was turned toward Mogh, his eyes fixed on him, but his face could tell nothing of the breaking of his heart.

"It's amazing what we can learn from writing things down," the healer continued, washing his hands in the basin.

The sedative's full impact had arrived. Connachen's eyes dimmed. In the thinning light he caught the hazy image of the Torrefact out of the corner of his eye. He was holding the hand of the child struck down in the courtyard. The boy smiled at Mogh and held up the wrung neck of the vulture.

Connachen's energy left him. His consciousness ebbed away and his world went to black.

CHAPTER 25

THE PARABLE OF THE CHILD

THE PRIESTESS ROCKED the bronze incense burner forward. A cloud of smoke burst from its vents. The smoke chugged up into the air and fell as the silhouette of the goddess Vestialis. She was nothing more than its vapors; she began where they began and ended where they ended. Vestialis extended her ethereal hand, bejeweled and emerging from a silk cuff, and caressed the crumbling old column.

"Frew the Elder himself carved these columns, girl. That he would render the image of a god other than Bragnal was a scandal. But you see, he fell in love with me. From the moment he set eyes on me. As do so many."

She pointed to the night sky beside them. The ruins of the temple of Vestialis sat on the tip of the Quardinal Rock, almost level with the stars. Beyond its columns and marble base was the sheer drop to the city's winding streets and alleys.

"He would have carved every inch of the Khallin Cliff in my likeness had I asked him to. And I should have. It would have held my visage to this day, mocking Bragnal's punishment as I lay in that crypt."

The priestess followed the gesture of her goddess. The view from the temple was expansive. The lands beyond the walls of Quardinal's Brawn were dotted with fires burning like bubbles in a thick stew, flaring and receding. The smoke they threw off reached as high as the temple. The priestess could have touched it if she'd leaned out into the night. But that would have brought her closer to them and the great lines of humanity burdened with overpacked wagons and mules snaking northward.

"Why are the people fleeing, my queen?"

"Because the race is on, my little dove. And those beyond the walls of Quardinal's Brawn find themselves in its path. But you must pay them no mind. You are destined for much greater things."

The smoke from the cloud of incense evaporated before Vestialis could bring her hand to the girl's trembling lips. "Go on, girl," Vestialis whispered, nothing more than a voice in the darkness now. "Burn it away. See what was. Before Bragnal imprisoned me."

The girl nodded. She touched her torch to the vegetation that choked the crumbling column. Dry and brittle as it was, it took the flame, and soon the exquisite artistry beneath appeared. The panel showed Vestialis in flowing robes and long lush hair dancing in the middle of a group of men and women prostrate before her.

"Look how the Elder depicted me. So beautiful. So beguiling. And look at their eyes, child. Full of awe and reverence. Let me touch it."

The priestess rocked another cloud of incense from the bronze burner. The vapored image of Vestialis appeared at the column, tracing her fingers over the sculpture. She did the same to the contours of her face. "He captured me perfectly, didn't he?"

"He did, goddess."

Vestialis reclined on the column, coy and alluring. "I was much courted in those days, girl. By gods as much as mortals. Go on. Burn more."

The priestess leaned in through the disintegrating cloud of her goddess and touched her torch to the column again. She teased another cloud of incense from the burner and Vestialis re-emerged as the growth burned away from the next panel.

A god was bent on one knee before Vestialis, a child in his hands. The young boy pointed above his head to a mountain chain in the distance.

"Your child, my queen," the priestess said. "The blessed child of Vestialis."

"Blessed?" Vestialis glowered. "You sound like all those braying supplicants who prayed to me when he was born. They were as incessant as maggots on a dead dog."

The priestess pointed to the carving of the man holding the child. "And is that… Corvii?"

"Aye. My blighted lover, the god of time."

The priestess lingered on the image. Her bottom lip trembled.

"Why do you hesitate, girl? Go on, show me more."

"I–I…" Tears filled the priestess's eyes. "It's just that you honor me so, goddess."

"No, girl, it is you who honored me. Calling out to me as you did. Your faith so strong while Bragnal imprisoned me in that crypt. You alone sustained me in my captivity. I shall never forget it."

"I–I only did as you directed, my queen."

"Now, now. It was more than that. It was devotion not seen since, well, since *The Parable of the Child.*" Vestialis smiled and pointed to the vegetation yet to be burned off above the last panel.

The priestess covered her mouth and her eyes went wide. "*The Parable of the Child?*"

"The very one. Your eyes will be the first mortuant eyes to see it in centuries. Would you like that?"

The priestess nodded, wiping a tear away with the back of her hand. "I will not let you down, Vestialis."

"Go on, then, girl. Illuminate what these barbarians have thrown into shadow."

The priestess torched more of the vegetation. Another panel

appeared showing a hundred men and women pounding against a tall wooden door. Corvii was head and shoulders above them, slamming his shoulder into it.

The priestess stumbled back. The light from her torch turned away from the column, drawing Vestialis's attention along with it.

She found the priestess staring off to the far end of the shrine. There, where the stairs up the Quardinal Rock led to the marble stairs of the temple, was a shattered wooden door buried beneath tree roots and vines.

"The very one," Vestialis said. The words brought the girl's attention back to her goddess. She produced another cloud of incense from the hanging burner, and Vestialis appeared twisting a lock of her hair in her fingers.

"Look at them." She nodded toward the column. "Clamoring for me. Screaming to the heavens. Yearning for the door of my temple to open. For me to appear. For me to reveal myself to them. A truer display of aching and longing I can scarcely imagine."

"Yes, my goddess," the priestess replied. But she was distracted. She leaned forward and illuminated the image of Corvii at the door.

"Why do you place your light on that skulking ingrate?" Vestialis hissed.

"Forgive me, my queen, but the texts of the *Parable* I have read… none of them mention Corvii. Have your divine texts twisted the story?" Her bottom lip trembled. "If they have, please forgive us," she whispered. "We did our best to interpret your divine meaning."

"And why should the parable mention him?" the goddess shrieked. "The *Parable* is to instruct, girl. To focus the mortuant mind on the matters that reign supreme in this universe. In this case, love—the love *of me!*"

Her words stunned the priestess. She relented with a confused nod.

"Good. Good girl. You are beginning to understand the truth. Now shall we burn off more of this dreck?"

The priestess nodded again and touched the torch to more decayed vines and leaves. They burned off and the next panel emerged. Vestialis had the child pinned against the altar of the temple with a dagger above the boy's neck.

The priestess dropped the incense burner. The embers spilled onto the broken marble floor. A chug of smoke poured out in their wake no higher than the priestess's knees. Vestialis appeared within it, sprawled like a spider and glaring up at her.

The priestess was looking at the ruins of an altar in the middle of the temple. She covered her mouth. "The boy," she whimpered as she imagined the scene. "You..."

Vestialis sneered from inside her smoky haze. "You begin to embarrass yourself, girl." She rose with the smoke. "The boy contained within him nothing less than the location of the Blackened Nevers. What mother would let that power stay buried in her child and thereby refuse the invitation to run?"

"No," the priestess whispered. "It cannot be love to kill your own child."

"What do you mean, *no?*" Vestialis hissed. "That *it cannot be?* I am a god, girl. You forget who you address."

The priestess fumbled to pick up the incense burner. "But in the *Parable*... it–it says you gave your child to bring love into this broken world, not to drain it away for your own advantage."

The thinning cloud of smoke was now insufficient to illuminate Vestialis's whole face. Her image was misshapen, threadbare, and grotesque. "Love? Did you really think me a cult of love, girl? No, love is what mortuants show *me*. It is *my* due, not theirs!"

The spark that had burned the last panel on the column flared and cleared the vegetation that covered the next scene. Corvii had the child in his arms and was running, running as fast as he could, toward a thick forest rendered by the Elder with deep gouges and ugly crosshatches. Filigrees off the forest reached out like arms toward them.

"Yes, girl. The fool ran to Bedlam's Thicket. To lose the boy in its dark corners. It is there we will find him, and we will carve from him the location of the Blackened Nevers once again."

The priestess clutched the incense burner to her chest and drew back from the column. She was soon at the temple's edge. Rubble from the crumbling floor dislodged under her heels and tumbled out into the air.

"What have I done?" She looked down at Quardinal's Brawn. "Oh, by the fates, what have I done?"

"*Shhh*, girl. You mustn't fret. We will find my boy again. Bockum is presently freeing my drudge, Pennylegion. They have started the work already. My boy will bleed the location of the Blackened Nevers once again and the race will be mine. And when I step into that gilded hall victorious"—what was left of Vestialis reached out to the priestess— "you shall sit at my right hand."

"No. No, I–I can't let this happen." She closed the valves of the burner, choking away its smoke, and waved her hand to dissipate what lingered. Vestialis disappeared, but the priestess' frantic efforts dislodged more rubble from under her feet. She stumbled, teetered, and found her balance again.

"What do you think, girl?" came Vestialis's voice on the wind. "Do you really think I'll let a mortuant hold my plans in the balance?"

Two men appeared from behind a crumbling column. A chill came over the priestess as she realized she had seen them before: they were the men who had rushed the platform in the town square.

"There, there, darling. Nothing bad's gonna happen," said one man, slicking back his hair and grinning.

"Yeah, just give it to us. That's a good girl. Give it here," said the other as he closed in beside his partner.

"No," the priestess whimpered. She clutched the burner close to her chest. "No, I can't. It's all a pack of lies. She's an abomination."

"An abomination?" The first man chuckled. He turned to his partner. "Our little priestess here has no idea what an abomination is, does she, Rec?"

The other man smiled. "We can't let her labor in ignorance, now, can we, Rol? Not fittin' for men o' faith."

The men lunged. The priestess screamed. The marble beneath her gave way. The incense burner split in two as she fell, its embers and smoke spilling into the air after her.

The men skidded to a halt at the temple's edge. They watched the priestess fall until, in the wisps of smoke from the broken incense burner, Vestialis appeared. She smiled at them and reached up with her arms, urging them forward. They looked at one another, blank and emotionless, and stepped into the air.

The ruins of the temple of Vestialis fell silent. Wind snaked through its crumbling columns and fanned the embers still clinging to the vegetation around them. The spark jumped to crinkled, desiccated leaves obscuring the last panel. They ignited, and the flame surged.

The dreck burned away to reveal Bockum standing before the temple of the Brothers of Digrir. It was consumed in flames. Digrir priests ran from the burning building with children under their arms. And in the corner of the panel Vestialis walked toward Bockum, dragging her kicking and screaming priestess behind her.

CHAPTER 26
THE AMUSEMENT OF ADALBANE

"PERHAPS YOU WOULD like to wash?" Bockum pointed to a marble basin filled with water. "I also arranged for some linens." He nodded to the pile of folded cloths on a tiny mahogany table then waited for the scream echoing down the hall to stop.

"And over there." He pointed to another table showcasing a collection of wood and bone trinkets. "I've placed some statues and beadwork of Digrir I collected while traipsing about with the 12th Leggat. I noticed his aspect changes the farther one wanders from Quardinal's Brawn. I don't mean to presume, but perhaps you'll find something in there to steel your courage."

He drew a handful of sand from the shallow wooden bowl beside him and threw it onto the stone floor. He leaned forward in his chair to examine the spill like a painter scrutinizing his canvas. "Take your time. I'll let you know when Vestialis arrives and starts to get impatient. She does get impatient, you know."

The brother of Digrir gathered himself up from the floor. They were in a hexagonal chamber of golden arches from which six hallways receded into shadows.

"Yes, you can run." Bockum nodded toward a hallway as he sifted sand from one hand to the other. "And I, for one, would say bravo. I would. It would display such vitality."

"What do you want with me?" the priest asked.

"What do I want? Me? Why nothing, friend. Oh, my good priest, if I had my way you would soak in ambrosia. You would fill your belly with figs. And then you'd be sent on your way with enough gold to buckle your mule's knees! To build another one of Digrir's temples, perhaps?" He gestured to the structure around them. As he did, another scream echoed down the halls.

Bockum scattered more sand onto the stone floor. He stared at it a moment. "She's catching her breath. Clapping the mud from her hands and throttling her mewling little priestess. You've still got time to work up your courage."

"Let me go," the priest said, scanning the room.

"You'll see it over there." Bockum gave a bored gesture toward the marble table and the ornate silver dagger lying in an open chest. He pressed proud of his chair.

"But rather than focus on that, why not try to enjoy the moments you have left. Don't adulterate yourself with base mortuant dread."

"Why have you attacked us?"

"Why have I attacked? I had no choice, now, did I? The Brothers of Digrir insist on keeping the boy hidden from Vestialis." Bockum let the words hang in the air a moment before he motioned to a chair. "Go on, sit. Rest while you think it through."

The priest sat down cautiously. "It isn't the Brothers who hide him. It's Corvii. He ran with the boy to Bedlam's Thicket. The boy is lost in his dark tangle with the rest of the scraps and curios he hides in there."

"You must understand, I believe none of that. Digrir is the god of wayward children. What more wayward a child could there be than the famous child of Vestialis?" He considered his point for a moment in the slow release of sand through his fingers.

"So? What name do I give you? What do you call yourself, friend?"

"Adalbane," the priest replied. "Brother Adalbane."

"Brother Adalbane. Splendid!" Bockum picked up a pitcher and hovered it over a chalice on the table. "One last drink, Brother Adalbane?"

Adalbane shook his head. Bockum poured nonetheless. He held up the chalice.

"You know I took this from, of all people, a woodland shaman. Can you believe that?" He rolled the stem between his fingers. "Look at the exquisite gold and sapphires." He held it higher.

"The 12th Leggat had interrupted his act of ceremonial slaughter. A mangy, emaciated goat, if I recall correctly, to be dispatched for the love of his god. On the edge of a swamp. Isn't that bizarre? That savage actually believed that his god has a taste for the blood of wet goat!"

Adalbane was still searching for his escape.

"I say, doesn't that just seem preposterous, Adalbane? That while Morven lived she would want the manna of a water-bogged goat."

Adalbane sprang from his chair, raced to the table, and picked up the dagger.

Bockum downed the water and calmly returned the chalice. "Such verve. Such determination." He slid forward in his chair, eyes twinkling like a child's. "Now I trust your courage is strong enough for you to run at me and try to strike me down?"

He drew another fistful of sand from the bowl, scattered it on the floor, and read its contents. "You have time. She is occupied tying down that screaming little priestess. Of course, I hope that word means 'tying down'. I often get it confused with the divine word for *butchering*."

Bockum raised himself in his chair and pulled down the collar of his tunic, exposing the top of his chest. "Go on, Brother Adalbane, strike me down! I'd relish it. You'd be a hero in my books, an absolute hero. For removing me from this vulgar role."

Adalbane let the dagger fall to his side. "By the gods, man. I am a Brother of Digrir. The patron of wayward children. What could you possibly want with me?"

"No!" Bockum slammed his hand on the arm rest. "You will not embarrass us. Stand firm, damn you. You are more than that." He composed himself.

"I'm sorry, Adalbane. It's just that I want to do everything in my power in these last minutes to mark you for something far more profound, as something far more dignified than a quivering victim. For you see, Brother Adalbane, you and I—right here, right now—have the opportunity to trumpet the full elegance of mortality. With such verve that *that goddess*," he pointed to the ceiling above, "will choke when she feels you hit her. And she will regret her station as a lowly god and not as one of us transcendent mortals. How does that sound, brother?"

He sat back, reached for more sand, and scattered it onto the stone floor. He read it quickly then looked up; his eyes were cold and focused now.

"She's done now, Adalbane. The priestess is restrained. It's time." He bent to the floor and rolled the chalice forward. It sang over the uneven stones.

Adalbane recoiled from it, knocking over the basin of water beside him. Cut marigold flowers spilled out with the water and settled on the floor. This sent Bockum to his feet. He covered his mouth as he stared transfixed by the arrangement of the flowers.

"She's beautiful, Adalbane. Such beauty as you've never seen. Such power. Such divinity. And yet Vestialis prays to you. *You*, Brother Adalbane. Asking for her child back. How she yearns for him." He turned his head for a new angle on the marigolds.

"She's wiping the sweat from her brow now, Adalbane. She's falling to her knees. *I can see her!*" He began miming what he spoke.

"She bows her head and her soft voice begins to pray." He brought his hands together in prayer. "'Brother Adalbane,' she whispers. 'Hear my solemn prayer. Tell me where to find my boy. To still the aching heart of a loving mother.'"

Bockum bounded from his throne. Adalbane lifted the dagger in defence.

"The race is on, Brother Adalbane. You and I are united in its raging current. But how we react to it, how we face it, *that* is how we show the universe who we mortuants are. Why, look at me." He pointed back to the chair.

"I am just like you. Bound in their knots. I was placed on this throne to sit and watch a daily stream of death and horror. The weight of the world on my shoulders. And do I wince? Do I cry? Do I look away? Do I surrender? Never! I saw my fate and I bent it to my will. With every ounce of strength and dignity I possess, I made it my own. It was *me* who started the race. Me! So you see what we mortals are capable of."

"This is madness." Tears streamed down Adalbane's cheeks.

Bockum rushed back to the bowl and scattered more sand.

"No, my brother. You don't understand. Look! The very goddess of love herself petitions you. She bends as a supplicant to you. She aches for you, Adalbane. You and no one else. And in this mess I want to give you dignity, Brother Adalbane! I want to give you the chance to scream out to those old, decrepit gods, on behalf of every mortuant soul that has ever been, that we mortuants are far more brave and mighty than the gods above. It is *they* who should pray to *us*."

"You're a fiend," Adalbane whispered, holding out the dagger. He kicked the chalice away. It spun to a stop between them.

Bockum sat back on his throne. "Think for a moment, Brother Adalbane. The race is on again, and in this divine maelstrom where do you find yourself? Sick in your bed? No. Skewered on a battlefield? No. Strung up in a noose by some bandits? No. In the midst of this chaos you hold a knife and are flush with the very blood a god waits so eagerly for you to spill. So she can receive the one thought that will propel her forward in this mad tumble: the location of her son. And you, and you alone, know it."

"B-but what of my family?" Adalbane said. "My children?"

Pennylegion and Chezepock suddenly emerged from the shadows behind Bockum's throne.

"You'll forgive me this rudeness, Adalbane, but tell me." Pennylegion braced herself on the throne. "What has that family, that bloodline of yours, done for you? The gods have toyed with it for generations, have they not? And what service have they done you? Where does your bloodline presently find itself? Sweeping the stone floors of Digrir's temple, that's where. With barely enough coins for a bag of barley. What does that say of your blessed family and their position in the cosmos?"

Bockum took over again. "But now, now a true god, one worthy to win this race, is waiting for none other than you, Adalbane. Vestialis, the goddess of purest love, longs for what you alone hold in your heart. For the divine knowledge that only you can deliver. To bring a wayward child back to his mother. And so, I ask you again, where is the boy, Adalbane? Where has Corvii hidden him in Bedlam's Thicket?"

Adalbane trembled as he prepared his lie. "I–I don't know."

Chezepock spoke now. "You would stand here and deny her, my son? You would force your fellow mortuants to wrench you to your knees and thrust you into Vestialis's loving embrace? What withered muse would you be then?"

Two Leggat guards emerged from behind a column and crossed their halberds.

Bockum threw another handful of sand. "Vestialis has begun to cry." He shot Adalbane a withering glare. "Her hands are stained with tears. Because of your thundering silence. How dare you?"

Pennylegion stepped forward, bending her old withered finger toward Adalbane. Her tattered doll dangled in her hand.

"In this cold, dark world, how can you refuse her prayers and yet still call this, *this creation*, good? You would leave a mother's petitions unrequited. You would stand there detached and aloof while a mother yearns for her child! What horrid omnipotence is this?"

Adalbane sprang off the column. They watched as he disappeared down the dark corridor. Bockum snapped his fingers.

"Find him," he muttered.

The two Leggatmen nodded and took off after the priest.

❧

Adalbane's robes billowed behind him as he flew through the darkened passages of the Digrir temple. He knew these corridors; he'd lived within this temple all his life. And so, even in the pitch black, he could stay ahead of the Leggatmen chasing him with ease.

He stumbled under the stone arch that separated the sanctuary from the inner temple. He steadied himself on the wall to gather his breath when he saw the arm of a dead Brother of Digrir.

Adalbane crept toward it. The chapel came into view. A dozen dead bodies littered the tiny sanctuary, draped over liturgy tables and pews or skewered where they stood. The rattle of the Leggatmen's armor snapped him away from the horrid scene.

My laboratory. They won't find me there.

He ran into the room, dodging the bodies of his brethren. The altar had been overturned and ransacked. The room was littered with debris.

A Leggat pikeman rifling through the pews looked up, his hands full of golden relics. He locked eyes with Adalbane and grinned. "Those racing gods are making a right mess, aren't they?" he sneered.

He let the golden artefacts tumble and grabbed his pike leaning against a pew. He lunged with it, but Adalbane managed to dodge. He raced behind the overturned alter.

"In here!" he heard the Leggatmen yell. Two more soldiers rounded on the entrance to the chapel.

"Do it, Adalbane," one of them yelled. "Give your mind to Vestialis!"

Adalbane stumbled back and was enveloped by the curtain behind the altar. He turned to pull it aside, revealing an ornate silver door. He was through it in a flash, locking it behind him just as it shuddered in its frame from a Leggatman's kick. The startle almost sent him tumbling down a set of steep stairs. He paused to gather his wits then began to descend.

He took the stairs carefully. Treads half an inch thick had been ground into the ancient rock. He negotiated the last withered step and saw the wooden door before him. Above he could hear the boots of more Leggat soldiers as they stampeded over the altar. With a quick prayer to Digrir he opened the door and slipped into the room.

His laboratory was untouched. Adalbane whispered a thanks to Digrir that the Leggat soldiers had missed it in their ransacking.

In the middle of the room a cauldron sat over a firepit that still glowed with faint flame. Next to the cauldron a golden lectern held a large opened book and a drawing of a small boy, surrounded by Adalbane's notes. Bottles of strange liquids, dusty jars, and old books lined the shelves of the walls. Dried herbs and flowers hung from every hook in the ceiling or were pressed under every book and bowl.

He snatched the book from the lectern then spied the golden cage on its side just as he heard a rustle of feathers. He turned to see a raven jump to a high shelf, dislodging books and herbs as it struggled to settle. In its beak was a key.

Adalbane looked from the raven to the squat half-sized door and its thick iron lock in the far corner of the room.

The passage to the garden. I can escape through it.

He turned back to the bird. "Here, my sweet. Here. Give it here."

Suddenly, the door to the laboratory shook. It loosened a cloud of dust from the ceiling above it.

"Please, my little sweet, give it to me." But the raven simply looked at him, key still in mouth, as it fussed with the feathers on its flank.

The door thumped again. He heard a crack from its spine. "Damn it, you stupid bird, *give me the key!*"

He lunged and the bird took wing. Adalbane grabbed a broom and swung. The raven dodged the blow but in its acrobatic shift dropped the key to the stone floor as it flew higher.

The door blew off its hinges. Three Leggatmen entered in a cloud of dust. An old swordsman zeroed in on Adalbane. He lunged at him as he clumsily tried to draw his sword. It didn't unsheathe in time; the old soldier swung his other fist as a contingency and connected with Adalbane's chin.

"Why do you run, Adalbane? The race is for the gods, not mortals," he sneered.

Adalbane collapsed. His world faded and threatened to extinguish itself completely but for the glint of the key. He summoned his strength and lunged for it, picking it up and getting to his feet. The Leggatman struck again and sent Adalbane stumbling toward the cauldron. He pushed it from its perch, scalding his hands, and a thick green boiling sludge spilled out toward the Leggatmen. It drew them off just long enough for Adalbane to drop to his knees at the lock of the squat wooden door.

He inserted the key as he stared over his shoulder in terror. The disarray of the Leggatmen evaporated. They saw their mark and they ran, pikes before them like elephant tusks.

C'mon, you blessed raven. Digrir, please.

The key turned in the lock. The door opened. Adalbane scrambled through and slammed the door behind him, sliding the bolt back into place in one fluid motion. It rattled from another Leggatman's kick. Adalbane pushed himself away.

"You will die, priest. I promise you. I did not betray my brothers at the Lomhar Pass so *you* could run! This is Bockum's race, not yours," the man screamed from behind the door.

Adalbane reached out to the sides of the passage. They were wet and earthy, like the inside of a mole's tunnel. His fingers traveled down them to the ground, and he began crawling into the tunnel as confidently as he could in the pitch black.

He could hear the Leggatmen striking and kicking the door behind him. Their assaults sent streams of dirt and dust down from the ceiling of the narrow tunnel. But if the Leggatmen still cursed him, their insults were nothing more than muffled voices now. As was the soft light that spilled into the tunnel from the base of the door. He had long since crawled beyond its stretch. The tunnel was pitch black now; his only measure of guidance was to trace the walls as he moved.

A light suddenly flashed above him. It struck so brilliantly he fell against the wall in shock. He reached for where it had pulsed, but his hand struck against the ceiling of the tunnel, falling well short of where the light had been.

A few feet further. Just a few feet, please, Digrir.

He crawled on, the rocks and dirt grinding at his knees. Another flash of light appeared ahead of him, then one behind it. It was as if someone had directed a sunbeam into the tunnel.

Another piercing ray flashed below him, then another above, and another below his left hand. His dark, subterranean world was lanced by brilliant light, and what was left of the soil and earth crumbled away.

He got to his feet. The floor was gone, but he didn't fall. All around him was white light. Then, as if he were a bird flying among the clouds, a vision slowly emerged below him.

Great stone structures and cities of glorious construction appeared. The vision dissolved like a reflection in a pond and was replaced by walls of water and flame. He saw crumbling statues, scrolls dissolving under desert sun, men clashing in armies as vast as the horizon.

He then careened downward. The motion was so abrupt and

realistic that Adalbane fell to his knees and closed his eyes. But no impact came.

He opened his eyes to see a woman in childbirth. His world drew back from the scene and soared into the air again; he looked down at a field filled with men and women holding hands.

The vision twisted and raced. He saw fanciful inventions: men on the wing of giant beasts, men descending to the depths of the oceans, cities cast in glass. He sailed higher into the air, bound for the sun. He shielded his eyes as the light flared and then went out.

He opened his eyes to a hawk standing before him with a snake in its mouth. Beside it was a cage on its side, its door wide open. On the other side of the hawk stood a tall, graceful heron, a ring in its beak. Its cage also lay on its side.

"W-what is happening to me?" Adalbane whispered.

The snake in the hawk's mouth suddenly came to life. The bird let it go. It dropped to the floor of the passage and reared up, hissing and darting its tongue toward Adalbane. A voice then flooded the room.

"Listen to me, mortuant. You are about to die and lift to the heavens as the dust of divine inspiration."

Adalbane's blood went cold.

"This is done and cannot be changed. But I implore you, mortuant, Vestialis cannot be allowed to find her boy."

The snake slithered closer. It adjusted its jaw to reveal a set of long, dripping fangs.

"Please," Adalbane said. "I don't want to die."

The heron dropped the ring from its mouth. It clattered to the ground with a crash, as if a metal sun had fallen from the sky. Adalbane winced at the sound, and the snake struck. Adalbane wrenched his arm back; a line of blood trickled down his wrist.

"Listen to me, Adalbane. Listen to me carefully as your life slips away and you set upon the ethers to rise to her ears. I am Methulla, god of truth. And in that capacity, I can do naught but declare to you that I want to win this race as any other would. But, in like measure, I reveal to you this: if Vestialis finds her child, this world will be doomed."

The snake struck again, this time on his other wrist.

"And so, I propose to you a bargain. I have brought my knight to the edge of Bedlam's Thicket. I can lead him into its weeds and tangles. Tell me where the boy is to be found and I will send my knight to him and Vestialis will be thwarted again. As she must be."

Adalbane shivered. He fell to his side. His world turned sideways.

"When this race truly begins, it will be you who will have seen truth triumph over wicked love. Over *corrupt* love. So, you must tell me, Adalbane: where is the boy? Where is the boy? Where is the boy…?"

Adalbane's world went to black.

⁂

Bockum stepped from the podium down to the sand he'd just thrown. He crouched by it, angling his head as he read further into it.

"She weeps tears of joy, Brother Adalbane. Absolute, pure… *joy*."

Bockum freed Adalbane's bloody dagger from the priest's fingers then grabbed up the chalice from the floor. He gestured for the Leggatmen to bring Adalbane's bleeding wrists over it.

"We found him in the yard just beyond the wall," said one of the Leggatmen as he wrenched Adalbane's arm up to the chalice. "Must have taken a leave of his senses. Found him rocking back and forth like a child."

"Gently!" Bockum said. He took Adalbane's chin, smiled sadly, and brushed away his hair. He lingered a moment with its strands between his fingers.

"Soon the location of the boy will be hers. And the race will soon be won," he whispered. "All thanks to the courage of Brother Adalbane."

Bockum stood up, carefully guarding the cup of blood. He set it down on the marble table, whipped open the folded white linen, and wiped the sides of the chalice clean.

He felt Pennylegion's hands on his shoulder; the old woman leaned in. "Where? Where is the boy, Bockum?" She took Bockum's hand gently and poured sand into it. He scattered it on the marble floor.

"The boy lies in Bedlam's Thicket."

"Still?" Her fingers fretted over her chin. "Are you sure?"

Bockum dipped his finger in Adalbane's blood and licked it. "The blood of the Brother of Digrir is gorged with truth."

"Then it must be," Pennylegion whispered. She turned to Chezepock. "We go to Bedlam's Thicket, and may the fates protect us from what that mad god Corvii has hidden under his rocks and knitted in his vines."

Bockum raised the chalice to the heavens and drank his mortal fill.

CHAPTER 27
FEFFERFEW HAS WORDS FOR YOU

LUMSDEN STROKED HIS old mangy dog. The fierce winds on the 13th Step took what remained of the warmth left by the crumb of Velveteen Cromide he'd manage to excavate from the lint and dirt in his pocket.

He had been a porter once. To an earl. He'd owned a soft cotton suit as well. And who knew what his old dog had once been? He knew as much about that dog's history as he remembered of his own. But whatever it had been no longer mattered. For whether prince or pauper, Fefferfew was now all Lumsden had in the world. He was his friend and his confidante and his woollen blanket. There were many nights where the cold on the 13th Step had threatened to snuff out Lumsden's vital fires completely. Had it not been for Fefferfew—the old dog more skeleton than anything else—wrapping up close and staring up at him with his warm eyes, Lumsden would have frozen to his death. And it was this same desire, this pure desire to please, that he had first seen in him when Lumsden had rolled over in the gutter, gasping for breath, a feather's stroke away from death, and felt that old mutt licking his face. A moment longer in his pitch torpor and Lumsden would have stopped breathing altogether. That dog had saved his life.

He moved his scratch to Fefferfew's ear. The old dog leaned into it, closer to him and closer to the other pitchies, as if he were leaning in for this new topic of conversation.

"I haven't seen him in days," Lumsden said. "Maybe he's gone and done it: finally tripped himself into oblivion."

They were huddled around a sputtering fire, under a roof of rotten wood, on the final step of the broad staircase that led from the tip of the Quardinal Rock, and what was left of the crumbling ruins of the temple of Vestialis, down to the heart of the city.

The good men and women of Quardinal's Brawn had long ago learned to avoid the temple and the staircase with it. And so the *other* men and women of Quardinal's Brawn had embraced it. First the brewers of Ginned Grin, their copper pipes tinkling in their crates, had moved in to occupy the first stair. Next came the huffers of Rat Reckon with their old, leaky wine skins and wrung-out pigeons. After them came the chewers of Quarrelfudge and their trays made of shattered caskets. After that, the lappers of Gloomwind and the growers of Speckled Frommorrow, delicately balancing the shoots growing on their tongues.

And with them all, in time, came a sort of pecking order, the lowest steps saved for the illegal, but socially acceptable, pitchies. The higher for the full warty rejects of the pitch, left to sleep off their fugues exposed to wind and rain.

"Well I heard he was taken into the Clovenstone. Got too careless about who he purchased his Velveteen Cromide from," said an old pitchie as he scratched at his forearm.

"Velveteen Cromide?" Young Vyren rubbed what residue he'd collected from his pipe onto his teeth. "No." He shook his head. "My guess is Madrigan found something a wee bit more interesting. Something he thought you dullards of the 13th Step weren't entirely ready for."

The other pitchies around the fire exchanged worried glances, passing their fright from one to the other like a pitchie pipe.

Vyren's eyes shined with delight. He pocketed his pipe and leaned in, taking the thin orange glow of the flames onto his cheeks.

"Shivery Coffinfit, that's what I mean," he whispered. He glanced about to see if anyone else had heard. Fefferfew's ears perked up and the dog rose to his haunches.

"Now you listen to me, boy." Lumsden said as he patted Fefferfew's neck. "Never mention that foul pitch again, do you hear me?" He glared at the other pitchies in rebuke. "None of you, understand? Or mark my words, 'twon't be the gendarme you'll be fearing." He turned his attention back to Fefferfew, broadening his strokes.

"'S'not pitch at all, if you ask me," he muttered. "It's miserable stuff. Takes you down, it does. Down into its filthy little pit. There it preys on you with all manner of visions. Linger there long enough and it'll swallow you whole!"

"Swallow you whole?" exclaimed a young man at the end of the circle. He still wore his gendarme graduation tunic, but it was filthy now, its deep crimson a faded, sickly brown resembling a rotting tomato.

"Aye, boy," Lumsden replied. "And who knows if you'll come back. No, stick with Velveteen Cromide. It'll never let you down."

"*Who knows if you'll come back?*" Vyren slapped his thighs. "Listen to him!"

"Aye, boy, who knows if you'll come back." Lumsden's tone was furtive and nervous. "Now that's just about enough said about Shivery Coffinfit."

Far below them, the acolytes of Methulla had begun to assemble in the main square of Quardinal's Brawn. They held all manner of birds made of parchment as long as a man's arm. The birds had elaborate wicks ready to be lit by one of the ornamental torches held aloft by the priests of Methulla.

The followers of the other gods were also starting to gather. Aelic's ascetics marched in from the south, their horsehair whips, long and black like Aelic's cords, snapping at passersby caught in a perceived ethical transgression.

From the east side of the square came the monks of Dhoorval, their open books resting on the crowns of their heads. Their leader held two rats in his hands and adjudicated their dispute with loud pronouncements of rat law.

Behind them were the silent men of Rawl, bare chested, straining to hold their large boulders. Their priest carried the biggest of them in his mighty arms.

From the west side of the square, four Keepers of Gollunt's Flame approached, holding a plank of wood between them. On the plank were four piles of brightly colored sand.

And keeping to the outskirts of the square, coy and skittish like a troupe of foxes, was a handful of Corvii's madmen. They huddled together, darting into the shadows, holding their burlap sacks tight to their chest, and hissing and cursing at the massing men and women.

A commotion rippled through the crowd as two figures draped in shadow, cowls pulled tight over their heads, walked through the square against the tide of humanity. The smaller of the two was forced on his trajectory by the other's prods and pushes. They reached the end of the square and the alley that led to the staircase. The bigger of them shoved the smaller one against the alley wall. He flattened against it and pointed to the stairs as if it would deter further blows. It didn't.

When they arrived at the first step, the battered man in front, spurred by his partner's wrenching of his collar, bent to the brewers of Ginned Grin. A whisper spread through them, and one rose, proud of his brethren. Shaking the last drop from his tin cup onto his tongue, he pointed up the steep staircase. The strangers began to climb.

"It just might be that Madrigan ain't the only one who's sampled a bit of Shivery Coffinfit," Vyren said through his toothless grin. He looked down from the 13th Step at the massing crowd in the square.

A low growl escaped from Fefferfew. Lumsden tugged on his leash. "Quiet, boy."

He glared at Vyren. "I said *enough* with that talk, Vyren. We pitchies should keep to our steps. Keep to the fugues we know."

"You sound like you've floated Shivery Coffinfit yourself, Vyren," the young man in the filthy gendarme tunic said.

Lumsden snorted. "Not likely. Remember what he did the first time he tapped his tongue into a bowl of Gloomwind? His bowels chugged like a blacksmith's bellows. You could follow his trail all the way to the Milkweed Market."

Vyren blushed. He looked askance. "That was a long time ago, Lumsden. I've twisted a few knots since then, believe me."

The pitchies chuckled as the memory finally presented itself to their muddled brains. It brought more blush to Vyren's cheeks.

"Enjoying your laugh, are you?" he sneered.

The two strangers climbing the steps were now past the lappers of Gloomwind, having burst through the dark gray smoke cloud that lingered over their stair. They were knocking aside wayward fists and kicks of the chewers of Quarrelfudge, who were brawling over a length of twine on the tenth step.

"Mark my words," Lumsden said, watching the strangers climb. "You'd best keep off that Shivery Coffinfit. I warn you, boy."

"Says ol' Lumsden. Old Velveteen Cromide Lumsden. Well, maybe some of us are tired of our Cromide."

Vyren turned to the rake-thin Dinafatari man beside him. "I'm through with it. Had my fill of blissed-out bubble-pits. Haven't you?"

The Dinafatari man was too far gone in his pitch fugue to understand what Vyren said. He nonetheless smiled and nodded obligingly. Vyren snorted and looked for agreement in the eyes of the other pitchies around the fire, but they were equally disappointing.

"Well then, guess I'm the only one among you all with a bit of ambition, is that it? A bit of moxy like Madrigan. Well, so be it." He reached into his pocket and drew out his hand. "Feast your eyes on *this*, you bunch of birds."

In the middle of his palm was a translucent egg. Lightning struck, fog swirled, sleet and hail sloshed and spun inside it. Even the pitchies long collapsed in the corner of the rough enclosure righted themselves, crawled forward, and were held rapt by the object in Vyren's hand.

Fefferfew growled, a low, threatening growl. "*Shhh*, boy." Lumsden tugged the dog to him. "Is that what I think it is?" He nodded to the egg.

"Aye, it most certainly is, you old coot. That there is a bit of shining Shivery Coffinfit, procured by none other than Vyren himself. And it's not the only piece I have. Who's the fool now, eh, old man?"

Lumsden struggled to hold Fefferfew. "*Shhh*, boy. What's gotten in to you?"

The old dog's hackles were up and he started barking. The warnings were thin and airy at first but quickly grew deeper and more pronounced; mean and menacing, aimed at Vyren.

"The heck is wrong with that mangy hound of yours? Does he want some? Is that it? You want some Shivery Coffinfit, eh, ol' Fefferfew?" He held up the egg.

Fefferfew's barks, deeper and more insistent, roused the form buried in the bundle of blankets in the farthest corner of the shelter. They slipped off her ancient, leathery face as she sat upright. She cocked her head as if to listen.

"Fefferfew has words for you," she said in a gravelly voice full of churning phlegm. Her index fingers pointed to the sky as if they were balancing two invisible plates.

"Enough from you, Molly," Lumsden snapped. "You can't tell the world from your fevered dreams any more. Leave off it!" But he wasn't as firm as he would otherwise have been, for Fefferfew was indeed acting strangely.

Molly crawled forward, shedding her filthy blankets. "I'm not bending, you old goat. I'm telling you, if you'd shut your yapping and listen. *Your dog is speaking*."

She was as old as Lumsden and he'd known her as long as he'd known the 13th Step. She was as close to a wife as he had at this point, and that familiarity made him want to snarl at her out of reflex. But as she sat back on her haunches, her chin quivering, her eyes adamant, and her filthy, index finger pointing at his dog, he thought the better of it. She was right. There *was* something amiss.

Lumsden bound Fefferfew's head in his hands and looked deep into the old mutt's eyes. "What the devil has gotten into you, boy?"

Fefferfew's barks grew even stronger. Lumsden looked at Molly, who nodded encouragement. He leaned in through the cloud of Fefferfew's moist, rotten breath and listened.

His eyes slowly widened. His jaw dropped slack. He righted himself, the color gone from his face.

"I told you," Molly said, seeing confirmation in his gaunt expression.

Lumsden's gaze fixed on Vyren. "By the gods—by the gods above, he's speaking, boy. To you! He says you're... you're lucky." Lumsden leaned in once more and once again looked up astonished.

"He says you're lucky that he doesn't, right here, right now..." His voice trailed off as Fefferfew released another flurry of barks.

"Doesn't what? The hell is that mangy dog saying?" Vyren drew away from the fire.

"Skull you for your insolence." The words tumbled off Lumsden's lips just as the two strangers reached the 13th Step.

They were silhouettes, the moon high behind their left shoulders lending them a dull halo. The smaller man was pushed forward, scattering the pitchies' pathetic little fire.

The dagger in Rothesay's hand flashed in the moonlight. The brute leaned into the gap and glared down at the pitchies in disdain. He nodded for Nyqueed to speak.

"Where is he?" Nyqueed demanded. "Where is Mulloch Furdie?"

The pitchies drew back. Rothesay rattled his dagger at Nyqueed again.

"Mulloch Furdie, damn it," Nyqueed said. "Where is he?"

Fefferfew got to his feet and leaned back in a deep stretch. It drew his leash to its length, and, in turn, turned Lumsden's focus from Vyren to the strangers.

"Mulloch Furdie? I haven't seen him in years," said the old pitchie.

"Doesn't visit the 13th stair anymore," added Lumsden as he drew in Fefferfew's chain. "Come here, boy."

But Fefferfew refused to budge. The dog's hackles were up. He growled and bared his fangs at the two men.

"What is wrong with your blasted mutt?" Vyren said. Fefferfew's growling increased and a froth came to his lips. It drew Nyqueed's attention to the dog. And that attention instantly grew quizzical, then astonished, then sneering.

"My guess is your dog has gone rabid as a skunk. Or perhaps he needs to relieve himself?" Nyqueed's tone was caustic, and he leaned down to Fefferfew's ear. "On the intricately crafted burglary plans of his accomplices, perhaps?"

To the astonishment of the pitchies huddled around that small fire, a voice bubbled up from deep within Fefferfew's belly. "Rabid? You suppose I'm rabid, do you?"

"I don't suppose anything, you flea-bitten mongrel. I hate supposing. What I like to do is *know*. I like to know things, like what time of day it is, or how much my pint of ale will cost. Or if my intricate plans are about to be foiled *by a complete moron!*"

"Intricate plans?" sputtered the voice inside the dog. "You call whistling for a load-bearing heron an intricate plan?"

"Well, the plan as conceived didn't exactly go as expected, now, did it? Hard to stick to meticulous planning when one's associate, who was supposed to have hidden lock picks in a monkey's cage, took his task too far and hid the lock picks, the monkey, *and the bloody cage!*"

"That was not my fault. Some prankster addled my soup with a triple packet of Finder's Weepers. I can hardly be faulted for that, can I?" Fefferfew turned his head and the voice repeated the question to the startled young pitchie beside him.

Lumsden was struck dumb by the exchange. He shared looks of

bewilderment with the other pitchies. They'd all heard it, and they'd all sobered in an instant.

Nyqueed vented his anger with a series of stifled mutters then turned back to Rothesay. He pointed at the old dog. "You wanted Mulloch Furdie. Well, here he is! He's got Salagrim's mouth now. Careful when you shake him, though. Our escape rope might tumble out of his nose."

"Lies!" Mulloch screamed from inside the dog's belly. "It was Ogham who left the rope behind. And can you blame him? What were you thinking? Telling an eight-armed god that a closet lay within that tower devoted solely to gloves!"

Rothesay's patience had reached its ebb. He wrenched Nyqueed aside and lunged for Fefferfew.

The old dog skittered away and lunged himself. But he was aimed for Vyren. He swallowed the Shivery Coffinfit in the startled pitchie's hand in a gulp and tore off down the staircase. The leash, still in Lumsden's hand, snapped taut, and he was drawn to his feet and off the 13th Step.

Rothesay growled and shoved Nyqueed off the stair after the dog.

Molly got to her feet, shaky and buffeted by the wind. She held up Lumsden's hat and rattled the meager haul of coins within it, but he was long gone. She shrugged and began picking through the coins, testing them between her teeth.

Lumsden landed on his back on the last stair. The tin cups of the Ginned Grinners clanged above him.

"Oooh, I can smell that Shivery Coffinfit from here," said a Grinner. "Smells meaty," said another. "So let's you and me share a wee dram, eh, boy? One for the ditch—*your* ditch.

Lumsden struggled to his feet and threw off their grasping hands. He staggered onto the cobblestones of the alley, half broken, half bewildered, struggling for breath.

He looked up the way he'd come. Rothesay and Nyqueed were stumbling over the stairs after him, scattering pitchies. Then, all of a sudden, he heard a noise, unearthly and bizarre, like the guts of a clock extruding from the nose of its cuckoo. It was the distant echo of hammering and ratcheting and scraping; the sound of gears turning over and steam releasing. He tried to find the source of the sound in the dim light of the alley. It was then his eyes settled on Fefferfew.

The old dog was a few yards ahead of him, sniffing at the cobblestones. To Lumsden's shock and horror—a shock and horror that drew him on his hands and knees to his old, mangy friend—Fefferfew's belly now glowed pale green. The glow illuminated Mulloch Furdie's silhouette inside standing before a table upon which was perched the sphere of Shivery Coffinfit. He hammered at it, tossed the hammer and drew a saw, tossed the saw and drew an axe.

"Fefferfew, old boy?" Lumsden ventured, bewildered. "What have you got there, my friend?"

Mulloch stopped mid-swing.

"An ax, you moron. What does it look like?"

At the bottom of the stairs the Ginned Grinners parted. Rothesay shoved Nyqueed off the last step and followed after him into the alley. The drudge arced his back to avoid Rothesay's dagger, which was pressing into his side, and blurted, "J-just give him the mouth, Mulloch!"

Mulloch's ax fell and split the Shivery Coffinfit. He hunched over the table as sparks of light burst from the sphere like the eruption of a miniature volcano. "Three-fifths of Hammered Dust. Of course! How did I not see it earlier?"

The shock of hearing language—actual language—spilling from that mangy old dog startled an old woman from her inspection of the Rat Reckon in her palm. She covered her heart and flattened against the alley wall as Fefferfew flew by her with Lumsden in tow.

Ruckus? At the bottom of the stairs? This ain't no place for a ruckus. No place at all, she thought. Little did she know what ruckus was coming.

CHAPTER 28

THREE-FIFTHS OF HAMMERED DUST

NYQUEED STUMBLED FROM Rothesay's push and knocked the woman aside, sending the piece of Rat Reckon into the gutter. Within a few strides, the alleyway gave them up to the busy main square.

The curious men and women of Quardinal's Brawn, the priests and shaman and monks and acolytes, the vendors hawking their wares to this miasma of penitents and onlookers, they all gave Lumsden and his old dog a wide birth. They threw up curses as the pair passed, drew in hems of dresses, shielded relics, covered urns, protected purses, settled their listing tables, and performed sacred gestures over forehead and chest.

Fefferfew suddenly skidded to a halt, nose fixed to the cobblestones. Lumsden dropped to his hands and knees, panting as hard as the old dog. "C'mon, boy. We'll have a nice, old bone. You and me. Is that what you'd like? I've got a few coins. How would you like a drak's thigh?"

Fefferfew looked up from his sniff, and Mulloch's angry voice echoed up from his belly. "I'm on the verge of it, you bloody buffoon.

That stupid pitchie Madrigan may have failed me, but this Shivery Coffinfit won't. It's about to yield up all its glorious secrets, and you think I'm inclined to part ways with that for *a bloody rancid bone?*"

The mysterious scent enticed again and Fefferfew was off. But a scream twisted Lumsden around where he stood. Rothesay and Nyqueed were parting a sea of Gollunt's acolytes. The mass gave way to them and filled the vacuum in their wake, only to be buffeted again by a human avalanche of chewers of Quarrelfudge, lappers of Gloomwind, sippers of Ginned Grin, huffers of Rat Reckon, and growers of Speckled Frommorrow spilling into the square and joining the pious crowd.

A shrieking chewer of Quarrelfudge knocked one of Methulla's birds from a penitent's hand just as he was gleefully lighting its fuse. It fell to the ground and exploded, showering a group of acolytes and onlookers with its blast of light. The Aelic's ascetics stampeded from the explosion first, joined by the priests of Gollunt close behind. The two groups bored through the crowd, gathering mass as they ran. The throng quickly grew beyond measure until its girth was such that it could not be stopped by mortal or divine measure: it took Frew the Younger's ice statue of Bragnal in its wake.

Bragnal teetered, and a terrific groan emanated from deep within the ice. The ascetics looked up at it. Had Bragnal spoken? No, but he seemed bent on suicide, for as they slowly parted, the statue staggered and crashed down to the square in an explosion of shattered ice. A chunk of that ice—Bragnal's hands up in front of him as if shielding his face from a blow—washed up at Lumsden's feet.

It was not upon the cobblestones long before a gendarme boot crushed it. Lostrus strode forward nose up, lips tight, filled with indignation at the chaos. With him were six gendarmes holding halberds.

He kicked off the chunks of the ice he'd shattered. "Just what in Aelic's straps is going on here?" he roared, knocking his heel on the cobblestones. But his wrath extinguished the instant his gaze settled on Nyqueed fighting his way against the tide of humanity.

"Well, as I live and breathe." Lostrus drew the back of his hand over his mouth. "Is that—why I think it is—Nyqueed! The mastermind of the Theft of Krosst's Thimble! Thought you got away with that, didn't you? Do you know how long I've been looking for you, little flotsam of the heavens? You're my last prize. I've kept a cell in the Daemonius Concentric nice and warm just for you!"

Lostrus stiffened as he took in the multiplying threats to the king's peace. He pointed and six more gendarmes came running through the crowd, dispersing toward the agents of violence all around them. Lostrus turned back to Nyqueed.

"And don't even think of running, Black Song Man," he sneered. "It'll only end worse for you." He brushed the lint from his gendarme's jacket. "Well? What's it gonna be?"

"Quarrel and bites and slaps and kicks!" screamed a chewer of Quarrelfudge as if in response. He lunged at a young gendarme, taking Lostrus's attention away just long enough for Nyqueed to run, with Rothesay chasing close behind.

"Aelic's straps, that brigand is running. He's actually running!" Lostrus shoved two of the gendarmes next to him forward. "Get him!" he shrieked. Then he drove his sword into the guts of the Quarrelfudge chewer. He withdrew it slowly, as his attention was taken by more pitchies racing from the alleyway. He wiped the blood on the dead man's tunic, righted himself, and adjusted his moustache in the reflection of his blade.

Turning to the frightened men and women of Quardinal's Brawn, he bellowed, "Enough, now! Go about your business, citizens. All is in hand!"

But it was useless. The square was lost to chaos. Even Lostrus could see that. He nodded to his feeble contingent of gendarmes and took off after Nyqueed and Rothesay.

Behind them, leaving a trail of mayhem, came the chewers of

Quarrelfudge, the lappers of Gloomwind, the brewers of Ginned Grin, the huffers of Rat Reckon, and the other pitchies besides.

The pell-mell careened out of the main square and down a street lined with shops and covered wagons. Doors blew from their hinges, windows smashed, and wagons exploded into the air as the throng poured down the street.

Fefferfew took the race eastward, turning at the first corner and barreling down the ring road. Then he bolted left down one of the tight passages that marked the Mayhemmed Narrows.

Suddenly, a high-pitched whistling came above their heads, followed by another, then another still. Three of Methulla's firebirds streaked up into the night sky and exploded. A great flash of light lit up the frenzied faces of the pitchies, gendarmes, drudges, and mortuants racing over the cobblestones as the shower of multi-colored twinkles fell back to the rooftops as ash.

Madrigan nudged the piece of Velveteen Cromide in his palm, nodding without listening to the man's concluding salutations. If he had paid attention, he would have heard the pitch dealer inform him, in no uncertain terms, how nice it was to see him again, how long it had been since their last transaction, and how pitiful Madrigan looked—that he should get some rest.

Madrigan had barely stepped off the rotten wooden step when the door slammed behind him. Madrigan didn't notice that either. His eyes were fixed firm on his piece of Velveteen Cromide, the anticipation of which was causing his forehead, upper lip, and palm to sweat.

Oh, my little dear. My dearie, dearie, dear. How I've missed you, old girl.

He stumbled, caught himself on the stone wall, and locked eyes with an old hag staring out the window above him. He flashed her a gummy, toothless smile.

Now, promise me, my little dearie, when you enter my veins you won't take umbrage at the foggy residue left behind by that horrid, nasty Shivery Coffinfit.

He startled at a whistle and looked up as a streaking Methulla firebird gained purchase in the sky.

Miserable stuff it was, my little dear. Horrible stuff. Made you doubt your senses. Not really pitch at all, if I'm honest. Thought I might never get out of it. But you'd never treat me like that, would you, old girl?

In the bright light cast by the explosion of the Methulla bird above him, he noticed something on the Velveteen Cromide: a little wiggle. He leaned in closer and prodded the wiggle with his finger. A weevil emerged from the little cube, and the Velveteen Cromide crumbled into dust in its wake. He tossed the weevil and dust aside and pounded on the door like a drunk. "Ket!" he screamed. "You've sold me a fetching."

A window above him slid open and Ket's grinning face came into the moonlight. "And you, my dear Madrigan, turned your back on old Ket, didn't you? Turned your back on all of us here in the Mayhemmed Narrows." This brought the shadowy jawlines of a dozen onlookers into the windows above them.

"Don't think I didn't hear," Ket continued. "You went to that Crummock bastard, didn't you? Well, consider this a punishment. Maybe now you'll think twice before going behind Ket's back." With that he slammed the window shut.

Madrigan gave another bang on the door, but it was a feeble effort. The pitch roil he'd fought off the entire time he'd slunk through the Mayhemmed Narrows, that he'd held at bay as he'd smiled at Ket and held out his coin, could no longer be ignored. His hands quivered and his vision narrowed. He leaned his head against the door, fighting for a clean breath of air.

Probably for the best. It's probably for the bloody best.

He brought his hands before his eyes.

You don't need it, Madrigan. You don't need any of it. It's just making you dumber and sicker.

He wiped the snot from his nose and gave a nod to the alleyway. He could hear the grinding of the vertebrae in his neck now.

Look what it's done to you. You're as filthy as a barn. Not a coin to your name. Elise wouldn't touch you now for all the gold in Harodim's Wish. And for what? To spin a bit of Velveteen Cromide? To chase after that Shivery Coffinfit? You should be ashamed.

A vision of his last spin of Shivery Coffinfit flashed before his eyes: the old overgrown bars of the crypt, the discordant music, the scent of perfume, the red claws bursting from the ground, and Rothesay grinning down at him haloed in the moonlight. He looked down at his fingertips and shook his head.

No. It wasn't real. It was an illusion, you stupid pitchie. A nasty dream. You need to pull yourself up by your britches, lad. You need to dust yourself off.

He slapped the dirt from his thighs. But the act was futile; if anything, it set the dirt even deeper into the weave.

You were a tutor's signature away from the gates of the Lyceum, for god's sake. A proper education. A proper station in this world. You could have been a magistrate, if you'd wanted.

The thought drew him down the alley on shaky legs.

You might have been a gendarme.

He chuckled at that as he stumbled.

You might have been a poet or a scribe, if you'd wanted. You can spin a pretty word now and then. And you can lie. You're a rank virtuoso when it comes to lies. You could've had any of that. Instead you picked the pitch.

He clung to the stone wall. It was all that kept him on his feet now as he pulled himself farther down the alley.

Right, it's decided then. You're kicking this pitch, Madrigan, old boy. You're kicking the pitch. Or, so help me, you'll die trying.

Just then a noise at the end of the alley shook him from his reverie.

Here. Now. Tonight. You begin your new life. Madrigan, old boy, you are leaving that pitch behi–

Fefferfew suddenly ran past him, leaving great chugging clouds of green gas in his wake. As Madrigan looked on in amazement, he saw the silhouette of Mulloch Furdie inside that old dog throwing down a giant lever.

"Mulloch?" Madrigan whispered.

"Madrigan!" Mulloch left the lever. Gears above his head whizzed freely, and great belches of green smoke filled the air. Mulloch slapped his hands against Fefferfew's belly and grinned.

"You needn't worry, Madrigan. I don't need you anymore, little pitchie. For I am the verge of it."

"The verge of what?" Madrigan called after him.

"Shivery Coffinfit, you little worm. *Shivery Coffinfit!*" Mulloch screamed as the dog slipped away into the darkness.

Madrigan drew back into the shadows and leaned against the wall. His heart pounded like a hammer in his chest.

Let him rot. This isn't your business anymore. You've kicked this foul pitch. There's nothing good that can come from him. Just let him go.

Madrigan ventured out from the shadows and watched as Fefferfew's glow disappeared.

Now you just put one foot in front of the other, nice and gently now. You just walk straight down that alley, find a warm corner of the square to curl up in, and you let this pitch roil run its course. You'll wake up the morrow all the better for it. To start a new day, Madrigan, old boy. A clean, clear new day. Free of all temptation.

It was then the great clattering sound came to Madrigan's ears. He looked up. The faces in the windows withdrew. He clawed forward, pushed himself proud of the alley, and looked down the street. His jaw fell slack.

Nyqueed and Rothesay appeared from out of the darkness, their boots clumping madly over the cobblestones, their faces stretched with worry, their brows wet with sweat. Nyqueed caught the glint of light off Madrigan's face instantly.

"What are you doing, you fool? They're coming. *Run!*" he managed between huffs and puffs.

"Who? Who's coming?" Madrigan said, but Rothesay and Nyqueed whizzed past him.

He ventured farther into the street and spun around. Were it not for the pitch roil boiling in his blood, he would have frozen in his tracks. As it was, he could only whimper "By the gods."

The clanging of the tin cups of the Ginned Grinners led the fray. Behind them were the shirtless bodies of the growers of Speckled Frommorrow. They were followed by the huffers of Rat Reckon and the lappers of Gloomwind running with their heads and necks lost in their clouds. And in the front of the mass, crouched like crabs, shrieking and screaming, rushed the chewers of Quarrelfudge.

Madrigan stumbled back. "But I'm kicking the pitch," he whispered. "*I'm kicking the pitch!*"

His stumble quickly transformed itself into a head-long dash. The ends of his robes bundled in his hands, he caught up to Rothesay and Nyqueed. He turned back and watched a huffer of Rat Reckon claw past a chewer of Quarrelfudge.

"Oh, this is a grim twist of fate, this is," Madrigan cried, his voice trembling like a jolted saucer. "Have the gods no pity?"

They careened down the street, punctuating the silence with their heavy breathing, all the while keeping the old, mangy dog in their sights. Fefferfew bolted down an alleyway and slipped through a door revealing a slant of flickering candlelight.

Skidding on the dewy cobblestones and clawing at the walls of the alleyway to keep themselves upright, the trio dashed through the door. They entered a foyer with a simple wooden desk upon which lay a candle and a chisel. Behind the desk was an ornamental arch with a fine dusting of white powder and rubble on the floor beneath it. The room beyond the arch was lost in shadow.

Nyqueed fell against the desk, gasping for air, rattling the chisel where it lay. Rothesay reached back, slammed the door closed, and locked it; the key snapped off in the lock. Nyqueed pointed to the trail of paw prints leading through the dust into the room beyond the arch, then—*thump, thump, thump*—three impacts shook the door. Rothesay stood back.

"You. Me. Them," hissed the rapid-fire voice of a huffer of Rat Reckon. "Rothesay? No sea I've known. And then the other. But why bother? And then us. And then a simple crust. And a simple crust leads to must. And from must we wiggle past to last. The last is *you*. Yes, you too!"

A brilliant flash of light from a Methulla firebird burst outside the windows beyond the arch. It bathed them in a strobe of light. In that brief flash, they saw a marble statue in the corner of the little antechamber. A clear likeness of Civiak towered above them, his long tongue stretching down to his midriff, his right hand holding a crown.

Another explosion of light flooded the room, followed immediately by another. The first flash: the statue of the Civiak had moved. It was through the arch. The second flash: the statue was gone.

Rothesay nodded to the room beyond the arch and readied his dagger.

~

Vyren fell to his knees in the rubble of Bragnal's statue. All around him was turmoil. Priests and acolytes, men and women, monks and shamans, ran from the dozens of blazes overtaking the square. But he was singularly focused on the little egg he held in his palm.

Lumsden saw it all. He'd reached the end of the square and was about to surge down the adjoining street after Fefferfew when he'd chanced to look back.

"Vyren, no! Don't do it, you fool!" he yelled.

"You *would* say that, wouldn't you, Lumsden?" Vyren screamed.

"Stuck in your old, pathetic ways." He held up the piece of Shivery Coffinfit.

"Don't be a fool, Vyren. Leave it alone!"

"Why are you not sick of it all?" Vyren spoke pleadingly. He pointed back to the staircase leading up the Quardinal Rock. "Wallowing on the 13th Step like some… some sewer rat! Well, I'm sick of it!"

He beheld the Shivery Coffinfit with profound reverence. "I want to soar as high as Madrigan. Over the tops of mountains. I want to blossom in the dahlias. I want to twist down the drain into the middle of the sea." He lowered the egg and locked eyes with Lumsden. "As you did once. Don't deny it. Before you became old and tired and broken, there was a time when you reached for it. I've heard the stories, Lumsden. It's no use denying."

"Then trust me, Vyren. That way lies madness," Lumsden bellowed. He was buffeted by a surge in the crowd.

"Liar!" Vyren presented the egg again. "Liar." He threw back his head and dropped it into his gaping mouth.

Lumsden fought the last of the throng and fell to his knees beside Vyren. He jammed his fingers into the young pitchie's mouth, struggling to find the Shivery Coffinfit and rip it free. Vyren mounted no defence.

"By the gods, Lumsden…" he whispered.

"Don't look at them, boy!"

Vyren's body jolted, and he would have fallen if Lumsden weren't holding him. The pitchie drew his hands before his eyes. His skin was turning translucent. Jagged rocks coursed in his hands and disappeared up his arms, like pebbles tumbling along a mountain stream. Vyren lifted one of his hands and pointed to the king's palace on the far side of the city.

Lumsden followed his gaze, steeled himself a moment, then leaned in to whisper.

"You need to understand something, boy. You'll die for this vision."

Vyren marshaled all his strength to turn his head and look at Lumsden. "I–I don't want to die," he cried.

"No. No, I don't believe you do. And by all accounts you shouldn't. But that's not the tale of the world, is it? You can't be faulted, boy. There's no hunger greater in our hearts than curiosity. And those sculptors know it. They use it against us."

Vyren fell forward onto his hands and knees. His arms buckled, and he crumbled downward an inch. A thin stream of white powder seeped from between his fingers.

"W-what's happening to me?"

"Your bones are beginning to fade, son, taking from you hope of running or fighting. Next you'll be taken by rot, aimed for your vitals. Your lungs'll harden like baked clay. Cuz the sculptors want you breathless when you look upon them."

Vyren retched. Rock dust and rubble fell from his mouth, landing on the powdered bone.

"You don't have much time, boy."

"Time?" Vyren whimpered. "Time for what? By the gods, Lumsden, make it stop." A steady flow of rubble out of his mouth impeded further words.

"You'll see them, boy, whether you want to or not. There's no turning back now. You've made your choice. You're about to look upon what few mortals ever get the chance to look upon. Few gods, even"

The bottom of Vyren's eyes began to fizz as if the blood and juices in his cheeks were coming to a raging boil.

"Aye, they're preparing your eyes now. Covering them with what's left of your spine." Lumsden drew closer to Vyren, whose eyes were fixed on the distant palace.

"Do you see them?" he whispered.

Vyren tried to lift his head, but his skull was suffering now like the bones in his arms. A long cut appeared down his forehead, and powder poured from the fissure. With it came a grotesque deflation.

"Where are they, Vyren? Which room? Where, boy? *Answer me!*" Lumsden looked down at the ailing man struggling for breath, eyes brimming with tears and wide with fear, and his heart broke.

"Forgive me, boy. Forgive me. You have moments left. And those moments should be used to look upon them as you see fit, not tracing a map for an old, sick pitchie. Go on, boy. Look upon them. Look upon the Blackened Nevers."

Vyren's eyes widened; he extended the obliterated, rotten stump of his arm up toward the palace in the distance when he was suddenly knocked sideways by someone in the rushing crowd. A blacksmith staggered, regained his footing, and continued his race from the square. Lumsden, though, was hurt and winded. He could manage little more than to turn his head as he lay ailing on the cobblestones.

The rot had reached Vyren's chest. His skin scrolled like a battered birch tree, and the bones of his rib cage spilled freely from the gaps. The vicious mechanism then overcame him entirely. What was left of his shell disintegrated, and the remnants blew off in the wind. The dying pitchie's dust mixed with the melted ice, blood, and ash in the square and was carried off on the soles of sandals and boots.

CHAPTER 29

THE POOLS OF DEATH'S RAIN

THE RUSTLE OF the tiny mouse woke Balkan. He opened his eyes to see the rodent seize upon a seed of wild barley. It turned the seed over and scoured it with its teeth.

Balkan was on his side, one arm bent behind him, one up and over his head. His cloak had split down the center. His belt had broken and his pouch was ripped, its contents scattered like a letter torn into pieces.

He groaned. His lungs felt as if they'd fallen out and filled with water, and he was dragging them behind his back. His joints and muscles and bones seemed to call out in a chorus of pain. He closed his eyes, looking for relief in the darkness.

The mouse threw down the husk of the seed and picked up another. Its nose quivered as it sniffed the air. The sounds of the forest took on outsized dimension. Every snap of a twig, beat of a wing, and buzz of an insect insisted on Balkan's attention. Above it all was the sound of the mouse razing its barley seed.

He retched and struggled not to dip into unconsciousness when the sounds stopped. It forced his eyes open again. The mouse was gone. Only the spent barley shell remained.

A wet heavy *thump* like a sack of potatoes thrown from a cart sounded behind him. Then came another and another.

He scanned the sideways world he occupied. Down by his feet he caught the eyes of the little Rowlach girl. She was sat up, hugging her knees to her chest, rocking back and forth. Her cowl was pulled over her head, and he could just make out her lips moving silently.

I can't hear you.

She wiped away the tears streaming down her cheeks and resumed her whispers.

Damn you, girl. Now you speak? I can't hear you!

A plume of leaves and dust lit up into the forest air behind her.

Behind you, girl.

Another mass of twigs and leaves flew up, spinning in flight. Another impact. Then another. Debris fluttered all around him.

Then a noise exploded directly above him, like a heavy clap to the ear, muffling the air, deadening sound for a moment. The resonance stoked the pain in his wounds and brought the agony back.

He couldn't turn his head, but he sensed that whatever sack or stone that had landed had landed on top of him. Yet he felt no impact. He tried to see what was falling, but the pain was too intense.

Back to the girl: her eyes were closed. The whispers still tumbled out of her mouth, but Balkan could not hear what she said.

Suddenly a body, broken and lifeless, landed beside the girl. Then another, its arms thrown up from the thundering impact like a rag doll's. She didn't notice. She was utterly absorbed in her trance, rocking back and forth.

Then, with the crushing impact of a hammer on a rotten plank, a body crashed onto the forest floor between Balkan and the girl, throwing off limbs and gore.

Balkan choked and struggled for breath as the broken corpse of a Rowlach woman, her throat slit and oozing blood, stared back at him, as the forest detritus settled back to the earth.

Another thump; another Rowlach body. This time a child, tears still wet on its cheeks, blood streaming down its forehead from a deep gash.

The sounds of impact came faster now. Debris seemed to blast like cannon shot on a battlefield. Clouds of soil ejected from the ground became a veritable tempest. Rowlach men were torn in half on impact, splitting at the chasm left by the killing stroke. Heads cracked, necks and spines bent and twisted, snapping like twigs. Balkan tried to close his eyes, but the reverberation of the impacts wrenched them open again and again.

Another *boom* sounded above. The body of an old Rowlach woman, armless and bent back upon itself, slid down off him. But he felt nothing. No sense of her on top of him, no pressure, no strain. As her broken face slowly sank away, he saw her deep-set eyes and pointed jaw frozen in a gasp of agony. Was there recognition in those eyes?

She slid closer the ground. Her eyes seemed to ask, *Why did you not save me? Why did you not save us?*

He tried to scream but produced only a pitiable whisper as the woman's mangled body slipped off him to pile among the rest of the ruined Rowlach. Wherever his gaze settled, he saw the face of a Rowlach man, woman, or child. Were they his family? Was that his cousin, his uncle, his sister, his brother? They all seemed to plead their case.

Why are they staring at me? Do they think I did this? Do they think I'm to blame?

His gaze returned to the girl. Like him, she was free of the falling mass, like an island in the midst of the broken flesh.

I must be dead. That's it. I'm in hell, aren't I, Kynon? He fixed his gaze on the girl again. *And this is all her fault.*

The body of a young boy added to the wall of corpses that had grown between them. It blocked Balkan's view of the girl. He shut his eyes as the bodies of his brethren, like chopped limbs of a dead tree, piled up in heaps around him. And he heard nothing. Not a sound from the world. No refrain for the loss, not a whimper, not a tear. Nothing.

Finally, mercifully, weak and exhausted from his sobbing, Balkan lost consciousness in the leaves, dust, blood, and dirt of that forest killing floor.

ꟹ

Balkan struggled to his knees beside the river. He cupped his hand and drew some water. The sun was beginning to set over the horizon. The trunks and branches of the thick, looming forest at the top of the riverbank filtered its light, as if a tiny child had scribbled over the sun with a piece of charcoal.

He took some water in his mouth and washed some over his face. He spit out some debris. It landed on the surface of the river, puncturing his reflection with ripples.

Well? Are you going to show yourself, Kynon? Or do you leave your dead to wander hell alone?

He got to his feet slowly and painfully and limped back to the rough shelter. The girl was sitting cross-legged before a tiny fire, more smoke than flame. Around her were pieces of rusted armor, straw mats, broken pottery, fabric and furs, all blackened by flame, dirt, or blood. He couldn't remember who had made the shelter. Maybe he had; maybe she had. They must have worked in silence, because he didn't remember anything being said. He knew only that sometime, somehow, the rain and wind had stopped beating him while he slept.

He sat down, stifling a groan. The girl held out a hollowed log. Steam escaped from a knot in the rough vessel. "Drink this. It will help your back."

Were these the first words between them? He couldn't remember. She read the reluctance in his eyes as she wiped her hair from her face. "It's called bruaichean."

"Is it?" Balkan snatched the vessel from her hand. "And who is it that calls it bruaichean?"

"The Rowlach."

"The Rowlach are dead, girl." He took a sip of the drink. "As are we."

"Then *we* will call it bruaichean." She picked up a small wooden carving from the pile beside her. "Even if we're dead."

"Even if?" Balkan replied incredulously. "We fell from the Khallin Cliff, girl. Do you think we can just stand up, dust ourselves off, and walk away?" He took another sip of the drink and stuck out his tongue.

"We aren't dead, Balkan. I saved us."

He chuckled. "Did you, now? And how about the others?" He nodded toward the bodies before taking another sip. "Were those ones not worth saving?" Balkan registered the drink's foul flavour again.

"I tried." The girl looked away to hide her tears. "But it was too hard."

"Was it, now?" Balkan nodded, unconvinced. He took another sip of the drink. To her credit, it did seem to help.

He took in the serene river. The light of the setting sun was twinkling on its gently rushing water. "Who are you, girl, anyway?" he asked.

"I'm Fignith of the Rowlach, daughter of Machlamorrinn." There was that word again.

"Why do you say it so often?" Balkan menaced.

"Say what?"

"Rowlach. What a pitiable word that is."

"Because that's what we are." She cradled the little statue to her chest.

"That's what we *were*, girl. Look about you. The Rowlach are gone and so are we. And more's the better for it." He cheersed with the log. "So ends the pitiful existence of the Rowlach. A people so horrible even their own god hated them." He finished the strange brew and tossed aside the hollowed log.

"We're not dead. And Krynon does not hate us." She held out the little statue. It had been carved into the shape of a tall, thin man hunched over and holding his knees. The deep-set eyes and thin limbs of the sculpture took on the glow of the fire.

"Does he not?" Balkan wiped his hands and turned to Fignith. "You see, child, I've done a fair bit of reading on our little Kynon. Is it not the case that the Rowlach believe that Kynon holds his hand out to the departed to lift them from the stream of death?"

Fignith nodded.

"Well, now." Balkan waved his hand over the riverbank. "I look around and, I don't know about you, I don't see any gesture from our god. Where is Kynon, hmm? Do you see him? No, of course you don't. Because he's turned his back on us. If we had any sense, we'd scamper through hell telling everyone we followed Mag or Methulla. Maybe then we'd get some service from the gods."

"What do you know?" Fignith replied angrily. "You don't even know the name of your people's god."

"Kynon is his name, you little wench!"

Fignith laughed. "It's Krynon, you fool. *Kry... non.* No wonder he doesn't hear you."

Balkan covered the space between them in a flash. Scattering the totem of Krynon, he knocked Fignith to the ground and slapped her hands away from her face.

"Are you mocking me?" he roared. "If you are, girl, I swear—I swear to Kynon or Krynon or whatever bastard god listens to us Rowlach—I will tear that tongue of yours out of your mouth and stake it to a tree."

Fignith slipped out his grasp and slid away from him. Tears welled up in her eyes. She grabbed a rock and held it up as a threat. It was enough. He recognized the fear he'd produced in the girl.

"I'm sorry, Fignith," he whispered. "I should never have done that. I'm sorry." He offered his hand to comfort her, but she shrank back.

"You're just like all the others," she sobbed as she ran away up the banks of the river toward the field of dead bodies.

Balkan shook his head as he watched her run. *Not only am I in hell, but now I find I'm the demon in it.*

He turned back to the fire. All was silent now save the hiss of smoke from the logs and the faint echoing of Fignith's sobs in the distance.

Bah! Let her cry. If only she'd said what I told them to say. Was it that hard? The court would have listened. None of this would have happened.

The sun was almost set. The bellies of the clouds were lit up with burgundy and ochre, saffron and amber. Balkan chortled as he took it in.

Maybe we aren't dead. You wouldn't be that big a bastard, would you, Krynon? To tease me with such beauty in hell?

A scream suddenly punctured his reverie. He pushed his broken body up from the forest floor and hobbled to the end of the rough shelter. "Fignith?"

She screamed again. It focused his vision. The stream had broken its banks. Like a rudimentary arm, the river bulged and surged over the mossy forest floor. It enveloped three broken Rowlach bodies, lifted them free, and took them into motion. They slid down to the river in its grasp.

Balkan stumbled to Fignith and offered an embrace. She pulled back in fear and this roused his anger.

"What did you do?" he barked. "It was that pig's bile you made me, wasn't it, you witch?" He grabbed his forehead. "You've poisoned me, haven't you?"

"I didn't do anything!"

Balkan's attention was taken by a *whoosh*. He turned to the river. The bodies had come to the surface, rising calmly and evenly. A tiny vortex appeared ahead of them. It turned the bodies in the water, pointing them head first into the flow.

Balkan hobbled to the riverbank, following the bodies as they coursed by. In the distance he saw that the stream narrowed. No vegetation grew in this part of the water. A large rock, smooth and perfectly convex, was submerged just enough that the river tumbled over it easily. The center of it, at the very point of its convex shape, was a brilliant brown circle, wide as a man's torso, speckled with green and blue.

Mud and rocks gave way under his foot as he stumbled toward it. He jumped back as a portion of the bank fell into the water. It didn't go unnoticed.

The colored center of the rock darted in the direction of the noise. Quivering madly for a few moments, the circle came back to the center and constricted as the first Rowlach body flowed over it. It darted over the length of the corpse, dilating and constricting as it worked, taking in every dimension, every nuance, every feature—the length and breadth of the broken bodies—but saving its closest study for their faces.

"We are truly in hell," Balkan whispered as he looked on in horror.

Fignith screamed again. Balkan dithered, his focus torn. He finally wrenched his attention away from the giant eye. The river was pulsing again, forming its limb of liquid up, out, and onto the bank to sink five more dead Rowlach.

Balkan ran to Fignith. Each stared transfixed at the procession of dead washing over the giant iris. Another surge of water pulled another set from the killing floor.

"What is this, girl?" Balkan said. "Who is it looking for?"

His words carried. The eye darted to the very limit of its sight and stared at them until another dead and mangled Rowlach body floated over it, and it began its examination again. No sooner was the body gone than the giant eye returned to watching their every move. Balkan drew Fignith back and pointed to the thick, dark forest ahead.

"But what about our things… our people?" she whimpered. She looked back at their rough shelter being engulfed in a branch of water.

Balkan locked eyes with the eye of the stream. "Let them go," he whispered.

The eye resumed its examinations as Fignith pulled Balkan in retreat. He didn't fight it, but neither did he submit. It was only when the thick vines and brambles of Bedlam's Thicket crowded out the horrid scene did Balkan finally look away. He took her little hand in his, and they ran into the folds of that dark forest.

CHAPTER 30
THE DAZZLING DUST OF THE GUDFIN

IT WAS MIDNIGHT before Phae and Chim reached the square in the middle of Sefton Skene. The translucent dome above them brought the moonlight into the belly of the mountain. It provided contour to the buildings lining the square that would otherwise have been buried in darkness. That same moonlight fell over Chim's face as he poked his head out from the shadows to see if they'd been followed.

"No one's there," Phae whispered. "Stop worrying."

I almost wish someone would find us.

The interaction with the gang played out in his mind. He winced at the memory: the squishy, hollow thuds, the sound of blood dripping onto the cobblestones, the ecstasy of Guindon when he stood up from his work.

He seemed to enjoy it.

Chim reached into his satchel and probed for the burlap wrapping. He found it and pressed the tip of the dagger into his finger as hard as he could.

I don't feel anything special. Nothing but pain. Why would anyone want more of that? He drew his hand out and looked at the red dot of blood. *Maybe it's different when you're kicking and stabbing someone else?* He put his finger in his mouth to dull the pain.

Phae was rifling through her own bag. She whistled as she worked, sending quills and parchment, cloth and tiny leather pouches up the wall of the bag.

"Would you be quiet," Chim whispered. She glared at him and whistled even louder.

In the middle of the square, bursting through the cobblestones, was the Gudfin. It stood forty feet high and fifty feet wide. It bent and torqued and tapered toward a summit that reached another twenty feet toward the dome above and the night sky beyond. It was the tallest thing Chim had ever seen. It seemed to him that if someone could climb to the tip of the Gudfin, and if they could reach through the translucent rock, they'd be able to step onto the twinkling constellations themselves.

At the base, on either side of the sloping path that led up the Gudfin Mountain, were two ornate copper lamps burning with blue flame. The path was sunk deep into the rock, creating walls from the mountain as it zigzagged toward the summit.

Phae fixed the latch of her bag and caught Chim taking in the mountain. "How odd. Truly, how bizarre. Correct me if I'm wrong, Chim, but I seem to remember reading somewhere that when the Gudfin blade is removed, the Gudfin is supposed to"—her voice changed as she began to recite from memory—"'split and sunder, to grit and sevens, as the axes of Aris, fall from the heavens.'"

She shot him a devilish grin. "Seems quite intact to me. Unless, of course, what I read was a bald-faced lie."

"Come on," Chim said. He walked out from the shadows and into the square. As he went, he half hoped his little sister would be consumed in the darkness. He pictured a set of gaping jaws slithering out of a doorway, creeping up behind her, and swallowing her whole.

But the soft sounds of her shoes over the cobblestones dashed his wicked vision.

They moved silently, ignoring each other, and soon reached the tiny stone wall that formed a perimeter around the base of the Gudfin Mountain. Chim climbed up the wall and dangled his feet over it. He lowered a foot tentatively, as though testing ice on a lake.

"What's wrong, brother? You look like a brae that's never touched the Gudfin rock." Phae jumped off the wall and ran on.

Chim held his breath. *This is it. There's no turning back now.*

He jumped and quickly discovered that the rock was as firm as any other. He hit his stride again and caught up to Phae at the base of the Gudfin. In the light of the blue lamps, Chim could see the recessed path clearly now. It was covered in white iridescent dust. The downy powder was suspended in the air above the path as well. It shimmered in the blue light but disappeared beyond its illumination. It was as though Chim stood inside the drink his mother made him when he was sick, freshly stirred and gritty.

As Phae made for the path Chim reached out and grabbed her arm. "*Arinestric nu estric nesim coll.*" He held her in place as he made the invocation.

She tugged her arm away from him angrily. "Really?" She rubbed her elbow. "You're going to recite it?"

"Yes," Chim said irritably. "Every one."

"Even the Midden, for god's sake?"

"Well, what is it without the Midden?"

"What is it *with* the Midden? That babble is complete nonsense. They teach it to brae in the nurseries to keep them from eating paste." She examined her elbow. "It's a waste of time."

"You don't even know what the benedictions say, so what do you know?" Chim's parry was enough to cool her fires.

He got down on one knee. It brought a tiny cloud of the white dust swirling around him. He touched the path, and the dust beneath his hand dissolved to the black scabrous veneer of the rock.

"*Arinestric nu estric nesim coll,*" he said under his breath.

As he withdrew his hand and stood up, the path regained its brilliant white lustre.

"I've been thinking about wastes of time, Phae. I think you're quite good at them. I bet you know this isn't the Gudfin blade you took, after all. I think you've just made this all up. You're enjoying this wild goose chase."

Phae's eyes narrowed. In the harsh glow of the blue lamp, her brother seemed almost a ghost. Its light robbed him of his vitality and vigor. His cheeks sank into shadows; his eyes retreated into pits. "Maybe it *isn't* the Gudfin blade," she replied impishly.

He snorted at his sister's callousness and shook his head. "What broke you into these awful pieces, Phae Wiscum?" He took his Gudfin Talen from his bag. The metal band, no bigger than his palm, was composed of a series of concentric rings made of flattened copper all linked to a dial in the middle. As he turned it, the rings of copper moved, and the various symbols etched into them came into alignment at the crown of the ring.

"You know exactly what it was," she spat. She held her elbow tight to her chest. It made her look vulnerable and wounded.

"Right. And so we all get to suffer?" Chim turned the dial one last click and held the Talen out toward the path like a surveyor taking a measurement.

"Yes, we all get to suffer."

They each went quiet as they fumed over the other's words. Before long, in the distance, the sound of a tavern door opening and its patrons spilling out into the street broke their silence.

"Sounds like we had better make haste, Chim. Wouldn't want anyone to find the Gudfin thief standing here with the Gudfin blade, would we?"

"No, I think you're right." Chim looked back toward the noise.

"So I suggest, if we don't want to waste any more time, you should stop your silly, childish benedictions and get to the task at hand. This is a path. We have feet. Let's use them!"

"Silly benedictions? Really? How would you even know? You don't even know what they mean. You don't even know what you're looking at."

"Don't be so sure, Chim Wiscum. You might know your blessed benedictions, but I've been up the Gudfin before, remember? And I learned a thing or two when I was there."

"Did you?"

"Yes, I did. And trust me, you don't want to hear what I learned."

"'Said the blight and darkness to the light and life,'" Chim whispered, reciting his favorite phrase.

"This is the Thoise," Phae said, blunt as a rock. She pointed back to the white path.

"So you know the Thoise." Chim crossed his arms. "And?"

"And? And what? I don't owe it any reverence if that's what you're expecting. It's a path. Up a hill."

Chim snorted. "A path up a hill?" He shook his head. "Don't worry, Phae. I don't expect any reverence from the likes of you."

"I told you not to press me, Chim."

Had Chim looked up he might have seen the tears welling in her eyes.

"Said the blight and darkness," Chim muttered under his breath. But Phae had heard the words.

"Fine!" She raced onto the path, turning the white dust into tiny mushroom clouds under her feet, and put her hands on the powdery wall.

"Look, Chim! This is *ash*, you fool. You can smell it. It's what's left over when a world burns. And that's exactly what Aris did. He raised up the Gudfin and burned it because he wanted to win the race so badly. He burned it before, and he's burning it again. And what I did has nothing to do with it!"

"And who told you that, Phae? Agajin, that mealy-mouthed little muhk?" He could see in her eyes that he was right. "Agajin Hiscum is a blasphemous fool. You'd risk waking the Gudfin—the destruction of everything we've ever known and loved—on the word of a damned fool?"

Phae blushed and looked away. Chim stowed his Talen and walked onto the path, joining her at the wall.

"Even a moment's thought can detect that he's wrong. No ash is this brilliant, this white. Look at it!" He rubbed the powder between his fingers and held it up to her. Phae tried to look away, but Chim stepped into her gaze.

"I camped when I went outwide. No fire left anything like this in the morning." He dusted off his hands. "And I'm the deluded one?"

Doubt flashed in Phae's eyes. And, as he had always done in the face of his sister's vulnerability, Chim relented.

"This isn't Aris's fire," he said softly. "This is his trove. It's the stuff of creation. Pure, clean, and whole. It's what we came from." His voice trailed off to a whisper as his eyes followed the path to the next corner. "And it's what we're about to lose if we let the Gudfin rise." He tried to measure his next words. "You'd know that if you had any reverence or respect for Aris."

"Reverence? Respect?" Her anger flared again. "Where was that for me?"

It was Chim's turn to avoid her gaze. A silence fell over them as if a bucket of cold water had tipped over their heads. Phae began to laugh. She pressed herself off the wall and walked backwards up the path, away from her brother.

"And how do you know any of this, hmm? I've been up this path before. I'm the Gudfin thief, remember?" She pointed to Chim's satchel. "Have you?"

The flush of color that came to Chim's cheeks was enough for Phae. Glee came into her voice. "Hah! Who's the blind fool now, Chim? You've been lied to, brother! But, of course, how would you even know? This humble, meek lamb of Aris hasn't even visited his temple!"

"Nonsense."

"We're not wasting our time here, Chim, not tonight. No. It seems one of us has been *wasting their whole life!*"

Chim fumbled with his Talen, trying to ignore her. But his sister's jabs dislodged the benedictions from his mind. His lip quivered; his concentration shattered. The words came out in waves of disjointedness.

"There are secrets on this mountain, Chim. I've heard them. I've seen the truth. It will shake you to your core. And the first is that Aris does not love us."

Phae crept farther away. "He watched as the world burned, all for his own advantage in the race." She reached the first corner of the path. "And by all that's right," she said, grabbing onto the rock wall, "we should burn again."

She darted around the corner, her laughter at him muffled now by the wall of the Gudfin path.

A vicious rage came over Chim Wiscum. He took the rest of the path in haste, spilling his benedictions and prayers as he ran, bent on visiting on his sister an anger that would have shaken Aris's temple to its foundations.

CHAPTER 31
A MAN FOR ALL SEASONS

MANION AWOKE. THE night had fallen, and the trail was silent. He watched the plumes of his breath drift up into the sky and stared at the stars. The river babbled quietly, and the reeds rustled in the wind.

A thrush landed beside him. As if the tiny bird carried a cord in its beak trailing back to the clouds, thick snow soon followed. The thrush took to the air and was lost from sight. Manion could no longer see his breath; the world had turned to white.

Methulla asked the fattened calf to take two breaths and give three back.

He strained to sit up. His head throbbed and his shoulder ached. His fingers felt wet and chalky. He worked them out and touched his face. Ice had formed around his nose and mouth and the sides of his eyes.

He stood up slowly; he teetered and fell back to the frozen ground. The images of what had happened crowded in on him: the merchant crumpled into a bloody mass, Verica, Cawthra's screams.

What have I done, Methulla? Lord, forgive me.

The wind whipped itself into a gust. The snow hit him horizontally now. He knew he had to move, and so he got to his feet, put a foot forward, and struggled to keep his balance as the storm's gales hit him flush. They seemed to want to push him back to Quardinal's Brawn, but he soon achieved a slow but steady pace, and so he walked.

He saw nothing but the endless snow rushing at him. But still he could sense that the surrounding forest had thickened and darkened. The bright moonlight above traveled on the backs of the snow flakes, illuminating them as they darted toward him. It gave Manion the impression he was moving through a cloud of tiny lights.

Like Calladen forging the Tarskavaig maul.

Soon the snowflakes were no longer cold to him. Nothing was. A warm glow had come over him, and his steps felt light. The snow no longer seemed to cut his skin. It felt soft and beautiful. Even the wound in his shoulder no longer throbbed.

The smells around him had changed too. He'd awoken to crisp river water, stone, dirt, and the scent of evergreen nettles. The snow that landed on his tongue and lips now seemed to taste of fresh bread and butter. The wind carried the smell of steaming potatoes, herbs, and dried firewood, as if it were all hidden somehow in the pockets and folds of the breeze.

He heard the thrush return. He could have sworn it circled above his head as if calling to him. He stretched his arm up toward it and felt a strange stillness on his fingers; nothing—no wind, no snow.

He walked a few more paces and again raised his arm. He could feel the stillness on his palm now. As he continued walking, more and more of his arm stretched clean of the blizzard. Soon the level of the snow fell to the top of his head, then to his eyebrows, and then below his eyes.

He blinked and rubbed the snow from them. He stared, his view unobstructed, into the night sky while the blizzard continued to run wild over the rest of his body. He could see nothing in it, nothing but the barrage of snow. It was as though he'd waded into a river.

But above this river, he could see a thick, tangled forest, overgrown with weeds and vines. Such a tangle he had never seen. In the distance, an old stone cottage stood with a thatched roof. He headed for it as the stream of blizzard fell to his chest, then to his navel.

By the time the storm ended at his thighs, he was standing before a young girl. She sat on a wooden bench in the garden of the cottage. In one hand she held a bouquet of dead dandelions. With the other, she brought one of the flowers to her mouth and blew. The white seeds burst out into the night as snow, swirling and diving in the air. By her feet was a gathering basket filled with more cut dead flowers.

"Georwrith! I haven't set eyes on you girl since–" A blade of pain suddenly pierced Manion's temple. He fell to his knees in agony, engulfed in the storm again. It might as well have scoured the rest of the memory from him for when he struggled back to his feet, all was confusion.

"W-who are you?" he whispered, holding his head in his hands.

"I am Georwrith, of course." She drew another flower from the bunch and blew the seeds into the air to feed the storm. "Don't you remember?"

"Child, I don't know who you are. But I need your help. I am hurt. I have walked for miles in the cold. I–I fear I'm dying."

"And what is the matter with dying? I think dying is beautiful. Do you not want me to take my turn?" She blew on another seed head.

"Your turn?" Manion frowned. "Girl, I need your help, damn it."

"My help? I'm no fool, Manion. I know for whose help you've come. He's inside. Father has just now retired to sleep. He's finished punishing him for his last escape. Take him. Father won't notice. And none of us will care." She blew again on her flower.

Manion grimaced; his strength was failing him. His shoulder ached, and he could feel the blood pulsing from the wound beneath his leather vest. The cottage was his only chance now, and so he stumbled off toward it. The little girl watched him leave. She then calmly reached down, took another dead flower, and blew more of the blizzard into the night sky.

ꟹ

Manion banged on the wooden door. It cracked open and another young girl peered out at him. She wore a dark-green dress cinched at the waist by a brown-leather belt. She had red hair and her face was pocked with freckles. The girl looked back into the house then ran from the door. As she did, tiny freckles fell from her skin.

Manion pushed the door open. Three children huddled against a wooden pillar. Manion tumbled inside and caught himself on a chair.

"*Shhh!*" the tallest girl whispered. "Father's sleeping."

"Please," Manion said. "I've been wounded. Please help me."

The tall girl bolted from the pillar and shut the door. She rounded back on him and tutted as she saw the red stain on his vest. "You need healing." Her words were not a question nor a statement, but a type of condemnation.

"Yes, dear. Please…"

"Well, who are you?"

The youngest of the three girls ran to her sister and wrapped herself in her dress. She peeked out to inspect the stranger.

"I'm Manion. Of the King's Watch in Quardinal's Brawn."

"I heard that's a filthy nest," the girl with the freckles whispered. "Filled with filthy mortua–" Her sisters turned and glared at her before she could finish the word.

"I'm f-formally a white knight of Methulla," Manion said through a grimace.

"You don't look like a knight," the tallest girl said.

"It was a long time ago, b-before you were born."

"No, I remember the knights," she said.

"So do I," said the girl who'd answered the door.

"Me too," came an insistent voice from inside her sister's dress.

"You are all very young to recall such a time," Manion said as another bout of pain hit him. He collapsed into the chair. "I–I feel as if… I no longer remember it myself." He dropped his head into his hands. "What has happened to me?" he whispered.

"You'll be needing Yaarach," the tallest of them said.

"Sowrug!" Yaarach said from the folds of her sister's dress, looking up to chastise her sister. Sowrug drew the little girl from her dress and lifted her chin.

"Show him your hedgehog, my little blue bud."

Yaarach gave Manion a wary glance and stayed fixed where she stood.

"Please, little Yaarach, my love. Please help me," Manion whispered.

The little girl looked around the room with one thumb in her mouth then bounded over to Manion and crashed against him. The old knight grimaced.

"I'm Yaarach," she said sweetly.

"Hello, Yaarach. I'm Manion. And I'm sorry, my child, but I'm… I'm gravely ill." He pulled the collar of his leather vest away to reveal his wound.

"Ouch! Does it hurt?"

"It does, my love. Your parents, are they—?"

"I have a pet hedgehog. Would you like to see it?" Yaarach ran over to a wicker basket in the corner of the room. She drew something from it, which she cradled in her arms. She rushed back to Manion and held it up.

"He's been sleeping. I woke him up. I wake them all up." She stroked the hedgehog's head. "The skunks are the sleepiest." She wrinkled her nose and frowned.

"My child, please, some water and a bandage. I feel light-headed and sick. And I'm so cold."

"That's because of Georwrith. She does that to everyone." Yaarach nestled her face into the hedgehog's belly.

"Yaarach, what do you do with the little peas?" Sowrug said over her shoulder.

"Right!" Yaarach replied, wide-eyed. She turned to Manion. "Do you have any peas? I always have to *find* them." She pouted then startled. "Oh, no. Wait. I have one!"

She dropped the hedgehog onto the table and rushed to the wicker basket. She dropped to her knees and rummaged through the box. "I have one. Sowrug, I have one!" She held up her tiny clenched fist into the air.

"Show *him,* silly, not me."

Yaarach nodded and ran over to Manion. She climbed onto his lap. "Watch," she said triumphantly. She turned her eyes to her sisters and saw that they weren't looking. "Sowrug, watch! You too, Forrar!"

Yaarach opened her fist to show a tiny pea. "Now, watch carefully." She touched the pea with her tiny index finger. It sprouted instantly, and within seconds a tiny flower with bright white roots appeared. "Georwrith tried that once and cracked the pea in half."

"Enough!" Manion roared. He was taking thin raspy breaths now. "Why do you devils torment me? Let me die in peace, then, if you won't help me." He fell into a storm of coughs.

Yaarach dropped the pea to the ground in fright. The flower split on the wooden floor, and she began to cry. She jumped from his lap and ran to Sowrug. "My flower is dead!" she wailed.

"It was new and beautiful, wasn't it?" Sowrug stroked her sister's hair.

"Not like him." Yaarach glared at Manion. He was slumped forward in the chair. "He's old and broken and brittle. Like Forrar's spillings," she cried with her thumb in her mouth.

Manion fell to the floor.

"But he found us. Here. In the Thicket," Forrar whispered, shedding more freckles as she turned to her sisters. "Maybe… maybe that means something?"

The sound of a sharpening stone running the length of a blade suddenly emerged from behind the door at the far end of the room. Sowrug looked back and forth between Forrar and Yaarach, chastising them with her eyes.

"Father will be very angry with you both," she said. She lingered on Yaarach. "Well? Are you going to help him?"

Yaarach's little face scrunched tight as she considered her sister's words. She nodded and ran to Manion. "Let's see Georwrith do this." She reached her tiny index finger forward and touched Manion's shoulder.

ঌ

Manion's eyes snapped open. It was dark inside the cabin now. He was lying in the corner of the room on a pile of blankets.

Seated cross-legged in front of the fireplace, illuminated in the fire's faint glow, was a young boy. His skin was bluish white. He had no hair and he wore no shirt, only a simple woollen blanket knotted around his waist.

Manion shifted, and the boy turned, revealing the scars on his neck. A dozen cuts were healed over in thick ridges. The shock sent Manion scrambling back.

"*Shhh.*" The boy put his finger to his mouth. "You'll wake father." He turned back to the smouldering log. "If he wakes, he'll punish me sooner."

"Who are you?" Manion whispered as he felt for his wound. It was no longer there.

"I am Louthe. And my father is Corvii, the god of time. He has gone mad, you know. He's hidden us all here in Bedlam's Thicket."

"W-what has happened to you?"

"Father is upset at me. I slipped out again. I went as far as the Lomhar Pass, can you believe it? But father said I was bad. Very bad."

"What are you talking about, boy? Where is your father?" Manion looked around the cottage with suspicion. His voice was starting to rise.

"Please. You'll wake him."

Manion heard a sound from the far corner of the room. Sowrug emerged from the shadows. She held a clay pot in her hands and tears streamed down her face.

"Do you see what he's done?" She slid the lid off the pot and tilted it toward Manion. Inside were what looked like the dull points of javelins. "They're dead. They're no better now than Forrar's spillings."

"Sister?" The boy turned from the fire to face her.

"I'm not your sister. I never will be."

The boy let his hand fall to the ground. From it rolled a tiny ball of light. It was no bigger than a pebble, but it shone with an outsized intensity.

"You took it from them, didn't you?" Sowrug held up the jar. "They're all useless now. Useless!" She threw the clay pot to the floor, smashing it into pieces, and glowered at her brother.

"Father is right. There is no room at the table for you, Louthe. There will never be room at the table. You are an abomination, and I hate you!" Sowrug sobbed as she ran to the cottage door and slipped out into the darkness.

Manion bent down to the burning pebble. "Boy, you'll burn the house down teasing your sister so." But though the pebble glowed as if a fire burned within, no smoke rose from the wooden floor. Manion braved to touch it, and a tremendous warmth came to his fingers like a bright summer's sun. He picked it up. The heat spread over his palm and the light snuck out between his fingers.

"This isn't fire, boy." He looked up in amazement.

"Would you like fire?" Louthe grabbed a flame licking up a log in the fireplace. He held his cupped palm out to Manion; the flame danced out the curl of his hand.

"You stay back!" Manion shouted, retreating from the boy. But the pain exploded behind his eyes again. He doubled over in agony.

"You would kill me, too, wouldn't you, Manion?" Louthe threw the fire back onto the log.

"Why am I here? W-what has happened to me?" Manion spied a knife on the kitchen table. He grabbed it and held it out.

"Wouldn't you like to remember who I am?"

"No, I would not!" Manion eyed the cottage door. To get to it, he would have to run past the boy.

"My father will punish me again, Manion. In the morning. He finds me. He always does. No matter where I go. No matter where I hide. He finds me. And once again I will pass unknown, never setting eyes on Methulla's birds, Mag's dice, or Bragnal's scales. Please, won't you help me?"

"Never," Manion looked around the room for another route of escape as the boy got up from the floor.

"Stand back, demon!" Manion pressed the knife forward.

"But I'm as natural as the rain. As familiar as a seed on the wind."

"You are nothing of the sort."

"You sound like father. Please. You must help me. Please, take me away before he wakes."

"Never." Manion eyed the door again.

"But I am wise, good knight. I see connections."

"I don't care what–"

"I see your son, Manion."

The air left him. His knees buckled. If he wasn't leaning against the wall, Manion would have tumbled to the ground. "Where?" he roared.

"*Shhh.*" The boy put his finger to his mouth. "Father will wake."

"Where is he?" Manion fought to contain his voice.

The floor boards suddenly creaked from behind the door.

"You've roused him," Louthe said. He looked at Manion pleadingly. "Help me, Manion. Help me, and I will help you. I will take you to your son. I know where he is, Manion. I spied him in the Lomhar Pass. He's a soldier now, did you know that? I can find him. If you let me."

The light of the pebble suddenly went out.

Footsteps sounded behind the door. Its latch lifted. Manion sprang off the wall and ran.

CHAPTER 32

THE PESTILENTIAL RATS

CHIM ROUNDED THE corner in a blind rage. He saw his sister ten paces ahead and ran toward her, fists clenched, when his feet suddenly caught. He tumbled to the ground.

"Falling on the Gudfin path, Chim Wiscum? What would Aris make of that?"

The wind had been knocked out of him. Chim rolled onto his back fighting for breath. The path had changed. The white ash of the walls and ground was largely gone. Wisps of the substance, aloft in the air, spilled out from the corner he'd just turned, falling as a light dusting on the path.

Chim felt for the scoush. It was gone. He looked around in a panic until he caught the glint of the blade tip having pierced through the burlap in its tumble. As he lunged for it, the path beneath him emerged in full relief. It was made of hundreds of fragments of bones: jaws, teeth, fingers, scapulae, skulls, femurs—all bound in the rock and covered in a dusting of the silky white substance.

No wonder I fell. I went running through a crypt.

He drew the scoush to his chest and got to his feet. Like the path, the walls encased the same skeletal remains. His shock was not lost on Phae.

"You see, Chim? I told you. This is proof!" She stretched her arms out and twirled.

"P-proof? How is this…?"

"It's all around you, dummy. Aris wanted to win the race so badly he burned his rival gods to dust. But he failed. He got most of them, but a couple tiny weeds managed to escape his fire!" She grabbed a loose femur from the wall, flipped it in the air, and plucked it mid-flight. "He's running alright. But he's not the only one in the race." She returned the bone to the hole.

Chim got to his feet, still struggling for his breath. "Th-that's a lie. Aris is the only… g-god in the heavens. And this…"

"Is a record." Phae finished his thought. "I like to think of it as a record of a frustrated god."

"What do you mean frustrated?"

"Well, what could be more frustrating than thinking the race was yours only to look back and see *that?*" Phae pointed up the path.

Within two paces, the color and relief of the path had changed. The cluttered, bone-encrusted dirt trail gave way to a solid green stair carved into it. The walls also took on the green hue.

"Amazing, isn't it, Chim? How quickly the runners got back on their feet." Her voice was full of awe and wonder. "Poor Aris never saw that coming, I'm sure."

Chim could finally breathe properly again. He straightened and saw that two more blue lanterns stood sentinel in this portion of the passage. It was Chim's turn to notice how different his sister looked in their light: thin and exhausted, shorter than he'd remembered. He stared up the path.

Phae nodded her encouragement, so he walked to the first step. It was clumsily carved, uneven, half broken. He reached down to touch it. Again it went black and scabrous under his hand, as the rock of the mountain had. Once again, when he lifted his hand it immediately regained its green hue.

He glanced to the next. It was smooth, still roughly hewn but better shaped. The third stair grew more uniform, more precise. The fourth was perfectly straight and embellished with runes and uneven symbols.

By the fifth stair, the work was brimming with rough drawings: animals, trees, and streams. The sixth was covered in a tapestry of symbols and shapes expertly carved into the iridescent stone. And the walls were no different—rough at first, then growing straighter until, by the sixth, they were covered in complex symbols and images.

Chim put the burlap sack back in his pouch. Phae stared at him intensely as she drummed her finger over a rib cage in the wall. Chim looked back to the corner of the path they had trekked then calmly bowed his head and closed his eyes.

"*Aris nu estec kholinestric, kholinestric nu esterc phaltinuc,*" he whispered.

"What are you doing? A benediction? In the face of this?"

Chim opened his eyes, took in her rage with contemptuous calm, and finished. "*Nu es Kullisc kollasc kollic nu Aris.*" He nodded contentedly.

"How can you? With all this… a benediction? Okay. Okay, then, Chim. Go ahead, tell me. What does your benediction say about this?" She removed the femur again and pointed to the stairs.

Chim took out his Talen. His tiny brae fingers turned the series of dials. "Why should I tell you?" he muttered.

She snapped the femur on the wall. "It doesn't say a thing about it, does it?"

"It most certainly does." Chim clicked the lever of his Talen into position.

"Bah! I've got eyes of my own. I can see for myself." She was pacing now. "We were lied to, Chim Wiscum. Simple as that. Aris doesn't run the race alone. There are other gods running against him. Gods that survived the Gudfin. Think about what that means. It means Aris can lose. Maybe he already has. Your benedictions are all lies!"

Chim bowed his head again for another invocation, but Phae grabbed his arms. Her voice fell to an earnest whisper. "Look around you, Chim. I know this is hard, but what we were taught was wrong. Aris is a spiteful god, ready to throw creation into flames for his own advantage in the race. That's how he won. That's why he raised the Gudfin. To win the race no matter the cost. And that's what he's doing again. Even if this *is* the Gudfin blade, it won't stop it rising!"

Chim gently pulled away. He smiled at her then lowered his head. Phae recoiled in disgust. She leaned against the wall, looking away from her brother. When he finished and not a moment earlier, Chim looked up at her.

"I don't believe that," he said calmly. He put his Gudfin Talen back into his leather bag.

"You don't believe that? Look around you, you fool!"

"I've looked, Phae Wiscum. Looking isn't the problem. Look." His voice softened. "It isn't my fault you're ignorant of the benedictions, sister. That you gave them up so spitefully. I am truly, truly sorry for that. I'm sorry that you're left with nothing more than your own, well... *guesses* to help you navigate the world."

"Guesses? Guesses? These are not guesses. Your benedictions, *those* are the guesses. And if they're so enlightening, then answer me: what do they tell us about this, brother? Hmm?"

Phae's eyes narrowed when he refused to answer. "You don't even know, do you?"

"Of course I know. This is where the first battle of the Gudfin clash occurred, dummy. Where Aris first marshalled the peoples of the world to destroy the evil Gudfin and bring peace to the world."

Phae burst out laughing. "You can't be serious. Look around you. He *burned* the world, Chim. Burned it to win the race; to sear his rivals. But he didn't get all of them. A couple gods, like pestilential rats, were lucky enough to escape his fire." She shook her head. "No, Agajin says–"

"Agajin Hiscum be damned! Speak that brae's name again, Phae, and I'll–"

"You'll what, Chim Wiscum? Strike me? With what? Your fist? Your foot? And here I thought you were the pious one."

Chim sneered at his sister.

"Don't think I haven't seen that spark growing in your eyes, Chim. The anger, the violence. You soaked it up from outwide, didn't you? Don't be afraid of it. I wasn't. It's as pure as water. Aris baked it in us, right from the beginning. And no tradition should have us deny it."

"Never!" Chim walked up the steps, sullen and angry. When he reached the corner he looked back at her.

"That's not all the benedictions tell us. They explain all of this. The how. And more importantly, the why."

They fell into silence. Chim waited for Phae's curiosity to break the quiet, but she refused; she was stubborn to the end.

"Ah, what's the use?" Chim said wearily. "Well? Are you coming?"

"I'm disappointed with you, Chim Wiscum." Phae did another spin on the path. It was her turn to turn a screw. "You'd walk past these runes and symbols and not stop to examine them?" She spun again and caught herself on the wall.

"I don't need to." A flush of color came to his cheeks. "I know what I know."

"They might prove me right," she said playfully.

"They might prove you wrong."

"You might read a god's poem of life as he crawled from the Gudfin fires."

"I might."

"One that forgot to include an account of Aris's noble virtues," she added in sing-song.

"Does that matter?"

"*Overwhelmingly.*" Phae gave a devilish smile.

"Well, it doesn't to me. And it wouldn't to you if you'd learned your damned benedictions."

A wind kicked up, and the blue Gudfin lamps began to rattle in their copper holders. A plume of white dust spilled out from the corner behind them. They stared at one another, each seeing the same sickness in the other, until Chim finally gave up. He adjusted his leather bag, turned from her, and walked around the corner.

Phae traced her fingers over the wall, fuming to herself, when they suddenly ran over a cluster of runes that felt different from the rest. She pinned the tip of her finger on the mark. But when she lifted her finger, there was nothing but smooth green wall. She reached out again. As her hands touched the wall and broke the exotic blue light of the Gudfin lamp, she could feel the runes once again.

She fumbled with her bag, parting vials and delicate tools, door handles and screws, bent nails and knotted herbs. The array of junk and discards swirled as if a tiny tornado had dipped its toe into her satchel. She found the parchment paper and reached down for a handful of dirt. She felt for the runes again and placed the parchment over the cluster. With her other hand she rubbed the dirt, imposing the image onto the parchment.

Phae stumbled back, staring at the image. The dirt in her other hand sifted away between her fingers. Off in the distance came a yell of drunken laughter. A tin whistle took up a tune. A door slammed. It snapped her back to reality. She curled up the parchment, threw it in her bag, and ran up the stairs after Chim.

CHAPTER 33

RUBBLE, GRIT, AND THE COBBLER'S CHAIR

NYQUEED SHUFFLED INTO the darkness beyond the arch. The little dome of light thrown off by his candle made him look like a jellyfish, and the giant room he entered the big, dark sea.

Both his candle's glow and the ambient light from outside, drawn in through the windows overhead, barely reached the layer of white dust and rubble beneath his feet.

He came upon the first of them when he trod on a chunk of rock and stumbled. The vaulting proportions of the room instantly gave up their purpose as his faint dome of light touched upon the colossal marble statue in front of him. The base was rough, as it had been when it first left its quarry, and it was cold to the touch, like metal out in the yard overnight.

The carver had chipped away everything above the base, leaving three shoots, thin as broom handles, twisting upward. When he pressed his candle into this bizarre marble grove, he saw the first of these shoots had been sculpted to bud what looked like a claw, and the second a tongue. The third was rendered heavily bent, like the end of a shepherd's crop, with an eye pressing proud of its vegetative bind. A copper plate had been nailed into the marble pedestal. In jagged script, it read: *Zernebruk, God of Harvest. Punished for the first race.*

Nyqueed heard an intake of breath and turned to see Madrigan.

"But Zernebruk was as strong as a lion, wasn't he?" The pitchie hugged his midriff, sweat coursing down his face. "And he had a wicker basket on his back. Full of wheat sheaves and apple seeds?"

Nyqueed nodded and finished the old saying: "'Seeds enough to fill a thousand fields.'"

They stared at each other a moment in mutual confusion. Nyqueed lifted his candle past the statue. The light caught the edge of another hunk of marble, and they ventured toward it, cautious as two thieves.

This statue was wider than that of Zernebruk. It portrayed an entire scene involving six figures. The first—the tallest and largest—reached well above them. His face was carved with a devilish smile and his head was cocked, eyes shut, mouth serene, as if he were listening to music. A giant hole had been bored from one ear to the other.

He held a lute. Its strings curled up and over his shoulder to the three sculptures behind him, much smaller than the first. These figures stared at the ground with vacant eyes and slack jaws. The strings led into their mouths where their tongues would have been.

At the feet of the horrid musician lay two braying female ghouls on their hands and knees. Another copper plate was sunk into this pedestal with the same jagged script: *Fitzhiff, God of Music. Punished for the second race.*

"But I thought Fitzhiff was a fat man, surrounded by dancing women," Madrigan whispered.

"No!" Nyqueed said. "The artist has captured him perfectly. Fitzhiff is a tortured god, a horror, rotten through and through."

He retreated from the statue and stepped into another pile of rocks. He followed the trail of rubble, and one more hint of white marble appeared in the dome of light.

It was nothing more than a pedestal. All the rock above the crisp corners of the plinth had been meticulously removed. All save the jagged middle. There the artist had carved an explosion, as if the subject that had once stood on the pedestal had broken from the rock and shambled away. Beside it, draped in marble dust and grit, was a cobbler's chair. On it was an old chisel and a hammer.

They heard a noise. They turned to see Fefferfew burrowing his head under a pile of burlap sacks. He rummaged for a moment then withdrew with a mouthful of rubble tumbling from his jaws. He threw back his head and swallowed it all.

The green light in Fefferfew's belly glowed back to life, and with it came Mulloch Furdie's silhouette. He held a bucket and looked up. The rubble suddenly fell into the belly, and he scrambled left and right to collect it. Satisfied he had caught every missile, he struck a match, tossed it in the bucket, and followed that with all manner of objects and liquids until the flame exceeded his own height.

Rothesay suddenly appeared from the darkness and collared Nyqueed. He pushed the drudge forward and gave a kick to the base of his spine. Nyqueed stumbled, sheltering the tiny flame of his candle as best he could. When he regained his balance, he crouched to the dog and looked back to Rothesay.

"He'll just follow you if you run, Mulloch. It's no use," Nyqueed pleaded. "Just give him Salagrim's bloody mouth. I hid it on you. Knowing how well you hide things, remember? But it's no use. Just give it to him."

But Mulloch eyes were on the bucket and the images contained in its rising smoke.

"*Shhh*, Nyqueed. Just you simmer down and watch. Because I think what's about to happen is going to be spectacular!" With that Mulloch kicked the bucket over and ran.

Fefferfew's jaws slowly parted. The old dog's tongue slid forward with Mulloch Furdie standing on it. He came into the light as if he were the stamen of an exotic flower blooming in jungle darkness.

The little god wore goggles made of fish eyes. They were up over his head. He'd taken a blast of thick smoke at some point, for he was covered in soot save an outline around his eyes where the goggles had been.

"What I'm about to show you now will be much more interesting than anything your thieving tricks could produce." He pointed back down Fefferfew's throat and glared at Madrigan. "And much more reliable than my sick, cowardly pitchies."

A *clang*, as if a giant steel gear had fallen, rose from the dog's belly. A terrible grinding and shuddering followed. Mulloch ducked to avoid the hinges and bolts and springs that shot out of the dog's throat.

Then it came. A chugging cloud of green smoke belched up from Fefferfew's belly. It rose over Mulloch's head. He crouched and watched it go. In its wake, floating in the air as if radiating from the divine core of the world itself, came an egg boiling with energy inside its transparent shell.

Mulloch delighted in their looks of surprise. "That's right! The great Mulloch Furdie, simple drudge of amphetamined mysteries, has created… *Shivery Coffinfit!*" He plucked the egg from the air and brought it close to his eyes.

He pointed a reprimanding finger at Madrigan. "No one dabbles in lysergic ministrations behind my back and gets away with it."

He tossed the Coffinfit into the air, fell to his knees, and swallowed it whole.

"I don't feel a thing," he wailed a second later. He raced to Fefferfew's snout, grabbed his whiskers, swung out, and pointed at the poor dog's eye.

"Your stupid pitchie friends have given me a fetching to work wi–" His body gave a jolt and he crashed to the floor.

The spell over the old dog broke. Fefferfew yelped, then, in a series of retches, spewed a half piece of hammered, punctured, sawed, saliva-drenched Shivery Coffinfit onto the floor. That was it; the dog was done. He raced out of the room, and all fell silent.

That is, until an eerie tapping emerged from behind Mulloch

Furdie. It came closer and closer. From the shadows emerged a hooded figure wearing loose-fitting robes cinched with a black cord at the waist and a series of golden pendants around its neck. The broad, heavy cowl that lay limp over the creature's head was oversized, as if meant for a colossus.

It walked to the middle of the room then snapped rigid as a box. It shimmered, and two more cowled creatures stepped out from behind it as if they'd been contained in its shadow. They came to stand on either side of the first.

A series of Methulla's firebirds suddenly exploded in quick succession—*boom, boom, boom*. Three flashes of light poured through the windows, and all was draped in light—including the statues of Fitzhiff and Zernebruk.

They were now staring at the cowled beings. Fitzhiff had given his lute to one of the ghouls at his feet, and Zernebruk's eye was proud of his pedestal like a probing antenna.

Another string of Methulla's firebirds exploded: *boom, boom, boom—boom!* Another intense burst of light buckled the room. As Nyqueed turned away from it he saw a flash of white marble in the shadows just beyond the arch. The statue of Civiak was now crouching in the corner.

The strange creatures shook. Their cowls widened and flared as if a hurricane bottled within their chests were roaring up their throats. They billowed to their length and breadth and fluttered like flags in a storm. The creatures leaned forward in perfect unison, and the pendants around their necks fired up and down like pistons, faster by the second.

In the black recesses of their cowls, the verge of one world met the cusp of another. The dark forests of Bedlam's Thicket took form. The sound of branches snapping, tree roots ripping, and footsteps battering through undergrowth echoed up from the deep inside the cowls.

Bragnal suddenly appeared in the first cowl in the line. His movement then played out in sequence across the next cowl until he stopped in the middle of the third. He breathed heavily and looked back the way he'd come, wary and nervous. He then faced the room. The face of Bragnal soon appeared in full measure, close on to the cowl. He drew closer still until only Bragnal's eye could be seen. He then startled and drew back, turning toward the way he'd come.

Vestialis appeared in the first cowl of the line. She walked slowly, curling her long flowing hair around her fingers. As she did, a string of firebirds exploded again: *boom, boom, boom!*

The statues of Fitzhiff and Zernebruk had changed again. Fitzhiff and his ghouls were glaring at Vestialis; Amariss and Juliet were pointing at her, their faces dark with recrimination.

Zernebruk's eye had drawn back as if in a startle, but the stalk that held his ear had drawn closer. For in this world beyond, captured in the strange creatures' cowls, Bragnal began to speak.

"I see you escaped my crypt, goddess," he said. "I shall bury my next prison under a mountain."

Vestialis draped herself over a tree and drew down her collar, fanning the beads of sweat running down to her cleavage. "It too will break, prince. They will *all* break, in time. We are gods after all."

"And what of the others?" Bragnal's tone was as blunt as a hammer. "Have they raced free from my crypt as well?"

Vestialis moved off the tree. "They have. All but one."

"And what of her?"

"Dead." But Vestialis would not be without artifice for long. Advantage, as always, dawned quickly on the goddess of love. "But I held her hand as she slipped away. It was to me that Morven spoke her final words."

Bragnal's eyes flashed at the mention of her name. "And what were those final words?"

"Soon enough, prince of gods." Vestialis looked past Bragnal and into the thick woods of Bedlam's Thicket. "For what time have we for idle chat? They will all come through Bedlam's Thicket. All of them. Racing behind you. Chasing you endlessly, like the steam off a kettle."

"Never have I had to run so quick," he said candidly, but that weakness, if weakness it was, was soon replaced by rage. "They cannot win, goddess. They are pale shades to me. As are you. Weak and corrupt."

Vestialis smiled. "Of course we are, prince of gods. None deserve to take your throne. Least among them those two other traitors now freed from your crypt, Zernebruk and Fitzhiff."

Another of Methulla's firebirds burst in the night sky beyond the room, drenching it in light.

Fitzhiff's face was a canvas of pure torment now, hands grasping at his neck in anguish. His ghouls at his feet had thrown their heads back like baying wolves and were struggling to release their hands from their marble binds. Zernebruk had produced five more shoots from the pedestal. Their disgorged claws curled into fists and were frozen hammering against the marble as a wailing child might.

Bragnal looked to the night sky. "The race is fierce. Fiercer than any other I have known. And fraught with… uncertainty."

Vestialis surged toward him. "It is, prince of gods. So, let me help you. It was what Morven wanted—it was her dying wish." Her cunning was sharp, and it cut deep.

"That was her wish?"

Vestialis nodded. "Even in the midst of your punishment, on the eve of her death, her only thought was for you."

She ventured to move from the first cowl to the second, then the third. She draped her long, slender fingers over Bragnal's chest, then turned and pointed back the way they had come.

"I could lay in wait for them. I could… I could *kill* the quickest among them. You are still the prince of gods, after all. You could permit it. You could permit a death outside Quardinal's walls. Just this one. And I would do that for you, prince. For you, and to fulfill Morven's dying wish that you succeed in this race."

Bragnal lifted her hand from his chest. "But you are the goddess of love," he said, his eyes narrowing. This produced a spark in Vestialis.

"And Methulla is the god of truth. And Aelic of fate. What of it? What honor do either of them do their element?" She regained her calm.

"Besides, you misunderstand me, great Bragnal. This will be a gesture of purest love. Love for you. Borne of Morven's love across time and space and"—she looked deep into his eyes— "the love that grows in *my* heart. Let me see you to victory."

Bragnal stared at her with suspicion. "And what would you have in return?"

Vestialis's tone became transactional. "To sit as your queen on your throne when you reclaim it. When you win the race to the Blackened Nevers."

"All this you would do for me?"

Vestialis nodded. "All I need from you is your indulgence, prince of gods. License. License to kill a god beyond the walls."

Bragnal slowly drew up the scale in his hand and placed his bicep on the weighing pan. Vestialis sensed his hesitation. She pointed again in the direction they had come.

"Do you not hear them, prince? They close on you. Full of greed and envy. And here you find yourself in the clutches of Bedlam's Thicket. Who knows what that mad Corvii has hidden in its leaves and streams?" Her rhetorical efforts appeared to be working, and Vestialis pressed on.

"Besides, you are not the god you used to be, Bragnal. The god who wrung the necks of those who tried to unseat you."

"You among them, if I recall correctly," he growled, lifting his bicep off the pan.

"Folly, prince. Folly of my youth," she said. "Before you blessed me with an eternity in that crypt to consider my wicked ways, and where I sit in this cosmic mechanism."

He returned his bicep to the pan. She found her track again. "You tire easily now. As do we all. The sustenance mortuants used to provide us daily now comes in dribs and drabs. And you struggle to find the finish line, don't you? I've seen your hesitation." She pointed one last time in the direction they'd come.

"But among that horde of divinity lie the most hungry. The most rested. The greediest! The chance to unseat you fuels them like the energy in the belly of a comet. Why would you take the risk? Let me help you. Give me your permission to kill the greediest of them and free you to fly to your victory." As if for emphasis, the sound of a tree root snapping came from the left-most cowl.

Bragnal slammed his bicep down; the opposite weighing pan rose and rattled when it hit its height. "Do it," Bragnal growled. He backed away from her, turned, and ran.

Suddenly, a loud bang was heard at the door beyond the arch. The handle rattled. Rothesay ran to it and leaned his bulk against it. A fist pounded on the door, and Lostrus's voice sounded at the keyhole.

"Please forgive me, Frew the Younger, sir. But I have every reason to believe that a pair of seditionists and thieves have just now invaded your shop. A pair of revolting heathens not fit to breathe the same air as a man of your majesty and talent. Now, if it isn't too inconvenient for you, sir, *open up this goddamn door!*"

CHAPTER 34

ON THE LIMITS OF QUARDINAL'S BRAWN

FIVE OF METHULLA'S firebirds swooped into the air and exploded. Their light blasted into the room once again. *Flash*: The statues of Fitzhiff and Zernebruk were gone. *Flash*: Mulloch Furdie lay comatose. *Flash*: Madrigan hugged his knees to his chest and rocked like a metronome. *Flash*: Rothesay ran back from the door. And *flash*: Nyqueed bent to the half piece of Shivery Coffinfit regurgitated by Fefferfew and slipped the slimy mess into his pocket.

Rothesay lumbered over to one of the giant burlap sacks of grain piled in the corner. He hoisted it onto his shoulder, hefted it to the door, and dumped it on the threshold. When he turned back to the room beyond the arch, he saw what he had done. The sack had obscured a ragged hole in the wall. A phosphorescent glow flooded into the room from it. And the worst of it: Nyqueed's eyes were fixed on this divine bit of providence and the possibility it held of quick escape.

The big man panicked. He darted back into the room and raised his dagger when another thump came at the door.

"Open this muhking door or so help me I will oil its hinges with your guts! Not you, Frew the Younger, of course. I do apologize for these ripe words, but they are an unfortunate necessity when dealing with such vermin."

The door shook in its frame again, and the force pressed the sack of grain back an inch.

"Thaltis has words for you, Black Song Man," Lostrus said through the keyhole. The door shook again. The sack slid back farther, providing more give for the ailing door.

But the door was the least of Rothesay's concerns now. He was standing under the arch; the hole's phosphorescent glow was closer to Nyqueed than it was to him.

He attacked. Nyqueed darted away easily, but Rothesay knocked the candle from his hand. Its flame washed against some crumpled linen sheets piled against the wall. They took up the flame and ignited into fire.

Mulloch Furdie sucked in a giant breath and his eyes flew open just as the door exploded off its hinges. Lostrus and six gendarmes rushed in through a cloud of dust.

The commotion startled Nyqueed, and Rothesay saw his moment. He lunged and this time reached his mark. He clamped his hands around the drudge and drew him off his feet, choking away his breath.

Meanwhile, Mulloch Furdie jumped left and right as if beset by devils with pitchforks. Then he saw the phosphorescent glow of the hole in the wall, and he ran for it.

Rothesay tightened his grip around Nyqueed's neck. The drudge struggled for breath, his world ebbing away, when all of a sudden Rothesay's pockets ripped free of their stitching and splayed out to the world like lazy tongues.

Nyqueed managed a weak smile as he slowly raised his clenched fist. Dangling from his fingers was an open locket.

"What w-will it be now, brute?" Nyqueed sputtered. "Their race… *or yours?*" With that he tossed the locket into the flames.

Rothesay threw the drudge aside. He knocked three gendarmes out of his path and dropped to his knees to search for the locket.

Nyqueed tumbled to the floor. A grinning gendarme stood over him with a pike. He drove it into Nyqueed's thigh. The drudge roared in pain and scrambled back, grabbed a handful of dust and grit from the workshop floor, and threw it into the soldier's face. The gendarme fell back, spitting and clawing at his eyes.

"Well, isn't this a bit of irony?" Mulloch yelped from the threshold of the hole.

Nyqueed turned just as Madrigan dove past Mulloch, producing a sound like coins swirling down a tube as he sank away down the hole. Mulloch locked eyes with Nyqueed and bowed.

"Look who has planned the *perfect* escape this time," the little drudge said as he jumped after Madrigan into the hole.

Nyqueed dodged another gendarme's strike. He got to his feet, raced toward the hole, and dove into it.

His world went dark; he banged against a metal pipe, tumbling and twisting until he landed in a puddle of gray water. The taste and smell of sewage hit his tongue and nose. He sputtered, got to his knees, and backed into the brick wall. The low curved ceiling of the pipe made him bend unnaturally.

"Sewers?" he whimpered. "I hate sewers. It's right there, in the third verse of my song. *I hate sewers!*"

Nyqueed touched his wound and raised his hand. It was covered in blood. He showed it to Madrigan, and the young pitchie's face blanched.

A flicker of lantern light appeared in the hole above them. Lostrus's head followed, bathed in the glow.

"A chase, is it? Alright, I'm game. But when I find you, I will carve those little divine hearts out of your chests, mark my words. *To me!*" he roared back to his men.

The light receded, quickly followed by the sounds of metal being scraped against, torches lighting, and bulk shifting and squeezing. The first of Lostrus's men crashed into the sewer.

Mulloch Furdie shoved Nyqueed and Madrigan into a run, narrowly missing the splash from the soldier's landing. They could hear Lostrus barking orders now and more of his men splashing in the water. They heard the whoosh of torches through the cramped air, and the sewage water splished and sploshed as the chase down the pipe began.

Lostrus called out to the two drudges as they reached the corner of the sewer pipe. "It's no use running, sprites. Gods, drudges, or otherwise—I throw them all into the Clovenstone. That's a promise!"

He barked a muffled order. Two gendarmes rushed forward, their flames bobbing as they ran through the knee-high water.

A few paces ahead of Nyqueed, a pipe broke off from the main line and disappeared into the stone wall.

"C'mon," Madrigan screamed, pulling Nyqueed into a headlong dash toward it.

Above the pipe on an old rusted plaque, a motto read *Look at the dung on which they clung; how words do fail the tongue.*

One of the gendarmes rushed around the corner in their wake. He grinned when he saw them and headed for them like a bullet from a musket.

Nyqueed scrambled up after Madrigan and Mulloch just as the gendarme crashed into the pipe. The swat of the man's torch singed the end of Nyqueed's cloak. "I'm going to burn you," the gendarme sneered. "Give you some scabs to play with when you sit in your cell."

Nyqueed scrambled to his feet in the slop and filth of this new pipe. Mulloch and Madrigan were gone. Splishes and sploshes echoed ahead of him down the pipe.

"Mulloch?" he whispered. Nothing.

Nyqueed bent low and walked ahead cautiously along the narrow pipe. Behind him, the gendarme struggled to enter, his armor and sword hampering his progress. Above Nyqueed's head, the exposed brick and mortar released drops of foul liquid. Mosses and spikes of hardened goo hung from the ceiling. Nyqueed bent to avoid them, but the cold sludge that dripped down was another thing entirely. Behind him he could see the bright nucleus of the gendarme's torch and the smoke chugging along the bricks overhead.

"Mulloch?" he whispered more insistently now. "Madrigan?" He stopped moving, strained to listen, but still heard nothing.

"Here, little drudge. Here, little flotsam," sang the gendarme behind him. He was closing, so Nyqueed ran for all his worth, dodging the dangling muck and sloshing through the slime. He saw light at the end of the pipe; the spikes of rot and filth hanging from the ceiling criss-crossed the glow like a serpent's fangs.

"Give up, drudge," called the gendarme. The voice was closer than it had ever been.

Nyqueed stumbled. A wave of sewage water splashed onto his lips. He could taste its foul, oily tanginess. He spit and sputtered but kept running.

"You're mine, sprite," came the gendarme's voice.

The light at the end of the pipe grew wider, and the bricks of the sewer wall beyond it were visible. It was on these bricks that Nyqueed set his attention as he ran with all the energy he could muster.

Suddenly, the roof of the tunnel peeled away like a jaw opening for a bite. He quickened his pace still. He could smell the smoke from the gendarme's torch now, hear the sloshing of the foul liquid in the soldier's boots. The lip of the pipe was in sight. He dove for it.

Just as he did, the gendarme reached out and grabbed Nyqueed's leg. He crashed down onto the sewage pipe and rolled over just in time to see the gendarme grin and draw his dagger.

The entire pipe then buckled. Nyqueed surged through the air and fell into the adjoining tunnel. The water was deeper here. He was submerged. When he surfaced, he shook the sewage filth from his eyes and looked up toward the pipe from which he'd fallen. The tip of it slithered back into the wall like a tongue. Then it was gone. All was brick and mortar now and a fine plume of dust.

"Nyqueed!"

He turned to see Mulloch bathed in light from the end of the tunnel. Standing next to him, wet as a drowned rat and shivering, was Madrigan.

"C'mon. I see moonlight."

Nyqueed tore off through the sewage water after Mulloch and joined him at the curl of the pipe. It led away through another wall and into the bright moonlight beyond. There the trickle of sewage fell away, and the pipe with it.

"Come on," Nyqueed whispered.

They moved like waterlogged termites. On either side of them, the walls of Quardinal Brawn draped them in a strange magical iridescence that glimmered off the sewage water. When they reached the end of it, they were outside the city. Before them stretched a vista of treetops, and the pipe upon which they stood ended, trickling its filth into the grasslands below.

Nyqueed grabbed Mulloch's elbow and urged him forward, but Mulloch shook himself free.

"Are you mad?" The little drudge braced himself on the side of the shallow pipe. "We can't leave Quardinal's Brawn! We'll…" He paled as the full implications rounded on him.

Lostrus's voice bellowed from the pipe behind them. "Well, well, well. What do we have here? Looks like it's the end of the line for the flotsam of the heavens."

Lostrus's face was illuminated by the walls' glow. The light also bathed the gendarme beside him, whose chest rose and fell as he caught his breath. Lostrus turned to this gendarme and nodded. The man smirked, raised his halberd, and moved forward.

Nyqueed ventured to the edge of the pipe and looked down. Lostrus caught it all.

"Hah! What are you going to do, drudge? Leave Quardinal's Brawn?"

Nyqueed and Mulloch locked eyes. Nyqueed lifted his hand from his wound and showed him the blood.

"This isn't how I die, Mulloch," he whispered.

"Speaking of dying, I have to say I don't have much interest in that either," Mulloch said as the gendarme closed in on them.

Nyqueed stole a glance at the forest beyond the pipe as he retreated. "Then we run."

"Run? You mean in the race?" Mulloch edged away from the approaching gendarme. "Are you mad?"

"What choice do we have? I'm not going back to the Clovenstone."

The gendarme rattled free some manacles from his belt. He held them up and grinned. The three fugitives stepped back, gobbling up what remained of the pipe.

"Let's do it, Mulloch. Let's jump and run. Let's win this race, you and me."

"What about this one? You want to a run the race with a mortuant?" Mulloch's words drew the blood from Madrigan's face. His threats now multiplied, he stumbled back from the two drudges without any sense of self-preservation. A gummed-up pair of shoes was the cost. His foot trod on them and their sludge bind gave way. Madrigan slipped and tumbled off the pipe after them.

Mulloch watched Madrigan crash into the grasslands. "But we're just drudges, Nyqueed. The race, it's… it's forbidden to flotsam like us."

The gendarme stabbed toward them with his pike. As Mulloch dodged, his balance deserted him. He would have careened over the edge if Nyqueed hadn't grabbed him.

"We're just the cogs and gears," Mulloch whimpered. "We… we have our place."

"Well, I'm sick of our place. And I'm sick of my song," Nyqueed countered. "And you should be too."

Mulloch stared at him dumbfounded. "But how the muhk would we do it? The Blackened Nevers are hidden from our kind."

Nyqueed dug his fingers into Mulloch's pocket and removed Salagrim's mouth. "Then we use *this*."

The little drudge looked at it baffled and amazed. "Is that…?"

Nyqueed nodded. "I stole it, Mulloch. I stole it! Now we can know what those gods saw when the race started. In the Lomhar Pass. Something happened there, I'm sure of it. That's where it all began. We just get this thing to talk and we'll know where the finish line is."

But the spell of wonder and excitement that overcame Nyqueed and Mulloch Furdie didn't last long. The gendarme lunged again.

The two drudges darted away from his blade. Arms flailing, mouths screaming, eyes wide in terror and breath stuck in their chests, they fell away from the magical city known as Quardinal's Brawn.

EPILOGUE

A DRUDGE'S EMPTY HUM

PHAE ROUNDED THE corner and fell into darkness. A hand covered her mouth. "Don't make a sound," Chim whispered. He removed his hand, and she pushed him away so violently she fell back and hit the wall of the path.

She felt Chim's hand on her shoulder now. "Would you stop!" he said. Phae heard the concern in his voice.

"My eyes grew accustomed while you were fiddling back there." She could also hear by the direction of his voice that he'd turned his head.

"You can't see it yet," he whispered, "but there's something at the end of the path."

Phae tried to force her vision through the darkness. "What? What's there?"

"I don't know." Chim slid in beside her and flattened himself against the wall.

"Is it coming toward us?" Chim hushed her. "Is it moving?" But he was gone. She could hear him sliding away down the wall. "Chim!" she whispered, reaching into the darkness after him.

Mercifully, the path began to settle into focus. Chim's figure came to her first; he'd moved a few feet away. She gazed past him and could now see a blurry object. "Is it…?" Again Chim hushed her.

"It's moving. Watch," he said.

She could see it now. A hooded figure knelt down to the stone path. It was clothed in a loose-fitting robe cinched at the waist, and a broad heavy cowl lay limp over its head. A stack of pendants hung around its neck. She could make out rhythmic movements of the creature's arms as well. It was drawing something toward it, hand over hand, in measured lengths, something buried beneath the rocky path. The creature's movements were slow and mechanical, as though there were a series of gears and cogs beneath its robes. Phae imagined them wrapped in rotted cords and drenched in thick, black oil.

"It's pulling something," she whispered.

Chim hushed her again. "Would you just listen?"

Phae reluctantly fell quiet, joining Chim in a feverish straining of senses. Her ears finally settled on the slow rattle of a chain. It was faint, but it was clear. She listened as the figure grasped the chain, arm over arm, and drew more of its length from the solid rock.

"It's a chain," Phae whispered.

"Coming out of solid rock?"

Phae leaned forward and cupped her hands around his ears. Her breaths puffed on his ear drums. "No, Chim, there's… there's actually a pit there. An awful, deep pit. I saw it. When I took the blade."

"I don't see a pit."

Phae's hands fell from his ears. "You don't believe me?" She sounded wounded.

"Well, I don't see a pit."

"Well, no wonder. Look!" She pointed to the dormant lamps swaying in the breeze. "The Gudfin lights have been snuffed out."

Meanwhile, unbeknownst to the little brae, standing in their fog of confusion on their little bit of rock in their mountain hideaway, the cusp of one world quietly met the verge of another. The Gudfin Mountain, upon which they stood, was no mountain at all. It was the hunch of the back and the bend in the neck of Madrigan. His robes pooled out to his sides over the grass and dirt like the flared base of the Gudfin Mountain.

On his knees in front of him, staring deep into the pitchie's eyes, as if scanning for the result of an act he'd just completed, was Nyqueed. As he watched with anticipation, his other hand fretted with the necklace given to him by the jeweler in Quardinal's Brawn. He cycled its tiles through his fingers like a rosary, drawing it up from his pocket and back down as he stared.

In the little patch of dirt and grass between them was a spent half shell of Shivery Coffinfit. The frost that jacketed the membrane was the same that now stained Madrigan's quivering lips.

"It's okay. It's okay," Chim whispered. "The benedictions speak of this. They do. They–"

"This must be a Gudfin priest?" Phae said in amazement. "I never saw one when I was here, mind you, but I heard them."

"Are you joking? Look at it," Chim said. "It's the size of three brae on end. And besides, what Gudfin priest would be out in the dark, cloaked like a bandit, doing, well, doing whatever that thing is doing?"

"A true priest of Aris, that's who. Not the fake ones you learned of in your nursery rhymes."

"This is no Gudfin priest," Chim said confidently.

"And how would you know?"

"The benedictions tell me so, that's how."

"Really? Well then, tell me: what do the benedictions say about this?"

"So now you want to hear the benedictions?"

Phae slapped his stomach.

"Fine." Chim struggled a moment to slow his racing thoughts. "The benediction of the third turn. The third turn. The third turn. Oh, what is it again? It's… wait, I've got it!" The little brae bowed his head.

"*Aris nu estric. Estric nu Aris,*" he whispered. "*Commen vilentic sommuc siklic.*"

The sound of the chain stopped. The creature's cowled head turned toward them. Its arms remained in the fashion of its activity, one arm outstretched beyond the other clenching the links.

Meanwhile, in the transcendence above them, Madrigan whispered the faintest of whispers. Nyqueed drew in close and his face turned white. He sat paralyzed for a full minute before he looked back at Mulloch Furdie to see if he had stirred. As his mind raced to decide upon his next move, his fingers resumed their fidgeting with the necklace. It was now half out of his pocket.

Chim and Phae held their breath and flattened themselves against the rock wall. "Does it see us?" Phae whispered. Chim glared at his sister to be quiet.

The creature lingered another moment, then it shot out its hand and clutched farther down the chain. It bent its head and slowly drew out another length from the rock. With this effort, a carved silver disc emerged from the rock like a bag from a cup of tea.

Phae pulled Chim close. "Look, Chim. What is it?"

Chim squinted. "It's a carving."

The disc rose on the chain. He could see it clearly now. It was packed tight with figures clawing and shouldering one another, running toward a series of mountains in the distance. Among them, in the corner of the carving, was Aris pushing his way through the horde, fighting to stand his ground, but he was losing.

"There's Aris, Chim. Look! Look in the bottom corner. He's running. *With others!* I told you. I told you there were gods that escaped the Gudfin. I told you he wasn't running alone. And look, they're all running toward a mountain."

"Nonsense," he replied. "W-we should turn back, Phae. Now!"

"Turn back? You can't be serious."

"At least until this thing is done what it's doing. Something evil has invaded the Gudfin. I can feel it."

"And how on earth would you know that, hmm? What do you know of the Gudfin? You've never even been here. Not once in your fourteen summers. You just sat on your stool, day in and day out, ignoring the Gudfin as it came and went with the kiltering." Tears welled up in Phae's eyes. "You ignored it, just like you ignored everything else."

"I never ignored it, Phae," Chim said softly, realizing the subject had shifted. "It's just, what were we to do?"

"You could have done anything!" she shouted.

Chim made to cover her mouth, but it was too late. The creature's movements stopped. It raised its head.

Meanwhile, in the transcendence, Nyqueed leaned close to Madrigan's ear. Checking once again that Mulloch was still asleep beside the smoldering remains of their fire, he whispered, his voice as trembling and fretful as his fingers cycling through the necklace in his pocket.

The creature at the end of the path took one hand from the chain and snapped its fingers. A terrible high-pitched scraping noise suddenly burst onto the path as a second robed figure emerged from the shadows. It wore the same limp, oversized cowl as the first. Its walk was slouched and awkward, for it was dragging a large square hammer that scraped over the path behind it.

The creature lumbered forward and fell to its knees beside the chain. It raised the hammer; it arced through the moonlight and crashed down onto the length of chain with a thunderous impact.

The creature that had drawn the chain from the rock got to its feet and threw back its head. Its cowl billowed broad as a swallowing whale, and a rush of air escaped it. The pendants around its head spun in perfect concentric orbits.

"You have the blade, don't you, little brae?" The words boomed into the path.

The creature crashed the hammer down again on the chain. Again the chain rattled and rumbled, and again the path flooded with the ominous booming voice.

"Bring it to me. Go on. *Bring it to me.*"

Chim turned to his sister. "They know we have the blade. Why? What have you done, Phae?"

"I told you, Chim. Aris isn't who you think he is." Phae tried in vain to hide her tears.

Chim stepped back from her. He fumbled with the latch of his satchel, testing that it was secure. "Phae, please, listen to me…"

Before he could finish his words, Phae lunged for the satchel. He slapped her hand away. "What are you doing?"

"Give me the blade, Chim."

"What? Never!"

In the transcendence, Nyqueed leaned in again to whisper into Madrigan's ear. And, in like manner, inside the mountain, on the tiny piece of path shared by Chim and Phae, the strange creature swung its hammer again, and Nyqueed's voice flooded the path.

"You did nothing wrong, Phae Wiscum."

The two little brae froze in their tracks. They locked eyes. Tears streaked down Phae's cheeks now. "You see, Chim. I told you. I did nothing wrong. Nothing! Now give me the blade."

Chim shook his head and retreated.

The hammer fell again. "I forgive you, Phae Wiscum," Nyqueed's voice echoed over the path.

"Chim, please. You don't understand. How could you? You don't know what I did."

"Of course I do."

"No, not taking the blade. What I did with it."

Chim stared at her, wide-eyed with shock. "What? What did you do? What did you do, Phae?" he screamed.

"Aris wants to forgive me. Why won't you let him?" she sobbed.

"Don't be silly. Of course I…"

Phae pounced. She thrust her hand into his satchel, slapping away his protests. She stepped back with the burlap and pulled the string. The wrapping fell from the dwarven scoush.

"Phae!" Chim screamed. He reached for her but she eluded his grasp, stepping to the middle of the path, and holding up the blade.

"I have it, Aris! I have it! I have the blade! Here!" She held it high above her head.

The creatures stopped their movements; the hammer drew down.

Meanwhile, in the transcendence, Nyqueed checked once more that Mulloch remained sleeping. Their tiny fire was now mere wisps of smoke. The night had reasserted itself.

He licked his lips and let the necklace drop into the recesses of his pocket. He felt for Madrigan in the darkness, his hands walking from the pitchie's shoulder, up his neck, to his face, to his ear. Nyqueed cupped it, then leaned in closer for his next whisper.

The hooded figure whose cloak had billowed with the unearthly voice crumpled forward like a desiccated sunflower. Bent now, its head cocked, it stretched out its thin hand.

"Bring it here, little brae," it hissed. "Bring it to your god." It fumbled at the air in front of it as though it were a blind man looking for the handle of a door.

Phae stepped forward one tentative step. The creature's head swiveled to follow the sound. "Good. Good, little brae. Bring it to me." It reached out again at an angle too high for the girl.

"You promise you will forgive me?" she sobbed.

"Of course I will forgive you, little brae. I am the Black Song Man. I know all about pain and redemption."

"Don't do it, Phae!" Chim yelled, stepping off the wall.

"Unlike some among you who are rotten to the core," the creature hissed, pointing its long crooked finger at the source of the new sound.

Phae's tears were sobs now. She held up the blade in her shaking hands. "A-and do you promise… do you promise to forgive the Gudfin thief?"

"Of course, little brae. This broken world should exalt its thieves, don't you think?" the creature hissed.

"You see, Chim," Phae said through her tears. "He..."

She turned to her brother and had time only to register his last step and the flash of his hand as he grabbed the scoush from her. "No!" she screamed.

Chim raced away and skidded to a halt before the hooded creature. It turned its head, the edges of its billowing cloak undulating like the flanks of a caterpillar, and twisted its shoulders, trying desperately to interpret the new sound.

"And what do you know of blades, eh, little brae?" it hissed as it sniffed at the air. "What do you plan to do? Offer your Aris another blasphemy? Give me the blade, you little fool."

Chim fumbled with the dwarven scoush, turning it in his tiny fingers, testing its edges.

Which bit cuts? Which end do I hold? His fingers instinctively wrapped around the pommel. *This must be it.* He looked up at the gruesome creature again. *Just enough to make it run away. Just to make it pop. Pop like a balloon. Or like a fork in a potato. That's it, a fork in a potato!*

The creature snapped its fingers. The other robed figure came alongside just as Chim let out his roar and started to run. The creatures twisted their bodies in a frantic effort to locate the danger, but it was too late.

His little eyes shut tight, his hands gripping the pommel of the dagger, Chim plunged the blade into the creature's belly. The dagger slid in as if settling into butter. The shock and speed of the motion knocked the brae sideways.

The creature dropped the chain. As the coils hit the rock they slid back toward the hole. Sparks and flames flew off the chain as it bounced over the rocky path. The creature with the hammer drew it back. But by now the chain had retreated past him. The hammer hit the path instead. It sent sparks up from the rock, which exploded into flames.

Meanwhile in the transcendence, Madrigan's trance broke. He gulped a mouthful of air and scurried away from Nyqueed, collapsing onto his back in the tall grass with thin tendrils of effervescence escaping from his lips. Nyqueed surged forward on his knees and bent close to whisper into Madrigan's ear. The young pitchie quivered as he lay on the grass, staring up at the bright moon, as Nyqueed spoke.

"The Black Song Man will not forget this embarrassment, little brae," the creatures hissed as the flames roared up around them. "You have not won. I will find you. And I will take your blade. Of that you can be sure."

Chim and Phae finally succumbed to the heat. They turned away from the blinding light, covering their eyes. And in the world beyond, Nyqueed raised his head and cursed the moon.

THE END

Here ends *The Woeful Wager*, book one of *The Race to the Blackened Nevers*. For more information about book two, *The Vulgar Victory*, please visit www.blackenednevers.com, or follow the author on Twitter at @DBainWriter.

For the free bonus chapters to this book: *The Lament of Besom* and *The Lament of Stewmull*, please visit www.blackenednevers.com/bonus.

Made in the
USA
Middletown, DE